Brad fr_____ to see what the distraction was. A tall, red-haired girl stood in the middle of the entry, and now she marched into the room like a warship under full sail. She had hair the color of a forest fire, pulled back in a tight bun under a plain dark hat, and she wore a dark, no-nonsense dress. This was a respectable lady, there was no doubt about that. Now what was a respectable lady doing in a place like the Texas Lily?

The silence grew as everyone turned to look at her.

"I demand to see Mr. Bradley O'Neal," she said in a back East accent that would cut glass with its sharpness.

Uh-oh. This couldn't be good. Brad stood up from the poker table with a sigh and turned his hand upside-down on the table. "Anybody touches my cards before I get back, I'll make him eat my derringer," he drawled and then stepped forward to greet the lady. "Brad O'Neal at your service, ma'am," he made a sweeping bow. "And to whom do I have the honor of—?"

"What is the meaning of all these shenanigans? This is no way to run a hotel. It must stop immediately."

"What?" He was seldom at a loss for words, but any man would wither under the glare of those cold green eyes.

"Mr. O'Neal," she snapped, "I am your new partner. I am Lillian Primm."

Oh, hell, his luck really had run out.

Also by Georgina Gentry

To Love a Texan

GEORGINA GENTRY

ZEBRA BOOKS
Kensington Publishing Corp.
www.kensingtonbooks.com

ZEBRA BOOKS are published by
Kensington Publishing Corp.
850 Third Avenue
New York, NY 10022

All Kensington titles, imprints, and distributed lines are
available at special quantity discounts for bulk purchases for
sales promotion, premiums, fund-raising, educational, or
institutional use.

Special book excerpts or customized printings can also be cre-
ated to fit specific needs. For details, write or phone the office
of the Kensington Special Sales Manager: Attn. Special Sales
Department. Kensington Publishing Corp., 850 Third Avenue,
New York, NY 10022. Phone: 1-800-221-2647.

Zebra and the Z logo Reg. U.S. Pat. & TM Off.

First Printing: January 2007
10 9 8 7 6 5 4 3 2 1

Printed in the United States of America

This story is dedicated to my sister, Stephanie Joyce, whose warm generosity of spirit and sense of humor have sustained this family through some very rough times. I love you, Sis, more than you know.

And also to Oklahoma's own movie star, James Garner. I drew on his Western movies, his television series "Maverick" and the "Rockford Files," featuring that dark, handsome wisecracking hero, to create Brad O'Neal.

Chapter One

They were burying Lil McGinty today and it was the biggest funeral this east Texas town had ever seen. It would have been even bigger, Brad O'Neal thought, if the local men hadn't been so chicken-livered and scared of their wives that they were afraid to attend.

So here he stood in the graveyard with the whores and card dealers, Delilah, the black cook, a billy goat named Herman, most of the single men of the town, plus cowboys from all over the county. Reverend Lovejoy was conducting the funeral, although his congregation might have something to say to him next Sunday. It was one thing to talk about redeeming the lowly and quite another to preach a respectable service for the biggest madam in the Lone Star state.

It was a warm day. Brad sighed and shifted the goat's leash to his other hand so he could wave away a fly. He really missed Lil; she'd been a great old gal.

Reverend Lovejoy droned on and on, attempting

to think of nice things to say about the sudden death of the owner of the most successful saloon and bordello in the county. Make that half owner. Because of Lil's generosity in letting him buy in, Brad now owned half of the Texas Lily.

The reverend motioned Lil's girls to come forward to sing. Unfortunately, none knew any hymns so they came out with an off-key chorus of "Hark, the Herald Angels Sing." Since it was spring, it didn't seem too appropriate. Besides, Lil, while good-hearted and generous, was hardly an angel.

Reverend Lovejoy said a final prayer and Brad reached down to pat Herman, who was now chewing the edge of Brad's frock coat.

"Oh, Reverend," lawyer Dewey Cheatum spoke up, "I wanted to inform all Lil's employees that in her will, Miss Lil left you each a hundred dollars so you wouldn't have to work the day of her funeral."

The customers moaned but the girls squealed with delight. "Now ain't that thoughtful!"

The preacher flushed and cleared his throat.

Dewey Cheatum walked over and put his hand on the preacher's shoulder, lowering his voice. "And there's five hundred dollars for the church." He nodded his gray, unkempt head.

"I don't know if my congregation—"

"Oh, I'll see that it's anonymous." The elderly lawyer assured him. "You know Lil was always generous with her money, covering everything from scholarships to charities."

Lovejoy nodded in agreement.

Brad started to walk away, still leading the goat, but Dewey caught his arm. "I need to see you and Delilah in my office."

"Sure." Brad nodded and took off his hat, brushing back his black hair as he handed the leash to one of the whores. "Reckon you girls can walk back to the Lily," he nodded toward the big Victorian house on a little rise at the end of the street. "Delilah, let's go to Dewey's office."

The wrinkled old cook nodded and wiped her eyes. "Mr. Brad, it just don't seem real that she's gone."

Lil was gone all right. Brad thought with a sigh, gone when she came over that rail of the open balcony last Saturday night—fiery red hair and bright purple skirts billowing—and landed on a billiard table, breaking one of its legs off. "Yep, she was one in a million." He took Delilah by the arm and helped her into his fancy buggy, looking back at the small graveyard at the edge of town. They'd covered the grave with Texas bluebonnets because the common orange day-lilies Lil loved so much weren't in bloom yet.

In the lawyer's office on Main Street, the two settled into chairs before the dusty, cluttered desk. Brad leaned back with a sigh and lit a cigar. He was feeling older than his thirty-six years today, probably because they were burying Lil. He had really cared about her, although she'd probably been almost old enough to be his mother. Before she'd taken him in and given him a fresh start three years ago, he'd been just another drifting gambler like his younger brother, Blackie.

Dewey cleared his throat and shuffled papers as he settled behind his desk. "Lil McGinty was one woman in a thousand. Too bad we know so little about her or where she came from." He looked at Delilah. "I hear tell you've been with her at least twenty-five years."

"She rescued me from a slave auction in Atlanta,"

the old woman wiped her eyes. "Wasn't nothin' I wouldn't do for Miss Lil."

Brad looked at her. "So you probably know more about her than anyone."

She gave him a steely look. "Not much. Some things maybe she didn't want nobody to know."

Brad shrugged. *What did the past matter?* He wondered if Delilah had taken the diamond pin he'd given Lil for her birthday only the day before her death. Or maybe it had been pinned to Lil's dress when they buried her and he hadn't noticed. Well, it made no difference now.

The old man shuffled his papers. "Here's the will—you two are mentioned."

"Us?" Both said in surprise.

Dewey ran his hand through his straggly gray hair, nodded, and began to read: "I, Lil McGinty, being of sound mind, do make this my last will and testament. I bequeath the employees of the Texas Lily one hundred dollars each so they can party instead of work the night of my funeral."

Brad laughed. "That sounds like Lil, all right."

The lawyer said, "She left the church five hundred and a little to other charities. Here's for you, Delilah: ". . . For my good and faithful cook and friend, I leave five thousand dollars—"

"Five thousand dollars!" Delilah's mouth fell open.

"Yep," Dewey nodded. "You're a rich woman, Delilah. The money's in my safe. You can retire and not work another day in your life."

"Humph!" the old woman said, wrinkling her nose, "and just what would I do with my time then? If Mr. Brad don't mind, I'd just like to save that money and keep workin' at the Lily."

"Sure." Brad grinned and puffed his cigar. "I don't know how I could run the place without you."

The old woman stood up and brushed her rumpled black dress. "Then if'fen you're through with me, I wants to inspect Miss Lil's grave and make sure the flowers are just right, then I got to get a roast in the oven. Folks got to eat, funeral or no."

Brad stood up and opened the door for the old woman. "You take my buggy, Delilah. I'll walk back after I'm finished here."

She nodded and left, then Brad took his chair again.

Dewey Cheatum reached into his desk for a bottle of bourbon and two glasses. "We lost a great woman with Lil McGinty. Let's drink to her." He poured the drinks.

"She was the savin' of me all right," Brad agreed and took his glass, clinked it with Dewey's. "I'm gonna miss her. She built the Texas Lily into the best gamblin' hall and bordello in all east Texas."

"You had something to do with its success," Dewey reminded him, "as good as you play poker. Anyway she left you something as well." He looked at Brad over his own glass of bourbon.

"I expected that someday but not yet. After all, I don't reckon she's got a relative in this world. At least, she never mentioned it. I don't even know if she was ever married or where she was from. She never talked about her past, but then, I didn't know her as well as Delilah did."

"Let her past die with her." Dewey frowned and lit his pipe. "Uh, Brad, she left you two things."

Her half of the Texas Lily, Brad thought. Hell, he'd rather have Lil back. He'd never thought she'd die in such an unexpected accident.

"No, actually she left you three things." Dewey studied the papers before him, fragrant smoke swirling about his gray head. "One is the goat. You're to look after her beloved pet, Herman."

Brad grinned. "That smelly old billy goat will probably outlive me. All he's good for is to chew up all the day-lilies growin' out front of the house."

"And she left you one thousand dollars in gold. It's in my safe; you know she didn't have much faith in banks."

"I know. There was always a rumor around town that she hid her profits in the walls of that big house."

Dewey shrugged and smoked his pipe. "I reckon that's just a local tale. Or maybe she did; but she didn't tell me. Also, she left you that big fancy iron birdbath out in front of the Lily, you know the one in the center flowerbed."

Brad nodded. He didn't care about the birdbath, although he knew Lil had set a great deal of store by it. She'd bought it in one of her rare trips to Beaumont and put it out among the orange day-lilies in the middle of the front lawn. Even now, he could close his eyes and see her in that big hat she wore to protect her freckled skin against the Texas sun. She liked to be out at dawn or sometimes dusk, gardening and planting flowers out front while the goat munched grass peacefully beside her. His mind went over what Dewey had just said. "Uh, Dewey, you said three things."

Dewey fiddled with his pipe. "That's three, ain't it?"

Brad began to get a sinking feeling in his gut. "What about the Texas Lily?"

Lawyer Cheatum took a deep gulp of his drink. "That's the hardest to explain."

"Try."

Dewey shrugged and read aloud from the papers in front of him. "I leave my half of the Texas Lily to my niece, Lillian Primm, a teacher at Miss Pickett's Female Academy in Boston, along with five thousand dollars."

"What?" Brad half rose from his chair and tossed his cigar into the spittoon. "What?"

"Now, take it easy, Brad, there's more. ". . . since I'm certain Lillian will not be interested in this property, indeed, I'd just as soon she never knew more than she already does about me, I suggest Brad O'Neal, my partner, offer my niece ten thousand dollars for her half out of what I've left him, thus making him sole owner."

Brad felt as if he'd been hit in the stomach. "Well, I'll be damned. A niece, and a respectable schoolteacher at that. Hell, I didn't know she had any family at all."

Dewey shrugged and wiped his mouth. "I reckon there's a lot we didn't know about Lil, even though she lived here for more than ten years."

"I don't know whether to be insulted or not that she didn't leave the Lily to me. If she left me one thousand dollars, how am I supposed to come up with ten thousand for the niece? The goat and the bird bath ain't worth ten bucks."

Dewey shrugged. "Reckon she thought you'd have the difference in the bank."

Brad frowned. "It'll be tough, but I can do it by borrowin' against my land. Why do you reckon Lil didn't just deed me the Lily and tell me to send the niece the ten thousand?"

"Maybe she knew you too well, Brad," the old man grinned, "and wanted to make sure the gal really got the money."

"I ain't that slick, even though maybe I used to be," Brad admitted, "but I been usin' my share of the profits to buy up land between here and Beaumont. Thinkin' of raisin' cattle in my old age."

Dewey nodded. "So it's simple. I'll write this niece a letter and tell her the deal, only I'll spare her knowing what the Lily really is."

Brad had a sudden, chilling thought. "Suppose the gal won't take it and tries to hold me up for more money? You know them damned Yankees."

"An old maid schoolteacher from Boston?" Dewey snorted. "Why, she'll jump at the chance to sell a property she's never seen. I'll write an official letter for you. I reckon by late May, you'll own the Texas Lily outright without ever having to meet this lady."

Brad heaved a sigh of relief and drained his glass, stood up, and set the tumbler on the edge of the desk. "Reckon I got upset for nothin'. Yep, you do that. Let me know when you hear from her." He opened the door and stood looking out, mumbling under his breath. He was more than a little annoyed with Lil, not trusting him to do the right thing by her niece. Not that she didn't know him pretty well. "A thousand dollars, a damned goat, and a bird bath. If that don't beat all."

"Oh, one more thing," Dewey called after him as Brad started out the door, "I almost forgot; Miss Lil said there was a box of stuff that's up on her closet shelf. She said Delilah would know what to do. Will you tell Delilah?"

"Sure, sure." Brad was only half listening as he closed the door and started down the wooden sidewalk. One thousand dollars, a goat, and a damned birdbath. Yes, by borrowing, he could afford to pay the old maid niece ten thousand dollars. The Texas Lily was profitable and he could soon be a rich man once he owned it outright, but he felt insulted and slighted. He'd thought Lil had had more affection for him than that. Oh, well, he was a helluva lot better off now than the poor white trash way he'd grown up. That thought cheered him as he started walking toward the big white Victorian house on the hill at the end of Main Street.

Miss Pickett's Female Academy,
Boston, Massachusetts

Miss Lillian Primm sat in her small, sparse room and reread the lawyer's letter as she poured herself a cup of tea. She felt little at the news of the death of her mother's younger sister and only relative, except that now Lillian was truly alone in the world. But then Lillian had met her namesake only one time as a child and barely remembered it. There seemed to be tension between her strict widowed mother and Aunt Lil, so she never asked about her.

Yesterday she had received notice from the Boston bank that the monthly stipends that had been arriving for ten years would now be ending. Her titled father's estate was exhausted, no doubt. Well, it had been a Godsend in helping Lillian and her sickly mother survive. Since her mother's death, Lillian had been helping pay impoverished girls' tuition by living frugally. Now this morning, this letter had come from Texas.

Did she dare add sugar to her tea? It was not a luxury Lillian allowed herself often, nor jam for her toast. A teacher barely got by on her meager salary, and she spent every extra penny helping poor students as she had been helped with a scholarship. Yet with this letter, she could afford to splurge. The three students she was aiding at the moment would graduate next month, ending that expense. Now five thousand dollars was hers and another ten thousand when she signed over her share of the hotel. She would be a woman of considerable means.

Brushing a wisp of red hair back into her tight bun, Lillian went to the window and looked out at the girls crossing the campus. She had hoped for a husband and children of her own, but it looked like that was not to be. In the years after she graduated,

when she might have met a nice young man, Lillian
had been busy nursing her sick mother so there was
no time for socializing.

Besides, as Mother had so often pointed out, Lillian was tall and thin and very plain to look at, with
undignified freckles across her nose. At thirty-two,
she had long since stopped hoping, although one
student's father had once hinted that he could be
very generous for a little warmth, wink, wink. She
had stopped him in his tracks with a frosty glare.
Mother and her aunt had both been redheads, too,
but both so much prettier than Lillian. Perhaps she
took after her highborn father, whose ship had
been lost at sea before she was born.

Outside, spring was still weeks away in this north-
ern state. She wondered what Texas was like.
Warm, most certainly, a vast place of cows and cowboys and savages, according to the books she
read—certainly more interesting and challenging
than spending year after year teaching rich spoiled
girls grammar and etiquette. A cool wind rattled
the building and she shivered in her plain dark
dress. So now she owned half a hotel in Texas. Or
she could take the money and stay in Boston.
Should she be daring? Lillian had never done anything daring in her whole life. Mother would have
frowned on anything that wasn't highly respectable.
Her sickly mother had been dead now five years.
She hadn't written Aunt Lil when her mother died;
she'd had no idea how to reach the woman.

On the other hand, Texas sounded full of possibil-
ities, and at least a change from her mundane life. At
that moment, Lillian made her decision. She would
journey to Fort Floppett and see this hotel herself
before deciding whether to sell or not. After all, her
aunt had also left her five thousand dollars and
school would be out soon. If she decided she didn't

like Texas, she could always sell out to her aunt's partner and be back in Boston in time for fall classes. Should she write this lawyer and tell him she was coming? No, she shook her head. She wanted to look things over before she announced herself. The Texas Lily. It certainly sounded like a strange name for a hotel.

Late May, the train station in Fort Floppett

It was sundown on a warm Saturday night as Lillian stepped off the train. The weather was so hot, she regretted wearing the dark serge, high-necked dress. She stood there holding her small carpet bag and looking around. It was supper time and there weren't many people on the street. Fort Floppett looked to be a prosperous town with many shops up and down Main Street. Behind her, the train whistled a warning and then began to puff and hiss as it started out of town. She had a sudden impulse to run after it and get back on, return to the safe, secure life she knew so well.

"Nothing ventured, nothing gained," she reminded herself, straightening her thin shoulders as she looked around, wondering where she could rent a buggy. But of course a hotel should be right in the heart of town.

A very respectable looking woman in a blue dress with a little boy in tow came out of a shop and walked past her.

"Excuse me," Lillian said, "Could you direct me to the Texas Lily?"

The woman stopped in her tracks and glared at her. "How dare you!"

"I beg your pardon?" Lillian blinked in confusion

and stepped back, but the woman only huffed and strode on, almost dragging the small boy.

A young army lieutenant had just stepped out of the tobacco shop on the corner and looked at her strangely. He was handsome but short, with brown hair and a wispy mustache. "Excuse me, ma'am," he took off his hat and bowed. "Perhaps I misunderstood what you asked?"

"I don't know why she was so upset," Lillian stammered, "I'm new in town and I was looking for the hotel—"

"Allow me to introduce myself," he said, "I am Lieutenant Buford Fortenbury of the Philadelphia Fortenburys. I can tell by your accent that you're not from around here."

"Hardly." Lillian said. "I am Lillian Primm, lately of Boston, and I'm looking for the Texas Lily."

"Indeed." First he looked confused, then mystified as his pale face turned a rosy blush red. "And may I ask what business a lady would have—?"

"No, you may not." Lillian snapped, and then regretted her peevishness. This officer was obviously attempting to be of service, but she was weary, hot, and a little cross now that darkness had fallen. "Now sir, if you would kindly direct me to the Texas Lily Hotel, I would appreciate it."

"You could have fooled me," the Lieutenant winked at her, "You don't look like the type Brad O'Neal hires to—"

"To what?" Lillian drew herself up to her full height, which made her taller than the foppish lieutenant. "For your information sir, I am the new half-owner of the hotel."

"The hotel?" He looked blank, then smiled. "My abject apologies, Miss Primm." He bowed again. "I was just running some errands for Major Bottoms so I have his buggy. Please allow me to drive you to the establishment."

Lillian smiled with relief. "You know my aunt's hotel?"

"Your aunt?" He took her suitcase and her elbow and they walked toward the buggy tied at the hitching post. "Lil McGinty was your aunt?"

Lillian nodded as he helped her up into the buggy. "I only met her once. I suppose somewhere along the way, she married some Irishman. Myself, I'm now establishing my lineage so I can prove myself eligible for Sisters Noble of British Society."

"Really?" Young Lieutenant Fortenbury took his seat next to her and smiled as he snapped his little whip. "What a coincidence. I myself am a member of Sons of British Society, the brother organization."

She warmed to him immediately. He might be a bit foppish, but after all, he was a blueblood and her mother had always stressed how important that was. It didn't matter if one were gently poor as long as one came from fine ancestors. Blood will tell, Mother had said over and over as she told Lillian of her aristocratic relatives. "Just what kind of town is this, anyway?"

He gave her a weak smile. "Oh, prosperous, with the fort and the ranches all around here. But they're really county bumpkins, most of them, and worse yet, Texans. I'm hoping for a transfer soon to Washington, D.C. so I can move up in the world."

Fine bloodlines and ambitious, too. She warmed to him even more. "Tell me about the Texas Lily," she asked. "Does it do a good business?"

He made a choking sound. "I—I really wouldn't know."

"Where is it, anyway?"

"That's it up ahead; that big white house on the hill at the end of Main Street."

"Oh, my." She breathed a sigh. It was a gigantic three-story white Victorian mansion with many turrets and gingerbread trim. A horseshoe-shaped drive encircled a large lawn and flowerbed of common orange day-lilies, centering around a big white iron birdbath. Lights streamed from all the windows and there were many buggies and horses tied out front. "It seems to be doing a landslide business."

"It always does on Saturday night," Lieutenant Fortenbury said, "Or so others tell me." He turned the horse up the horseshoe-shaped drive toward the ornate stained glass front doors.

"Is that a goat out among the day-lilies?" She blinked, not quite sure what she saw.

"Oh, that's Herman, the billy goat. He was Lil McGinty's pet."

The goat glared at them, waggled his gray beard, and returned to munching day-lilies.

"I thought billy goats were always named Billy?"

The officer laughed. "This one is named for the fort's founder, Major Herman Floppett. I understand there's a resemblance. Well, here we are." He reined in the buggy out front. From inside came the sound of laughter and music.

"My," said Lillian, "they seem to be having a good time."

"They usually are." Lieutenant Fortenbury said. "Miss Primm, I think you should know . . ."

"Yes?"

"Never mind. Uh, let me help you down, Miss Primm."

He came around and assisted her, then hesitated. She started toward the steps. "Aren't you coming in?"

He shook his head. "I—I think I'll wait for you in the buggy."

"Oh, but I'll be staying since I'm now half-owner."

He hesitated again. "Miss Primm, about the Texas Lily—"

"What?"

He hesitated again.

She was a bit put out with him, thinking him rude for not assisting her up the steps like any proper gentleman would. She lifted her skirts, went up the steps, and rang the bell. From inside, she heard loud music and men talking. A woman laughed somewhere inside. Her limited experience with hotels made her puzzle over the racket. Of course, she'd heard Texans were rowdy by nature. She wondered about the other owner. Perhaps he was some old Texas rancher or maybe a back east hotel man. At the very least, he must be Irish. Lillian wrinkled her nose. Hadn't her mother often told her how vulgar and low-class the Irish were?

She heard footsteps and then a small, elderly black woman in a maid's uniform opened the door. The smell of cigar smoke enveloped them both, and beyond the woman, Lillian could see crowds of men and girls dressed in short, gaudy dresses. "What in the name of goodness is going on here?"

"Just who is you, lady?" The elderly woman inquired.

Lillian pushed past her into the hallway. The inside was as large as a ballroom with an open balcony overlooking the room. The drapes were gaudy red velvet and through the swirl of cigar smoke, she saw men at tables playing cards or leaning against an ornate bar. An off-key piano banged away at "Buffalo Gals." What kind of behavior was this in her deceased aunt's fine hotel? She marched into the room and stood looking around, confused and outraged. As the raucous crowd seemed to notice her, they moved and quieted.

Brad felt good tonight. It was about time his luck changed. In his hand, he held a royal flush. He hadn't had one since the night Lil McGinty crashed through that railing and came sailing off that balcony and landed on a billiard table. Yep, his luck was running wild tonight. Just as he was about to bet, he realized the room was growing quiet and heads were turning toward the door. The music quit mid-note. *Now what the hell?*

Brad frowned as he craned his neck to see what the distraction was. A tall, red-haired girl stood in the middle of the entry and now she marched into the room like a warship under full sail. She had hair the color of a forest fire, pulled back in a tight bun under a plain dark hat. She wore a dark, no-nonsense, severe dress and she was skinny as a rail and looked stiff as a poker, her face frowning, a few freckles scattered across her nose. This was a respectable lady, there was no doubt about that. Now what was a respectable lady doing in a place like the Texas Lily?

The silence grew as everyone turned to look at her.

"I demand to see Mr. Bradley O'Neal," she said in a back-East accent that would cut glass with its sharpness.

Uh-oh. This couldn't be good. Brad stood up from the poker table with a sigh and turned his hand upside-down on the table. "Anybody touches my cards before I get back, I'll make him eat my derringer," he drawled and then stepped forward to greet the lady. "Brad O'Neal at your service, ma'am," he made a sweeping bow. "And to whom do I have the honor of—?"

"What is the meaning of all these shenanigans? This is no way to run a hotel. It must stop immediately."

"What?" He was seldom at a loss for words, but any man would wither under the glare of those cold green eyes.

"Mr. O'Neal," she snapped, "I am your new partner. I am Lillian Primm."

Oh, hell, his luck really had run out.

Chapter Two

He managed to close his mouth and made a sweeping bow. "Oh, Miss Primm, we weren't expectin' you."

"Evidently." She glared at him although she had to look up to do so. He was tall and wide-shouldered, dressed in a stylish frock coat and a red satin vest. His black hair fell down over one eye as he bowed low and his dark eyes issued both a challenge and an invitation. There was something very primitive and male about him that made her take a step back. Oh, he was one of those Irish rogues her mother had warned her about; no doubt about it. "There will have to be some changes made. This is no way to run a fine hotel."

Around them, men had gathered out of curiosity and now a chuckle ran through the crowd. Lillian saw nothing funny at all. A blond girl in a red satin dress that was both too short and too tight swaggered up, swinging her hips. She held a slender cigarillo in her hand and smoke encircled her head. Lillian could only stare. She had never seen a woman smoke before.

"Hey, Brad, honey," the blonde sneered, "what's

the problem?" She put her hand on his broad shoulder a bit too familiarly, which annoyed Lillian although she wasn't certain why.

Lillian glared at her. "This does not concern you."

"Why, you—"

The Irishman caught the girl's arm. "Now Sadie, there's been a big misunderstandin' here. "Miss Primm, I think we need to retire to my office and—"

"You've been drinking," Lillian snapped as she took a sniff. She was acutely aware that she was surrounded by the type of people she'd never met before in her very sheltered life. They looked like rowdies. "Worse yet, you reek of cheap perfume."

"That ain't cheap perfume!" The blonde put her hand on her hip. A customer brung that to me all the way from St. Louie."

"Brought," Lillian corrected.

"What?" Sadie looked bewildered.

She had had enough of this nonsense. "Mr. O'Neal, I will see you in the lawyer's office in the morning."

"What?" He scratched his head.

"You heard me." She turned to go.

"Tomorrow's Sunday." He gave her the most devilish grin.

The crowd laughed and Lillian felt foolish. "Then I shall return Monday with the lawyer." Lillian said and then she wheeled, her head high as she marched out of the Texas Lily. She was close to tears, but of course a person of good background did not give way to emotion. Hadn't her dour, cold mother taught her that? Yet she was shocked, horrified, and downright exhausted after her long trip. All her dreams about Texas and a fine hotel and then to discover what she'd inherited was evidently a—a—she couldn't even say the word. And from her own aunt. She blinked and swallowed hard as she went out the door and down the steps into the darkness.

Lieutenant Fortenbury hurried to meet her. "I am so sorry, Miss Primm. I didn't know how to tell you."

"I'll be fine." She managed to keep her voice steady, but inside, she was a wreck. She imagined that pretty Sadie creature was snickering at her even now. For this, she had given up a safe, secure job in faraway Boston. "Take me to the hotel. I'll decide what to do later."

He helped her up into the buggy, his delicate hands moist. "I'm sorry, Miss, but there is no hotel. It burned down last month."

"What? Where do visitors stay then?"

"Well, if they don't have relatives in town, they've been sleeping under a tree or staying at the fort until someone builds a new hotel. I'll take you there."

As they drove away, she looked back over her shoulder at the lights and music streaming from the fine mansion. "I had no idea. I was told it was a hotel."

"I didn't know how to warn you, Miss Primm. I never go in there myself—it's full of rough louts, typical Texans."

She warmed to the gentleman as they drove past the big white birdbath and the goat raised its head, bleating at them. "I should have accepted the offer, I suppose. No wonder my mother disapproved of Aunt Lillian. And her partner, why, he looks like a rascal of the worst sort."

"Low-class Texas trash," Lieutenant Fortenbury agreed. "No one knew you were coming, I presume?"

She shook her head. "Lawyer Cheatum wrote that it was a hotel, and that Aunt Lil had left me her half, but that rascal, O'Neal, wanted to buy me out."

"So do you intend to sell?"

"I—I don't know. Certainly I'm not one to run from a fight."

"Perhaps you could buy that gambler out," the young officer suggested as they drove along the quiet street.

"And own a—a bordello? I think not. Besides, I only have a small sum. I couldn't afford to buy him out."

"Well, said the officer, "there's always been a legend that Miss Lil hid a lot of money inside the house somewhere. If you owned the place and found that, you could certainly afford to buy the place and do whatever you wanted with it."

"I am not one to chase after pie in the sky," she answered sternly. "I am a realist."

"Still it was a shame to make such a startling discovery for one of such fine lineage. If there's anything I can do to help you, Miss Primm, I am at your service."

She smiled at him and felt better already. "Thank you, Lieutenant. But I could expect no less from a member of Sons of British Nobility."

"Of course not." He smiled back at her. "Here's the fort straight ahead. There's a social and dance tonight. I'll take you to the major's wife. She'll be very sympathetic, I'm sure."

They drove past the parade grounds and the barracks. The scent of roses drifted on the hot Texas air.

"Roses at a fort?" She asked.

He nodded. "Major Bottoms' passion—along with parades. Why, he wanted to bring out the marching band for Lil McGinty's funeral, but the respectable ladies of the fort would have. . . ." He let his voice trail off and cleared his throat in the awkward silence. "Well, here we are."

He drew up before a large building. Lights and sedate music drifted from inside. He stepped down and handed his reins to an orderly. "See to the lady's luggage and the horse."

"Yes, sir." The young private snapped a salute and took the reins.

The lieutenant came around to help Lillian from the buggy.

She hesitated as she stepped down. "I'm not really dressed for a ball."

"Nonsense." He let her take his arm and they strode toward the building. "You are lovely, although it's presumptuous of me to say so."

She felt a rare blush. "My, you are very kind." Lillian was confused and a little uncertain. Men had never noticed her before and yet tonight, here the lieutenant actually seemed to be flirting with her.

Inside, a sparse crowd danced to the sedate music or stood around the room with cups of punch. The ladies seemed to be visiting while most of the men looked bored.

Lieutenant Fortenbury led her up to an older, plump couple. "Major and Mrs. Bottoms, I have the honor to present Miss Primm, lately of Boston."

Lillian curtsied, although she was awkward at it.

"Delighted, my dear," said the major. "Did you see my roses as you drove in?"

"Now, Gilbert," his gray-haired wife scolded. Then to Lillian she said, "Don't pay any attention to my husband, my dear, he has only two interests in life, his roses and his parades. Are you visiting someone in town?"

Lillian took a deep breath, wondering how to explain.

Lieutenant Fortenbury said, "Miss Primm is a

teacher from Boston and is joining the Sisters Noble of British Society, the elite S.N.O.B.S."

"Snobs?" Mrs Bottoms looked puzzled.

Lillian took a deep breath. "This is a bit humiliating but I'm in town to inherit a hotel."

"Hotel?" The major said, "we have no hotel."

Lillian bit her lip and the Lieutenant rushed in. "Miss Primm is the late Lil McGinty's niece."

"Oh, dear me." The lady's mouth dropped open.

The major cleared his throat in the awkward silence. "Of course, family resemblance, and all that, I mean, so I hear . . ." he sputtered into confused silence.

"Red hair runs in the family," Lillian said, feeling like an idiot.

Couples on the dance floor seemed to be straining to hear the conversation.

The way everyone was staring at her, she knew what they all thought of her aunt and the Texas Lily. No wonder the relationship between her proud mother and her aunt had been torn asunder. "I thought I would come out and see the hotel," she sputtered.

"Hotel? What hotel?" The major said again.

"Hush, Gilbert." Mrs. Bottoms patted Lillian's arm. "You poor dear."

"I drove her out to the Texas Lily," Lieutenant Fortenbury shrugged helplessly, "I didn't know quite how to tell her."

Tears came to Lillian's green eyes but she blinked them away. "I—I haven't quite decided what to do. It was such a shock."

The motherly woman gave her a sympathetic look. "Well, you don't have to deal with that tonight, my dear. You look tired and I have a spare room."

A chubby civilian wearing thick glasses and

leading a dumpy woman walked over just then. "Is this a stranger in our midst?"

Mrs. Bottoms made the introductions. "Miss Primm, this is Lester Osburn, owner of our weekly newspaper, the *Fort Floppett Bugle,* and his wife, Gladys."

"Delighted to meet you," the gentleman smiled. "We call our paper the *Bugle* because of the army and the fort—"

"I get it, I get it," Lillian said, and nodded politely to his dumpy wife.

"Maybe I can add your name to our society column," said Mr. Osburn, "who are you in town to visit?"

"Uh, Lester," said the major, "Miss Primm is Lil McGinty's niece."

"Oh, dear," said dull Mrs. Osburn, and her mouth dropped open.

Lillian wanted to go through the floor.

"I think," said the major's wife in the awkward silence, "I'd better take Miss Primm to her quarters."

"But I was hoping to dance with the lady," The chubby major protested.

"Oh, stop it, Gilbert, you old goat. Come, my dear. Do you have luggage?"

The lieutenant said, "I had one of the privates take charge of it."

Lillian murmured an awkward good night and followed Mrs. Bottoms off the dance floor.

"Such a fine young man," Mrs. Bottoms nodded approval as she led Lillian away. "I wish we had more like him. You see how few are at our dance? I imagine most of them are over at the Lily."

"There were quite a few there," Lillian admitted as they walked away. Behind them, she heard the buzz as word spread through the room about who she was. She kept her head high and ignored it. After all, she was from a fine and highborn family. She couldn't be responsible if her aunt had done the unthinkable, marrying an Irishman and owning a bordello. Still, it was humiliating. In her genteel poverty, her family pride was all that had sustained her. There were a million questions she wanted to ask Mrs. Bottoms, but she feared to hear the answers.

In the hallway of the building hung a large oil painting of an elderly officer. His hair was parted down the middle and he was slightly cross-eyed, with a gray mustache and a straggly beard. Lillian paused and stared at it.

"The fort's founder, Major Herman Floppett." Mrs. Bottoms explained.

"He really does resemble the goat," Lillian said without thinking.

"Oh, you've met Herman? He's sort of the town mascot, but mostly he grazes the lawn and the orange day-lilies out in front of your aunt's place. I presume you met the handsome devil at the Texas Lily, Brad O'Neal?"

"What a rascal!" Lillian said as she followed Mrs. Bottoms to the officers' quarters.

"But a charming one," Mrs. Bottoms murmured with a sigh. "He could convince a sparrow to fly right into a cat's mouth."

"I saw nothing charming about him," Lillian snapped, "and I'll have to talk to Mr. Cheatum about what my legal options are."

"Dewey?" The lady laughed as she showed Lillian to a room. "If you'd asked around, you'd have probably seen him at one of the poker tables at the Lily tonight. He and Mr. O'Neal are friends."

Lillian's spirits sagged. Evidently if Mr. Dewey Cheatum was a good friend of the gambler, he would be no ally to her.

"My dear, the easiest thing to do would be to sell out to Brad and leave town."

"My mother told me the Primm family has a proud heritage dating back to the Earl of Primley who was a hero at the Battle of Waterloo against the French, so I am not one to cut and run before a low-class Texas hooligan."

"Bravely spoken." The major's wife smiled and nodded. "I imagine there aren't many women who can stand up against Brad O'Neal's lure."

"This is one respectable lady who is immune to his oily charm." Lillian sat down on the bed.

"Brad O'Neal is a formidable opponent, my dear. But that can all wait until tomorrow." With that, she said her good nights and left Lillian to ponder her next move. She had liked the Texas landscape the train had taken her through, and she'd been excited about a new life and the new career of running a first-class hotel. And what she'd found was a slick rascal and a whorehouse. There, she'd said it. How could Aunt Lil have fallen so low? She bit her lip to keep from breaking into sobs and got ready for bed. Tomorrow she would decide what to do.

The next morning, she had breakfast with the major and his wife out on the veranda of their quarters, where she could admire the roses around the lawn. "Steak for breakfast?" She couldn't hold back her surprise.

"After all, my dear," the major said, "this is Texas. They have more cows than people and the local ranches keep us well supplied."

Lillian was used to a cup of weak tea and a slice of toast. The coffee was strong enough to float a horseshoe. Along with the steak came scrambled eggs and hot biscuits. She tried not to gobble, but the food was so good. "Tell me, Major, just what function does the fort serve?"

The major looked uncomfortable and cleared his throat. "Uh," he said, "originally, it was built to protect the stage lines from bandits and Indians."

"Is there a stage line?" Lillian asked, "I thought the train—?"

"Not in forty years," Mrs. Bottoms smiled, "and the Indians in this part of Texas were never much for war parties anyway."

"But what about the War?"

Major Bottoms shook his head. "Occupied by the Union and played no part in the war—sort of the backwater of the fight."

"Then why does it even exist?" Lillian asked.

"The truth is," Mrs. Bottoms lowered her voice and leaned closer, "there's really no reason for Fort Floppett's existence except that it's a comfortable post and the town relies on it for business. It's a wonder Congress hasn't closed it already and sent all these troops to where they're really needed— Arizona, to fight Apaches."

The major shuddered. "Don't even think about it. Arizona. No water for roses, nothing but heat, dust, cactus, and bloodthirsty Apaches. No, the soldiers love Fort Floppett, and the town of Fort Floppett loves the army. Let us hope members of Congress never come here to look around."

Lillian ate one more biscuit with homemade wild sand plum jelly and put down her napkin. "What time is it?"

The major pulled out his big gold watch. "10:30."

"I imagine that scoundrel will be up by now at the Texas Lily." Lillian said.

The major laughed. "Brad? I wouldn't bet on it."

His wife gave him a warning frown, then to Lillian, she said "My dear, do you really want to confront him? Perhaps you should arrange a meeting in lawyer Cheatum's office tomorrow instead."

"I've decided I would like to get this settled today," Lillian said, gritting her teeth. She was nothing if not New England stubborn.

"Be careful around that gambler," the major grinned. "They say he could talk a cow out of her calf or a dog off a meat wagon."

"I beg your pardon?" Lillian said.

"Oh, honey," Mrs Bottom said with a dismissing wave at her husband, "that's Texan for beware of the rascal's gift of gab. You wouldn't be the first girl Brad's talked into—never mind. Another cup of coffee, my dear?"

Lillian shook her head. So Mr. Brad O'Neal was a ladies' man? Humph, she certainly didn't see him as charming. The genteel and highborn Buford Fortenbury was more to her taste. "May I borrow your buggy, Major?"

"You're really going over there this morning?"

"Yes, that is my plan."

"But it's Sunday and as late as they were all up, the girls working so late—"

"Gilbert!" His wife glared at him.

His beefy face turned bright red. "I meant, they are probably all still asleep and will be 'til noon."

"Good." Lillian said curtly, "then I shall wake them up." She imagined that Texas rascal sleeping soundly and being disturbed by her ringing his bell over and over. It would serve him right.

However, she was a bit less certain as she left the driver with the buggy and marched up the steps to the elegant stained glass front doors. She rang the bell. And rang and rang. Then she resorted to pounding. She was not going to be treated shabbily by that rascal. "Brad O'Neal, I know you're in there. Open this door immediately!" She pounded some more.

About that time, the door was opened by the wrinkled black maid. "Yes?"

She mustered as much dignity as she could, considering she was puffing from her exertion. "I am here to see Mr. Bradley O'Neal."

"He don't usually see visitors this early in the morning, Miss."

"I am not surprised. I assume he is sleeping off a hangover?"

"No, ma'am, he's in the kitchen."

"What? Then I will go to the kitchen." Lillian pushed past the old woman and looked about. The delicious scent of strong coffee and frying ham drifted to her nose. She marched toward the kitchen with the small maid trailing in her wake.

It was a spacious kitchen and the scene as she entered caused her to stop short. Seven beautiful but sleepy-looking young women in various stages of dress sat about a big round table. Brad O'Neal, needing a shave and in his shirt-sleeves, worse yet, wearing an apron, stood at the stove. He turned and grinned. "Oh, hello, Miss Primm. Would you like some breakfast? I cook on Sunday sometimes."

"He's great at flapjacks," the blond girl volunteered and lit a cigarillo.

"No thank you, I've had breakfast. Mr. O'Neal, we need to talk—"

"Well, I haven't, so you'll have to wait. Delilah, get the lady some coffee."

She wasn't about to accept hospitality from this rascal. "Thank you, but I'm here on business—"

"You might as well have a cup, Miss," the black maid said, "Mr. Brad is right stubborn."

Stubborn? She'd show him stubborn. His oily

charm might work on weaker women, but not on a Primm descendant. However, Lillian accepted the coffee and stood there awkwardly.

"Sit down," O'Neal ordered, gesturing toward the table, but the whores didn't look too friendly.

"Thank you, but I prefer to stand. I am here on business."

"Suit yourself." He shrugged and returned to his cooking. He had pots boiling and ham frying along with his flapjacks.

She didn't know what to say. "I didn't expect you to be the cook."

"It's just one of my talents," the rascal said, winking at her, and the girls around the table giggled. "I like to keep my hand in; learned a lot in New Orleans, but all but Sundays, the kitchen belongs to Delilah."

She watched him dish up food. Something in the big bowl looked like mush. "What in the name of goodness is that?"

"Grits." Brad grinned. "You know you're in east Texas when they serve you grits with your eggs. In north Texas, its more likely to be fried potatoes and along the Mexican border and in west Texas, it'll be beans and tortillas. Want some?"

"I said I had already eaten." She answered frostily.

The girls were digging into their heaping plates.

"Oh Brad, honey," a brunette smiled at him, "you got so many talents."

"Evidently, Miss Primm doesn't think so." He grinned and dished himself a plate of food, then poured himself a cup of coffee. "Very well, Miss Primm, if you'll precede me, we can talk in my office while I eat, if you don't mind."

The girls set up a moan. "Aw, Brad, honey, we thought you was gonna eat with us."

He winked at them. "We'll have dinner together. Remember, I've got a roast ready to go in the oven and Delilah, you'll watch my coconut cake, while I visit with Miss Primm, won't you?"

"Sho 'nuff, Mister Brad, you gonna want seven minute icing with that?"

He nodded as he pulled off his apron. "Get the eggs out of the root cellar now. You know the whites whip higher when they're room temperature."

"Well!" sniffed Lillian. "Is there no end to your talents?"

He winked at her. "Ask the girls."

They all broke into giggles while Lillian's face burned. Oh, she wanted to grab the syrup pitcher and pour it all over his head, but of course, a lady of quality would not lower herself to that. Besides, rascal that he was, he might return the gesture. "We have business to discuss," she reminded him with a frosty tone.

"Come, Miss Primm," he commanded, leading the way out of the kitchen, food in both hands.

She followed along behind with her coffee cup as he led her into a large office in one wing of the big mansion.

He set his plate and coffee on his desk and gestured her to a nearby chair. Instead, she chose to take the one directly across the desk from him. She set her cup on the desk with a bang as he dug into his food, eating heartily. "Are you sure you wouldn't like some, Miss Primm? You look like a rack of bones."

She felt herself flush. "It is not polite to make such personal comments and a gentleman should not greet ladies in his shirt-sleeves."

He grinned at her and a lock of black hair fell down over one eye. "Let's get one thing straight, lady, I never claimed to be a gentleman. I'm a

Texan and a gambler and I was a very good friend of your late aunt's."

"How good?" She asked without thinking.

"Now who's being rude? She was almost like a mother to me, if that's what you're askin'."

"I—I beg your pardon." She realized that he was right. She might have to change her attitude to get anywhere with this rascal. Evidently, he was accustomed to dealing with women, if not ladies. Well, his oily charm wouldn't work on her. "Mr. O'Neal, you must understand that I am rather startled to discover my aunt's past."

"You ain't startled, lady, you're shocked out of your drawers." He put a bite of ham in his mouth. "Lil was a great old gal and you can only hope to be half the woman she was. You goin' out to visit her grave?"

"Certainly not, and I will not sit here and be insulted." She felt herself flush and half rose from her chair.

"My dear Miss Primm, I don't know what you are doin' in either Texas or the Lily. I offered to buy you out to spare you from ever knowin' the hard facts of life that your aunt evidently hid from you."

She didn't know whether to cry or throw her coffee cup at him. "I will admit I've lived a very sheltered life. I had hoped to make a new start in the hotel business here."

He laughed and sipped his coffee. "The Lily is not exactly a hotel."

"So I'm now aware." She set her jaw and glared at him.

"So just where is this conversation headed, Miss Primm? We seem to be caught in a Mexican standoff here."

"A what?"

He leaned back in his chair and sighed. "It's

Texas talk which is like no other in the world. It means we're at loggerheads. What do you have in mind? It seems quite evident that we'd be unlikely partners."

"Me? A partner in a—a—?"

"See? You can't even say the word." He grinned at her. "You should have accepted my generous offer and stayed in Boston."

"I wish I had," she snapped back, "but I had no idea—"

"But now you do, so my offer still stands—no, I'll sweeten the pot."

"What?"

"It's a poker term. I'll give you eleven thousand dollars if you let me buy you out and keep the Texas Lily and you go back to Boston."

She was nothing if not shrewd. "So what was worth ten thousand is suddenly worth eleven? Could it be worth even more than that?"

He sighed and lit a cigar without even asking her permission. "Do not toy with me, Miss Primm. Take my money and go away. It's a fair offer. Although I'll have to borrow the money, it's worth the extra thousand to get you out of my hair and out of town."

She coughed politely and waved a little lace hanky in front of her nose, but he seemed to pointedly ignore her as he continued to smoke. "If it's worth that much to you, sir, perhaps it's worth that much to me, although in good conscience, I cannot imagine running a—a—a bordello for a living."

"Oh, Lord," he blew smoke in the air and looked skyward. "Lil McGinty, what were you thinkin'? I thought you liked me." Then to Lillian, he said, "all right, Miss Primm, then you buy me out, and shut the place down."

"Are you insane? I don't have ten thousand dollars."

"Ah, I thought we were talkin' eleven? However, to break this partnership, I'd accept ten thousand and move on. No, I might even take nine thousand. I've been run out of better towns than Fort Floppett anyway." He put his boots up on his desk and smiled at her.

"I do not have even nine thousand dollars and I do not want to own a—a—" She still could not even bring herself to say the word.

He smoked his cigar and grinned at her. "So you will accept the ten thousand and return to Boston."

"You said eleven." She glared at him.

"You are a tough one to deal with," he smiled in grudging admiration. "All right, eleven. There's an evenin' train—"

"No." She said and glared back at him.

"No? Did you say no?" Evidently, from his expression, the handsome rogue had never heard that word from a woman.

"I said no. The Primms have a long history of resoluteness," she snapped. "We do not run from adversity. We did not run in the Revolutionary War and we did not run when our dear President Lincoln—"

"Oh Lord, I'd forgotten you are also a damned Yankee." He leaned back in his chair and sighed.

She was horrified. "Don't tell me you stood with the South in the Rebellion—"

"I served with Terry's Texas Rangers and proud of it, right along with my cousin, Waco. Matter of fact, my Pa lost a leg at Shiloh."

She took a deep breath and decided on a different tack. This scoundrel was as stubborn and determined as she was. "I do not know what the answer to this conundrum is, Mr. O'Neal, but—"

"This what?"

"Conundrum."

He sighed. "A damned Yankee and a school-teacher. I came up through the school of hard knocks, Miss Primm, as did your aunt."

She winced. "I am embarrassed by my aunt. I cannot imagine she needed money so badly that she would stoop to this."

He gave her a cold look. "You should live to be half as warm and generous as Lil McGinty. In Texas, we say don't judge anyone until you've walked a mile in their boots."

"This is getting us nowhere, Mr O'Neal. I think we should arrange a meeting with this despicable lawyer who wrote the letter—"

"Dewey?" He grinned. "He's really a good old boy."

"I have another opinion of him—hotel indeed." She sniffed. "I understand he is an acquaintance of yours so you'll know how to contact him. Let us say about four o'clock this afternoon?"

"On a Sunday?" He paused, cigar in mid-air. "I think Dewey is usually takin' a nap or playin' pinochle with Dimples and Pug on Sunday afternoons."

"Who? Never mind. Send him a message to forego his afternoon pleasures and we'll meet at his office at four o'clock sharp. We'll let him mediate this mess." She stood.

"What?"

"Try to straighten it out." She walked briskly to the doorway. "I shall see you in Mr. Cheatum's office, which I presume is on Main Street. This problem must be resolved."

He sighed. "I was plannin' on goin' noodlin' for catfish this afternoon afore supper."

"What?"

"It's a Southern thing," he explained, "you dive down and feel along under the river bank until you stick your hand in and find a big catfish lyin' under the bank in the mud where it's cool. Then you grab him and toss him up on the bank. Last one I got weighed fifty pounds."

"It sounds dangerous and primitive."

"Just like me." He grinned.

"Well said. I could not agree more. Now good day to you, sir."

"Well, it was until you showed up," he answered.

"Humph!" And she went sailing out of his office, out the door and down the steps, fuming. Brad O'Neal was primitive, but she wasn't certain how dangerous he was. The way the girls at his establishment had sighed and smiled at him, he certainly thought he was God's gift to women. Well, this was one woman who was immune to his oily charm, even if he was a big, handsome man. Or at least some women might think so, Lillian sniffed as she got in the buggy and ordered the driver to return her to the fort. She was not going to let that rascal win this!

Chapter Three

Brad sighed, got up, and went to the window to watch the red-haired spinster marching down the front steps and into the buggy. "Lady, what am I gonna do about you?"

Sadie came into the room behind him. "You talkin' to somebody, Brad, honey?"

He turned and looked at her. She had last night's lip rouge smeared across her mouth and her neck looked dirty. She reeked of stale tobacco. Miss Primm had smelled of soap and her face had been shiny clean and scattered with freckles, rather undignified for a strait-laced schoolteacher. "Naw, Miss Primm just left."

Sadie laughed. "Ain't she a hoot, though? Skinny, homely, and probably never had a man in her bed."

"You got that right," Brad said, watching the buggy go up the driveway. "But there ain't many girls that would go toe to toe with a man. She's as stubborn as I am."

Sadie leaned against his desk and gave him a provocative smile. "I got a good idea what to do with the afternoon."

He was suddenly bored with Sadie. She was good

at what she did, but he'd never get any interesting conversation or challenge out of her. Hell, was he loco? Who expected sass or interesting conversation out of a woman? "No can do, Sadie," he winked and shook his head. "Miss prissy Primm wants a meetin' with me and Dewey this afternoon. Maybe he can talk her into sellin' out."

"You couldn't?" she snorted. "That ain't like you, honey, not to be able to charm a gal out of her drawers."

Brad didn't like having that rubbed in. He turned away from the window. "I don't think that will work with our Yankee schoolteacher, she's smart and hard-headed."

Sadie tried to slip her arms around Brad's neck, but he shook her off. "Smart and hard-headed may be good things in a man, but that ain't what a guy's lookin' for in a girl, is it?"

"Hell, no. She's my worst nightmare, a lady, a real lady who's as savvy and stubborn as a man. Dewey has his work cut out for him on this deal. Maybe he can reason with her, but she's the most unreasonable woman it's ever been my bad luck to come across." He went outside and plopped down in the porch swing, trying to think. He'd send José, the little stable boy, with the message to Dewey. Nope, Dewey wasn't gonna like his afternoon interrupted, either. Just what was it gonna take to rid himself of this skinny, fiery-haired pest?

Lillian returned to the fort for a Sunday dinner with the Bottoms, who had invited Lieutenant Fortenbury to join them. It was a pleasant meal on the patio among the wealth of blooming roses. They dined on fried chicken, a dish called black-eyed peas and another called okra, and a strange bread known as corn bread, the Bottoms told her.

She explained her predicament. "So we're meeting with Dewey Cheatum at four. Perhaps I should hire my own lawyer."

"Isn't another one," the major said as the Mexican maid brought in another huge platter of fried chicken and fresh vegetables. There was mashed potatoes and cream gravy, homemade pickles, hot rolls, and big pitchers of cold milk and iced tea.

Lillian had never seen so much food in her life. She had always lived so poor that she hadn't imagined that anyone ate like this.

Lieutenant Fortenbury wiped his wispy mustache on his linen napkin. "Miss Primm, I do sympathize with your dilemma. That Brad O'Neal is such a low-class ruffian."

"But a handsome one," Mrs Bottoms said as she passed the pickled peaches.

The lieutenant frowned. "I wouldn't call him handsome."

"Well, he is, don't you think, my dear?" Mrs. Bottoms asked Lillian as she poured more iced tea.

Young Lieutenant Fortenbury frowned. "I'm sure he wouldn't appeal to a high-class person like Miss Primm."

"Of course not," Lillian agreed. In her mind, she remembered the gambler's grin and the way his black hair fell over his dark eyes. He probably had some Indian blood, which made him even more dangerously appealing . . . well, to some women. He was virile and wide-shouldered, and had a whole harem of women at his beck and call like a stallion. She wondered suddenly if he serviced them all. He was probably able to do so. Horrors, what was she thinking?

"Are you all right, my dear?" The major inquired, "you appear flushed."

"It—it—the afternoon is so much warmer here than in Boston." she stammered while the others seemed to look at her strangely.

"No place hotter than Texas," the major said, nodding as he helped himself to another piece of chicken. "Locals take pride in it."

He droned on, but Lillian's mind was racing again, seeing wild stallions running free across the Texas prairie, a whole herd of mares running with him. Some wild stallions were not meant to be tamed or even controlled.

". . . so what do you think, Miss Primm?" The younger officer said.

"What?" She started, embarrassed that she'd been thinking about rearing stallions while ignoring the obvious interest of a respectable, eligible gentleman like Lieutenant Fortenbury.

"I said, the major is planning a band concert soon and I'll be playing the tuba," the officer wiped his wispy mustache again. "I do hope you will come hear our concert."

"Uh, certainly—if I haven't returned to Boston. What's the occasion?" She tried to smile and concentrate on young Fortenbury again, but all she could see in her mind was the short man struggling to carry a big brass tuba.

The major cleared his throat. "I understand we're getting some congressmen coming through on a fact-finding mission—or maybe just looking for a vacation."

"Too bad we don't have a hotel anymore." Fortenbury said.

"Did they ever decide why it caught fire?" Mrs. Bottoms asked.

The major shook his head. "No, but we'll do our best with rooms here at the fort."

"What time is it?" Lillian asked. "I have to meet with the gambler at four."

"My dear," Mrs. Bottoms cautioned, "I don't know if I'd confront that gambler alone again, he's supposed to have a way with the ladies . . . or so I hear."

Her husband frowned at her. "Now what would you know about a man like Brad O'Neal, Edith?"

"Women talk." Now her face flushed and she kept her head down and seemed suddenly engrossed in her salad.

"Anyway," the major snapped, "she won't be alone. Dewey will be there."

Mrs. Bottoms smiled. "If you think you can't deal with that charming rascal, you could take the lieutenant here along."

Lillian saw the sudden tremble of Buford's dainty hands. "I—I was thinking of practicing my tuba this afternoon, Mrs. Bottoms, or otherwise, I'd be delighted—"

"I don't blame you, son," said the major as he ate his fried chicken with his hands, "I'd be afraid of Brad, too. I've seen him in a fistfight."

His wife gave him an inquiring, annoyed look. "Now just when was that, Gilbert? You told me you'd never been in the Texas Lily."

A sweat broke out on the major's face. "It—it was out on the driveway one time, my dear. I had gone there to retrieve some young soldiers who were too drunk to make it back to the fort."

"Disgusting!" Young Fortenbury drew himself up proudly. "That place should be closed down."

"Now that would upset the soldiers and all those cowboys who come into town on Saturday," the major said. "Men have to blow off a little steam now and then."

In Lillian's mind, the big powerful engine raced into town, its engine working and its pistons going up and down, up and down, blowing its whistle while women smiled and swooned. Power and muscle and danger.

". . . Miss Primm?" Young Fortenbury said.

"What?" Lillian started.

"I asked," the younger man said patiently as he wiped his wispy mustache again, "if you thought there was anything to the story about gold being hidden in the Lily?"

She shook her head. "I really have no idea."

Mrs Bottoms looked intrigued. "You know, I've heard that tale, too. They say Lil McGinty didn't trust banks."

The major snorted and threw down his napkin. "Oh, Edith, I'm sure that's an old wives' tale."

"Well," the lady defended herself, "there's lots of nooks and crannies and walls to hide things—maybe some boxes in the attic just full of treasure."

"Hmm," said the lieutenant, "If there is, my dear Miss Primm, you wouldn't want to sell out too cheaply. Why, he'd probably offer you a lot just to get rid of you so he'd have free rein at hunting the gold."

"Well, he did his best to talk me into selling out to him," Lillian admitted.

"Ha!" The young officer crowed triumphantly, "I knew it! Watch out for him, Miss Primm, they say that gambler could charm a bird out of a tree."

"I doubt that," Lillian sniffed. "I don't find him charming, only annoying."

About that time, the conversation was interrupted by the maid carrying a hot berry cobbler topped with homemade ice cream. Lillian protested she couldn't eat another bite, but the cobbler tasted so good, she managed to eat a big bowlful anyway, just as the others were doing. My, these Texans certainly knew how to eat!

After dinner, she said good-bye to the lieutenant at the door. He seemed suddenly taller, although not nearly as tall as Brad O'Neal. Of course, not many men were.

"Honestly, Miss Primm, I really would accompany you this afternoon and protect you from that randy brute, if I didn't need to practice my tuba so badly."

"Yes, I understand. He seems to loathe me, so I'm not afraid of him, Lieutenant."

He took both her hands in his soft ones. His palms were moist. "I—I know we barely know each other, Miss Primm, but I do wish you'd call me Buford."

"Buford?"

He nodded. "Buford Arthur Reginal Fortenbury. I'm named for important ancestors. You know, I told you I was a member of the Sons of British Society."

She smiled at him. "How could I forget? Good afternoon . . . Buford."

"Now remember what I told you about not letting yourself be done out of any hidden treasure in that house."

She didn't like being admonished like a small child. "I've been looking out for myself for several years now, Lieutenant, ever since my mother died, five years ago."

He hesitated in the doorway, his prominent adam's apple bobbing as he swallowed, evidently getting up his courage to speak. "If—if I'm not being too forward, Miss Primm, I hope you may soon grant me the divine privilege of calling on you?"

What man used the word 'divine'?

"Let me give that some thought, Buford. This is so sudden."

"Of course. Well, I'll be off. Ta ta."

She watched him walk away. What kind of real man said 'ta ta'? Then she realized why he seemed taller. He was wearing new boots and they had such high heels, he seemed unsteady on his feet. She imagined marrying him. Yes, he was highborn and certainly rich. Mrs. Buford Arthur Reginal Fortenbury, Her linens and silver would be monogrammed B.A.R.F. Somehow, that didn't seem very appealing.

Lillian went to her room and tidied up for her appointment at the lawyer's office. She recombed her tight, severe bun and put a dab of delicate lavender scent behind her ears. Not that she thought she had any feminine wiles to weaken Bradley O'Neal's stubborn resolve, but maybe the lawyer might be swayed and if so, maybe he could sway that Texas scoundrel. Lillian needed every edge she could get. She wasn't a beauty and she knew it, but her mind was as sharp as any man's. Unfortunately, men were swayed by big bosoms and rounded bustles, not brains. She looked in the mirror again and sighed. Then she took a deep breath of resolve and marched out to the waiting buggy.

At precisely four o'clock, Lillian reined in her borrowed buggy before the lawyer's office. Nothing moved along Main Street. The whole town must be napping or playing pinochle on a warm Sunday afternoon. A spotted hound lay out in the middle of the road, asleep. There was a black stallion tied to the hitching rail. Of course it would be black, Lillian thought in annoyance, just like his hair. Silver trim shone on the fine leather saddle and bridle. No doubt it was the mount of that gambling rascal. Lillian took a deep breath and went through the door with the lettering, DEWEY CHEATUM, ATTORNEY AT LAW.

A rumpled gray-haired man sat behind a cluttered desk and Brad O'Neal sat to one side. Both had drinks in their hands and stood up when she entered.

"I thought this was a business meeting. Alcohol on a Sunday afternoon?" she frowned.

"Would you like a mint julep?" The Irishman grinned at her.

"Certainly not. I want my wits about me when I am conducting business." She nodded to the older man. "Hello, sir, I am Miss Lillian Primm, Mrs. Lil McGinty's niece."

"How do you do?" Lawyer Cheatum gestured toward a chair. "I never realized your aunt had been married."

"Well, obviously somewhere along the way to some Irishman." She frowned at the gambler. "The maiden name on my mother's side is Winters."

Brad O'Neal sipped his drink and sighed. "I told you what she was like, Dewey."

She glared at him and then turned her attention to the lawyer. "I think you are guilty of subterfuge, sir."

"Subterfuge?" Brad said, "Tsk, tsk. Why, Dewey, I knew you had sinned a lot, but I didn't reckon you had committed subterfuge."

Oh, he was maddening. "I meant," she almost gritted her teeth to hold her temper, "that Mr. Cheatum misled me about what I was inheriting."

The lawyer fumbled with his glass. "I'm really sorry about that, Miss Primm, but I just couldn't imagine writing a lady like yourself and telling her she had inherited a—well, you know."

O'Neal snorted. "If instead of being so hard-headed, lady, you had accepted my offer, you would not have had to know about this."

"I am not hardheaded," she answered, her voice cold enough to cause a blizzard, "but I give everything a lot of thought. I am not a silly female who lets herself be ruled by whimsy and passion."

Brad snorted. "Do you even know the meanin' of the word?"

"Certainly. My dictionary says—"

"That's not what I meant and you know it."

"You are a cad, sir. Now, do you know the meaning of that word?"

Lawyer Cheatum pulled out his pocket watch and sighed. "This is getting us nowhere, folks, and they're holding up a game of pinochle over in the back of Pug's store waiting for me. We need to resolve this."

"Ha!" said Brad, "Dewey, if you can convince this stubborn old maid—"

"I beg your pardon!" Lillian snapped.

Dewey Cheatum sighed and poured himself another drink out of the bottle on his desk. "I reckon I can forget about a fast settlement. I wish I'd told Pug and Dimples and the others to start without me."

Lillian had brought a list. Now she got it from her handbag and sat poised with a pencil. "Just what do you own of the Lily, Mr O'Neal?"

"We own the house jointly. It was once the mansion of a Yankee carpetbagger who came to Texas hoping to make a livin' in cotton and went broke. I understand Lil bought it at a good price from him more than ten years ago."

"Hmm. And what did you pay her for your share?"

"What business is that of yours?" He sighed and reached for the bottle.

"I'm trying to decide the house's value. I suspect she gave you a real good deal."

"She did at that." He grinned. "Didn't anyone tell you? I'm charmin'."

She frowned. "Somehow, that eludes me. How did the business operate?"

"I handle the saloon and the gamblin' downstairs. Lil kept the upstairs runnin'. So you've inherited the upstairs and the girls."

She felt the blood rush to her face. "I do not intend to make my living off girls selling themselves to men."

"Miss Primm, you are givin' me a headache."

"Are you sure it's not a hangover from last night's riotous living?"

"You are givin' me a bigger headache by the minute." He gulped his drink and looked beseechingly at the lawyer, who lit his pipe and sighed.

"Miss Primm," Dewey smiled at her. "Perhaps Brad could be convinced to offer you a little more than ten thousand for your share—"

"I already tried." O'Neal said.

"Perhaps," the lawyer said, "he might offer you a lot more—"

"Now wait just a damned minute!" Brad put his tumbler on the desk with a bang.

"Out of the question," Lillian snapped. "I cannot accept dirty money that those girls have earned by . . . well, you know." She felt her face burn.

Brad glared at her. "Then you buy me out, sister, and do whatever you want with the place."

"I have considered that," Lillian chewed the end of the pencil. "I have only the five thousand that my aunt left me. However, if you would let me pay you off in installments—"

"No way, sister," Brad snapped, "In God we trust, all others pay cash."

She thought a moment. "Very well, if I control the upstairs and the girls, I think I am going to move in."

Dewey Cheatum choked on his drink and burst into spasms of coughing while the gambler stood up so suddenly, his chair went over backwards. "What? Hell, you can't be serious."

She gave him a steely green stare. "Mr. O'Neal, swearing is the measure of a small vocabulary."

"Lady, I reckon you could make a saint swear."

"Which you definitively are not."

"I never claimed to be. Your Aunt Lil liked me just fine as I am."

"We've already determined that my late aunt had questionable taste in lifestyle and men."

Brad turned a pleading look toward the lawyer.

Dewey put down his pipe, somewhat reluctantly. "Bradley, I think we need to have a talk. Can you wait, Miss Primm?"

She smiled, feeling like she was in the catbird's seat. "Certainly."

"But, Dewey—"

"Come on out on the sidewalk, Brad, we need to talk." He grabbed the gambler by the arm and dragged him out front, carefully closing the door behind him. Lillian sat waiting, mildly amused by the angry voices and gesturing she could see through the office's big front window.

After awhile, the pair returned inside, Brad slamming the door so hard, the glass rattled.

They both sat back down.

Dewey leaned on his desk and smiled at her. "Dear Miss Primm," he began, "Mister Bradley O'Neal has generously decided to—"

"I saw you almost twisting his arm out there."

She said, "I think what he'd really like to do is throttle me."

"Oh, sister, don't tempt me," he growled.

"Now, now." Dewey made a soothing gesture. "This is getting us nowhere and I have a pinochle game I'd like to get to before tomorrow night. Oh, where was I?" He seemed to give it some thought.

"My offer," Brad said through gritted teeth.

"Oh, yes." The lawyer nodded. "Miss Primm, your partner, after much thought, has decided to offer you the very generous sum of twelve thousand dollars for your share of the business."

She leaned back in her chair and smiled. "No."

"What do you mean no?" Brad's voice raised. "Didn't you hear that I'm offerin' more money?"

"I heard. You seem very eager to be rid of me, Mr. O'Neal."

"Oh, lady, you don't know the half of it." He reached for the bottle.

"Tsk! Tsk! You'd better keep your head clear or I might best you in this deal." she said.

"Miss Primm," he warned, "I have never been bested by a woman. Do not try my patience."

"You are trying mine."

"Now, now," Lawyer Cheatum gestured frantically, "Let's keep our mind on the goal. That's a lot of money, Miss Primm."

"I know that." Lillian shrugged. "Mr. O'Neal seems too eager to be rid of me and there's rumors around that my aunt hid a large treasure somewhere in the house."

Brad leaned back in his chair and groaned. "That old story? Miss Primm, I live in that house and I never—"

"But of course I wouldn't expect you to level with me. You'd want the gold for yourself. I hear my aunt didn't trust banks," Lillian said.

The older man cleared his throat and picked up his pipe. "Miss Primm, I was your aunt's lawyer, and she never said anything to me about money hidden in the Texas Lily. Now even considering that faint possibility, Miss Primm, we might work out a contract that if you sold out and Mr. O'Neal ever found such a treasure, you'd have some prior claim—"

"Ha!" Lillian snorted, "you think I'd trust that sleezy rascal to let me know if he ever found anything?"

The lawyer sighed and pulled out his pocket-watch again. He looked resigned to being here for the foreseeable future. "She's right, Brad, you ain't exactly what the average citizen would call a model citizen."

"I thought you was my friend, Dewey. Hell," he snapped, "there ain't no money hidden in the house, that's just an old tale. If there was, I'd think Lil would have told me or left it to somebody in her will, wouldn't she?"

Dewey shrugged and looked at Lillian. "He's got a point there, Miss Primm."

"I see we are getting nowhere." Lillian said briskly, looking at the tiny lapel watch on the front of her severe dress. "Lawyer Cheatum, I am a teacher and I was touched by the plight of those poor, unfortunate girls—"

"They ain't poor, Miss Primm," Dewey leaned across the desk confidentially, "why, on Saturday nights, there's a waiting line—"

"Mister Cheatum!" She felt her face burn.

"Or so some of the men tell me," Dewey said hastily and took out his handkerchief and wiped his face.

"Nevertheless, I feel duty bound to help them." Lillian said.

Brad looked puzzled. "By doin' what?"

"I said I was a teacher," she said. "If those girls were

educated and knew a little etiquette, they could fit into society."

Both men looked puzzled.

"I mean they could find respectable jobs and perhaps get married."

"Married?" The gambler said the word as if speaking the name of some dread disease. "Who'd marry a wh—?"

"Mister O'Neal, she said, "I understand there is a shortage of women in all the Western states. If I could reform the girls, they could find husbands and—"

"You mean," croaked Dewey, "Close the upstairs rooms at the Texas Lily?" He looked a bit faint.

"We shall see," Lillian said.

Both men jumped to their feet, their mouths hanging open.

"Speechless?" she asked. "That must be a first for both of you. Mister O'Neal, if you will get a locksmith to put a strong lock on my aunt's bedroom door, I shall move in sometime tomorrow."

"Move in?" Brad opened and closed his mouth like a fish gasping for air.

"I said move in, didn't I? How else am I to reform these unfortunate girls?"

"Fif—fifteen thousand," Brad croaked, "I'll give you fifteen thousand for your share."

Lillian smiled. "Save your money, Mr. O'Neal, I cannot be bought off."

"But you can't be serious about movin' in?"

"Never doubt a New Englander," she said and stood up herself. "Aunt Lil also left me a little money. I intend to close down the brothel section and use that cash for the benefit of these poor unfortunate girls."

"But that will effect business downstairs!" His voice rose.

Now it was her turn to smile. "That is not my problem. Gambling and drinking are bad for the community."

The lawyer had turned pale. "Miss Primm, I think I can get the local men to make up a pot, maybe twenty thousand—"

"I cannot be bought." Lillian said, "I only wanted to see how the game would go. Good afternoon to you gentlemen. Tell Delilah to set an extra plate at dinner tomorrow."

Dewey Cheatum was almost sobbing. "Miss Primm, if you turn things upside down, there is no telling what the men who frequent the Texas Lily might—"

"Mr. Cheatum, they might stay home with their wives and play pinochle with their children. What this town seems to need is a good hotel, not a bordello."

"Tell that to the soldiers and cowboys!" Brad seethed.

"You tell them." She started out the door. "Remember about the locksmith, won't you?"

"And suppose I don't?"

She smiled at him. "Then everyone in town will gossip that you are lusting after the old maid schoolteacher and are intending to take her virtue."

Brad shuddered. "I'll put the damned lock on the door."

"Thank you. Good day, gentlemen." Then she sailed out of the office and stepped up into her buggy, smiling to herself. When she looked back through the big glass window, the rascal was gesturing wildly and the lawyer was running his hands through his gray hair.

Yes, she was going to save those unfortunate girls. After that, she had no plan, but if what she was doing annoyed Bradley O'Neal, it was a very good day.

Chapter Four

"Hell!" Brad muttered as he watched Lillian Primm sashay to her buggy and get in. She was the damndest woman he had ever met. Worse yet, she intended to ruin him financially by meddling at the Lily and thereby cutting into his business. He watched her drive away, head high. She reminded him of her aunt, not very pretty, fiery red hair and stubborn as an army mule. "Lil, what a joke you played on me."

Or had she? Certainly Lil McGinty had really expected the school-marm to accept the money and never find out that her aunt was the madam of the most successful bordello in all east Texas. In point of fact, he was a little miffed with Lil. He had thought she would leave him a lot more than she had because they had been such good friends.

Dewey shook his gray head and smoked his pipe. "You really think there's anything to that old tale about Lil hiding money in the house?"

Brad made an exasperated sound. "Oh, hell, she never said anything to me, and who knows what she did with all her profits? For all I know, she put it in a bank in Beaumont or Dallas to fund a home for stray cats."

"No, some of it funded . . ." Dewey started to say something, seemed to think better of it. "You're right about one thing, Brad, I never saw such a stubborn woman. Wait 'til the local boys hear about her plans. There'll be more hell raised than the alligator did when the lake went dry."

"Oh, she ain't gonna reform the girls." Brad snapped as he returned to the window to watch Miss Primm driving down the street, posture straight and head high. Inside, he wasn't so sure. Besides being stubborn, Miss Primm seemed like a very determined and opinionated woman. Worse yet, she had morals and principles and hadn't turned into a giggling, swooning idiot who went to mush when he smiled at her.

Dewey stood up. "Reckon I'd better not tell the boys at the pinochle game just yet. We don't want the whole male population to go into a panic."

Brad reached for his Stetson. "Don't tell 'em," he snapped, "because it ain't gonna happen. I'm in charge at the Lily and if Prissy Primm thinks she's gonna change things, she's got another think comin'. She'll find out Brad O'Neal ain't a man to be messed with."

"She beginnin' to get under your skin?" Dewey grinned.

"Hell, no," Brad growled, "I ain't gonna give her another thought. She ain't pretty and she's too damned smart for a woman."

The two walked to the door.

Dewey said "I don't envy you, my boy, having to deal with that stern old maid."

"I may just kill her," Brad thought aloud.

"They'd throw you in jail."

"Not if the jury met her," Brad said. "They'd probably want to give me a medal. I reckon I can make it so miserable for her at the Lily, she won't stay long. In the meantime, I reckon I'd better get the locksmith."

"Luke will be at the pinochle game," Dewey reminded him.

"Oh, hell, I forgot about that. Well, tell him to come over tonight or first thing in the mornin'. I ain't about to have anyone in town think I might want to get into that old maid's drawers. I got a reputation to uphold. See you later, Dewey." He went out and swung up into the saddle of his fine black stallion, then rode toward the big Victorian house at the end of the street. As he neared it, he saw Herman, the goat, munching day-lilies and grass out near that damned old rusty bird bath. Why would Lil have thought he wanted that? No, Lil had played a joke on him, all right. And to think he'd given her that little diamond lily pin to celebrate her birthday.

He rode to the stable around back, turned his horse over to the young Mexican boy, José, and went in through the back door. He walked into the main room and stood studying the open balcony over the big gambling room. The railing Lil had fallen through had been repaired. Funny she should have fallen when she had walked along the balcony a thousand times. However, that hall light had been off; maybe it had run out of kerosene and maybe she'd tripped in the dim light. Even now, he could remember looking up when she screamed, and seeing her coming down to hit one of the billiard tables. She might have been okay except her head caught the eight ball. Rotten luck.

Brad had scrambled to his feet and rushed to the table, but there was nothing that could be done. Immediately, girls and their customers had run out of upstairs rooms to peer over the balcony, screaming and asking what had happened. Brad had even thought he'd seen that damned Lieutenant Fortenbury among them, although Brad wasn't certain. If so, the lieutenant must have sneaked in, because the Texas Lily had been off limits to the young twerp after Brad had caught him cheating at cards and the officer had welshed on a number of gambling debts.

And now Brad was going to have to deal with Lil's niece. The Lily was quiet this Sunday afternoon with the girls probably napping in their rooms. The ironclad spinster school-marm had indeed given him a headache. He went behind the bar and poured himself a stiff drink, which was unusual for Brad. He seldom drank because he was certain it affected his poker game. "Miss Primm could drive Reverend Lovejoy to drink," he observed dryly as he sipped it. What was he going to do? He had to get rid of Miss Primm, but he wasn't certain how to accomplish that. She wouldn't sell out and she couldn't afford to buy him out. "A woman with principles," he snorted and leaned against the bar, "I ain't used to dealin' with that."

He rubbed his square chin. And now, she was going to move in. Even the thought made him cringe. Maybe he could annoy her so much, she would pack up and leave town. Not likely. Miss Primm seemed as determined as any female he'd ever met. She certainly wasn't like most women, or any woman he'd ever met.

"You can say that again," he grumbled under his breath. If he couldn't drive her away, what else could he do? He thought about it a long moment, then smiled. "Okay, so she's a pain in the ass, and stubborn, but she's a woman, ain't she? There's my answer."

He knew that he could play women like the strings on a fiddle. He'd certainly used his skills on enough females. He'd left a trail of broken hearts across the Lone Star state. Not that he did anything underhanded; he was always right up-front, telling the gal he would not be tied down. That message always acted like a red flag to a bull and they charged in, determined to hog-tie him and put a wedding ring through his nose. Oh, there had been one beauty after another, but none had taken his heart and never would. He was a Texan to the core and he valued his freedom and independence. Besides, why buy the cow when he could always get free milk?

He sipped his drink, smiled, and began to make plans. Maybe even an old maid schoolteacher from Boston could be vulnerable to his virile male charm. "Oh, yeah, when hell freezes over," he grumbled. Miss Primm seemed too smart, or too strait-laced to fall for a man's wiles. But then, she had never been charmed by the champion ladies' man, Brad O'Neal.

He wandered back toward his downstairs bedroom. From upstairs, he heard the girls laughing and talking. Although pretty and very talented on a mattress, suddenly they seemed stupid and inane to him, and he'd had them all. None of them offered a challenge like the quick-witted old maid. He winced at the thought of bedding her. She was too skinny and not pretty at all; at least, not what he considered pretty. Her dress was modest and severe and she wore her fiery hair pulled back in a plain, no-nonsense bun. "Well, after a few drinks, all women are beauties," he muttered. Now if she'd just keep that educated mouth shut while he made love to her. Not likely. No doubt she'd never even been kissed, but she'd still try to instruct him on how to do it.

He plopped down in his favorite chair and lit a

cigar, grinning. "All right, Miss Primm, you have thrown down the gauntlet to the biggest ladies' man in east Texas. If I can't buy you out or scare you out, maybe I can charm you out of your share of the Texas Lily." He thought for just a moment that it really wasn't fair or gallant to seduce an innocent. Then he thought about how she'd probably wreck his business if he didn't get her out of town.

Oh, if only she was prettier so the task would be appealing. Miss Primm was definitely coyote bait, the worst kind of Texas insult. "Yes, my dear lady, if you dare to go toe-to-toe with me, you may find yourself losin' your virginity besides losin' your share of the Lily."

He shuddered again. He had no doubt he could charm her drawers off; the question was, could he stand to bed the stern spinster? "Anything to save the Texas Lily," he promised himself and he meant it.

Lillian had driven away from the lawyer's office gritting her teeth. Oh, that damned Texan thought he was so smart and was so sure of himself. Just the way he had looked at her let her know he thought he was God's gift to women. Not that Lillian knew anything about men. Her stern, cold mother had been very strict and now Lillian understood why. She must have been afraid her daughter might turn out like her Aunt Lil. Lillian had never even been to a ball, although one of her young students at Miss Pickett's had taught Lillian how to dance.

Not that any young man had come to court her anyway. The two or three who had acted even slightly interested when she was young had been run off by her strict mother. Then Mother had gotten sicker and every spare moment was dedicated to her care, leaving Lillian no time for a social life. By the time Mother finally died, Lillian had resigned herself to teaching other people's daughters and never having one of her own. Her life had been planned in a long, dull line with no surprises. Now Aunt Lil's will had turned her life upside down. What to do?

She had no one to ask, really. She drove down the street and back to the fort. It seemed everyone she passed stared at her curiously, even though she nodded politely as she passed. No doubt the story had already made the rounds of the whole town. Out on the parade grounds in the late afternoon shadows, Major Bottoms conducted his marching band. The soldiers didn't look too happy about spending their Sunday thus engaged, but of course they couldn't buck authority. Some of them looked sour and headachy and she assumed they had been at the Texas Lily until late the night before. Then she noted Lieutenant Fortenbury playing the tuba. She sighed as she nodded to him in passing. He should have chosen another instrument; the tuba only emphasized his height—or lack thereof.

Out on the Bottoms' veranda, the major's wife was serving iced tea to a group of ladies and invited Lillian to join them. "This is Mrs. Pugsley, her husband owns the General Store and this is Mrs. Darlington, her husband owns the livery stable." The ladies nodded politely. "Edith has been filling us in, you poor dear," dumpy little Mrs. Pugsley said.

Somehow, her patronizing tone annoyed Lillian. "How do you do? I assure you, I'm quite capable of dealing with it."

"Oh, my dear, that gambler, he's s-o-o-o charming," gaunt Mrs. Darlington sighed. The other ladies looked at her. "I mean, so I hear; a charming rascal, someone told me."

"He's a rascal, all right." Lillian frowned as she sipped her iced tea. She wondered if Brad

O'Neal was presently in the back of Pug's store, playing pinochle.

About that time, they were joined by the major and Lieutenant Fortenbury. "Good afternoon, ladies," the major said, "you should have been there to see our parade."

The younger man frowned and looked exhausted. No doubt that tuba was heavy.

"I saw it in passing," Lillian said politely, "very good job."

The major beamed. "We've got important people coming in on the train next week, I hear, so we'll have to put on a parade, of course."

The ladies all turned their attention to him. Obviously, Fort Floppett didn't get many important visitors.

"Congressmen from Washington." The major seemed as puffed up as a toad with his own importance.

"Oh, dear," said his wife. The other ladies looked apprehensive.

"Now, don't start getting too excited," the major made a calming motion with his hands. "It might not mean anything at all, especially if the visitors see what an important post this is."

Lillian spoke without thinking. "Is it?"

The others all turned and stared at her. "It is to us," said young Fortenbury. "Why, if they should decide the fort is not needed—"

"Don't even say it," Mrs. Pugsley's chubby face turned pale. "The whole town depends on the fort for our livelihoods—everyone knows that. Should it close, we'd be in desperate straits."

"Not as desperate as the soldiers," the major snorted. "Our next post would be the middle of Arizona, chasing Apaches."

Young Fortenbury went into a spasm of frenzied

coughing. Evidently, being shipped to that hostile desert was his worst nightmare.

Mrs. Bottoms looked about helplessly. "Let's talk about something more cheerful."

"All right," said the major, turning his attention to Lillian. "How did your meeting with Brad go?"

"Brad?" the other three women asked simultaneously.

"Uh, I meant, that rake who runs the Texas Lily," the major coughed and then busied himself sipping his tea.

"Gilbert," his wife said, "that's really none of our business." Then she stared at Lillian with frank curiosity.

Lillian felt herself flush and shifted uneasily in her chair. "Rake is a good description of him, I'm afraid. He's being completely unreasonable."

The plump matron leaned even closer. "So what do you intend to do? The whole town is wondering—"

"Now who's sticking their nose in other peoples' business?" the major said.

"It's all right," Lillian hastened to say, although she really didn't want to talk about it, but she was aware the whole group was leaning forward so as not to miss a word. "It seems we are at loggerheads. I can't afford to buy him out and I refuse to accept his offer. The morality of accepting the wages of sins seems to me—"

"You wouldn't think of closing the Lily?" The major paused, his eyes wide.

His wife peered at him critically. "Now why would you care, Gilbert?"

He avoided her eyes, busying himself with reaching to break a dead blossom off the nearest rosebush. "Well, I was thinking of economics, my dear. After all, if it were to close, the local cowboys would have to ride down to Beaumont and our poor soldiers—"

"Would take up more wholesome pastimes like playing croquet or joining the weekly nature walks my ladies' club puts on."

"To be sure," said the major.

The three matrons nodded.

"Well," Lillian said," I've given this a lot of thought and I'm nothing if not decisive—headstrong, my mother called me."

"Just what every man dreams of—a stubborn, headstrong woman," the major muttered.

"What?" Mrs. Pugsley asked.

The major cleared his throat and fiddled with his drink. "I—I said, just what every man dreams of, a resolute, decisive woman. Good for you, Miss Primm."

Lillian set her glass on a side table. "After much thought, I believe there is no course left to me but to move into the Lily and see if I can reform those poor, unfortunate girls."

"What?" Lieutenant Fortenbury turned pale.

"I mean it," Lillian nodded. "My aunt left me a little money and I am a teacher of both grammar and etiquette. I feel I could lead these poor girls to a better way of life and maybe find them respectable jobs or even husbands."

"You mean, close down the upstairs at the Lily?" The major's plump cheeks went ashen.

"Good for you!" The three matrons nodded approval, and Mrs. Bottoms declared, "That's something the ladies of this town have long hoped for. Then the neighboring ranchers and our young soldiers might be more interested in our local respectable girls."

"Not likely," the major muttered and sipped his iced tea.

Lillian was now on fire with her idea. "Yes, I shall

reform the girls and clean up or close that sinful establishment. Perhaps it is my destiny."

"Hip hip hooray!" Mrs. Darlington shouted. "Ladies, we should drink a toast to this brave young woman!" The other two reached to clink their glasses together.

"What does Brad think about this?" the major asked.

"Don't ask." Lillian sighed. She thought she heard young Fortenbury groan softly.

The major said, "that only leaves the Bucket O' Blood Saloon to entertain the troops and cowboys, and it's a dirty little dump."

His wife stared at him. "Now how would you know that, Gilbert?"

"Uh, the soldiers tell me," the major said and avoided her glare.

"Nevertheless," Lillian announced with new determination, "I cannot do anything about how that terrible rake operates his part of that house, but I can do something about closing down the upstairs."

"Hurray!" The older ladies looked at her as if she were Joan of Arc. "My dear, every respectable woman in the county will want a statue of you in front of the courthouse."

"And every man will want you hanged in effigy," the major muttered.

And so it was that early Monday morning, Lillian packed up her few belongings, and borrowed the major's buggy and a driver again. Mrs. Bottoms hugged her and wished her Godspeed and told her all the ladies in town would be forever grateful for her courage.

However, Lillian did not feel quite so brave as once again, she marched up the steps of the big white mansion and rang the bell. After a moment, Delilah answered the door.

"Oh, Miss, you is back?"

"I certainly am and I'll be moving into Miss Lil's room. Didn't Mr. O'Neal tell you?"

"Yes, ma'am, he did, but I didn't believe it, and I'm not sure he did, either. Mr. Brad ain't gonna like that."

Lillian shouldered her aside. "I don't imagine he will, but he knows I'm coming."

From somewhere in the back of the house, she heard that deep male voice. "Delilah, who's at the door?"

"The new owner of half the Lily." Delilah drawled and Lillian was uncertain whether the maid was being sarcastic or not.

"What?" Brad O'Neal came striding into the entry hall, but by now, Lillian and her little carpet bag were already half-way up the winding stairs. He peered up at her. "I thought you were bluffin'."

She glared at him. "I always say what I mean and do what I say."

He was freshly shaven and dressed in a fine black coat and string tie. Even from here she could smell the scent of shaving soap and a fragrant aftershave.

"I am moving in as I said." She announced.

"You can't do that! The locksmith hasn't gotten here yet—"

"Have you even called him?"

"Well, no," he stammered, "I didn't really think you'd have the gumption—"

"I've got gumption, Mr. O'Neal. Delilah, send a message to the locksmith to come over and put a stout lock on Miss Lil's door."

The black maid looked at Brad.

"You heard the lady," he snapped.

"Thank you." Lillian dismissed them both with a

polite nod and continued up the stairs. Half-dressed girls poked their heads out of their rooms, eyes wide, mouths open. They were of all heights and hair colors, all of them pretty.

Lillian gestured to one of them, a petite redhead. "You, please direct me to Miss Lil's room."

Instead, the girl looked helplessly over the open balcony. "Brad, honey, what should I——?"

"Pansy, show the lady to Lil's room!" He thundered from below. He sounded furious. Good.

"Thank you." She smiled down at him.

"You are not welcome!" he shouted. "By the way, Miss Primm, we serve dinner around here at precisely noon, so we can open the Lily in the late afternoon for the first customers."

"Fine. Set a place for me."

The girls were still staring open-mouthed as the petite redhead led her into a large bedroom. "This is Miss Lil's room, but——"

"And now it is *my* room. I am Lillian Primm, Miss Lil's niece and you are?"

"Pansy." The girl said and stared in curiosity as Lillian put her suitcase on the bench at the end of the bed.

"I think we are going to be friends, Pansy." Lillian looked around.

"We are?"

"Despite what Mr. O'Neal may have told you, I am here to champion the cause of the working girl."

"Huh?"

Pansy wasn't the sharpest pencil in the box, Lillian thought sympathetically, but then, probably none of these girls had any education or any home-making skills. No doubt, all their skills were directed toward a mattress. "Pansy, it is not polite to say 'huh'? A lady says 'I beg your pardon?'"

That pretty, sneering blonde sauntered in and leaned against the door jamb, smoking her cigarillo. "We ain't got no ladies here."

This one would be a major challenge, Lillian thought. She smiled at her anyway. "You can all be ladies with a little training."

Pansy looked hopeful. "We can?"

"Certainly." Lillian smiled at her.

The redhead looked hopeful. "You hear that, Sadie?"

"Don't get your hopes up, kid." The blonde frowned. "We gotta good place here and we don't want it changed."

Lillian was not one to be pushed. She had a backbone of steel. "We'll see about that. You two can go and we'll talk at dinner. By the way, ladies do not smoke."

"I ain't no lady," the blonde said.

The girls both left and Lillian inspected the door as she closed it. It was a heavy, sturdy door that would be impossible to break down once a good lock was put on it. Not that she thought any man would break down a door to get to her. She sighed. She couldn't even imagine a man bothering to turn the doorknob. At thirty-two, she had long ago resigned herself to being an old maid. The Civil War had left many widows and unmarried women in the North and even some of the prettiest, which she definitely was not, were not finding husbands. Many had immigrated west where there was a shortage of marriageable women.

Lillian looked around the room. It was a large, pleasant room but overly done in wine and pink brocades and silk. A thick Persian carpet covered the floor and the scent of perfume still lingered. It looked like a room decorated by a madam, Lillian thought, then was shocked to realize that she liked the decorating. She had never had anything but a sparse, bare, small room of her own. She shook out her two other frayed dresses and wished she had something nicer to wear. When she hung her few clothes in the closet and placed others in the bureau, she discovered a wealth of expensive gowns, shoes, and delicate lace underwear. Her Aunt Lil's things. She sighed and stroked one of the fine silk gowns. Paid for by the wages of sin, she thought. She had never really known her aunt and wondered how and why the woman had ended up in this life. What was it Brad O'Neal had said? Don't judge someone until you've walked a mile in their boots. Yet she was ashamed and angry at Aunt Lil for embarrassing her and her mother with her terrible lifestyle.

She leaned against the ornate bedpost and remembered the scent of his aftershave and the passion in those dark eyes. Careful, Lillian, she admonished herself, this is a terrible rogue, and there's no telling what will happen when he realizes you really are closing your share of the Lily.

Lillian rang for the maid while she laid out a plain, high-necked, dark blue dress. She thumbed through the racks of Aunt Lil's clothes. There were lots of satins and silks in many shades of blue and green. The woman had been much more voluptuous than Lillian, that was for sure. Even if she wanted to, Lillian couldn't wear any of those fine gowns without gaining some weight.

What was she thinking? To be proper, Lillian should be wearing mourning. Now, what exactly was proper attire to mourn the co-owner of a whorehouse? She shuddered at the thought. She couldn't even force herself to visit her errant aunt's grave.

Delilah brought water to fill her pitcher and bowl. "I don't know about you taking over Miss Lil's room," she muttered.

"I'm sorry, but there isn't any other place for me," Lillian smiled. "Were you with my aunt long?"

"More than twenty-five years. She rescued me from a slave auction. I know more about her than anybody else in the whole world and I know about you. . . ." Her voice trailed off.

"Oh, did my aunt speak of me?" She really didn't know much about Lil McGinty except that she was the black sheep of a very proper and highborn family.

"More than you know." The maid abruptly departed the room.

That puzzled Lillian. Since Aunt Lil had only come to see them once and had not ever corresponded with her mother, Lillian had not even known how to inform her aunt that Mother had died. In the earliest years, Lillian and her mother had struggled to survive, her mother too fragile to work. Mother had said there was trouble over the legal aspects of Father's estate. That must finally have been straightened out, because small amounts began to arrive and about ten years ago, much larger, regular stipends from the Boston bank had enabled the two to live comfortably, if frugally. Lillian had reasoned bitterly that Aunt Lil never gave them a thought. She was too busy with her rich, wastrel life.

And here Lillian was right in the middle of that life. Her mother would probably be horrified that Lillian was actually going to live in a whorehouse. "It's that no more," she assured herself as she washed and dressed for dinner.

The little French clock on the bureau was chiming noon when a bell rang downstairs and the maid called. "Dinner's on the table, ladies."

Lillian looked at herself in the long mirror by the closet door and sighed. Sometimes she forgot her plain looks and middle age, but it was hard to forget in a house full of winsome beauties. At least, in her high-necked dress and sensible shoes, she was respectable. Oh, so very respectable. It was going to take a great deal of courage to deal with these poor soiled doves—and especially with Bradley O'Neal—but she had had a grim, joyless life as long as she could remember, so she was used to adversity.

She went out her door and paused, looking down. Except for the poker tables and the billiard table and the ornate bar off to one side, it was a magnificent room that lay below her, with its stained glass and dark, waxed floors. It looked like the waiting room of a fine hotel. She paused at the railing, noting it had been repaired, and wondered about it.

Below her, Brad O'Neal appeared. "Miss Primm," he said, looking up, "we are holdin' dinner for you."

"Oh, I'm sorry, I didn't mean to be rude."

"You lookin' over where Lil fell?"

"She fell? From here?"

He nodded. "About where you're standin'."

Lillian took a step backward. "Oh, my."

She came down the stairs and the gambler waited for her at the bottom. He held out his arm and she took it awkwardly. He led her into another magnificent room with a stained-glass light hanging directly over the big, round, golden oak table where the girls were already seated. "Ladies, may I present Miss Lillian Primm? She's gonna to be with us a day or two."

"Or maybe more." She smiled at the curious beauties. "Good day, ladies."

"We ain't ladies." The blonde, Sadie, glared at her and put both elbows on the table.

"She said we could be," Pansy, the little redhead, said.

The blonde snorted. "You dummy, don't believe everything you hear. Don't ya know a do-gooder when you see one?"

Brad said "Behave yourself, Sadie." He pulled out Lillian's chair so she could sit down.

Sadie subsided and poked food in her mouth with her spoon.

There were seven young beauties at the table. Besides Sadie and the red-haired, petite Pansy, there was a tall, black-haired girl, a pair of brown-haired twins, a strawberry blonde, and a Mexican girl. They stared at her with bold curiosity.

There was an awkward silence as Brad sat down at the head of the table. "Miss Primm, I hear you've met Pansy and Sadie. The tall one is Fern, the twins are Ella and Etta, the strawberry blonde is Flo, and the exotic beauty is Rosita."

Lillian nodded and smiled. "How do you do?"

Sadie glared back. "Just what do you think you're gonna do here?"

The others waited, watching.

Lillian forced herself to smile. "I haven't decided yet, but when I do, I'll discuss it with all the ladies."

"I'm the most popular among the local soldiers." Sadie offered.

"Says you!" The twins challenged her.

"Ladies!" Brad glared at them.

Lillian said, "I'm sure we'll all get to be good friends. I have such plans."

Again they looked at her curiously while Brad smiled ever so slightly. "Ladies, Miss Primm is Lil's niece from Boston. She's inherited Lil's half."

Sadie glared at her. "She don't look like she can hold a candle to Lil."

Lillian stared her down. "We'll see."

At her elbow, Delilah stood with a giant bowl of mashed potatoes and Lillian helped herself. She'd already had more food in the last couple of days than she usually got in a week in Boston. She took big slices of roast beef when it was passed to her. "Did you cook it, Mr. O'Neal?"

"No, but I raised it. I like to cook, but usually, I only take over the kitchen on Sunday." He gave her a dazzling smile. "Please call me Brad. All the ladies do."

"And you may call me Miss Primm." She gave him a cold stare. She looked around. All the girls were dressed in fine, low-cut gowns. She had never felt as dowdy and homely and middle-aged as she did right now. "Some men would feel their masculinity threatened by an apron."

He simply grinned again. "Now, Miss Primm, do I look as if my masculinity was lackin'?"

"I can promise you it ain't," Sadie said, and all the girls laughed.

Lillian felt her face flush. "It was not a personal inquiry, I can assure you, Mr. O'Neal."

Delilah came through the kitchen door just then carrying another giant tray of meat. It looked like half a cow. That was followed by hot rolls and gravy, all sorts of vegetables and huge glasses of iced tea.

Brad dug into his food like a man who likes to eat. But then, probably all his passions were big, Lillian thought critically. He was probably like Falstaff in that Shakespeare play—with a huge appetite for women, food, and drink. The girls were now chatting with each other while Lillian ate daintily.

The gambler frowned and gestured with his knife. "Miss Primm, I think you're as skinny as a rack of bones. Eat up, there's plenty more."

"What is this?" She stared down at some of the food as she helped herself.

"Fried green tomatoes and fried okra," he explained. "Later in the summer, we'll have watermelon."

She hadn't meant to, but she found herself eating heartily. She, who had always struggled to exist on thin soup and stale crackers, hot tea and weak coffee, now almost couldn't believe how much food there was in Texas.

The girls were too busy eating to pay much attention to her. They talked and laughed like a bunch of magpies. Lillian winced at their table manners and their grammar. There would certainly be a lot to teach them to turn them into respectable women.

Just when she thought she couldn't eat another bite, here came Delilah with a huge chocolate cake. "I really don't think—" she began, but Brad ignored her words and gave her a thick slice. "Eat up," he commanded, "you're as skinny as a snake."

The girls all giggled and smiled at the gambler. Evidently, in their eyes, the rascal could do no wrong.

"Mr. O'Neal," she said coldly, "It is quite rude to comment on a lady's physical—"

"I'm just worried about your health," he grinned at her. "After all, if something happens to one of us, the other gets both halves of the Lily. By the way, Lillian seems very stuffy. I think you look more like a Lily."

"My name is Lillian, but you may call me Miss Primm." She kept her voice frosty, which was difficult between bites of the delicious cake. "Mr. O'Neal, we need to talk."

"Again? And call me Brad." Again he gave her a charming, warm smile that was so full of animal magnetism, it made Lillian's hand shake as she sipped her iced tea. Well, that might work on these young, daffy girls, but she was a mature woman, not easily taken in by some four-flusher.

The girls had been chattering with each other. Now they all got up and left the table without even asking to be excused or waiting for the host and hostess to get up from the table first. Yes, there was a lot to teach them. They all seemed friendly enough except for Sadie, who had glared at Lillian all through dinner. She seemed to see Lillian as some kind of interloper, competing for the gambler's attention. As if Lillian would even consider . . . in her mind, she was naked in his bed and he was kissing her roughly, his big hands pulling her to him—

"Miss Primm, are you all right? You're tremblin'." He was staring at her as if he could read her thoughts.

She felt blood rush to her face. "It—it's cold."

"Cold? It's almost June."

"Never mind," she snapped and let out her breath. "Mr. O'Neal," she said, "after much thought, I have plans for my part of the establishment."

"Good." He wiped his mouth and lay his napkin next to his plate. "Your aunt had a head for business. If we must be partners, I'm glad to hear you're takin' an interest."

"More than you know." She smiled at him.

He shifted in his chair, a bit uneasy. Obviously, he didn't trust Lillian. "The locksmith sent word he'd be here right after dinner."

"Good. I'm pleased to hear that."

He leaned toward her and smiled as she took a deep breath. The sheer animal magnetism of the man made her uneasy and she shifted in her chair. "Surely, Miss Lily, you wouldn't think that I would push myself toward a lady. I am a Texan and I do have some sense of propriety."

She snorted. "I doubt you know the meaning of the word."

He grinned broadly. "Whatever I lack in formal education, Miss Primm, I'm sure I make up for it in the school of Hard Knocks. I come from a white trash moonshiner's passel of kids in the Big Thicket."

"The what?"

He tipped his chair back and lit a cigar without even asking her permission. "The Big Thicket. It's a wild, swampy area in southeast Texas. My Pa was married three or four times and there's a dozen kids scattered over Texas."

Lillian waved her dainty lace hanky before her nose, but he didn't take the hint. "My family comes from a long lineage of dukes and earls. We were never rich but very respectable. As a matter of fact, I'm hoping to become a member of S.N.O.B.S."

"Snobs?"

"No, you dolt," she snapped, "Sisters Noble of British Society."

He grinned and smoked his cigar. "Sounds like the same thing. I always reckoned a man ought to be judged by his actions, not his ancestry."

"In that case, sir, you should probably have been hanged by now." She gave him a cold look as she stood up. "As I said, I have made a decision."

"Good." Now his smile seemed genuine. "I've got a few ideas myself on improvin' business and—"

"No, no, Mister O'Neal, you don't understand. I wasn't bluffing. I intend to close the upstairs and help these poor, unfortunate girls find husbands or honest work."

Brad O'Neal's dark face went pale and he dropped his cigar in his plate. "What?"

"You heard me. From now on, the upstairs is off

limits to men. I shall go inform the ladies that tonight, we will have classes in my room instead."

"Miss Primm, you will ruin my business."

"Oh, but I'm not bothering your share, Mr. O'Neal, and remember, I own the upstairs. Good day to you."

He was cursing behind her as she walked briskly toward the stairs.

Chapter Five

He was going to murder that woman, even if they hanged him, Brad thought grimly as he watched the locksmith come down the stairs. No jury that had met Miss Primm would not blame him—they might even help him.

"All right, Brad," the lanky workman wiped his hands on a rag, "I got the lock on the door for the lady. I got to charge you extra since it's Sunday evenin'." He turned and looked up the stairs. "She's something, ain't she?"

"She sure is, Luke," Brad chewed his lip, "but I could think of more appropriate names to call her."

"A respectable woman like that really gonna live here?"

Brad sighed. "She says she's gonna save the girls."

"From what?"

"A life of degradation, whatever the hell that means."

Luke scratched his lanky frame. "The boys ain't gonna like this."

Brad snorted. "You think I do?"

"You know she's moved furniture around in her

room, setting up chairs? She says she's gonna teach the gals."

"I reckon they could teach the old maid a thing or two."

"Not her—too staid and respectable. Well, I'll send you a bill and—"

About that time, as they watched, Lillian Primm marched down the stairs carrying a big red ribbon. As the two stared in stunned silence, the spinster tied it to one bannister, strung it across the stairs and tied it on the other side, thus blocking the stairs. A sign hung on the big red ribbon. It read, "UPSTAIRS CLOSED TO MEN."

She gave them each a nod and went back up the stairs, head high.

"Well, I'll be damned," Brad swore softly.

Luke stared at the ribbon. "Does that mean what I think it means?"

Brad nodded. "She's got principles. I don't know how to deal with that, and the damned stubborn woman won't get on a train and leave. She's as ornery as old Herman the goat."

Luke shrugged and grinned with snaggled teeth. "I thought you was the stubbornest person I ever met. I don't envy you, Brad. It ought to be very interestin' to watch."

"For you, maybe." Brad snorted.

"The boys is layin' bets."

"Tell em not to bet against me," Brad seethed, "I ain't gonna be done in by some old maid schoolteacher."

"She's got red hair," the other said. "Red-headed women is damned hard to reason with."

"You think I can't see that? That don't mean nothin'. Brad O'Neal ain't never met a woman he couldn't charm and this one ain't no different."

"Folks around town say she is."

"Folks around town got too much time on their hands to talk," Brad grumbled.

Luke left and the rest of Sunday evening was tense. The Lily wasn't open on Sundays, so Brad stayed in his office and played solitaire. He could hear the girls upstairs reading from a primer—all but Sadie. She came into his office and tried to flirt, but Brad ignored her.

"Hey, honey," she lit a cigarillo, "you think she's bluffin'?"

"Be careful with that smoke," he grumbled, "you'll burn something down someday. Does Miss Primm look like the kind who bluffs?"

Sadie turned and looked toward the stairs. "So when we open tomorrow night, that red banner stays?"

"We'll see." He considered ripping it down himself, and remembered she owned the upstairs.

At precisely seven o'clock on Monday morning, Lillian dressed in one of her no-nonsense plain dark dresses and went downstairs to find Delilah quietly sipping coffee on the back steps. "Delilah, what time do you usually serve breakfast?"

"The gals and Mr. Brad ain't never up before almost noon—you know, they work late at night."

"Well, there's going to be a few changes made around here now that I'm half-owner. What did my aunt like to do with her mornings?"

Delilah stood up, looking sad. "Miss Lil, she liked to get out and work in her front garden early before anyone else was up—her and old Herman goat."

"Yes, I've met the goat." She didn't think much of her aunt's gardening. All that grew out front around that big bird bath were those common orange day-lilies. Aunt Lil could have at least grown something fancier, like maybe roses. "From now on, Delilah, things will change around here. I'm going to start classes for the girls, and from henceforth, breakfast should be served promptly at seven."

The black woman looked incredulous. "In the mornin'?"

"Of course in the morning—like the rest of the world."

"Mr. Brad ain't gonna like that. I don't reckon he'd get up that early for the end of the world." Delilah shook her gray, frizzy head.

That thought pleased Lillian. "Mr. Brad is no longer in complete control here. Now, I'll wake the girls and you get breakfast ready."

The old woman sighed and threw the dregs of her coffee into the grass. "Yes, ma'am, but Mr. Brad—"

"I know, I know, he won't like it." Lillian smiled and wiped her hands briskly on her skirt. "And oh, by the way, here's something else Mr. Brad won't like: I'm closing the upstairs and going to try to find husbands or honest jobs for the girls."

"Ma'am?" The old woman's eyes widened.

"You heard me." Lillian lifted her skirts and turned to go back inside.

"But Mr. Brad ain't gonna—"

"Now that's just too bad," Lillian said, "but the upstairs is my property."

The old woman shrugged. "Miss Lily, I'd advise you not to tangle with Mr. Brad."

"On the contrary," Lillian said as she paused in the doorway, "you'd better advise him not to tangle with me."

Delilah nodded, a slight smile on her wrinkled face. "You know, I reckoned you only looked like

Miss Lil, but maybe you acts like her, too. She didn't take no sass off nobody."

Lillian winced at the comparison She wanted to distance herself as much as possible from her wayward aunt. "I shall now awaken the household." She marched inside, found the dinner bell and went to the bottom of the stairs. She rang the bell as hard and rapidly as she could.

Upstairs, doors flew open and pretty girls stuck their heads out of their rooms. "What the hell's happenin'?"

"Is the house on fire?"

Several girls started screaming.

Lillian waited at the foot of the stairs, looking up as the girls ran out of their rooms, pulling on robes. "Everyone calm down—there is no fire or any emergency."

Sadie blinked and ran her hand through her bleached hair. "Then what the hell's goin' on?"

Lillian said, "Profanity is the mark of a small vocabulary and ladies do not use it."

"Huh?" Now all seven of them were hanging over the railing blinking at her.

"Never mind," Lillian shrugged, "we'll discuss that later. Now, Delilah will be serving breakfast soon."

"Breakfast this early?" Pansy acted as if she did not know anyone ever ate before ten o'clock.

About that time, Brad stumbled out of his downstairs room, blinking and pulling on his shirt. "Delilah, what's goin' on? Did someone say the house is on fire?"

Delilah frowned and gestured toward Lillian. "Ask her. She say breakfast gonna be served this time every morning from now on."

Brad paused in buttoning his shirt and stared at

Lillian as if he'd never seen her before. "Oh yes, you. What in the name of hell—?"

"This is the time respectable people get up, Mr. O'Neal. You do know about respectable people?"

"Reckon not as much as you do," he complained.

Sadie called down the stairs. "Brad, honey, tell that woman that we don't hafta—"

"I am half-owner of the Texas Lily now," Lillian said, "so I can make some of the rules. Now, everyone come down to breakfast. I have some announcements to make."

The gambler looked a little worse for wear. "Couldn't your announcements wait 'til about noon?"

"'Early to bed and early to rise makes a man healthy, wealthy, and wise,'" Lillian said.

Brad swore under his breath. "I ain't even got my boots on yet."

"Then go get them," Lillian said.

Grumbling and complaining, the girls and Brad O'Neal stumbled to the dining room where Delilah was now putting out plates and pouring coffee.

Brad plopped down in his chair. "Miss Primm, this is outrageous. Why, nobody gets up at this time of the day except roosters and—"

"Now how would you know?" Lillian said a little too sweetly, "I doubt if you've ever been up at this time, unless you had never gone to bed after a long night of poker."

"You've got that right." He sat down at the table and reached for his coffee.

Lillian took her place and motioned for the girls to do the same. They were a tired, bleary-looking lot with hair undone and old makeup still smeared on their faces. "Tomorrow, ladies, you will come to the table dressed and with your hair combed and your faces washed."

Rosita looked at Lillian. "Ma'am, I think you missed your callin.' You ought to be warden at a woman's prison."

"I have been the head mistress at a girl's school, which is not much different." Lillian said and sipped her coffee.

"What'd you say about bein' somebody's mistress?" The gambler seemed to be coming out of a sleepy fog.

The girls giggled and Lillian frowned. "Mr. O'Neal, do your thoughts never get above your belt buckle?"

He grinned and sipped his coffee. "I was just tryin' to imagine the picture of you in a compromisin' situation."

She felt her face burn. "I would never allow myself to be in a compromising situation."

"Ain't it the truth?" Brad muttered and the girls laughed again.

She decided to ignore him. She looked around the table, favoring the unkempt girls with a smile. "Today, ladies, we begin classes."

"We ain't ladies," Sadie snapped as she reached across the table for the sugar bowl in front of Lillian.

"All of you should aspire to become ladies," she announced as she sipped her coffee. "And Sadie, to be polite, you should ask me to pass you the sugar."

"Why? I managed to reach it myself."

Lillian took a deep breath for patience while the girls giggled again. "I have decided I cannot in good conscience make a living off unfortunate girls who are at the mercy of a bunch of lustful men."

"What?" The girls looked at her blankly.

"No!" said the gambler.

"Yes!" said Lillian and sipped her coffee.

"What?" asked the girls again.

"What Miss Lily means," Brad frowned, "is

that she thinks you shouldn't get paid for screwin' no more."

Lillian winced. "Please watch your language, Mr. O'Neal, and don't use double negatives."

The entire table gave her blank, puzzled looks. This was going to be more difficult than she thought. "How many of you girls can read and write?"

Pansy and the twins, Ella and Etta, held up their hands.

"The fellas don't care if we can read or write," Sadie complained, "so why should you?"

"It would keep you from being cheated out of any money," Lillian said.

Brad slammed down his cup. "Nobody cheats my girls," he said, "or they deal with me."

All the pretty young things turned and looked at the gambler and sighed with adoration. That annoyed Lillian.

"May I remind you that they aren't 'your girls'? Now ladies, education will be the first order of business," Lillian said briskly, "With that, you can get a good job."

"I got a good job already," Sadie griped.

"I mean a *respectable* job," Lillian said. "Or perhaps some of you would like to get married?"

"Married?" The gambler said the word as if it were dirty.

"Married?" Now all the girls but Sadie looked at her, their faces hopeful. Then their faces fell.

Pansy said, "Men don't marry gals like us—we're whores."

Lillian winced at the harsh word. Yet that was what her aunt had been. How could Aunt Lil have fallen so low? Why couldn't she have remained respectable like her older sister? "Well, if you looked like ladies and behaved like ladies, each of you could get a husband or at least a better job."

"And just how in the hell, pardon my French," Sadie poured her coffee in her saucer and slurped it, "are we supposed to make a livin' while you're teachin' us how to be respectable?"

"Yeah, how?" Brad leaned back in his chair and grinned at Sadie's logic.

Lillian took a deep breath. "Besides half the Lily, my aunt left me five thousand dollars. I will pay your expenses for several months while you change your lives."

Both Brad and the girls looked at her in astonishment.

The tall brunette, Fern, said, "You'd do that for us?"

"I will. In fact, I feel it is my duty to help you out of this life of degradation and—"

"Now wait just a damned minute," Brad glared at her. "The Lily is one of the best in Texas, ain't it, girls?"

"Yeah," Sadie nodded. "We like life here, don't we?"

"See?" Brad said with smug satisfaction and sipped his coffee.

"That's because these girls have never known a better life. Like I told you before, Mr. O'Neal, the upstairs is closed to men. I own the upstairs, so I get the final say."

Brad sighed heavily and rolled his eyes. "You do realize, Miss Primm, that if the girls don't mingle with the customers, lots of men will avoid the Lily and go down to the Bucket O' Blood for drinks and gamblin'?"

"I can't be responsible for that," Lillian said. She turned to the maid who stood, mouth open. "Now, Delilah, you may serve the oatmeal and after that, we'll begin classes."

"Well, I'll be damned!" Brad muttered.

Lillian smiled. "You probably will be, Mr. O'Neal, but keep in mind, I'm technically *not* interfering with your half of the business."

"The hell you ain't! No man's comin' in for a drink and a little gamblin' if there's no girls to take upstairs."

"That's your problem." She smiled coldly. "Ladies, enjoy your breakfast. Classes begin at nine o'clock in Mr. O'Neal's office. My room is too crowded."

"Hell, no, you ain't takin' over my office—"

"Well, I suppose we could set up chairs around the poker tables. Of course, that might interfere with the gaming."

Brad sighed audibly. "All right. Use my office."

Sadie slammed her cup down. "Well, I ain't gonna read no books like some prissy schoolgirl, and nobody can tell me how I'm gonna earn my livin'. Ain't that right, gals?"

The others were silent except the strawberry blonde, Flo. In a soft voice she said, "I always wanted to learn to read."

Lillian regarded Sadie calmly. "You may do whatever you wish, my dear, but there'll be no men upstairs tonight or any night. However, any girl who doesn't like how I intend to run my half of this business is welcome to move out."

"Brad, honey," Sadie said, "you gonna let her talk to me like that?"

The gambler shrugged in defeat. "It's her half of the business."

They ate breakfast in stunned, sleepy silence. Only the gambler grumbled as he ate, about 'damned Yankee women.'

Lillian ignored him. She was already making her plans. She had been teaching grammar and etiquette to rich, high-born girls for years and she could certainly teach these less fortunate ones and help them better their lives, even if she spent all her inheritance to do so.

By eight-thirty, everyone had left the table and retreated to their rooms, Brad still muttering under his breath. Lillian went up to her room and gathered a few pencils and notebooks. At promptly nine o'clock, she went to the bottom of the stairs and rang the dinner bell. "Ladies, it is time."

Everyone but Sadie trooped down the stairs, most looking a little uncertain. They wore tight, revealing dresses.

As they stood at the foot of the stairs, Pansy said, "You really think you can learn us anything, Miss Lily?"

"Teach you—and of course I can, Pansy," she assured the redhead with a pat on the shoulder, "This isn't that difficult and I'm sure you're a smart girl."

"I don't own no books."

"I don't own any books," Lillian corrected.

"If you don't own none either, what we gonna study?" Etta asked.

Lillian sighed. This might be a bigger task than she thought, but she was determined. "Never mind, I'm sure I can find some around town and maybe out at the fort. Don't you ladies have any other clothes?"

They examined their bright dresses and shook their heads. "We don't have no reason to wear nothin' else."

"I shall find a dressmaker," Lillian said. "Now, let's get to work."

The gambler was seated behind his desk, but now he retreated outside to smoke a cigar, leaving his office to the women. Lillian passed out paper and pencils. "Some of you might become teachers or nurses."

"Who'd hire a bunch of whores?" Ella asked.

Lillian winced at the word. "But you aren't that anymore. From now on, you'll be ladies and you'll get a fresh start. And when you leave here, no one will know of your past."

Etta looked hopeful. "You mean, men might actually marry us?"

"Certainly. We can put ads in the papers out West where maybe you could be mail-order brides."

"But you ain't married," Fern pointed out. "What good does it do to be educated if we end up like you?"

"I have chosen to be a single woman," Lillian said loftily. That wasn't quite true, but these girls didn't know that no one had asked her. Besides, Lillian's standards were incredibly high. She was looking for a well-bred and polished gentleman. From where she stood by the window, she could see Brad out on the garden smoking a cigar and rubbing the head of the old gray goat. A well-bred and polished gentleman. The gambler was the furthest thing from that. Maybe Lieutenant Fortenbury . . .

She found a couple of dusty old books on a shelf in the office, and showed the girls the letters and explained how they connected into words. Then she had them draw some of the letters on their paper.

Etta held up her hand. "Miss Lily, can we stop now? I got to pee."

Lillian grimaced. "A lady would never say that, Etta."

"Well, I got to anyways."

"Very well, everyone is dismissed until after dinner. The proper thing to do is excuse yourself, Etta. You don't have to explain such a private matter to the whole world."

The girls scattered, and Lillian sat down behind the desk with a sigh. She enjoyed teaching, and the girls seemed pathetically eager. Dealing with the Texan was her biggest problem. She didn't think he'd let her cut into his profits without a fight.

It was almost noon. She heard Delilah ring the dinner bell. This was as good a time as any to work on table manners. If these girls were ever to be able to blend into society, they would have to learn table manners.

Everyone was already gathered around the table as she joined them. "We had a good class this morning, ladies. I'm going to assign you some homework and dismiss you for the afternoon. Now, as Delilah serves, we'll learn how a proper lady eats."

Sadie glared at her. "We know how to eat."

Fern said, "She's teachin' us to be ladies, Sadie."

"I don't wanta be no lady."

"At this rate, you never will be," Lillian said, "especially unless you get your elbows off the table."

Sadie defiantly kept her elbows on the table.

Lillian said, "now, girls, you don't tuck your napkin in the top of your clothes, you spread it on your lap."

All eyes turned toward Brad, who had tucked his napkin in the top of his shirt collar. He reached up and yanked it out. "I knew that," he said.

Delilah began serving bowls of chili. Fern started eating as soon as hers was put before her, as did Brad.

Lillian ignored the gambler. "Fern," she said softly, "it's polite to wait until everyone has been served before you begin to eat. And dip your spoon away from you."

Sadie and Brad glared at her, but the others complied. "Look," Etta said, "are we doin' it right?"

"You could all eat soup at the best hotel in Boston without embarrassing yourselves."

"I ain't embarrassed," Sadie snapped. The other girls turned and glared at the blonde.

Pansy said, "Miss Lillian is teachin' us manners."

Sadie snorted. "Then you'll still be nothin' but whores. Who you kiddin'?"

"That's not very kind," Lillian said.

"And who are you kiddin'?" Sadie snapped, "your aunt was the biggest whore in Texas."

Lillian heard the others draw a quick breath and she felt tears come to her own eyes.

Surprisingly, Brad stepped in. "Shut up, Sadie, Lil was a helluva lot better person than you'll ever be."

With a curse, Sadie stood up from the table and ran out of the room and up the stairs. There was an awkward silence.

Lillian looked at the gambler. "Thank you."

He shrugged. "I didn't do it for you. I don't like nobody judgin' Lil McGinty. She did whatever she had to do to survive and take care of others."

She was a whore, Lillian thought, not being as charitable as O'Neal. It was embarrassing to be Lil's niece.

They finished dinner in silence and the ladies scattered throughout the house. Lillian went upstairs to get her parasol, then she went to the kitchen and looked in the door. "Delilah, dinner was lovely."

The old woman grinned at her. "I don't have to work here, you know. Miss Lil left me plenty of money."

"I know. Thank you for staying on."

"I owe it to Miss Lil," the old black woman said. "We all owe her a lot."

Lillian didn't say anything. Finally, she said, "I'm going out. I'll see about finding a dressmaker."

"For them gals?"

Lillian nodded.

"You want I should get José to bring the buggy around?"

"No," she shook her head, "it's a nice day, I'll walk."

"Miss Lillian, for what it's worth, I think Miss Lil would have closed down the upstairs, too, but she had big obligations to pay."

"What kind of obligations?"

The old woman hesitated, then got very busy at the sink. "Never you mind."

Lillian waited, but Delilah said nothing more. "You aren't going to tell me?"

"If Miss Lil had wanted you to know, she would have told you." She gave Lillian a long look. "Sometimes the past just needs to bury itself."

That didn't make any sense, but Delilah said nothing more. After a moment, Lillian opened her parasol to protect herself from the warm sun and went out on the front porch.

Brad glowered at her from the porch swing. "You self-righteous prig. You don't really think you can change those girls' lives, do you?"

"I'm at least going to try, which is more than you've done, Mr. O'Neal."

"Most of them were already workin' here when I came and they're glad for the job."

"I think they're eager for a change," she sniffed.

"Look, lady, if they weren't workin' here, they'd be on their backs in some saloon worse than this one."

She felt her face flame. "You're just sore because I'm about to cut into your profits."

"A-ha—you admit it."

"Your profits are not my problem." She went down the steps and walked briskly down the street, past the big ornate bird bath and the goat,

Herman, now happily munching the common orange day-lilies in the front yard. Lillian found her way to Pugsley's General Store and walked in. The little bell on the door announced her arrival. A short man with a face like a bulldog and bushy eyebrows came out from the back. "Oh, you must be Miss Lillian. My wife said she met you at the fort."

Lillian smiled. "Yes, nice lady. You have yard goods?"

He nodded, his blue eyes bright with curiosity. "You actually moving into the Lily?"

"I already have."

"I'll bet Brad don't like that." He wiped his plump hands on his white apron.

"Everyone seems very concerned about what Mr. O'Neal likes; everyone but me."

"He ain't used to having women buck him, ma'am, mostly they just swoon and do whatever he wants."

She smiled a little too sweetly. "Well, here's one who won't. Now I'd like to see some yard goods, please, and can you give me the name of a dressmaker?"

"Yes, ma'am, Miss Webble does sewing. How many dresses you want made?"

"Oh, I think they should have at least two each. I'm dressing the girls at the Lily a little more modestly."

"Oh, Brad ain't gonna—"

"Like that? There are changes to make at the Lily."

He nodded. "Dewey already told us."

"Does everyone in town gossip about everyone's business?" She was slightly put out.

"Now, what else we got to do?" He grinned and began to pull bolts of cloth off the shelf. "What you intending to do about them gals, Miss?"

"I'm going to turn them into ladies."

Pug turned around slowly. "Ladies?"

"Ladies." She said firmly, examining the fabric he lay before her. "I think I'll take some of the pale blue gingham and some of that with the little pink flowers, and that green lawn is nice, too. Hold that for me and direct me to Miss Webbles' and the *Weekly Bugle*."

"We're hoping someday it'll be a daily paper," Pug said, "we call it the *Bugle* because of the fort—"

"I get it, I get it. Now point me the way, please."

She left the general store, went to the *Bugle*, placed an ad in the mail-order bride section, and then found elderly Miss Webble to discuss making suitable dresses for the girls at the Lily.

The old woman peered at her over the top of her gold-rimmed spectacles. "Dress 'em modest? Brad ain't—"

"I know, I know. But it's something Mr. O'Neal is going to have to learn to live with, as I'm as stubborn as he is." And Lillian meant it.

Chapter Six

Late that afternoon, Clyde the bartender and his two faro dealers arrived for the evening shift. All three Texans stood staring at the big ribbon across the stairs. "What the hell—?"

"Don't even ask," Brad snapped, "I'm just fixin' to go upstairs and deal with this." He yanked the red ribbon aside, found it was tied too tightly, stooped to go under it, and took the stairs two at a time. He banged on Miss Primm's door. "Hey, in there!"

Miss Primm came to the door and opened it. "Yes?"

Past her, he could see the girls, all but Sadie, sitting around her room with paper and pencil in hand. "About your damned banner on the stairs—"

"Tsk, tsk. Did you know swearing shows a limited vocabulary?"

"So you've told me." He brushed past her.

"I did not invite you into my room, sir."

He ignored her. "You girls, why ain't you gettin' into your costumes? Customers will be arrivin' soon."

They all looked toward the old maid.

"She's learning us to be ladies," Pansy said.

"Teaching," Lillian corrected gently.

"Oh, hell," Brad said.

"A gentleman does not swear around ladies," Miss Primm drew herself up and frowned.

"These ain't ladies, they're—"

"Not anymore," Miss Primm said. "And we're having classes, Mr. O'Neal. As I've already told you, the girls will not be coming down tonight or any night. Also, any man who tries to come up the stairs, and that includes the back stairs, will wish he hadn't."

"What?"

"We're already discussed this," Miss Primm said. "Are you forgetful or stupid?"

"I didn't think you meant it. Girls, think of all that money you'll lose—"

"Miss Primm is usin' her own money to help us," Etta said and her twin nodded. "We're all gonna get jobs or maybe find husbands and be respectable like Miss Primm."

The lady had a slender neck. Why had he never noticed how graceful and creamy white her neck was, almost like a swan's? For a long moment as Brad fought to control his temper, he imagined putting his fingers around that neck and giving her a good shake. "You can't do this," he said.

"But of course I can. Now you leave my sign on the stairs because if any hooligan comes up here, I intend to whack him myself with one of Delilah's big frying pans." She gestured toward the iron skillet on her dresser. "Now would you return to your whiskey and your cards, Mr. O'Neal? We're going to conjugate verbs for the next several hours."

"That sounds dirty," Brad said.

"Only to you. Your grammar could use some improvement, too."

He looked past her at the whores. "Don't listen to her. You all got good lives, don't you? Why would you want to get married? You'd be working a helluva lot harder than you do now."

"All women want to get married," Ella said. "We're all gonna be mail-order brides."

"Brides? Brides? So now we're in the matrimony business? Miss Primm, I will talk to my lawyer—"

She smiled. "We've already done that. Remember? I can assure you I'm within my legal rights—"

"But the guys won't come for drinks and cards if there's no pretty ladies—"

"That's not my problem," Miss Primm said and turned her back to him. "Now class, let's get back to our studies. Remember, a lady never uses the word 'ain't'. You won't attract a real gentleman if you do."

"Brad uses 'ain't,'" Pansy pointed out.

"Exactly," Miss Primm said. "That's my point."

He was speechless, and that was unusual for him. It had never even occurred to him that the girls didn't love their jobs and would rather be housewives. He had thought they were happy to work here. And he had thought that in a showdown, Miss Primm was bluffing. Evidently not. Brad turned and stomped back down the stairs, stooping under the red banner.

The two faro dealers and the bartender were still standing there. Lem, the piano player, had joined them.

"Don't even ask!" Brad snapped.

"We ain't gonna have no girls tonight?" Clyde, the bartender asked, stroking his handlebar mustache.

"No, they're learnin' to conjugate verbs."

"That sounds dirty," Lem said.

"There ain't nothin' dirty about Miss Primm, she's got principles." Brad stomped over to the bar. "Give me a whiskey."

Clyde came around behind the bar. "You sure? You don't usually drink, Brad."

"The lady is drivin' me to it. Now pour."

A handful of men were already leaning on the bar: a couple of townsmen, a cowboy, two soldiers. Since there was a long-standing tension between cowboys and soldiers, they were eyeing each other suspiciously.

Lem, still wearing his derby and bright shirt garters, sat down at the piano and began playing "Beautiful Dreamer."

"Hey, Brad," drawled the cowboy, "what's the meanin' of the banner on the stairs?"

"Now what does it look like?" Brad grumbled, putting one fine boot on the brass rail. "Lil McGinty's niece has taken over her share and she's closin' down the upstairs. If you're gonna get any, you'll have to marry it."

"Marry?" All the men at the bar said in unison and turned pale as toads' bellies.

"We got poker and keno and music and good booze," Brad said, "that's more'n you'd get any place else."

One of the young privates stepped away from the bar. "If'fen there ain't gonna be gals, I ain't gonna stay. I could drink beer over at the sutler's store at the fort." He turned and left.

"And I could go down to the Bucket O' Blood," said the cowboy, "it ain't much, but it's got whores."

"Boys, I got no answers for you; at least not now." It was going to be a long night, Brad thought as he took his drink over to the poker table and sat down. "Hey, Lem," he yelled, "play something lively."

"Anything in particular, Brad?" The little piano player paused and pushed his derby to the back of his bald head.

From upstairs, Brad could hear the girls reciting their ABCs. "Just make it lively and loud."

About that time, Sadie came down the stairs, climbing over the red ribbon. She wore about enough tight red satin to cover a broom handle, Brad thought. The men let out a collective sigh of appreciation. "Evenin', fellas." She waggled her hips as she crossed the floor and came to the bar. "Now, who wants to buy me a drink?"

There was a stampede to do so and Brad breathed a sigh of relief. "See? The others will come down soon."

But they didn't. Only Sadie amused the boys at the bar, and drifted from table to table, but even she didn't attempt to take anyone upstairs.

They had a fair crowd that night although some left when they discovered no more girls would come down. One drunk did defy the red banner and went up the stairs. Brad watched from his poker table as the poor devil was chased back down those same stairs seconds later by the angry and protective Miss Primm and her frying pan. He tripped over the red banner and fell on his face on the floor. "And stay out!" She screamed at him.

The piano player stopped playing and there was an uneasy silence, broken only by the girls' voices from upstairs; ". . . the rain in Spain falls mainly on the plain. . . ."

"Lem, play something fast and loud," Brad ordered.

"Yes sir," he said and began belting out "Camptown Races," not well, but with vigor.

Brad had a difficult time keeping his mind on his poker game. He began to lose, which was unusual for him. It did nothing to improve his mood.

Dewey Cheatum came into the Lily just then and

looked around. Then he ambled over to the poker table, looking up the stairs as he did. "Brad?"

"Don't even ask," Brad muttered.

"This is serious," Dewey said, pulling up a chair.

"Tell me about it. You see how small the crowd is tonight?"

"It'll get smaller when word gets around there's no upstairs action."

"Dewey, shut up. You ain't tellin' me anything I don't already know."

Lem had stopped playing the piano to have a beer and in the sudden silence, the faint sound of girls singing "Mary Had a Little Lamb" drifted down the stairs.

Dewey's mouth fell open. "Just what the hell—?"

"Don't you know cursin' shows a limited vocabulary?" Brad snapped.

"Huh?" Dewey said, fumbling with his pipe.

"Miss Primm is turning our whores into ladies," Brad said, "or tryin' to." He frowned at his hand. No good.

"Miss Primm strikes me as pretty determined," Dewey said, "the boys is all takin' bets—"

"I already heard. Someone reshuffle that deck so I can get a decent hand for a change."

"Wait just a damned minute," Dimples Darlington smiled, showing his famous dimples, "I got four aces." The livery stable owner laid out his cards and everyone groaned.

Dewey frowned. "This woman is serious about ruining the local economy. I think I'd better round up the boys and let's have ourselves a little meeting tomorrow morning, maybe at the general store?"

"That okay with you *hombres?*" Brad threw in his cards and leaned back in his chair.

"I reckon so, although I don't know what we can

do about Miss Primm. Maybe you could offer her more money for her share." Dewey suggested.

"We tried that, remember? I only got so much money, Dewey, and besides, that ornery old maid probably wouldn't take it if I offered her a hundred thousand, which of course I ain't got. She says she's got principles."

"What's that?" asked Luke, who had just joined them.

"Not anything any of us knows much about," Dewey said. "Okay, I'll tell the rest of the boys and I'll get the message to the major, too."

From upstairs came the sound of the girls doing arithmetic. ". . . If Susie needs four apples to bake a pie, but apples cost five cents each, how much—?"

Brad groaned aloud and yelled at Lem. "Play something to drown that out."

The music started again. Business was really slow tonight. It would get worse as word spread. "Luke, can you come to a meetin' in the mornin'?"

"Wouldn't miss it for the world," Luke said, "after I put that lock on her door and—"

"There's a lock on the lady's door?" Dewey grinned and ran his hand through his unkempt gray hair. "What's the matter, Brad, losin' your charm?"

Brad bristled. "I ain't—am not losin' my charm. You seen the lady, ain't—haven't you? She's so plain, she'd make a freight train take a dirt road to avoid her. No ladies' man would want to get into her room."

"Especially if she's got a lock on the door," Dewey winked.

"I could have her if I wanted her," Brad said, "I just ain't—am not that desperate."

"That's right," Dimples nodded, "after all, there's

all them pretties that work here. If you live in a candy store, why would you eat plain cornbread?"

All the men guffawed.

Brad said, "Remember, the old maid has put a lock on the candy counter, too. She's gonna marry the girls off."

"Marry?" He hadn't heard such a shocked tone since some Yankee insulted the Alamo and the locals tarred and feathered him.

"That's right, *marry*. Any man gets any goodie around here, is gonna have to marry it."

A long moment of silence followed, as each of them contemplated whether any man needed loving that badly.

Dewey said, "Brad, I think you're gonna have to offer her more money to get her to leave town."

"I'll contribute," said Lester Osborn as he joined them.

"Me, too," said Pug.

"And me," said one of the local ranchers.

All the men were reaching in their pockets, but Brad waved them away. "The lady has her mind set, and we got to be smart. Now you all come to the meeting tomorrow and we'll discuss it."

"How we gonna get away from our wives for this meeting," one asked.

"The way I sneak off to come here," Lester nodded, pushing his wire-rimmed spectacles back up his thin nose. "It'll be a town beautification meeting we're holding. Ladies is always in favor of improving the town."

"You ain't lyin'—it'll be much improved if Miss Primm leaves," Brad said. "Now let's call it a night, fellas, I'm tired."

They closed early because business was slow anyhow. Even Sadie hadn't been able to drum up much interest when the men realized that they would have to run the gauntlet past Miss Primm's iron skillet to go to Sadie's room.

As stragglers paused for one last drink, Sadie leaned on the bar, smoking a thin cigarillo and pouting.

Brad wandered into the kitchen where Delilah was laying out bread to rise for breakfast.

"Mr. Brad, how is you?"

"Do you need to ask?" He leaned against a cabinet.

She grinned and poured him a glass of milk and handed him a fresh oatmeal cookie. "She kinda gettin' your goat?"

He shook his head. "I'm not sure what to do about her, she's turnin' things upside-down; she's so stubborn and determined."

"She's a lot like Miss Lil, ain't she?"

"Yeah, and she even looks a little like her. I reckon there was a whole family of tall red-headed women. I never realized Lil McGinty was from high-class stock."

"I don't know about that," Delilah muttered as she wiped up crumbs from her baking, "I thought she was shanty Irish."

"Naw," he shook his head. "The maiden name was Winters. Reckon I know about shanty Irish, that's my background—that and a little Indian. My biggest ambition was to be 'lace curtain Irish.'"

"What's the difference?"

He grinned. "Lace curtain Irish has flowers in the house when nobody's dead and fruit in the house when nobody's sick."

"Well, I reckon it don't matter none what her background was."

"That's right. Here in Texas, we don't give a damn about background and fancy bloodlines—we judge people differently."

Delilah nodded, her face sad. "She was a generous, kind-hearted woman and she did what she had to do to take care of those she loved."

"You think Lil did this to me as a joke?" He took another cookie. They were crisp and still warm from the oven. The milk tasted cold and rich, and he dunked the cookie in the milk and savored it.

The black woman shook her head. "No, sir. I can guarantee Miss Lil thought the world of you, Mister Brad, and she wouldn't have wanted her family to find out about her. I'm sure she thought Miss Lillian would take the money and never come to Texas."

"Delilah, you knew Lil better than anybody. Do you think she hid money somewhere in this house?"

The woman shook her head. "She never said nothin' to me. 'Course she had her secrets, and I only knew some of them."

He waited, but the old woman said no more, busying herself around the kitchen. Brad thought about the diamond pin, started to ask, decided against it. If Delilah had taken it or had it buried with the body, it didn't matter. She was welcome to it. He finished his milk and started out of the kitchen.

"Mr. Brad," Delilah said behind him, "one thing, I didn't know Miss Lil was ever married."

He shrugged. "Must have been before she met you, and who knows who this McGinty was? I imagine the old girl had a lot hidden in her past."

"More than you know," Delilah muttered.

"What?"

"Never mind. I was just talkin' to myself."

He was already thinking about tomorrow's meeting. His mind on other things, he nodded vaguely and left the kitchen. The saloon was deserted, the bartender locking up, but Sadie still sat at a poker table nursing a drink.

"Hey boss," Clyde said, fingering his handlebar mustache. "we didn't do so good tonight."

"I ain't blind. Maybe tomorrow night will be better."

"It had better be," Clyde shrugged and went out the back door, following the faro dealers and Lem.

Brad paused at the foot of the stairs. It was finally quiet upstairs. There was no light under Miss Primm's door.

"Well, now, looks like we're the last two up." Sadie got up from the poker table and sidled over to him, put her hand on his arm. "Hey, Brad, honey, what are we gonna do about that bitch?"

Somehow, inside he winced at the epithet. "She's respectable, Sadie. I'm just poor Texas trash myself, I don't know how to deal with a lady."

"But you know how to handle a woman," she pulled and pulled his face down to hers and kissed him. For a moment, his hunger took him and he returned the kiss, enveloped in her cheap perfume.

"We could go to your room," she whispered and she kissed him again.

His pulse seemed to be roaring in his ears and he needed a woman bad. Roughly, he pulled her to him.

"Well!" said a cold voice and they broke apart and looked up. Lillian Primm stood at the top of the stairs in a modest green wrapper, looking down at them.

The moment was gone. Brad stared up the stairs while wiping Sadie's lip paint off his mouth. He remembered that Lillian Primm didn't wear lip paint and her scent was light, like soap and faint lavender; a lady's scent. "I was just headed to bed," he said.

"Whose?" Miss Primm asked pointedly.

"Now that ain't none of your damned business!"

Sadie snapped. "I'm goin' to bed." She marched up the stairs past the lady.

Brad kept looking at the slender girl on the stairs. Lillian had taken her hair from its tight bun. Now it fell in soft red curls about her small shoulders. She looked fragile and vulnerable, like a willow branch. "What are you doing up, Miss Primm?" Brad asked.

"I couldn't sleep. I thought I'd come down for some warm milk." She came down the stairs and brushed past him, headed for the kitchen. Without thinking, he reached out and caught her arm. It was soft through the pale green robe.

She turned toward him and looked up and he realized her eyes were bright green and her lashes long. "Sir, unhand me."

He just kept staring down into her face. Her skin shone clean and delicate, a smattering of freckles across her nose. *Why had he ever thought her plain?*

Her full mouth turned into a grim, thin line and she yanked her arm out of his grasp. "I am not one of the girls," she reminded him and turned, nose in air, and headed for the kitchen. Tall, nevertheless, she moved with grace. He had a sudden vision of long, slender legs under that robe and he felt sweat break out on his virile body.

Brad watched her go, both surprised and unnerved. He must need a woman worse than he thought to feel a sudden rise of interest in the prim old maid. Yet his mind lingered over what she must look like under the long green robe. *Damn, Brad, old boy, you're more desperate than you thought.*

He went to his downstairs room. After he blew out the lamp and lay down in bed, he could hear Lillian Primm going up the stairs. He remembered her scent and the softness of her arm, and the way she had looked up at him. She was so innocent.

Maybe that was the challenge. He was used to experienced sluts who really knew how to give a cowboy a good ride. Now that he looked back at all his bed romps, he didn't remember ever having a virgin, a woman that no man had touched.

"Brad O'Neal, are you loco?" he whispered to himself. "That cold old maid is coyote bait."

Yet, there had been a fleeting expression in those green eyes as if there was something warm and vulnerable hidden there. He knew then how he could win against Lillian Primm. He couldn't buy her, he couldn't bully her. "Brad, the answer is clear," he muttered. "What's your best talent? Lovin' women. They fall like timber after a few minutes in your arms and it don't seem like that one has ever been in a man's arms. The answer is as plain as the nose on your face: you seduce her, make her fall in love with you, and then she'll do anything you want."

He grinned in the darkness. Was it a rotten, villainous plan? Of course it was, but his living depended on claiming her half of the Lily. He had come up from a starving, hard-scrabble existence— him, and all his brothers and sisters, in the roughest part of Texas, where only the strongest or trickiest survived. Miss Primm with her blue-blooded background couldn't possibly know how hard life had been for him, and he wasn't going to stand by and let her wreck it all. Satisfied with his plan, he finally dropped off to sleep.

Lillian had peeked around the kitchen door to make sure the gambler was no longer in the main room, then she went up the stairs and into her room. She made sure the lock was bolted and got into bed, but she could not sleep. She lay staring at the ceiling and wondering if Sadie was even now in Brad O'Neal's bed. She shook her head to wipe out the images that came to her mind of the big man naked, his strong arms wrapped tightly around the blonde as he brought her to ecstasy.

Lillian sighed and moved restlessly. She had seen the way the Texan's muscular arms had pulled the girl to him and the way their mouths had melted together. Lillian had never even been kissed, much less held in a passionate embrace. That virile stallion of a man surely knew how to thrill a woman with his touch and conquer her until she was writhing under him, moaning in surrender. She broke out into a light sheen of perspiration as she pictured it and threw the sheet off. It seemed very hot for early June.

Gradually, she dropped off to sleep. In her dreams, Brad O'Neal pulled her to him and kissed her, not like the fine gentlemen did in the romantic novels she read, but roughly and powerfully—subduing her mouth until her lips opened and she clung to him, wanting everything he had to give.

I want you, he murmured against her ear. *I need you.* Then he swung her up in his arms and carried her to his bed. *And I shall have you tonight, my sweet one. . . .*

She sat up in bed, abruptly awake and panting, still covered with a sheen of perspiration. She was furious with herself for her fantasy. *Brad O'Neal? Was she going insane?*

Chapter Seven

The Town Beautification Committee met next morning in the back of Pug Pugsley's General Store over a bottle of bourbon. Even Caddo, the Indian who was the telegrapher at the train station, sat in.

"First things first," Dewey said, pouring a round of drinks all around. "Everybody here?"

Luke said, "Not everyone—Doc's at the Johnson ranch deliverin' a baby and Brad ain't here yet."

Almost in answer, the bell on the front door jingled and Brad O'Neal strolled to the back. "Relax, gentlemen, I've got it figured out all ready."

"Then why are we here?" Dimples rubbed his pink, dimpled face.

Dewey frowned. "Now you've got a drink in your hand; you need any other reason?"

"Good point," said Pug, "but I think the womenfolk are gettin' a little suspicious about all these meetin's."

Lester Osborn snorted and pushed his wire-rimmed spectacles back up his nose. "That's just women. They always want to step in and stop it when you're havin' fun."

"But we don't ever accomplish anything." said Caddo, his brown face thoughtful.

"We've killed a lotta bottles of bourbon," Dewey ran his hand through his unkempt gray hair.

"That's true," Brad nodded.

"I tell you what," Pug, who was also the mayor, said. "Let's think about puttin' out some flower boxes of petunias to beautify the town."

The others looked at him.

"Well," he shrugged, "women like flowers, and that gives a reason for meetin'."

"True," said Lester. "I'll do a front-page story that the Beautification Committee is taking the flower boxes under consideration. That's what they do in big cities to stall any action."

Everyone breathed a sigh of relief.

"How about a game of pinochle," someone said.

Brad shook his head. "I ain't—don't have time. I just came down to bring you the message that the problem at the Lily is solved."

Dewey surveyed him as he lit his pipe. "You come up with enough to finally buy her out?"

Brad leaned back in his chair. "Now, Dewey, you know that woman can't be bought—she's got principles."

"What's that?" Pug asked.

"Nothin' you'd know anything about," Lester grumbled. "I saw you putting your fat thumb on the scale last time I bought beef here."

"Gentlemen, gentlemen," Brad grinned. "The answer is simple: I'm gonna make a concerted effort to seduce the old maid until she gives me or sells me her half cheap, and leaves town."

"I don't know, Brad." Dewey shook his head and smoke circled his gray hair.

"You doubtin' me?" Brad said. "Ain't I the womanizin' *hombre* in this town?"

The others all looked at him with admiration.

"Reckon that's true," Dimples said. "Brad just looks at a gal and she sighs and starts droppin' her drawers."

"But Miss Primm has principles," Dewey reminded them.

"But Brad has know-how," Pug pointed out. "Even a damned Yankee old maid probably can't resist him."

"What do you mean, probably?" Brad snapped.

"I put a big lock on her door," Luke said, "and she ain't asked me to take it off."

In the silence that followed, all the men looked at Brad.

He shrugged. "I didn't say it would be easy and it sure won't be fun. I shudder just thinkin' about lying on that bag of bones, but I think I can make myself do it for the good of the Texas Lily and Fort Floppett."

"Speakin' of the fort," Caddo said and sipped his drink, "didn't someone invite Major Bottoms?"

In the distance, they heard the faint sounds of band music drifting on the warm summer air.

"Never mind," Caddo winced. "Someone pour me another drink."

"Caddo," Dewey said, "we could all be in trouble for giving you a drink at all. It's against the law to give liquor to Injuns."

Caddo laughed. "I been a member of the Town Beautification Committee for many years."

"That's right," Brad said, "pour the man a drink."

"It's the last one," Dewey said and after pouring, held up the empty bottle. "Well, I reckon the mayor can offer a motion to end this meeting, leastways 'til the next shipment arrives."

"I so move," Pug said solemnly. "Do I get a second?"

"We got seconds?" Luke looked around at the shelves.

"No, dummy." Dimples said, "I second the motion."

"All in favor?" The mayor said.

"Aye!" answered the Fort Floppett Beautification Committee.

"Well, gentlemen," Brad stood up. "I'll let you know when I have scaled the wall."

"What?" Pug scratched his bulldog face.

"When he gets her drawers off," Lester said.

The men all laughed and that riled Brad. "Listen, you horny bastards, I'll bet I can charm her out of her drawers and get the Lily back the way it used to be."

All the men looked at each other.

Dewey said, "I'd never bet against you, Brad, but I've met the lady, and you're gonna lose."

They all nodded.

Brad grinned. "My honor as a real ladies' man is at stake here, so watch me work." And he strolled out of the store, his Stetson at a jaunty angle. Once outside, he was not quite so sure of himself. Maybe nobody could seduce the strait-laced schoolteacher. He didn't think it would be much fun to try, but the commerce of Fort Floppett and his own rakish reputation depended on his virility. Yes, he was up to the challenge.

A week had passed and Lillian was pleased with her girls' progress. One man had tried to sneak up the back stairs one night, but Lillian had met him with her frying pan and he had fled, howling like a scalded hound. Now she had the girls reading the *Fort Floppett Weekly Bugle* and discussing the Town Beautification Committee's idea about putting flower boxes full of petunias downtown. Lillian smiled and nodded with approval. Flowers meant

civilization and if ever she'd seen a bunch that
needed it, it was Texas men.

She noted business downstairs was still dropping
off, but Brad O'Neal seemed incredibly cheerful
about it and never missed a chance to be civil and
friendly to her. That made Lillian very suspicious,
and she avoided him.

Sadie was still causing trouble, but Lillian wasn't
one to give up on a difficult student.

Today, Lily had Delilah giving cooking lessons in
the kitchen. She looked over the girls with satisfaction. All except Sadie looked fresh-scrubbed, their
hair pulled back in modest buns, their blue gingham dresses becoming. Sadie wore tight red satin,
but Lillian decided to ignore that. "Now ladies," she
said, "to snag a husband, you'll need to cook."

Sadie laughed. "We know what it takes to interest
a man, and it ain't fluffy biscuits, right, girls?"

Nobody answered. They looked at Lillian, hope
in their eyes. "Believe me," she said. "There comes
a time when fluffy biscuits will be more interesting
than anything to a man, especially when you're
old."

"I ain't never gettin' old," Sadie said and lit a
cigarillo.

"Put that out," Lillian said in a no-nonsense
schoolteacher tone.

Silence fell over the little group. Everyone
seemed to be holding their breath.

Sadie gave her a defiant grin. "Make me."

The silence grew even more strained.

Abruptly, Lillian reached out and jerked the cigarillo from Sadie's carmine lips, and tossed it in the
sink.

"Why, you—!" She came at Lillian, but the other
girls grabbed her. She shrieked and clawed while
they held her.

"When you regain your composure," Lillian said with cool dignity, "we'll discuss the new rules. "Now let go of her, girls."

They let go of her and Sadie stood there, defiant and confused as she looked around. "You dummies gone over to her side, have you?"

"She's teaching us to be ladies," Pansy said.

"Yeah!" said the girls. "Like Lillian."

Sadie sneered. "You ain't ever gonna be ladies, you're just a bunch of whores."

"Good-bye, Sadie," Lillian said, "I believe you have just been voted out of the Lily."

"What?" The blonde backed away from the group. "You can't do this to me, I'll tell Brad."

"Remember Brad is not in charge of the upstairs," Lillian said. "Now, I'll give you a little money to make a fresh start and—"

"I don't need your damned money, I can still earn my own way flat on my back. I can go to work down at the Bucket O' Blood." She marched out of the kitchen, hips swinging in defiance.

Well, she couldn't help Sadie if the girl didn't want her help. Lillian looked her little group over with satisfaction. She had won a moral victory here—the girls were now solidly aligned with her. "My, my. Now that that's over, let's get back to our lesson. We may also bake a cake and this is where that arithmetic may come in handy, when we have to measure ingredients."

Delilah looked doubtful. "I don't know about this. These gals ain't ever even boiled water for coffee."

"But they can learn, and we'll have what they cook for dinner."

Pansy clapped her hands, and her red hair bounced. "Can we really?"

"Of course. Imagine how pleased your future husband will be when you cook."

Delilah shot them a dour look as she got out mixing bowls and pans. "If'fen they don't kill off those husbands with their first meal."

"Delilah, don't be so glum. We're going to surprise Mr. O'Neal with our meal today."

"Oh, I'll bet he'll be surprised, all right," Delilah predicted.

He appeared shocked as they all sat down to dinner around the big table. "What in the name of God—?" he said to Delilah.

The maid rolled her eyes. "The ladies is learnin' to cook."

"Is that what it is?" He seemed to be dismayed as he surveyed the burned mess before him.

"Do not hurt their feelings," Lillian admonished, "It's really delicious. See, I'm eating it. Mmmmm." She choked only a little as she smiled at the anxious young cooks.

Brad looked at her, then around at the six girls. "What happened to Sadie?"

"Sadie is moving out," Lillian said.

Pansy piped up. "She was being a smart-alec, and she lit a smoke, and Lily told her to put it out."

"Miss Lillian took on Sadie?" His tone told her he didn't think it was a good idea. "That's a pretty tough gal."

"She's a coward," Lillian said and touched her napkin to her dainty lips. "Besides, the girls helped me."

The expression on his rugged face told her he thought the girls had gone over to the enemy. He began to eat, although, it appeared, reluctantly. "You girls have changed," he grumbled, "you look like a bunch of missionaries in them high-necked dresses. What happened to all the jewelry and face paint?"

"Ladies don't dress like that," the twins said in unison.

He gave Lillian a startled look. "I don't reckon I know much about ladies, but—"

"Oh, by the way, girls," Lillian interrupted, "after dinner, I have a surprise for you."

Brad said, "I reckon in the last several weeks we've had all the surprises we can stand."

Lillian ignored him. "I've gotten two letters answering the ads I put in several papers."

"Mail-order bride papers?" Flo asked.

"Yes, and now that you all can read and write a little, someone can answer them."

Brad played with his fork. "I don't reckon that will be you, Miss Lily?"

"Of course not, I'm not looking for a husband."

"More's the pity," he muttered.

"What?"

"Never mind." He seemed to grit his teeth. "Miss Lily, I think what you're doing is wonderful—all these improvements you've been makin' around here."

"You like the flower boxes and the porch swings I put in yesterday afternoon?" she asked. "I got the idea from the town beautification story in the *Bugle*."

He started to say something, then he sighed.

Just then they heard footsteps on the staircase and all turned to see Sadie coming from upstairs with her valise.

She marched into the dining room. "I am moving out," Sadie announced in a tone that would cut ice. "This ain't what I signed on for."

"Now Sadie," Brad said, "you can't leave—"

"Oh yes, I can. Now, when that damned Yankee goes, I might come back."

"I am not leaving," Lillian announced, "I am half-owner here."

Brad actually looked dejected as he looked from his plate of burned food to Sadie and back again. "Miss Primm, I reckon I could raise my offer——"

"Won't do you any good," Lillian said. "I will not accept your dirty money when I have set myself the task of helping these young girls."

"Well, you ain't gonna help me!" Sadie snapped. She whirled and went out the front door, slamming it so hard, the house rattled.

There was a moment of silence and all the girls looked from Brad to Lillian.

"Oh, my," she said briskly, "where were we? Oh, yes, now our meal may not be perfect, but——"

"Perfect?" Brad seemed to lose his temper, "the biscuits are like cannonballs. If General Lee had had these in the war, he could have won."

"If you can't say something nice," Lillian said, "don't say anything at all. As I recall, Mr. O'Neal, you are a better than average cook, why don't you give the girls cooking lessons?"

"Are you insane? Why do you think we have Delilah?"

The old black woman came into the dining room just then, bristling. "Now I'm gettin' damned tired myself of bein' taken for granted, Mr. Brad. You could at least give these gals a chance. Miss Lily has taken on a big job here."

There was a long moment of silence.

Brad sighed and threw down his napkin. "You've even turned my own cook against me. Lily, you're as stubborn and hard-headed as your aunt."

"I'll take that as a compliment." Lillian said.

"It wasn't meant as one." He got up from the table.

"Delilah, the Town Beautification Committee will be meeting here this afternoon about three o'clock."

"Good," Lillian smiled, "our ladies will serve them cake and tea."

"Cake the girls baked?" He seemed to be struggling for self-control.

"That's right."

He sighed again. "I'm sure the boys will be very glad to hear that, Miss Lily." And he wheeled and left the room.

The girls looked at her, awaiting direction.

"Well," she said briskly, "you see how pleased he was?"

"Didn't seemed pleased to me," Pansy said.

"Oh, but I'm sure he was. This afternoon, we'll feed the gentlemen the cake you made and I'll teach you the proper way to serve a formal tea."

Fern said, "I don't think any of those men drink tea, except maybe iced on a hot summer day."

"They can learn. I realize Texans are not too civilized, but they can be taught."

"My mama said," ventured tall, black-haired Fern, "that you can always tell a Texan, but you can't tell 'em much."

"Isn't that the truth?" Lillian muttered to herself, but she gave her ladies a brave smile. "Besides, if any of you don't marry, you could work in a fine hotel and make good money."

Etta blinked. "I thought you said we was through with all that?"

"I meant, serve as waitresses. Why, the Lily would make a fine hotel and the town doesn't have one."

"That'll be over Brad's dead body," Ella volunteered.

"Don't tempt me," Lillian said. "Now, let us go up to my room and read these two letters. Maybe there's a marriage in it for one of you."

Upstairs, one letter was indeed promising. A

rancher and his brother over in New Mexico Territory were looking for brides. The twins Etta and Ella decided to answer them and Lillian helped them with their writing.

Unfortunately, the other was from a sheepman in Wyoming. Lillian read it aloud.

I have money in the bank, ten thousand acres, and a thousand sheep and would like to meet a woman. Object matrimony.

"Who's interested in this one, ladies?"

The other four shuddered.

"A sheepman wed a Texas gal?" Fern shook her head. "I may be a whore, but I ain't low enough to marry a sheepman."

"You Texans," Lillian said. "Sll right, we'll throw that one out. Twins, you get your letters written and I'll take them to the post office for you. Then this afternoon, we'll serve tea and cake to the gentlemen."

"They ain't gentlemen, they're Texans," Pansy said.

"Well, maybe they've got eligible brothers or cousins, so let's put our best foot forward, shall we?"

Lillian helped the twins with their letters. An hour later, she was headed out the door for the post office, twirling her parasol and pleased with herself. She could have the stableboy, José, get out the rig, but it was a pleasant June day and she decided a brisk walk would do her good. She even stopped to pet the ragged old goat out munching lilies on the front lawn. "Eat up, Herman," she laughed, "I think your meal is better than what I just had."

She mailed the letters, went to the telegraph

office, and visited with the telegrapher, Caddo. She found more information about out-of-state newspapers and arranged to place some ads. Once the ladies got correspondence, there were many eager men in the West who wanted a wife.

She came out of the telegraph office and bumped into Reverend Lovejoy. "Good day, Miss Primm. I've been a bit worried about you living up there in the Lily."

"Brad O'Neal has behaved like a gentleman," she said. Then she realized she was defending the scoundrel. "Besides, there's a sturdy lock on my door."

"The ladies of this town are behind you one hundred percent," he said, "but the men aren't too happy."

"Just what kind of town is this," Lillian asked, "that has no hotel but a first-class bordello?"

He fumbled with the brim of his hat and shook his head. "Like most Texas towns, I reckon, that have a lot of soldiers and cowboys and not enough women to go around."

"Then we should import some respectable women from back East, Reverend. You know there are too many single women and widows because of the war—"

"Begging your pardon, Miss Primm, but these men aren't looking for respectable women—"

"Well, they should be." She drew herself up proudly. "Fort Floppett will never be a peaceful, truly civilized place as long as men can have their cake and eat it, too."

"Well said," he agreed and tipped his hat and walked on.

About that time, Lieutenant Fortenbury came out of the general store with some packages, walking a little uncertainly in his high-heeled boots. He was still short. "Miss Primm, what a pleasure to see you again."

She warmed to him as he bowed. He was nothing like that sleazy gambler at all. "I'm happy to see you, too, Lieutenant."

"I had hoped to see you again, but I don't go into the Texas Lily," he drew himself up proudly.

"It's nice to meet a man who realizes what a den of evil the place is."

"It's a terrible place for a lady," he said, "I've worried about you. That rascal, Brad O'Neal—"

"He's been a prefect gentleman." Again she found herself defending the scoundrel and was annoyed with herself.

"If he does anything to offend you—"

"You'll thrash him?" she asked.

"Uh," he hesitated, "well, I'd probably report it to the sheriff."

"Oh." She was a bit disappointed. Perhaps she'd read too many romantic novels in which the hero whipped the villain for daring to even look at the lovely heroine. *What was she thinking?* Fisticuffs were uncivilized, and besides, she knew the tough Texan would wipe up the floor with the young officer.

"Here, let me give you a ride. I've got Major Bottom's buggy." He stepped over to the buggy tied at the hitching rail and put the packages in the back. Then he turned and helped her up to the seat. His hands were too soft and too sweaty. "I had hoped that the low-class gambler would admit defeat and sell out to you. Then you could turn that awful place into a fine mansion and live there."

"Oh, you don't understand, Lieutenant. I have little money and couldn't buy him out. Anyway, I certainly couldn't afford to live in such a grand manner."

"Oh." Did he sound disappointed? "If you found that hidden treasure, you would be a rich woman."

Lillian laughed as he climbed up beside her and snapped the reins. The old horse started down the street at a slow walk. "I think that's just a tale that's grown and grown. Mr. O'Neal doesn't seem to think there's any treasure."

"Of course he would say that because no doubt he's looking for it, too."

Of course he was, Lillian realized suddenly. That was why he was so eager to hang onto his half and buy her out. She was more determined than ever to keep her share.

The Lieutenant drove her back to the big white mansion and reined in, looking about uncertainly. "Is that gambler inside?"

"I imagine he is," Lillian said, "there's a meeting of the Town Beautification Committee here this afternoon."

He seemed to be in a hurry to leave as he came around and helped Lillian down. "I've got to get back with Mrs. Bottoms' parcels," he said, "and the major needs his buggy. I think he's coming to the meeting. There's a rumor that important congressmen are coming to town."

"Oh?" Lillian shrugged. "That doesn't seem very important. I imagine Major Bottoms will put on one of his parades and Mrs. Bottoms will hostess a social for them."

"You don't understand," The lieutenant took her hands in his small, damp and soft ones. She couldn't help but compare them to the Texan's. "They might be coming to assess the fort and maybe close it." He shuddered in spite of the warm day.

"What?"

"If they close the fort, they'll ship all the soldiers to other forts—most likely to Arizona to fight

Apaches." Sweat broke out on his pale face. "It's a fate worse than death."

Herman raised his head and glared threateningly at them, bleating, lilies hanging out of his mouth.

"Terrible, smelly animal," the officer sniffed. "He ought to be barbecued."

"But he's a pet," Lillian protested.

"Some pet. Every time I've ever gotten close to the beast, he's tried to butt me."

She tried to pull away, but the young officer held her hands and looked up at her, his pale eyes earnest. "Miss Primm, I know we don't know each other very well, but well, you've stolen my heart."

"What?" She was taken aback. "Lieutenant, I've never done anything to encourage you—"

"Yes, but I'm still bewitched by you. I hope you might let me call on you?"

"Call on me?"

"Very honorable, of course," he hastened to add, "with the object of future matrimony."

"Oh, my. I—I don't know quite what to say." She was a bit bewildered.

"Don't say anything yet, dear Miss Primm. Give it some thought. After all, we are both from blue-blooded families, so it would be a good match. I've known from the first time I saw you that we were the same kind of people, well-bred and unappreciated in a sea of Texas savages—especially that hooligan, Brad O'Neal."

In her mind, she saw Brad O'Neal. His hands weren't soft and moist and he wouldn't stand here like a pantywaist holding her hands and jabbering on and on. He'd just grab her and kiss her, holding her so tightly she couldn't breathe. She remembered the primitive way he had held Sadie in his embrace. No doubt kisses from Lieutenant Fortenbury would be chaste and wet. On the other hand, she didn't know anything about kissing.

"Miss Primm?"

"Oh, yes, what you say is true. I—I'll give it some thought."

"You've made me a very happy man, dear lady." He bent his head and kissed her hand with a wet kiss as his wispy mustache brushed along her knuckles. She almost laughed at the sensation. His hair was thinning on top, she saw as he bent over her hand. "I have been burning with passion from the first moment I saw you."

She couldn't imagine Lieutenant Fortenbury burning with anything. She looked up. Was that Brad O'Neal glowering out at her from behind the lace curtains? He looked like he might come out here at any moment, although she couldn't understand why he looked so annoyed. "I'd better go in. I think Mr. O'Neal knows we're out here."

The lieutenant seemed to blanch. He dropped her hands and ran around the buggy, clambered up on the seat. "Ta ta," he tipped his hat and drove away in an unusual hurry.

She stared after the disappearing buggy a long moment. Herman raised his shaggy beard as the officer passed and seemed to shake his head, bleating again.

Lillian sighed and went inside. Brad stood in the entry hall.

"You let that young popinjay give you a ride home?" He seemed angry.

"Now that's hardly your business, is it? Lieutenant Fortenbury is a perfect gentleman."

"Then he's got you fooled. He used to be one of our best customers."

"I don't believe you!" She snapped, green eyes

blazing, "You're jealous because he's from an old, well respected family, something you can never be."

His head snapped back as if she had struck him and she was suddenly ashamed of herself.

He caught her wrist. "You're right about that, Lily, I'm just a common Mick who's had to fight my way through the world, not had it handed to me on a silver platter like Fortenbury has."

"I—I'm sorry, that was rude of me." She tried to pull away from him. His grip was so much stronger and more masculine than Buford's. The way he was glaring down at her made her freeze in position, looking up into those dark eyes. Electricity seemed to crackle like lightning. For a split second, she thought he was going to kiss her and she held her breath. All she had to do was slap him or insult him again, and yet, she only stared up at him, waiting.

Instead he laughed and turned her loose. "The lieutenant is after your half, don't you see that?"

She felt stung. "Is it so unbelievable that he might actually like me?"

He shrugged. "Don't be fooled, Lily; you can do better."

"Maybe not—at least, not among you uncivilized Texans." She flung her head back and marched up the stairs. She sat on her bed, trembling and trying to compose herself, remembering the power of his hand on her wrist. He had been close enough for her to smell his tobacco and aftershave.

Fern stuck her head in the door. "The men are arrivin' downstairs, Miss Lily. We gonna serve cake and tea?"

She took a deep breath. "Of course, Fern, it'll be a good learning experience." She got up and started downstairs even though she dreaded facing the gambler again.

The men were standing around a poker table awkwardly.

"Gentlemen always remove their hats indoors," she smiled at them, and they hurried to comply like young schoolboys.

Lillian and the girls set out a slightly burned cake and dainty porcelain cups. "Sit down, gentlemen, and I'll pour."

They fell into their chairs.

"Now, ladies," Lillian said, "notice I offer the cup of tea as I ask 'Cream or lemon?' and then say, 'Sugar? One lump or two?'"

Pug looked at the tiny cup as it was handed to him. "What the hell's this?"

Brad said, "Hush up and drink it, Pug, don't hurt the ladies' feelin's."

"Ladies?" Luke grinned, but Brad gave him a hard look and he shut up.

Lillian shot Brad a look of thanks and he nodded. Then the ladies proudly served their cake around the table while the men stared at the burnt offering askance. She murmured instructions to her girls and shooed them out of the room.

"You gonna stay for the meetin', Miss Primm?" Pug asked.

"Would you like me to? After all, I'm half-owner here."

The men looked at each other as if they didn't know what to say. She recognized most of the men. Dimples Darlington really did have dimples and a complexion as smooth as a girl's. If he'd had long hair instead of that pale blond thatch, with a little padding, he could have passed for a woman. "My, Miss Primm, we've all heard a lot about you."

Nothing good, she thought, but she only nodded.

The bell rang just then and Delilah escorted the

major into the room. Major Bottoms had brought her some roses.

"Why, thank you, major." She buried her face in the red blossoms and sniffed their perfume.

"Uh, Miss Primm," Brad glared at her, "this is a really a man's meeting."

"Then why isn't Reverend Lovejoy here?" she challenged. "He's an important man of the community."

"Hmm," said someone, and they all looked at Brad. He sighed. "The reverend is rather inflexible on some things—"

"Principles?" She said archly. Delilah came in and Lillian handed her the roses. "Please put these in water."

Brad shot her a murderous look. "Be reasonable, Miss Primm, we can't invite a preacher to a gambling house where we're all gonna be having a drink . . . that is, after we drink your nice tea and eat the cake the ladies made."

The others looked dubious.

Lillian paused.

"Gentlemen, let's get down to business." Brad sighed and gestured. "I think Miss Primm was just leavin' us."

"No, I'm not." She pulled out a chair and the major rushed to aid her. They both sat down.

Delilah had left with the roses and now returned with a big plate of sandwiches and homemade pickles. "Just in case you men need something more than cake and tea. I also got deviled eggs and potato salad."

The men dived in like they hadn't eaten in a week, some wiping their faces on their sleeves.

"I have napkins," Lillian offered.

"Miss Primm, we are doing just fine, thank you very much." Brad shot her another annoyed look.

"Mmmm," sighed Dimples who was more than a little pudgy. "You barbecue this yourself, Brad?"

"'Course he did," said the cook, "can't nobody beat Mr. Brad when it comes to barbecuing."

Luke, the locksmith, had his mouth full as he turned and spoke to Lillian. "How's that lock workin' for you, Miss?"

"Just fine."

Brad said, "It ain't like anybody's tryin' to break her door down to get in."

"No one would dare," she said.

"Miss Primm, don't you have some mendin' to do?"

"I think I'll stay for the meeting, since I'm a part owner of a business in this town."

The other men all looked uncertainly at Lillian, then at Brad. He was taking deep breaths.

Lillian said "Delilah, please bring me some iced tea."

"Yes, ma'am." She left the room.

"Are you sure you want to stay?" Brad said as he finished his sandwich ad wiped his face on his sleeve.

Lillian winced at his manners, or lack thereof. "I said I was, didn't I?"

Luke looked longingly toward the stairs where the NO ADMITTANCE sign still hung. "Where'd the girls go?"

"I just sent them out on a nature walk," Lillian said, "gathering blooms to press and dry in their scrapbooks."

"What?" said all the men in unison.

Brad shrugged. "I reckon it's something prissy ladies do back East."

"But them ain't ladies," said Pug, "they's wh—"

"Shut up, Pug," Brad thundered. "If Miss Primm says they are ladies, they are ladies."

"Anything you say, Brad." He looked as puzzled as the other men.

She warmed toward the gambler and sent him a look of gratitude. Like Sir Galahad, he could be very courtly.

Brad shrugged. "It ain't my doin'. The Lily still got good liquor and gamblin'."

"But no girls?" White-haired Doc sighed.

"Well, much as I hate to give a plug to the competition, Sadie's moved down to the Bucket O' Blood." Brad dug into his chocolate cake and winced as he took a bite. "Miss Primm is gonna reform the rest of 'em and marry them off."

"That's cruel to every man in the county," Dewey declared and all the men looked at her like she'd stomped on a baby rabbit.

Delilah came in to bring Lillian a tall glass of iced tea and carry away the plates as the men finished.

"Before we get started," Brad said, "I'll mix up some juleps." He got up and went over to the bar.

"You'd better mix a big pitcher," Major Bottoms warned, "we got a very serious problem."

"In that case," Brad grinned, "I'll make enough to last until evenin'."

"I don't know how much serious work you can get done if everyone gets snockered," Lillian said.

Again they all looked at her.

Brad said, "We're Texans and Texans think better when they've had a few drinks to oil 'em."

"Remember the Alamo," Dewey said reverently and they all scrambled to their feet, hands over their hearts and tears in their eyes.

"I don't even know what that is," Lillian complained and again, they looked at her in horror.

"Tsk, tsk." Brad brought a tray of drinks over to the table. "Miss Primm, people have been lynched for less than that. Why, Texas babies know about the Alamo. Remind me to educate you later." He passed the drinks around and smiled at her. "Would you like one?"

"No, thank you." She sipped her iced tea and began to wish she'd skipped this meeting. Whatever was going on, she probably wasn't going to approve.

"Well," Major Bottom took a big gulp of his julep. "This is serious, boys. A passel of congressmen, Yankees of course, are coming to Fort Floppett next weekend."

"On a junket?" Lillian asked.

"A what?" Luke asked.

"An official trip," Lillian explained, "usually at taxpayer's expense."

Brad eyed her. "Is there any other kind for congressmen?"

She frowned at him. "Don't be so cynical."

"What?" asked most of the men.

"Never mind," The major leaned closer. "Gossip says they're talkin' budget again in Washington and it's election time, so they got to look good to their voters."

All the men paused and stared at him.

Brad said "You don't mean—?"

"I do," the major nodded. "They might decide to close Fort Floppett."

A hushed sigh of dismay went around the table. Dimples said "That'd wreck this town. We all make a livin' off supplyin' the fort."

"It seems to me," Lillian put in, "that the fort doesn't serve any useful purpose. I understand it used to protect the stagecoach lines from wild Indians and bandits, but there's a train now and the town's so peaceful, a dog can sleep on Main Street all day without anything bothering it."

Now they all turned and glared at her.

"Young lady," said the major, "half the forts in the

country serve no real purpose except helping the businesses in town and giving the army parade grounds to march on. Most of the businesses in town may close, including yours, if the army shuts down the fort."

Brad snorted. "Miss Primm is doing a pretty good job of shutting us down now."

"I am against making money off sin."

The men all regarded her with a sigh.

"Miss Primm," Brad said, "you don't belong in this meeting any more than the other ladies and Reverend Lovejoy."

She ignored him.

"You two stop that quibbling," the major snapped. "This is serious. Why, if they shut down the fort, they'll probably send me and all my soldiers to Arizona to fight Apaches." He shuddered at the thought. "Any of you ever been in Arizona?"

They all shook their heads.

"It's hotter than Texas," the officer said.

"No place is hotter than Texas," Brad protested proudly. "Texas is hotter than hell with the lid off."

"Arizona is too dry to raise roses," the major continued. "Instead of putting on parades, I'll be out in the cactus and scorpions being shot at by savage Injuns."

Caddo said, "I resent that. My people been civilized for years. Most of the Caddos around here speak better English than the white men."

"Apologies," the major nodded. "Caddo, I'm gonna need your peoples' help—we all are. Brad and I have already discussed this and he's got an idea. Tell 'em about it, Brad."

Lillian began to get a feeling that there was something crooked afoot. Of course, if Brad O'Neal was involved, she wasn't surprised.

"Well," Brad sipped his julep. "We'll entertain

'em royally, maybe a parade and the band meetin' the train."

"A parade? I like that," The major grinned.

"They'll have to stay at the fort since we ain't got no hotel." Pug said.

Lillian winced at his grammar and almost automatically corrected it, but realized Brad was giving her a look, daring her to say anything, so she didn't.

"Anybody ever figure out how the hotel caught fire?" Doc's white hair fell across his pink forehead.

They all shook their heads.

"Never mind." The major said. "We'll show 'em a real good time," he seemed to warm to the idea. "Brad'll cook up some of his famous barbecue and all the ladies will bring their best dishes. We'll have a party and a dance for the whole town."

"Just to entertain a bunch of damned Yankees," Pug said before he remembered Lillian was there. "Excuse me, Miss, I keep forgettin' there's a lady present."

"Think of me as just another business owner," she said, smiling at Brad, who glared back.

Brad said, "Now I've got an idea as to how to convince them east Texas really needs this fort to protect this town."

"Protect it from what?" Dimples laughed, "Herman the goat maybe butting someone?"

"Does he do that?" Lillian asked.

"Now and then," Brad admitted. "Now you all hush up and listen. I figure about the time the congressmen are leavin' on the evenin' train, we'll have a stagecoach arrivin' in town with important mail—"

Dewey shook his unkempt head and puffed his pipe. "We ain't had a stage running since before the War of Yankee Aggression—"

"You mean the Southern Rebellion?" Lillian asked pointedly.

Brad sighed. "We ain't got time to refight the War right now; we got plans to make. So, here comes the stage at full gallop—"

"We got no stage," Caddo said.

"No," said the livery owner, Dimples, "there's an old one in back of my barn, missin' a wheel, though."

"Can you get it runnin' by then?" Brad asked.

He nodded. "Reckon I might could."

"Okay," Brad said, "So here comes the stage agallopin' with lady passengers inside screamin' to be saved and the stage is being chased by war-painted savages. That's where you come in, Caddo."

The squat Indian bristled. "My people never were into war paint. That's an insult."

Brad looked exasperated. "Well, couldn't they just this once to save the fort?"

"I reckon," Caddo nodded. "But they won't like it."

"Then," Brad said, seeming to warm to his story, "the army comes gallopin' to the rescue with bugles soundin' the charge, like General Custer."

"Custer was annihilated," Lillian pointed out dryly.

"Sounds thrilling," the major said. "I'll tell all the soldiers to shoot up in the air. You think the congressmen will buy that?"

"I think they'll be so scared, they'll wet their drawers," Brad said.

"I beg your pardon," said Lillian. "And besides, it sounds dangerous. Where will you get ladies to ride in this galloping coach? They might get killed."

Brad smiled and looked at her. "Are you volunteering?"

"My goodness, no! No woman will consent to do that, not even to save the fort."

"I wouldn't let 'em anyway. No true Texan would put a woman in harm's way. But we do need a lady in that coach screamin' her head off—gives it a good effect." Brad looked at Dimples. "Hey, you remember that time you dressed up in your wife's clothes for Halloween?"

There was a long moment of silence as all the men stared at Dimples.

"No!" Dimples said. "N-O. I ain't gonna be some prissy girl ridin' in the coach."

"It would make it more realistic," Brad suggested.

The other men murmured agreement. "You got to do it, Dimples, to save the fort."

"I wanta be one of the cowboys or soldiers who come riding to the rescue."

"We need a gal in that coach worse," Brad said. "When it's all over and the congressmen leave on their train, they'll realize how much we need the fort and leave us be. I'll throw a party afterwards—free drinks on the house."

"Now for that, I might do 'er," Dimples said.

Lillian sighed with exasperation. "I can't believe this. Are all of you in favor of this subterfuge?"

The other men looked at Brad. "Is that a dirty word?"

"She don't know any dirty words—she's a lady." Brad shrugged. "Don't mind Miss Primm, she used to teach English, you know."

"What I am saying," Lillian raised her voice, "is that this is crooked and dishonest. Don't you upstanding men have anything to say to this—this sly rascal?"

There was a moment of silence as all pondered her words. Finally they all turned and grinned at Brad. "Thanks, Brad, old buddy, this is a plan that denotes a true Texan. Three cheers for Brad O'Neal!"

"I've had enough!" Lillian got up and flounced away from the poker table. Behind her the men shouted, "Hip hip hurray! Hip hip hurray! Hip hip hurray!"

The meeting was breaking up as the girls entered the front door with their little baskets of flowers. The men's eyes gleamed. Lillian rushed to meet her ladies, escorting them past the table. The men sighed as the girls went by.

"Dang it," Pug muttered, "it's like dangling candy in front of a baby and then snatching it away."

The others murmured in agreement.

Brad looked at Lillian. "Of course, there's some sour lemon drops in the bunch. Well, let's break it up, fellows, it's time for the regulars to start driftin' in. We'll work on our plan and talk more later. Dimples, you get that stage coach runnin'. I'll be the driver and Dewey can ride shotgun. Lester, you get word around to all the ranches."

"The cowboys and the soldiers ain't never got along well," Lester reminded him.

"We need 'em all, this time." Brad said.

"And I'll get the dance scheduled and the band practicing," the major promised.

Lillian took her little flock up the stairs and then watched over the balcony as the men left. It was a crazy and unprincipled plan and only that Texas rascal could have dreamed it up. Besides, it couldn't possibly work . . . could it?

Chapter Eight

The congressmen were due into town on the Saturday morning train, which of course gave Major Bottoms a perfect opportunity to stage a parade and have his band waiting on the platform, brass buttons shining, as the engine puffed into town. Most of the townfolk and the outlying ranchers came to the station to welcome the visitors.

Lillian had been eating well these past weeks and might be adding a few pounds, she thought, as she tried to button her plain dark dress. She was eating her way out of her clothes. What to do? She dug around in her aunt's closet and found a green plaid traveling costume that was not quite as gaudy and revealing as most of Lil McGinty's clothes. Wearing a perky little hat, the ladies assured her she looked beautiful. Even Brad O'Neal looked startled as she came down the front steps where he waited with the buggy.

Brad blinked as he watched Miss Lillian come down the steps. Not only did she look a lot like her aunt, she was almost pretty. Pretty? Was he going loco? She was only appealing because he'd been so long without a woman, he told himself. "You look nice," he stammered and then put his hands on her waist to help her into the buggy. She still was slender enough that he could almost put his hands around her waist. "You did something different to your hair."

"The hat wouldn't fit with a bun, so the girls pulled it back in ringlets." She seemed pleased he had noticed.

The twins, Etta and Ella, came down the steps carrying valises and chattering like jaybirds. Brad helped them in. "Where you two goin' with the luggage?"

"Didn't Miss Lillian tell you? We're catchin' the train out to go to New Mexico Territory. We're getting married!"

He frowned at Lillian. "Miss Lily doesn't tell me much of anything." he grumbled.

"José is bringing the other girls to the station in the wagon," Lillian said.

"So now we'll only have four girls?" Brad said.

She nodded and smiled as he snapped the reins to start the drive to the station. "I got more letters in yesterday, so maybe others will be leaving soon."

He seemed to be gritting his teeth. "I hope you know what you're doin.' My business is still slidin'."

"Since you're such a great cook," she said, "maybe you should be offering barbecue and other food along with your whiskey and gambling."

"I ain't runnin' a café."

"It's not a bad idea," she said.

As usual, Herman was out of his pen and munching day-lilies out on the front lawn next to the white bird bath. He raised his head and shook his curled horns at them as the buggy passed. If they could just get through today and get the congressmen on the train tomorrow night, Lillian thought, maybe everything would be all right. She had no faith in the shenanigans planned as the congressmen got on that outgoing train. In the distance, Lillian heard the whistle of the train's engine as it puffed toward town. Immediately, the army band struck up an off-key rendition of the "Battle Hymn of the Republic."

Brad groaned. "Seems like he could have chosen something livelier than that Yankee tune, like the 'Yellow Rose of Texas.'"

Lillian decided to ignore that comment. She turned toward the twins in the back seat. "You both look lovely—quite respectable. I hope you'll be very happy."

They giggled with pleasure.

Etta said, "I'm gonna name my first little girl after you, Miss Lillian."

"Well, thank you, I'm honored."

"And Brad, I'm gonna name my first little boy after you," Ella said.

"You might want to reconsider that, my dear," Lillian said.

"Now what is that supposed to mean?" Brad snapped.

"Nothing." She looked toward the back seat. "I'm only sorry you two are going to miss the dance tonight."

"The girls from the Lily are invited to that?" Brad asked.

"*The Bugle* said *everyone* was invited," Lillian reminded him, "and our girls are now ladies. Some rancher at the party might take a liking to one of them."

Brad snorted, but Lillian decided she would not rise to the bait. Their buggy moved at a brisk pace down Main Street and arrived as the congressmen were getting off the train. Brad tied the buggy to the hitching post and helped the women down.

"My," Lillian said, "there's such a crowd. Come,

ladies, I'll help you get your tickets. Mr. O'Neal will bring the luggage."

He seemed about to say something, sighed, and got the luggage, wending his way through the crowd behind her on the station platform. Ahead of him, her little bustle waggled enticingly. He couldn't take his gaze off it as he pushed through the crowd. Several members of the Town Beautification Committee were standing next to the station door. Dewey hooked his thumbs in his vest. "Well, if it isn't Romeo, now carryin' suitcases like a hired hand."

Brad glared at him. "The twins is leavin' town," he snapped, "and somebody's got to carry their stuff." He ignored the grinning men and followed the three women into the station. Caddo had moved from his telegraph board and was selling tickets.

Lillian bought the tickets and led the girls to the train, Brad following along behind. The band still played as the congressmen shook hands all around. She hugged the girls, wished them luck, and promised to write. The gambler set their luggage on the train and then hugged the girls himself, a little too tightly, Lillian thought with a frown. Then she and Brad waved their good-byes and went to mingle into the large, boisterous crowd. Pug, the mayor, stepped forward, shook hands with all the congressmen, and tried to begin his speech, but the band continued playing. Mrs. Bottoms finally had to step forward and touch the major's arm to end the music. There were three congressmen: a short one, a tall one, and a young one.

Lillian leaned over and whispered to Brad. "Are you men still planning that silly raid on—"

"Hush," he commanded, "you're interruptin' the mayor's speech."

"I take that as a 'yes'?"

Brad didn't answer.

The mayor cleared his throat and began again. "Friends and fellow townspeople of the great town of Fort Floppett, we are honored today to have three important congressmen come all the way from our nation's capitol to visit us."

"Austin?" Someone asked, and the crowd cheered.

"Washington, D.C.," the mayor said, unruffled. "They are here on a fact-finding mission to see how important this fort is in protectin' our local citizens from the attacks of vicious savages and bandits."

Some of the citizens looked baffled and one actually said "Savages—?"

But before anything else could be said, Brad shouted, "Hurray for Major Bottoms and our brave soldiers who put themselves at risk every day to protect us in this dangerous, wild land!"

"Hip hip hurray!" shouted the crowd. "Hip hip hurray!"

Lillian sniffed. The most dangerous thing she'd heard of the major doing lately was pricking his thumb on one of his prize rosebushes and bleeding a little, but she kept her mouth shut.

"And," Pug continued, "these soldiers are almost as brave as those who went down at the Alamo!" This led to more cheering. Texans, it seemed, always cheered when the Alamo was mentioned.

Of course some of the cowboys in the crowd had been celebrating early. It didn't take much of an excuse for cowboys, especially Texans, to celebrate. Many of them were more than a little drunk, so they cheered every time the mayor paused to take a breath.

Then the major had to welcome the visiting congressmen and Reverend Lovejoy's little daughter stepped forward and presented them with bouquets of roses from the fort and orange day-lilies from the Texas Lily. Then the congressmen had to make speeches, which no one listened to, of course—because they were Yankees and nobody thought anyone from north of the Red River had a lick of good horse sense—but it was expected.

Finally the major said, "we're taking the visitors on a fact-finding trip this afternoon to see how valuable our fort is in protecting the townspeople and then tonight, the whole town is invited to a big dance out at the fort."

That really got the cheers going.

A cowboy yelled, "Does that mean free beer?"

"Courtesy of the Texas Lily," the major nodded, and there were more cheers than there had been for the Alamo.

Brad stepped forward and shook hands with the three congressmen. He couldn't decide if they looked bored or just stupid, but after all, they were Yankees. "Welcome, gentlemen. I just hope there won't be any Indian raids or bandit attacks while you gentlemen are in town."

All three looked uneasy. "Is that a possibility?"

The major stepped forward. "Not with our brave soldiers ever on the alert to protect this town."

The crowd cheered again. Lillian thought most of them looked like they didn't know what they were cheering for, but maybe they were excited about the free beer.

About half the band looked to be asleep, Lillian thought. Of course a few of them had been at the Lily playing cards until late and maybe the rest had been down at the Bucket O' Blood, doing whatever it was men did in dives like that.

The crowd began to disperse and the train

pulled out, Etta and Ella leaning out of the window to wave good-bye.

"Good luck! And remember to be ladies!" Lillian shouted and waved.

The tall congressman sidled up to Brad and lowered his voice, although Lillian caught his words. "Ahem, we hear there's a lot of fun to be had at this place called the Texas Lily."

Brad grinned. "Well, we have a good bar, and if you favor poker or keno——"

"I meant women," the congressman winked.

Brad looked toward Lillian and frowned. "Uh, not any more, but we'll have some lovely ladies at the dance tonight."

"*Respectable* ladies?" He looked disappointed.

"Afraid so," Brad said with a sigh.

The gathering broke up then, the mayor and the major escorting the important visitors around town and out to the fort to show them the defenses against all those marauding Indians and bandits.

Caddo had come out of the telegraph office and stood watching the ceremony. Now as the crowd dispersed, he wandered over to Brad and Lillian. "You think they'll buy it?"

Brad shrugged. "All we can do is try. They'll be stayin' at the fort tonight. We'll hustle them out of town tomorrow night, and that's when we'll stage the attack. You got your people ready?"

Caddo nodded. "They ain't too happy about having to play the savages. Some of them wanted to be the cowboys."

"We got plenty of cowboys, and Dimples is gonna be the lady in distress."

Luke joined them. "I understand they got the coach repaired."

"Good," Brad said.

"Major Bottoms alerted all his troopers about what we're doin'?" Dewey asked.

Brad nodded. "We're gonna put on a show that makes one of those Wild West shows look like a kid's play."

Lillian drew herself up and frowned. "This is deceptive and will have ruinous results. I heartily disapprove."

The men looked from her to Brad. "Does she ever speak English?"

Brad shrugged. "She's a Yankee schoolteacher, you can't expect too much."

"I beg your pardon." Lillian stuck her nose in the air and strode away through the crowd.

She saw Lieutenant Fortenbury hand his tuba over to another band member and hurry to meet her. He tipped his hat and bowed low. "Good day, Miss Lillian. How did you like the concert?"

"It—it was wonderful, Lieutenant." She was a lady and a lady was always polite.

"Do call me Buford." He smiled at her and his wispy mustache wiggled. "Are you attending the dance tonight?"

She nodded. "Of course, I wouldn't miss it."

"Then I shall monopolize your whole dance card," he promised. "Well, ta ta, I must be off." He wobbled a little in his high-heeled boots as he walked away.

Brad strode up just then, scowling. "Is it my imagination, or is that prissy officer gettin' taller?"

"Don't be rude," she snapped. "He asked to be put on my dance card tonight."

"You'll be lookin' down at the top of his head all evenin'," Brad snorted.

Luke walked up. "Did you hear him? He said 'ta ta,' What kind of a man says 'ta ta'?"

"Well, he ain't a Texan, that's for sure," Brad said.

Dewey had just joined them. "If'fen a Texan said 'ta ta,' the boys would rope 'im and drag him through a cow lot."

"He's a gentleman," Lillian said, "and you are all just jealous. I'll be happy to save him dances tonight. Now, I'll be waiting in the buggy." She stuck her nose in the air and marched away.

Behind her, the men stared after her. Her little bustle wiggled enticingly as she walked. Brad was mesmerized by the sight.

"Damn," Luke sighed. "Is it my imagination, or is she gettin' prettier than a speckled pup in a red wagon?"

The way the men were staring after her like hungry hounds after a rabbit annoyed Brad for some reason he couldn't be sure of. "Ya'll quit gawkin' after Lily that way. She's a lady."

The others had gathered now and Dewey nodded in agreement. "She's a lady, all right. She's saving dances for that prissy lieutenant? Our Romeo lost his charm?"

"When hell freezes over," Brad snapped and adjusted his Stetson, "I just ain't—haven't had time to really turn my charm on her yet."

Lester had joined them. "She's a big challenge, is she, Brad?"

"Hell, yes, contrariest woman I ever run across. She don't seem to notice how charmin' I am."

"Let us know when you get her drawers off," Luke grinned.

"No contest," Brad snapped and headed for the buggy. His reputation was at stake, as well as his business. Tonight at the dance, he'd have to out-charm that prissy young officer. He strode over, climbed up in the buggy and snapped the reins at the startled old horse. "If'fen I was you, I wouldn't promise all my dances to that prissy Yankee."

"I shall not listen to your attacks," Lillian defended the officer gallantly, "he's a gentleman and a blue-blood."

"I'll bet it runs red as anyone's if he ever got into a fight."

"Fight?" Lillian gasped, "I'm sure Buford's not a low-class saloon brawler."

"Like me?" Brad said.

"I didn't say that," she sniffed.

"So it's Buford now, is it? You two are gettin' mighty friendly."

"That's hardly your concern." She stuck her nose in the air as the buggy moved along. "He asked to call on me."

"That nancy-boy comes into the Lily, I'll throw him down the steps," Brad glowered at her.

"He's too respectable to come into our place as long as it's a low-class saloon."

"Maybe because he's been told he ain't welcome since he cheats at cards and welshes on bets."

"How dare you! The lieutenant is a high-class gentleman."

"The gentleman is after your share of the Lily," Brad said.

She turned and glared at him. "And you're afraid I might marry him and he'd get it," she snapped, green eyes blazing. "We've had this conversation before, Mr. O'Neal. I know you don't think it's possible a man could ever want to marry this old-maid schoolteacher, but maybe the lieutenant is different." Tears came to her eyes and she blinked rapidly.

Brad pulled up before the Lily and she hopped out, lifting her skirts and running up the steps. He sat in the buggy looking at her. He could have sworn she was sobbing as she jumped out of the buggy and he felt bad about that. "Well, you stupid ass, reckon you didn't help your cause none just now. Bed her? You'll be lucky if she don't throw rocks at you tonight."

He had seen José driving the other girls home so now he called for the stable boy to come take the buggy around back. Then Brad sat in the porch swing and lit a cigar. The Lily wasn't going to be open tonight because of the big dance at the fort.

Dance. In his mind, he saw the snotty lieutenant dancing with Lily, holding her close while he entertained her with sophisticated conversation about society back east. Brad had always charmed women, but now he felt at a distinct disadvantage. What did a hard-scrabble Texan know about behaving like a gentleman? In his mind, the pair waltzed and laughed and then the Lieutenant whirled her out the doors of the big hall and into the darkness. Out there, he'd kiss her.

The thought upset Brad so, he found himself clenching his fists. It was only because he had a bet on with the boys, he told himself, and he intended to seduce the naïve girl before the lieutenant got a chance to. Yes, that was what was bothering him. If the lieutenant kissed her, he might get her lace drawers off and . . . that picture really upset Brad. Lily was a lady and how dare a nancy-boy like that try to take advantage of her? Well, tonight, he promised himself, he'd outcharm the young officer, and if anyone was going to kiss her, it was going to be Brad O'Neal.

The girls were all aflutter on this warm summer night as they got ready for the party. "Guess what?" Fern said. "A new rancher was flirting with me at the train. He said he'd be at the dance tonight."

"Remember to behave like a lady," Lillian admonished. "You can't sell the candy store by giving away sweets."

"What?" asked Pansy, blinking her eyes.

Lillian sighed. "Never mind, Pansy. I think Fern knows what I mean."

Fern nodded. "I do, Miss Lillian, and I'm mighty grateful to you for all you've taught me."

Lillian smiled and patted her arm. "I only want what's best for all of you. You've almost become like daughters to me."

"You ain't that old," Pansy said.

"Aren't old enough," Lillian corrected gently. "Sometimes I feel like it, though." She thought about marriage with a wistful sigh. Mrs. Buford Fortenbury. Should she settle for that, if he asked her? There might not be many fireworks, but she'd be part of a blue-blooded family. Her mind went to the night Brad had caught her arm and her heart had hammered at his touch. Her common sense told her the gambler was not only wild, but dangerous to a respectable woman. Yes, the lieutenant would be a sensible match.

Lillian had thought she'd wear the dress she'd worn to today's welcome ceremony, but the girls would have none of it. "Miss Lily," Fern said, "you could look so much better than you do. I'll bet one of Lil's dresses would fit you."

"Oh, I don't think—"

"You can at least try," Pansy urged. "We'll look to see what Lil had or what one of us owns."

"Oh, I don't think—" Lillian said again doubtfully, but the girls were already looking through each other's closets, attempting to find a ball gown for Lillian.

It was in Lil's closet that they found the dark green silk. "This will be perfect with your red hair."

"Oh my, it's so much fancier than what I'm used to," Lillian protested, "and it's so low-cut."

However, the ladies insisted. They spent as much time getting Lillian dressed as they spent on themselves.

Lillian stood blinking at herself in the full-length mirror. "I'm afraid I've put on a little weight."

"It looks good on you," Pansy assured her, and the others agreed. "Now you need some jewelry and something done to your hair."

"What's wrong with my hair?" Lillian touched it defensively. "It's very practical this way."

"It needs to be a little softer," Fern said, "I'll get the curling iron. You others find her some jewelry and some scent."

They all scattered with Lillian calling after them in protest. "Scent? I never wear scent except for soap. I'm not sure it's respectable for a maiden lady my age to curl her hair and soak herself in perfume."

"Hmm, hmm, ain't you somethin' now?" Delilah had come upstairs and now stood waiting, nodding in approval. "You looks like Miss Lil in that dress, Miss."

Lillian turned toward her. "What—what was she really like? My aunt, I mean?"

"Generous, kind." The old woman said. "She just had a hard life, Miss."

"I don't really know anything about her except that my mother didn't approve of her, especially, I think, that she married some Irishman—"

"Miss Lil was never married," Delilah muttered.

"What?"

"Never mind."

"Well, maybe it was before you met her," Lillian said. "I think she must have been quite young."

Delilah bit her lip and looked away. "Maybe I was mistaken."

"I'm sure you are," Lillian said. "Her maiden name was Winters."

"Is that right?"

"We're related to royalty," Lillian nodded. "The earl of Primley, Mother said. Blood will tell, you know."

"Seems to me actions is more important than bloodlines, unless of course, you're breedin' cattle or horses."

"But of course it's important," Lillian defended herself. After all, she was not pretty. If she didn't have her fine bloodlines to comfort her, she was nothing. "I do agree that my aunt must have had a hard life. The family was poor and my aunt even worked as a servant for a while for a rich, low-class Irishman who lived down the street. He owned a saloon and was the worst kind of fellow, Mother said."

Delilah didn't say anything for a long moment, then shrugged. "Well, I got food in the oven for tonight's big dance. You look right pretty, Miss Lillian."

"You think so?" She stared at herself in the mirror. "My mother frowned at vanity."

As Delilah left the room, the girls reappeared with a string of pearls and a curling iron. "Now, Miss Lillian, you let us do something about your hair. And here, Pansy has a bottle of rose scent. That's not too much scent for a lady."

Lillian protested, but she was overwhelmed by the much younger girls who took down her hair and began to redo it with giggles of delight.

Downstairs, Brad finished shaving and frowned as he slipped into a fine black broadcloth coat that had been custom-made for him. He slapped on a little aftershave and stared at himself in the mirror. He was still youthful at age thirty-six and his hair was still black and thick, thanks to some Indian blood back somewhere in his lineage.

There were going to be some pretty girls at the dance and normally, Brad would help himself to the feast of beauties, but tonight, he must concentrate on Miss Lillian. Lily, he thought with a smile. In spite of her stern demeanor, she was really naïve and defenseless in a tough world. He felt suddenly protective of her. Then he remembered that she was ruining his business and he had a bet on with the boys—his reputation as a charmer was on the line. No, Lieutenant Nancy-Boy was not going to monopolize her evening if Brad had anything to say about it.

It was turning dusk outside his window. From upstairs, he heard the girls giggle again. *What was going on up there?*

José came in the back door and announced that the big open buggy was out front and ready. Brad nodded and went to the foot of the stairs. "Hey ladies," he shouted, "you ready for the party?"

The younger women came down together. Lillian must have had a hand in their outfits because they wore little face paint and their dresses were demure. He made an exclamation of surprise. "Why, you girls look like real ladies," he said before thinking.

"We are ladies and entitled to respect," Pansy said. "Wait until you see Miss Lillian."

"Uh huh." He said without enthusiasm, not expecting much. She always looked as prim as her name, and she hardly ever smiled.

"We'll get in the buggy," the girls said and trooped past him.

"Hey up there!" he yelled up the stairs. "Are you coming, Miss Primm?"

Her door opened slowly and she came out on the landing and stood there hesitantly.

Brad took a surprised breath. "Well, I'll be damned!"

She paused at the top of the stairs. "Do I—do I look ridiculous? The girls insisted on helping me."

He couldn't say anything; he just stared. She looked a lot like her aunt, but much prettier in that green silk. Miss Primm had put a little weight on her skinny frame over the past weeks, and the dress was very lowcut. Her skin was the color of cream and her graceful neck was emphasized by a string of pearls. And her hair. . . .

She came down the stairs, blushing. "Do I look that bad?"

"You—you look pretty," he stumbled over his words. "What did you do to your hair?"

She reached up to touch it with a nervous hand. "The girls insisted on pulling it back in curls, weaving a green ribbon through it. I feel like a fool. After all, I am thirty-two and past trying to gussy myself up like some young girl."

"No," he shook his head, spellbound, "you don't look like a young girl."

"Oh, my. I—I was afraid of that. Perhaps I should go upstairs and change." She half-turned and he caught her arm.

"No," he said, "don't change. Uh, there isn't time." He smelled the faint scent of roses and realized how green her eyes were—and that the sprinkle of freckles across her nose only made her more appealing. He had a sudden urge to drag her to him and kiss her there in the darkened hallway, but then realized she'd probably slap him. Lieutenant Fortenbury would probably kiss her tonight out on the veranda at the hall. The thought made him grind his teeth.

"You look upset, Mr. O'Neal. You don't have to be nice to me, I know how much you dislike me."

"Then maybe I'm the one who has been a fool," he smiled gallantly and offered her his arm. "Shall we go?"

She blushed again as she took his arm.

He nodded, still a bit speechless over her appearance. Once she had looked like coyote bait and now she was almost pretty. *Almost?* He patted the dainty hand she put on his muscular arm and smiled down at her again. "I shall be honored to escort you, Lily. And while I know you've promised all your dances to young Fortenbury, I shall fight him and all the others off and insist you save me a dance."

She flushed. "Please don't make fun of me," she whispered. "I know you're only after the Lily."

Could he deny it? He was as confused as a calf in a roping pen. Somehow, he could not lie to this soft paragon of virtue. "Well, save me a dance anyway."

They started out the front door and Delilah called after him "Mr. Brad, I put a coconut and a chocolate cake in the back of the buggy as well as a ham."

"Thanks, Delilah, doesn't Miss Lily look nice?"

The old woman came out into the hallway and stared at her, nodding, a smile on her face. "She sure does. Miss Lil would be mighty proud. The girl looks just like—"

Lillian turned around, a question in her eyes.

"Uh oh." Delilah shooed them on out the door. "You have a good time at the dance tonight." She stood on the porch and waved good-bye to the buggy as it pulled away. Then she headed back to her kitchen to pour some coffee and put her feet up. "Black gal, you gonna have to watch your big mouth," she scolded herself. She had almost said too much. If Miss Lillian only knew everything there was to know . . . but of course she must never find out any of Miss Lil's secrets. Delilah didn't think even *she* knew them all.

As far as Mr. Brad, Delilah knew him all too well. She'd seen the way he smiled at that naïve girl just now. He was going to try to charm her and probably the poor thing had never had a man court her. Miss Lillian would be like a baby chick in a wolf's mouth; that gambler was a lady's man.

"Uh uh," she shook her head in disapproval. Delilah used to like Mr. Brad much better until the diamond pin disappeared. She knew he'd given it to Miss Lil only the day before she died. But when Delilah had looked for it to pin it on Lil's dress for the burial, she couldn't find it. Had the gambler done the unthinkable and taken it out of her jewelry box the day of the funeral? That was incredibly cheap and not like Mr. Brad at all. He'd always been kind and generous. No wonder Miss Lil had loved him better than a son. If he'd been a little older or she'd been a little younger . . . well, that was water under the bridge now.

Delilah sat in the dark kitchen sipping her coffee and wondered about what he'd done with the diamond pin. He'd probably given it to one of the whores or even Miss Lillian, trying to charm her to drop her suspicions of him. She shook her head. "Yes, the poor little thing is a baby chick in a wolf's mouth and Mr. Brad will get what he wants. She'll end up in his bed like all those other women."

She'd warn Miss Lillian, but the girl wouldn't believe her anyway. "Miss Lil," she looked up toward the ceiling, "If'fen you can hear me, you better step in, or they ain't gonna be no happy ending, no sir!"

* * *

As the buggy pulled up before the big hall at the fort, the girls in back giggled with excitement. "Oh, look at all the buggies and horses. Half the county must be here tonight!"

"Whoa, horse." Brad reined in and stepped down, handing the reins to a young soldier. It was a warm night, and lights and music streamed from the big hall.

Lillian glanced at him. He looked handsome tonight, and he'd been so polite, and the way he had looked at her back in the hallway had made her pulse pound. He smiled at her and started to get out of the buggy, but just then, Lieutenant Fortenbury came out of the darkness and bowed low. "Allow me, Miss Lillian. My goodness, but aren't you pretty tonight?" He helped her down as Brad sat there scowling.

"I was going to help Miss Lily down," he yelled. But the officer had offered Lillian his arm, and they were walking toward the hall.

She looked back over her shoulder. The gambler scowled blackly and then turned to help the girls from the buggy.

"My," Lillian said to the lieutenant, "I thought you were afraid of that gambler."

"Who, me?" He smiled almost arrogantly. "Of course not. Besides, I knew he wouldn't create a scene with ladies present—at least *one* lady."

"Oh." Of course, Lillian thought, Brad was gallant that way. Her thoughts went again to the way he had looked at her as she came down the stairs.

"And so what do you think?"

"About what?" Lillian paused and looked at him blankly. She realized she hadn't been listening, she'd been thinking about the gambler.

"About the concert at the train station?" The lieutenant asked. "Didn't you think the way I played the tuba was outstanding?"

"Outstanding," Lillian echoed, although frankly, she couldn't remember the music.

Buford beamed at her as he escorted her into the hall. "You look beautiful tonight. I'm so pleased to be your partner. You probably shouldn't have let that scoundrel drive you over."

"Since you didn't have a buggy," Lillian said, "I didn't have much choice—"

"But he's such a low-class rascal," Buford said as he took her over to the table where the buffet had been spread. "You can't turn a sow's ear into a silk purse, now, can you?"

"Of course not." But somehow, the Lieutenant's snootiness annoyed her. Brad came into the hall just then, Pansy on one arm, Fern on the other. Rosita and Flo brought up the rear, carrying Delilah's cakes. Brad frowned at Lillian and her escort, and turned his attention to his ladies.

Lillian nodded toward her girls. "They look nice, don't they?"

"Miss Lillian, if I may be so bold, everyone will be scandalized that you brought them here."

"Then let them be," she snapped, a little annoyed with the officer. "They may not have the pedigree that you and I possess, but they deserve a chance." *What was it Brad had said about walking a mile in a person's boots before judging them?*

She and Buford filled their plates in the buffet line. About that time, the major gestured for them to join his table. Around it sat the major, his wife, and the three congressmen. The men scrambled to their feet.

"Oh, do sit down, gentlemen," Lillian hastened to say.

Major Bottoms smiled. "Miss Primm and Lieutenant Fortenbury, may I present our distinguished guests from back east? This is Congressman Whittle, Congressman Nosely, and Congressman Tuggle."

"Delighted," Lillian nodded, although she sighed, thinking it would be a very dull evening.

All three grinned at her. "Wow," said one, "if we'd known how lovely the ladies were in this town, we would have come before."

"Oh, but it's a dangerous place," the major warned. "Why, people who come here have to run through a maze of wild Indians and bandits."

Lillian saw him punch his wife's arm and Edith said, "oh, goodness yes, gentlemen. The ladies just worry all the time about being carried off by ruffians or savages."

"Really? It looks like a very peaceful town," the tall, thin one said.

The lieutenant leaned closer. "Looks are deceiving, gentlemen. Why, Fort Floppett is a fortress of civilization in the midst of bloodthirsty savages and bandits. East Texas is a dangerous place to live. Only the army prevents bloodshed."

Lillian decided she wasn't about to get involved in this deliberate fiction. She turned her head slightly. Brad was sitting at a table with the four girls. They were laughing and seemed to be having a wonderful time. Of course the scoundrel could be pretty charming, she admitted to herself.

The short congressman, Whittle, said, "Bloodshed, really? Fort Floppett looks like a sleepy, safe place. So far, we haven't seen anything that looks—"

"Don't be fooled," the major warned. "Every few weeks, we fight Injuns off as they try to burn and ravage our town. When it's not them, it's bandits. Why, we might even get attacked while you're here."

The three congressmen looked nervous. "Good thing we're leaving on tomorrow night's train."

"Don't worry," the lieutenant said, "I will personally protect you in case of attack."

Lillian brought her napkin to her mouth to hide her smile. Just how Buford would do that while carrying his big, shiny tuba, she wasn't sure.

Congressman Tuggle said, "I was expecting to see lawmen and Texas Rangers that we've heard so much about."

Major Bottoms said, "I've got a brother who's a lawman out in west Texas, Sam Bottoms. Maybe someday he'll come visit and you can meet him then. That is, if the fort hasn't been closed."

The young congressman coughed and didn't meet his gaze. "That's still up for discussion—the national budget, you know."

The tall congressman looked across the room. "Now there's a likely fellow and he's escorting four beauties all by himself."

Lillian turned her head. It was Brad and the girls. Buford opened his mouth as if to say something and Lillian glared at him and then said "Oh, would you like to meet the ladies, sir? I just happen to know them."

All three congressmen grinned.

"That little redhead," said the short one, "really takes my eye."

"I presume you are unmarried?" Lillian asked pointedly.

"As a matter of fact, I am. But of course, the right girl could change that and become Mrs. Albert Whittle."

Lillian looked at him. He was balding, but no doubt he was from a fine family, and rich. "After supper I'll introduce you," she said.

The band begin to assemble on the bandstand. Lillian said "Lieutenant, aren't you playing tonight?"

He shook his head. "For dancing, there's no need for a tuba."

She fervently wished there were. At Brad's table, they looked as if they were having fun.

The music began and couples started toward the dance floor. Brad took Flo and led her out on the floor.

The others at her table were talking among themselves except for young Fortenbury. "Look at that gambler, bold as brass," he muttered. "Acting like he's respectable when we all know what he is."

"Let's introduce the congressman to Pansy, shall we?" She stood up and all the men jumped to their feet. "I think you should meet my friend," she said to the short congressman.

He nodded. "I'd be delighted."

Poor Buford could do nothing but trail in her wake as she took the congressman's arm and led him over to where Pansy sat at a table watching the dancers. "Miss Pansy Jones, may I present Congressman Whittle?"

"Charmed, I'm sure." He bowed to Pansy. "Would you care to dance, Miss Pansy?"

Lillian held her breath, hoping the girl remembered what she'd been taught. She did.

Pansy fluttered both her fan and her eyelashes. "Why, sir, I'd be pleased."

The congressman took her arm, grinning like a possum eating grapes, and led her out onto the floor. He was clearly smitten with the redhead and maybe he'd never need to know her past. Lillian watched with satisfaction, although Buford frowned. "Well, he's certainly buying a pig in a poke."

"Oh, Buford, don't be such a snob."

"How can you say that, Miss Lillian? You know

breeding counts. She's probably Irish, just like that low-class gambler."

Wasn't this her own thinking? Then why was she so annoyed with Buford?

"Would you care to dance?" he asked, and she nodded. He whirled her out on the floor, but he didn't dance very well. Maybe it was because of the high heels on his boots. He didn't even dance as well as she did, and Lillian was not a good dancer—but then, she'd had little social life. She frowned, looking over Buford's head. That Texas rascal danced smoothly as he whirled the strawberry blonde, Flo, past her. A tall handsome cowboy was now at the table asking Fern to dance. Good, her plans were working.

The music ended and the couples applauded. The night was warm, and someone had opened all the French doors leading out onto the back veranda. "My, it is warm, isn't it?" she said, watching Brad lead Flo back to his table.

"Would you like a cup of punch?" Buford asked.

"That would be nice." She nodded.

Buford left and she stood there alone, waiting.

Abruptly the music started and Brad crossed the floor in long strides. "I believe this is my dance, Miss Lily."

"But I'm waiting for Lieutenant Fortenbury."

"No, you're not, you're dancing with me." And he whirled her out on the floor, holding her tightly even as she protested.

Chapter Nine

The gambler was holding her much too tightly. "Really," she said, quite annoyed, "my escort went to get me a cup of punch."

"I know," he grinned down at her, "I watched him leave, then I pounced on you."

She had to look up at him and that made her feel small and vulnerable. "Then that was incredibly rude."

He grinned and pulled her even closer. "Did you expect any better from me?"

She stifled a rude reply. *I will not lower myself to this rascal's level.* He smiled down at her and she took a breath of his shaving lotion and noted how square his chin was. His big hand enveloped hers and his strong arms held her even tighter as she struggled to put a little distance between them. "What will Lieutenant Fortenbury think?"

"What do I care?" He whirled her about the floor smoothly. "Even if he takes offense, what can he do about it?"

She glanced over to one side where the young officer stood with two cups of punch, looking helpless and pathetic. Of course if someone had snatched

Brad O'Neal's partner, he'd confront the man and take her back. She looked at the wilting Buford and sighed. He wouldn't confront anyone. Of course, that only showed how civilized he was.

Everyone seemed to be watching them, looking toward Buford and smiling. She threw the officer a silent plea with her eyes. The lieutenant put the two cups of punch on a table, squared his thin shoulders, and marched across the floor, tapping Brad on the arm.

"I—I'm cutting in." His voiced almost squeaked.

Brad glanced down at him. "No, you're not. The lady is dancing with me." Then he whirled her away, leaving the shorter man looking helpless.

"That was rude." Lillian said.

"He could challenge me to a fight out back, but I don't think he wants to dance with you that badly. I do." He shrugged those big wide shoulders and his body was so warm against hers, she suddenly imagined they were both naked.

What on earth was she thinking? "Fighting solves nothing."

"A man who wants a woman will fight for her." His fingers seemed to tighten on her waist.

"Buford is a civilized gentleman," she defended him.

"Uh-huh. So let him stand on the sidelines with his cups of punch."

The Town Beautification Committee seemed to be mesmerized on the sidelines, and most of the ladies looked envious as the couple danced past them.

"Why are you doing this?" Lillian demanded. "Do you take me for a fool?" He couldn't possibly be attracted to a plain thing like her.

He gave her a hard look. "Anyone who would take you for a fool, Miss Lily, is underestimatin' you. You're clever and smart and stubborn, just like me."

"I am nothing like you, you scoundrel."

"Scoundrel?" He grinned down at her. "I am that."

They were near the open French doors and abruptly, he whirled her out onto the veranda. The moon was full, and the June breeze pleasantly cool although the night was warm. A soft whisper of roses wafted by. This man was all male. He was a threat to any woman because there was something so magnetic about him, something primal. He stopped now, still holding her.

"Take me back inside, this instant."

"Are you sure you want to do that?" He smiled and his hand enveloping hers felt strong and masculine. *Did she? Was she out of her mind?* He held her so tightly, she suspected he could feel her nipples pressing into the fine fabric of his coat. "Certainly. Everyone inside will be gossiping and Lieutenant Fortenbury—"

"Will do what? You think Junior will come out here and challenge me?"

Of course he wouldn't. No man in his right mind would challenge Brad O'Neal. He was looking down at her in a way that made her so nervous, her hands began to sweat. Why had she never noticed how full and sensual his lips were? "Please," she whispered and then wasn't sure what she was pleading for.

In that instant, he let go of her and bowed low. "I'm a fool for a lady's pleas. Allow me to escort you back inside, Miss Lily."

He hadn't kissed her. She didn't know whether to be relieved or upset. After all, she'd never been kissed, so maybe she wouldn't like it at all. As she took his arm, she imagined him bending her back, claiming her mouth as his own, kissing her deeply, thoroughly while his tongue played along her lips, begging them to open while his big hand reached to caress the front of her low-cut dress and then slip inside.

"Why, Miss Lily, you're tremblin'." He sounded genuinely concerned as he led her through the French doors.

"I—I—it was cold out there." She felt like an idiot.

"Of course. It's always freezin' in June." He smiled ever so slightly.

Was he mocking her? It seemed to her that everyone was watching them and she did see several ladies lean over and whisper to other women. The Town Beautification Committee almost seemed to be jumping up and down and grinning like a pack of idiots, but she couldn't imagine why. "Now see what you've done, you've ruined my reputation."

He led her across the floor. "It takes a little more than two minutes on the veranda to ruin a lady's reputation. You are so innocent, Miss Lily."

She felt humiliated. No man had ever desired her, so of course her reputation was as intact as her virginity.

Brad led her back to her table and bowed again. "Thank you so much, Miss Primm, it was my pleasure." He nodded to the major's wife. "You're looking lovely tonight, Mrs. Bottoms."

The older woman giggled like a schoolgirl as Brad turned and strode away. "Oh, Lillian, we all saw you go outside with him. Half the women in here would give anything to have that handsome rascal ask them to dance."

Lillian looked around. Sure enough, most of the women in the crowded hall were looking at Brad and sighing like hungry hounds after one bone.

Lieutenant Fortenbury hurried to the table. "Are you all right, Miss Lillian?"

"Of course. Why wouldn't I be?" She was annoyed with the timid young man.

"He's such a masher," Buford said. "Good thing I'm a gentleman who can hold my temper or I might have wiped up the floor with him. Of course I daren't create a ruckus at the major's party."

Brad would mangle him. Lillian managed not to smile. "How thoughtful of you, Buford."

He asked her to dance again and she nodded, watching miserably as Brad danced with one lady and then another. If she hadn't protested so much, what would have happened out there on the veranda? The rascal was virile, masculine, and dangerous, which made him twice as appealing. She noted he danced with many ladies, but he didn't dance anyone else out the French doors. When they passed him on the dance floor, he winked boldly at her.

"The nerve of him. Did you see that," she seethed.

"Very ill-mannered," Buford said. "Why, even if he could qualify as a member of the S.O.B.S.— which of course the rascal can't—we'd toss him out."

"I'm sure that would worry a man like Brad O'Neal tremendously," she said sarcastically.

"Now, my dear, what would you like me to do, fight him like some rough, low-class Texan?"

A man will fight for the woman he wants.

"No, of course not, Buford. He'd wipe up the floor with you anyway." she murmured.

"What?"

"Nothing. Let's talk about something else. No need to let that Irish scoundrel ruin our evening."

"All right, let's." Buford began talking about his

family, his future in Washington, D.C. when he got transferred, his tuba, his background.

Lillian stifled a yawn. Buford was incredibly boring—he only wanted to talk about himself. She glanced toward Brad's table. He must have said something witty because the girls were laughing and leaning closer to him, and women at other tables kept looking his way. She reminded herself what a wonderful pedigree Lieutenant Fortenbury had, and his high social background. That was important . . . wasn't it?

Finally the dance ended as the little band played "Goodnight, Ladies." The four girls from the Lily stood gossiping and laughing as Brad paused and turned, heading toward Lillian's table.

As Brad was approaching Buford said, "I can borrow the major's buggy, and I'd like to see you home, Miss Lillian—"

"Nope," Brad appeared at the table, grinning. "I'll see her home."

"Now isn't that up to Miss Primm?"

They glared at each other, then both looked at her. She was speechless, never having had men practically dueling over her before. If there was a fight, the Irish brawler would turn the young officer inside out, and she knew it. "Uh, Buford, I think I'll ride home with Mr. O'Neal. I wouldn't want to put you to any trouble."

Buford said, "It wouldn't be any trouble—"

"You heard the lady, sport," Brad said and took her elbow, steering her toward the door.

"You are being incredibly rude," she snapped.

"And you are bein' incredibly stupid," Brad drawled. "He's after your share of the Lily."

They were outside now, walking through the darkness toward their buggy.

"As are you," she shot back.

"Of course," he grinned down at her. "But at least I'm honest about it and would pay you for it."

They were standing next to the buggy, and the girls were not there yet. "Are you saying no man would ever find me desirable enough to want me for myself?"

He still held onto her arm and now he pulled her to him. "I didn't say that, Lily."

They were standing so close, she could feel his warm breath on her cheek and smell his aftershave. She stood there, looking up at that full sensual mouth while her heart began to hammer. *He's going to kiss me,* she thought. And she found herself holding her breath and starting up on her tiptoes to meet him half way. The moment was charged with electricity as they stared into each other's eyes.

At that instant, she heard the laughter and chatter of the girls as they approached the buggy. She pulled away from the gambler, breathing hard. He looked slightly puzzled.

"Oh Miss Lillian, guess what?" Fern laughed, "My cowboy wants to marry me."

"Congratulations," Brad said and turned to assist the beauty up into the buggy.

Lillian took a deep breath. "It is not good form to congratulate the lady; you congratulate the man and offer best wishes to the bride."

Brad scowled at her. "You certainly know how to take the joy out of everything, don't you?"

Pansy said, "That congressman, Mr. Whittle, wants me to leave town with him tomorrow night."

Brad laughed. "Good for you, Pansy, just don't give away the milk until he buys the cow." He lifted her up into the buggy.

Lillian said, "Could you be any more crude?"

He laughed. "Of course I could be, but I won't, in

deference to the ladies." He lifted the others up into the buggy. Then he turned back to her. "Ready?"

Ready for what? The way he was looking at her made her take a deep breath.

"Here we go." He put his big hands on her small waist and lifted her. It felt like his fingers were burning through her dress. He sat her on the seat and went around, then got up into the buggy. It seemed to her that he was sitting much too close to her. She felt perspiration break out on her skin. Of course that was just because the June weather was so warm.

Buford stood forlornly on the edge of the grass, staring up at them. "Good night, Miss Primm."

"Good night, Lieutenant." She favored him with a smile and a polite wave as the horse broke into a brisk trot.

Brad snorted.

She was annoyed now with Brad O'Neal. He had ruined her evening with Buford and made her feel emotions that she had never felt before. Lillian was not used to dealing with emotions. Listening to the heart rather than the brain was frowned on by her cold, distant mother.

When they reached the house and he helped them all down, she almost ran up the steps and inside. She didn't want to be left alone with him. She wasn't sure if she was afraid of him or herself. She hurried up the stairs and into her room, locked the door, and leaned against it, breathing hard.

She heard the girls passing her room, laughing and talking about their evening. After a few minutes, the house grew quiet and then she heard his heavier step on the stairs. Lillian tensed and leaned against the bedpost. No doubt he was going to go to one of the girls' rooms and any of them would let him in. In her mind, she saw him kissing a younger, prettier girl, kissing her slowly and languidly while she gasped and whimpered with urgency. Then he would remove her dress and—

"Lily?" He whispered against the door.

She started. She hadn't expected this. There was only a slab of wood between them, that and the lock.

"Lily?" he whispered again.

"What—what do you want?"

"Do you have to ask?"

She held her breath, her mind awash with mixed emotions. She knew very well what that big male animal wanted. She remembered the way he had held her out on the veranda, the heat and the strength of the man. Then again at the buggy, when she was certain he was going to kiss her and she had not known what she was going to do if he did.

"Lily?"

She did not answer. She had never even been kissed, and now this man was offering, no, maybe demanding something more. Her hand trembled in mid-air, trying to decide what to do. All she had to do was unlock that door and let him in to begin the most exciting adventure of a lifetime.

Lillian, you're a fool to think he might care for you, she scolded herself. You know he's trying to seduce you out of your share of the Lily and nothing else. Tomorrow, he'd probably laugh about it with the other men.

As she hesitated, the decision was made for her. She heard him walk away from the door and she sighed, both with relief and regret. He would take his passion to one or more of the younger, prettier girls down the hall, and no doubt they wouldn't be clumsy and amateurish like she would—they would know how to please a man.

Instead, the footsteps seemed to move down the stairs. *What?* She unlocked the door, went out into the hall and looked down. She saw him go down the stairs and around the main hall toward his room. She stood there blinking. He had gone to his room . . . alone. For a split second, she almost ran down the stairs and into his room. She wanted to call out, *teach me, oh, teach me.*

Was she losing her mind? She was no strumpet to throw away her virginity on that Texan. Quickly she returned to her own room, locked the door, and leaned against it, breathing hard. In her mind, she saw the two of them naked on her bed, in a violent thrashing of passion, all covered with perspiration—his hot mouth on her bare skin.

The image and her own reaction to it horrified Lillian. She undressed, put on a modest nightgown, and got into bed. She pulled the covers up to her nose even though it was a warm night. *Naked and thrashing about, indeed.*

Brad wasn't quite sure why he had gone to Lily's door, it had been something about holding her in his arms out on the veranda. She was so fragile and innocent, yet as spirited and stubborn as himself. She had seemed almost beautiful to him tonight. *Beautiful?* He just needed a woman, that was all. While she would not answer, he had a feeling she was just on the other side of that door, listening.

Hell, he wasn't a man to beg—he'd never had to beg a woman for her favors. He was annoyed at the refusal. He turned and looked down the dim hall, thought about returning upstairs. Any of the girls would welcome him into their beds, no doubt. They were all younger than Lily and much prettier, but tonight, he wanted something else—something challenging and unobtainable. As far back as he could remember, he didn't think he'd ever had a virgin. Of course that Yankee old maid would probably talk through the whole thing and correct his grammar. So why would any sane man desire her?

Was she really smitten with that pip-squeak, Lieutenant Fortenbury? He almost growled at the thought of that Nancy-boy in bed with her. Buford Fortenbury couldn't satisfy a woman like that. Once a man ignited the passion flowing deep in her green eyes, he would have a wildcat on his hands. Or maybe not.

Of course Miss Primm was so innocent, she needed protection against a villain like Buford. Hell, protecting the virtue of the Yankee old maid wasn't Brad's problem. What was his problem was that the rotten pip-squeak might end up with her half of the Texas Lily. Brad shuddered at the thought.

He undressed slowly, annoyed with Lily and himself that he had made a fool of himself just now, begging at her door like a hungry dog sitting up for a bone. He wouldn't be that stupid and weak again. He went to bed and lay there sleepless, something he never did. He wished now he had kissed her when the urge had been so strong in him. She might have slapped his face, making him feel like a fool. No woman had ever refused his kisses, but who knew what the prim old maid was liable to do? Surely what made her so suddenly interesting was the challenge of the unattainable.

He'd better forget about all that and concentrate on tomorrow night. There was a lot riding on the fake Indian attack. If Congress closed Fort Floppett, the Texas Lily would go belly up and the whole town would be ruined financially.

After a sleepless night, Brad rose on Sunday morning and began to cook flapjacks and ham.

The girls wandered down the stairs in their house-coats, yawning and chattering.

Of course Lily came down dressed in a modest dark dress, her hair once again in a tight bun.

"Good morning, ladies," he said in a tone heartier than he felt. "Remember this is going to be a challengin' day for all of us. If you get a chance to talk to any of the congressmen, tell them how terrified you are of Indian and bandit attacks."

The girls all giggled but Lily made a face and poured herself a cup of coffee. "I am opposed to lying. Besides something is bound to go wrong."

"Be positive," Brad growled and handed a plate of hotcakes to Delilah.

"Humph!" Lillian snapped as she accepted the plate from the maid, smothered it with butter and sorghum syrup and reached for the big thick slices of ham. She had never eaten so well as she had here in Texas, where everyone ate like hogs at a trough.

"Lily," he said as if speaking to a child, "we must save this town and I don't have any better ideas. Do you?"

"We might petition Congress—"

"Yep, and how far would that get us?" Brad grumbled as he served up more hotcakes. "I know this is a big gamble, but we must save the fort."

Brad watched Lily. He was sober this morning and she still looked good to him, even if she was back in her old uniform of modest dress and severe hair. Maybe he wasn't sober after all.

Delilah poured more coffee. "Mr. Brad, you do your best tonight. Is you in any danger?"

Brad shook his head. "No, the cowboys and the soldiers will make a lot of noise with their guns, but they'll all be shooting over everyone's heads. However, it'll look real to the congressmen. They'll be so scared, they may wet their pants."

"Ahem." Lily scowled at him.

He bowed. "Oh, excuse me. I forgot there was a lady present."

Pansy made a face. "And what are we? Chopped liver?"

He found himself staring at Lily. She was blushing. There was no doubt this was a real lady, much too high-class for an Texas saloon brawler like himself. "Girls, I meant no offense. Now let's get through here. Delilah, you cook your best dinner for the congressmen, and girls, you keep them amused all afternoon while the boys and I work on the stage coach and costumes."

Lillian's face flamed. "Not in this house."

"Oh hell," Brad muttered, "then girls, take them out for buggy rides or over to the livery stable; there's a barn full of hay there."

"I object," Lily said and slammed her coffee cup down.

Brad paused with his ladle in midair. "Miss Lily, I'm not askin' you to personally amuse the congressmen, and I'm not tellin' the girls what to do. I'm only sayin' keep them busy 'til train time if you have to play cards with them."

The girls all giggled.

Lillian sighed audibly. "Mr. O'Neal, you have no conscience, you are an unmitigated scoundrel."

"Thank you." He smiled and nodded.

"It's not a compliment." She almost screamed at him.

He winked at her. "I'm just a stupid Texan, how would I know?"

"Ladies," she said, "take the congressmen driving or maybe play a game of croquet with them."

"We don't know how," Pansy said.

"Well, let the gentlemen teach you," Lillian said. "And if all else fails, you can defend your virtue with your mallets."

Brad snorted. "That's sort of lockin' the barn when the horse was stole long ago."

"Mr. O'Neal," Lillian seethed, "could you be any more crude?"

He grinned at her and flipped a flapjack. "I don't know, want me to try?"

"No." She poured herself another cup of coffee and retreated to her room. Why had this ruffian seemed so appealing last night? She must have been moonstruck.

Lieutenant Fortenbury cleaned his rifle and looked up at the sun. It was mid-afternoon and he knew the congressmen were over at the Texas Lily having dinner. He scowled, thinking about last night. That damned gambler had seemed randier than that billy goat, angling to charm Miss Lillian. Of course, he was after her share of the Lily, but Buford intended to have that, and after tonight, there would be only one owner anyway.

He smiled to himself and his own cleverness. The fake attack was supposed to take place at dusk as the congressmen got on the train. There would be lots of shooting, shouting, and confusion. He examined his rifle critically. Buford was not a good shot, but since he didn't intend to end up in Arizona, his life hardly depended on his shooting.

What he'd like to do was own a fine saloon and bawdy house like the Texas Lily. Then, in two years when his enlistment was up, he'd live an easy life with all the liquor he could drink, plenty of income, sleeping with all the girls upstairs. After that, he might sell the bordello at a profit and head home.

Maybe his father would forgive him and think twice about disinheriting his youngest son for getting that society girl in the family way and deserting her.

It would be horrible to go through life poor, and that certainly was not in Buford's plans. He frowned. To end up with the Lily, he had to get rid of Brad O'Neal so Miss Primm could inherit the gambler's half, then Buford would charm her into marrying him. That might not be so easy—he'd seen sparks fly between those two at the dance last night.

Buford checked his rifle again. The troops had been given orders to make a lot of noise with their weapons tonight but shoot over the fake Indians' heads. Now, if Brad O'Neal accidently got shot and killed in tonight's adventure, no one would know who did it. Buford grinned. He might not be a great shot, but he could shoot well enough at close range to kill that damned Texan.

Chapter Ten

It was late Sunday afternoon. After dinner, Lillian had insisted that her girls not leave unescorted with the congressmen, so now they were out on the lawn playing croquet. They didn't look too happy about it, especially after the fat one from Maine leaned over to eye the ball and Herman couldn't resist that wide target.

Lillian looked out the window and saw what was about to happen. "Look out!" she screamed. But Herman made a mighty thud as he caught the congressman squarely in his . . . striped pants, leaving him sprawled on the grass with Herman standing over him, bleating and shaking his curled horns. "Oh dear."

This wouldn't help the congressmen's dispositions at all, but then Brad invited them up to sit in rockers on the porch and served them mint juleps. They had to put a feather pillow under the man from Maine.

"Ah, this is the life," breathed the short one, finishing his drink. "Must be the most peaceful place in the world."

"Yes," said Tuggle, "no need of a fort here anymore."

Brad frowned and watched Herman contentedly munching on the orange day-lilies out front. "This area can fool you, gentlemen. Why, you just never know when we'll have another Indian attack and put voters at risk of their lives. Here, let me get you each another drink."

If they were well oiled when they headed toward the train station, it might be more difficult for the men to know whether it was a fake attack or not. He hopped up and got them each a big tumbler of that tasty Southern drink.

Lillian frowned at him as he came in and went behind the bar. "You'll have them so drunk, we'll have to pour them on the train."

He grinned at her. "Lily, that's not a bad thing— good memories of the wonderful town of Fort Floppett."

She frowned. "This whole thing is liable to backfire on you."

"Aw, you're as nervous as a church deacon with his hand in the collection basket. It'll work—everyone knows what they're supposed to do. If Pansy's all packed, have José bring the buggy around."

He returned to the front porch where the four men drank and watched the sun moving lower on the horizon. The randy old goat glared banefully from the front lawn, seemed to decide the tempting targets were all out of his reach and returned to chomping on flowers around the big bird bath. In the distance, the bugler at the fort announced the folding of the colors as the flag came down for the night. The Texans still didn't like the Yankee flag flying over Texas ground, but they did like the green of Yankee money.

"Well, gentlemen," Brad stood up, "it's been a

good weekend, but I think your train will be arrivin' soon. And here comes José with the buggy."

"Is my lady ready?" asked Congressman Whittle.

Pansy came out the door carrying her valise. "Here I am, Albert, honey."

"Let me bring along a pitcher for the road," Brad said and yelled inside the house, "Lily, would you bring out some more juleps? And if you're going with us, we're ready to leave."

In a moment, Lily appeared with a pitcher of mint juleps. She looked none too happy about it. "It was an honor to host you gentlemen," she said with a smile. "I do hope you'll come again sometime and bring your friends."

Brad looked daggers at her. What the town didn't need was any more nosy congressmen from back east snooping around.

"We'd love to," said the one from Maine. He seemed to be having a difficult time focusing his eyes as Brad helped him to the buggy. "Next time, maybe the town will have a hotel for us to stay in."

"Maybe so," Lillian took the second one's arm and led him toward the buggy.

Pansy trailed along with the third congressman, and he beamed at her like he'd just won the prize at the state fair.

In the distance, the train whistled again as it crossed the prairie toward the station.

Brad said, "Well, gentlemen, it's been a pleasure. José here will drive you. I've got important things to do."

Lily frowned and let the Mexican boy help her up into the open barouche. It was almost dark as they drove toward town. Over on the station platform, the cavalry band had struck up a tune, "Dixie," not seeming to remember their visitors were all Yankees. Of course, Lillian thought with a sigh, their repertoire was pretty limited. Most of the town was gathering to see their important visitors off.

Lillian frowned. It was dusk now as she stood on the crowded railway platform, watching. The major had turned leadership of his band over to a pompous captain, but no one seemed to notice because the band didn't play any worse now than they ever did. This time it was an off-key version of "The Yellow Rose of Texas," sans the tuba player and many of the others who would be part of the fake attack.

The congressman from Maine said, "Oh, before I leave, I think I need to send a telegram."

Uh oh, thought Lillian, now there would be a problem. She knew Caddo was the only one who could send a telegram, and no doubt he was already gone, getting dressed for his part in the attack.

The major's wife said, "Oh, but you might miss your train. Can you send it from the next station?"

The congressman thought about it a moment while Lillian held her breath, then nodded that he thought he'd better do that. José began loading their luggage on the train.

Where were the men? Lillian thought. *What had happened to the fake Indian attack?*

"Such a nice, peaceful town," said Congressman Tuggle. "There doesn't seem to be any need for a fort here."

She was going to have to get involved, even though this whole thing went against her principles. "Oh," Lillian said stepping forward, "you just never know when there'll be another blood-thirsty attack or maybe some bandits trying to rob the bank."

The man from Ohio looked out at a brown

hound-dog sleeping in the road near the station. "Looks peaceful enough to me."

The train blew its whistle, warning that it was almost ready to leave. Mrs. Bottoms looked frantically at Lillian, but Lillian shook her head. She had no idea what had gone wrong either. Then, in the distance, gunfire erupted.

"What was that?" One of the congressman asked.

The whole crowd seemed to draw a deep breath of relief.

"I think," said one old codger, "we may be in for another Indian attack."

Pansy played her part well. She threw her arms around Albert Whittle's neck and began to scream, "Protect me! I don't want to die!"

Sweat broke out on the man's face. He looked like he might run, but of course Pansy was hanging onto him. "Good Lord, how dare they attack a U.S. congressman?"

The band stopped playing and the major's wife shrieked, "Oh, but Congress has been cutting our budget, we may not have enough bullets to protect anyone!"

The women all began to scream. "We'll be ravished and carried off!"

In your dreams, Lillian thought cynically. Most of the local women were hefty as Hereford heifers.

The band looked about uncertainly. The captain snapped to attention. "We'll do what we can to protect you, ladies, if they kill us down to the last man!"

The shooting and shouting grew closer. The crowd milled and screamed. She hadn't seen such a good job of acting since back in Boston, where she'd seen a melodrama about a dastardly villain tying the heroine to the railroad tracks.

Congressman Whittle pulled out a derringer and put his arm around Pansy. "I'll protect you, honey."

Oh my goodness, someone was liable to get hurt, Lillian thought, and she rushed forward, grabbing the man's shaking arm. "Protect me, too!" she screamed, and managing to knock the gun from his hand.

Down the street in the darkness came the stage-coach with Brad as the driver and Pug riding shot-gun. Dimples Darlington, dressed in his wife's old pink flowered dress and bonnet, hung out the window of the stage, screaming for help in a high falsetto. Caddo and some of his friends, half naked and in bright war paint, chased after the stage, shooting and whooping. Behind them came Major Bottoms and his cavalry, accompanied by some of the cowboys from the local ranches, all shooting and yelling.

It wasn't a bad presentation, Lillian thought with grudging admiration. She even saw Buford riding with the cavalry, gun blazing and shouting with the rest of them. He wasn't a very good rider, she thought, but he was doing his best.

"Oh my God," said the congressman from Ohio, "they're coming straight for us!"

"The cavalry will try to keep them from reaching you and taking your scalp!" Mrs. Bottoms screamed. "Maybe you'd better get on that train and get out of here!"

"Good idea!" said the tallest of the three, "Engineer, get this train moving!"

From his seat high on the stagecoach, Brad cracked his whip and drove his galloping stage. It was turning dark rapidly, but he could see the crowd on the station platform. The congressmen, even at this distance, looked terrified.

He glanced sideways at Caddo and his cousins,

riding next to the galloping stage. "Give us another warcry, old buddy!"

"Now what the hell do I know about war cries?" the plump Indian complained, but he tried to oblige.

Brad glanced behind him and to each side. The cavalry, even young Fortenbury, was doing an excellent job of hot pursuit, shouting and shooting. He looked forward and saw the congressmen rushing to get on the train. He pulled his plunging stage horses up near the platform in a cloud of dust and he and Pug jumped down, shooting at the circling Indians.

Dimples jumped from the coach, lifted his skirts and ran up on the platform, screaming in a falsetto, "Help! Save me! Some brave man, please save me!" Dimples ran up to the congressman from Maine. "Oh, kind sir, the fort is doomed! They just don't have enough bullets."

The congressman slipped his arm familiarly around Dimples' shoulders. "My dear, I'll save you."

Lillian saw him pinch Dimples on his generous rear and at that moment, Dimples hit the man with his pocket book, almost knocking him off the station platform. "Masher! I'm not that kind of girl!"

Everyone was scattering in the noise and confusion while the fake savages circled the platform in the darkness and the cavalry and the cowboys shot at them. The congressmen and Pansy scurried aboard the train and now they hung their heads out the windows watching with horrified fascination as the Indians began to retreat, still firing. A soldier fell from his saddle with a groan.

"I think we're doomed," Brad yelled, kneeling on the platform and firing away. "For Floppett doesn't have enough men and munitions, but we'll protect the train with our lives!"

"Oh my God," shouted the fat congressman, they're killing people!"

Now as Lillian watched, Brad threw up his hands, grabbed his chest, yelped, and fell on his face. He was a pretty good actor, she thought.

The major jumped up on the platform, still shooting at the fake warriors who by now, were retreating. The engine was pulling out, smoke billowing. The major yelled after the trio, "We've got to keep this fort open or the savages will massacre all the citizens!"

"You'll get the money!" the one from Ohio yelled, "we'll see you get an even bigger budget."

The crowd cheered and the Indians began to retreat. The train huffed and puffed, pulling away from the station. Pansy stuck her head out and waved a handkerchief at Lillian and she nodded and waved back. The train picked up speed as it pulled out of town.

The major wiped his sweating face and grinned at everyone. "Damned good job, folks, if I do say so myself."

The crowd cheered but a cowboy reined in and complained, "those damned soldiers let their bullets get a mite close. That happens again, we'll have to wipe up the street with 'em."

"Didn't either," said Lieutenant Fortenbury as he reined in and dismounted. "We were all shooting above everyone's heads just like we were told."

Brad still lay sprawled on his face on the platform. Lillian walked over and looked down at the motionless man. "You can get up now. The congressmen are gone."

He did not move. She was annoyed and nudged him with her foot. "I said you can quit acting now, they're gone."

He still did not move.

The whole crowd gradually grew quiet.

"Brad? Stop this, it isn't funny."

No answer. Dimples, in his pink flowered dress, ran over and tried to lift him. Then he turned an ashen face framed by his big pink sunbonnet toward Lillian. "Oh my God, he's been shot!"

Women screamed and men crowded closer as the major pushed his way through the crowd. "Somebody get Doc, quick!"

Lillian took a deep breath. Brad O'Neal had been killed in this fake fight, just as she had warned that something might go wrong. She ran over and stood looking down at him even as Sadie pushed her way through the crowd and knelt, cradling his dark head in her lap. Sadie began to sob and stroke his face. "Oh, Brad honey, speak to me."

Lillian shook so badly, she could hardly speak, but she managed to get control of herself. *Hysterics won't do any good.* She leaned over, picked up his hat, strode off the platform to fill the hat with water from the nearest horse trough. Then she returned and threw it on him. He came awake, his eyes blinking as he coughed and sputtered.

Doc pushed his way through the crowd and knelt by Brad's side. "Looks like a bullet in the foot."

"Is that all?" Lillian said with a sigh of relief.

Doc nodded his white head. "Yep, think he hit his head when he fell. We need to get him home."

"No, take him to my place," Sadie begged.

"No," Lillian stepped forward and knelt next to the gambler. His dark face was pale as a fish belly, but he managed a grin. "You rascal. You aren't dying, you got shot in the foot."

"Lord, did it ruin my new boots?"

Only a Texan would be more concerned with his new boots than his flesh. Lillian surveyed his bloody boot. He had small feet for such a big man. "Well, the right one now has a big hole in it."

"Oh, hell." He tried to sit up, but his face was pale as fresh milk.

Lillian shoved Sadie aside and cradled him in her arms. "He's my partner, let's take him home."

The major paced up and down the platform, cursing. "Don't know how this could happen, I told everyone to shoot high."

Lieutenant Fortenbury strode up on the platform, took off his hat and wiped his sweating face. "What a tragedy! Is he going to die?"

Brad's eyes flickered open. "Don't you wish!" he muttered.

"Hush!" Lillian commanded. "Now Buford, you and some of the men help him up into my buggy and Doc, you climb up on the seat beside me. I think I can drive this rig."

People clustered around. "What happened?"

"They say someone shot the gambler."

"Well, as much shooting as was going on, it's a wonder more weren't kilt."

Caddo frowned. He looked ridiculous in a breech cloth, Lillian thought. "Miss, soon as I get this paint off and get some pants on, I'll help you."

"Never mind," said Dewey Cheatum, "Boys, let's get him in the buggy, lay him flat in the back."

Everyone ran to help. Lillian had a smear of blood from him on her dress but she didn't have time to faint now. "I'll drive. Doc, you get up here with me and let's get him home."

Sadie stood nearby, pouting. "I'm sure he'd rather go with me."

Brad's dark eyes flickered open. "Ohh, Lily, I think I'm dyin'. Everything seems to be goin' dark."

"It *is* dark," she snapped, not wanting him to know

how concerned she was. She spread her shawl over him. "If you hadn't come up with this fool stunt—"

He groaned again and looked up at her. "Are you an angel? Have I died and gone to heaven?"

"That's the worst acting I ever saw," she complained as Doc climbed up in the wagon. "You've been seeing too many melodramas."

"Oh, Lily, Lily." He grabbed her hand and kissed it. "Did—did it work? Did we save the fort?"

"Did it work!" The major leaned over the side of the buggy. "My boy, it was brilliant. They're going to see we get even more money!"

"Good," Brad whispered and promptly fainted away.

Now Lillian was really worried. She leaned over him, touched his face gently.

Buford came to her side of the wagon. "Miss Lillian, is he dying?"

"I don't know." She shook her head. "He's lost a lot of blood even if he was shot in the foot."

"What a tragic accident." Buford said. "I didn't like the rounder, but I'm sorry it happened."

Sadie yelled, "don't let her take him away; no tellin' what she'll do. If he dies, she gets full ownership of the Texas Lily."

"How dare you?" Lily seethed and she almost came out of the wagon to slap the girl silly, then remembered she was a lady. Besides, it was important to get Brad home right now. José took over the driving. He snapped the reins and took off at a trot, some of the men following on horseback.

Brad lay with his head in Lillian's lap and she stroked his black hair. "It'll be all right," she said as the buggy moved up the road at a fast clip, "just as soon as we get you home."

The riders carried Brad into the Texas Lily and

laid him on his bed. Everyone gathered around to stare.

Doc said, "I can't work with a crowd in here."

Lillian turned and said in a tone that brooked no argument. "Everyone has to go. We'll let you know how he's doing. Someone get Delilah."

Doc turned up the lamp and examined his bloody foot. "I'm gonna have to cut that boot off."

"New boot," Brad groaned, "don't—"

"Oh shut up," Lillian snapped, "it's ruined anyway, has a hole in it and it's all bloody."

Delilah hurried into the room, mouth open. "Lord a mercy, what happened?"

Lillian ordered, "get some hot water and some clean rags, Delilah, the rascal's been shot."

"Everybody else get out of here," Doc roared.

The crowd seemed to leave reluctantly and Delilah ran to get hot water. Lillian leaned over the gambler. For once, he looked helpless, and it scared Lillian. She was used to him being in charge, a man who knew what he wanted and went after it.

Doc labored to cut the boot off Brad's foot. "Keep him occupied, young lady. I might have to probe for that bullet."

Brad's eyes flickered open, and he looked at Lillian. "Lily," he gasped, "you ain't gonna let me die, are you?"

"Aren't," she corrected without thinking.

Brad groaned again. "Even a dyin' man can't escape from the Yankee's naggin'."

"I am not nagging," Lily snapped.

"Both of you put a sock in it," Doc grumbled, ripping Brad's shirt open.

What a masculine chest with rippling, powerful muscles, Lillian thought as she hovered in the background. "May I do anything to help?"

"Yep," Doc nodded as he ripped Brad's pant leg.

"Get a sponge and some cool water, and keep sponging him off in case he gets feverish."

"She'll drown me if she gets a chance," Brad complained, "then she'd own all the Lily."

"The very idea!" Lillian fumed. "Besides I wouldn't do you in in front of all these witnesses."

Delilah came in just then with a pan of water and some clean rags. "Who shot Mr. Brad?"

Lillian took the things from her and shrugged. "Nobody knows. With all those men firing and half of them drunk, it could have been anyone. He had a snoot-full of mint juleps—he might even have shot himself."

"I heard that," Brad said.

"Oh, hush," Lillian returned.

Doc had cut the pant leg and was mopping away the blood. "Brad, I gotta probe for the bullet. You game?"

He nodded. "I was hurt worse than this in the War, Doc."

Doc's grizzled face looked strained in the lamp light. He turned to Lillian. "You women might want to step out. This may get gruesome."

"Hmmph!" Delilah snapped, "I done experienced more in slavery than this. Let me get him a slug of whiskey first."

Brad grinned as she left the room. "Now there is an angel of mercy."

Lillian took a deep breath. She could smell the coppery scent of the scarlet now staining the sheets. "I—I trained to be a nurse toward the end of the Rebellion, so I can help."

". . . War of Yankee Aggression," Brad corrected in a whisper.

Doc laughed without mirth. "He ain't so bad that he's forgotten he was one of Terry's Texas Rangers. Miss Primm, you sure you want to stay?"

She nodded and took Brad's hand. He clasped hers strongly and she looked at it, marveling what a big, strong hand it was.

Doc said, "what happened to Delilah with that whiskey?"

Lillian frowned. "He's already got a snoot ful."

The old man glared at her. "I meant for m

Delilah ran in with a full bottle and four glasses. he filled them all. "Miss Lillian, you might ought to drink this."

"I'll be all right." She leaned over and cradled Brad's head, held him so he could drink the water she held to his lips.

"Angel," he whispered, "red-haired angel."

"O'Neal, you're drunk."

He grinned up at her. "Don't leave, Lily."

"I won't."

Doc gulped his whiskey and then began to probe the wound. Brad's face turned paler still and he gritted his teeth. Lillian wavered, feeling faint, but she dipped a sponge in cool water and wiped his face. "Brad, it's almost over."

Doc said, "I got it," and she heard the metal bullet hit the pan.

Brad heaved a sigh of relief.

She'd never seen such bravery. "Maybe—maybe I could give him a little whiskey."

Sweat stood out on Brad's handsome face. "Thought you'd never ask," he whispered.

"I'll have another," Doc said, "and don't be stingy."

She poured Doc a tumbler full and put it on the bedside table. She poured another for Brad and held him up while he sipped it. His body was wet with sweat. Without thinking, she brushed his black hair from his forehead. He looked so pale and defenseless, like a little boy. Her heart went out to him as she lay him gently on his pillow. He closed his eyes.

Doc looked at her. "He'll sleep now. I think you'd better have some of that whiskey, Miss."

"No, I—yes, I think I will." She took a big gulp and felt it burn all the way down. "You're a good doctor. And as for Brad, that was the bravest thing I ever saw."

"You were pretty brave yourself, Miss Primm. Brad's had a tough life," Doc muttered as he began to gather his things and clean up. "Nobody ever did much for him. He sort of raised himself. Old man's a drunk and the mother died. Them O'Neal kids is scattered all over Texas."

"He's lost a lot of blood. Will he be all right?"

Doc looked up at her and smiled. "I think it will take more than a stray bullet to finish off this rascal. I'll bandage him up and get Delilah to change the sheets. You go out front and tell everyone he's okay."

She nodded and stumbled out of the room, sighing with relief. It was dark outside but there was a big crowd standing on the front lawn and the drive. The outside air felt cool against her skin and she gulped in deep breaths of it. "He—he's going to be all right, Doc says."

A cheer rose from the crowd, and some of the cowboys and soldiers began to sing: "For He's a Jolly Good Fellow." If nothing else, Brad O'Neal was a very popular man.

The major came up the steps to her. "I'll investigate what went wrong. I reckon some of the men was shooting wildly."

Young Lieutenant Fortenbury hurried to offer her his handkerchief. "Are you sure he'll make it, Miss Lillian? Sometime these cases get blood poisoning and die even if it's a small wound."

She nodded and wiped her face. "Doc thinks he'll make it—he's tough."

"Well, thank God for that." the lieutenant said, but he didn't sound relieved. "Even though he's a scoundrel, the whole town would be upset if he died. Miss Lillian, are you aware you have blood on you?"

She looked down at the smear on her dress. "I—I must have gotten it while I was holding him for Doc."

Lieutenant Fortenbury frowned. "Really, Miss Lillian, I would think dirty work like that should be left to the maid, Delilah."

"Oh hush, Buford," she muttered, "you're such a snob."

"What?"

"Uh, I'm tired and I think I'd better go see if Doc needs anything. Major, can you get the crowd to disperse?"

The cowboys and the soldiers were shoving each other and bickering about which side should take the blame for shooting the town's best-loved gambler. The problem between the two groups was that most of the soldiers were Yankees, and the cowboys were mostly Southerners, namely Texans.

She went back into the house and Doc was coming out of Brad's bedroom. "I'll be back tomorrow. See if you can get some food into him, maybe some broth."

She stopped by the kitchen and Delilah nodded. "Got some steak soup. I'll bring it in."

She tiptoed into Brad's room. His foot was bandaged and propped up on a pillow, but he looked pale as death. She looked down at him and his eyes flickered open.

He grinned. "Looks like you don't get sole ownership of the Texas Lily yet."

"How dare you, after I got blood all over me trying to help?"

"Yeah, Doc told me." He smiled, his voice faint. "You got more grit than I gave you credit for, Yankee lady."

"What's grit?"

He tried to shrug. "Western word—means you won't turn tail and run in a showdown. Texans admire that."

"I'm not a Texan," she reminded him.

"You're becomin' one, Lily."

She took the sponge and gently wiped his face. "Delilah's bringing in some broth."

He frowned. "Rather have chili with some peppers, and a cold beer."

"That's not what you're getting." She kept her voice firm. That was the only way to deal with this gambler, going toe to toe with him.

"Miss Lily, did anyone ever tell you you're stubborn to deal with? You must be Irish."

She drew herself up proudly. "I am not Irish. I am related to the sixth earl of Primley. My father was a very important man and nobility besides."

"So what?" he grinned, "In Texas, that don't make no never mind. We judge people on what they are, not their blue-blooded relatives."

Delilah came in with the broth. "I can feed him and look after him, Miss. Lieutenant Fortenbury is still waiting out front for you. He reminded me it ain't really proper work for a fine lady like you to be playin' nurse to a gambler. One of the girls can do it."

Lillian looked up to see the curious faces of the Texas Lily's girls in the doorway. Suddenly, she didn't want any of them feeding him and sponging him. "Never mind. I'll do it."

"You gonna poison me?"

"Don't give me any ideas, rascal." She looked

toward the door. "Everyone can go to bed. Delilah, go tell the Lieutenant that I can manage just fine without his advice. No," she shook her head. "Uh, just tell him I'll talk to him later and don't give him any details. It's not his business anyway."

"You can say that again." Delilah nodded and left the room, taking the girls with her.

Brad winked at Lillian as she sat down on the edge of his bed. "What will young Fortenbury think?"

"Lieutenant Fortenbury is hardly your concern. Now shut up and eat this soup before I pour it on you."

"You'd do that, pour hot soup on a defenseless, wounded man?"

She smiled. "Don't tempt me, Texan."

Chapter Eleven

Two afternoons later, the gambler seemed to be much better, although he insisted on having Lily feed him. "How—how'd our business do last night?"

Lillian hesitated.

"That bad, huh?"

"Well, with me not allowing the girls to, you know, and you too hurt to deal cards—not so good. Also, our bartender has quit and gone back home to Iowa."

He tried to get out of bed.

"What do you think you're doing?" She restrained him and he looked up at her, their faces close.

"Can't lose the Lily—worked too hard all my life not to be an average bum."

Just settle down," she commanded. "You can't do anything about that right now. We'll talk about it later."

He settled back against his pillows with a sigh and reached to touch his unshaven face. "I need a shave."

"Maybe I can get the barber to come here."

He shook his head. "Not likely, even for a good friend. Why don't you do it?"

She snorted. "Aren't you afraid I'll cut your throat? Then I'd own the Lily outright."

"I trust you." He grinned up at her.

"More fool, you." She went to his dresser and got the straight razor, looked at it dubiously. "You know, I have absolutely no experience with this. Maybe we'd better call in Delilah."

"If you say so," he nodded.

"In the meantime, I need to go up to town for supplies. Want anything?"

"How about some of those good cigars?"

She frowned at him. "Cigars are bad for you."

"Lady, I've got scars all over from bullets and knife fights and my insides are probably rotted already from cheap whiskey. Get me some cigars."

"All right." Some things weren't worth the argument. "I'll have Delilah come shave you and clean you up."

"Oh, I was hopin' you'd do that." he winked at her.

"Mister O'Neal, I've done just about everything I intend to do for you." She kept her tone icy, too aware of how charming he was and how vulnerable, too, weak and wounded. She went upstairs and got her purse.

Fern caught her in the hall. "That rancher asked me. He really asked me!"

"Oh? Good for you. He knows and doesn't care?"

She nodded and smiled. "He says I'm gettin' a fresh start and the past doesn't matter."

Lillian put her arm around the tall brunette and hugged her. "I'm so happy for you, Fern. We can put on a wedding right here."

Then she stuck her head in the girls' rooms and said, "You need to get up and start cleaning this whole house, Delilah can't do it alone. I'll be back to help."

"Clean?" Flo, the strawberry blonde, raised her head and blinked.

"Yes, clean. We may have Fern's wedding right here and the place should look presentable."

She stopped to give Delilah instructions about shaving the gambler and cleaning him up. If this were one of her romantic novels, the heroine would wash his naked body and then they would kiss.

This wasn't a romantic novel. The rascal could just stay dirty for all she cared. After all, if he hadn't been involved in that trickery, he wouldn't have gotten shot by some drunk cowboy.

Since it was a fairly cool mid-June day, she decided to take a walk, and got her parasol. Herman grazed across the large lily bed that bloomed like orange fire. Bluebirds played and sang around the big white bird bath. The billy goat raised its head and stared at her.

She shook her finger at him. "Don't you even think about it, you beast, or you might end up in the stew pot."

Instead, the goat trotted over and nibbled on the edge of her blue dress. She patted his head. "I'm glad we've come to an understanding."

Herman bleated at her and returned to his lily-munching as Lillian walked briskly toward town. It was a slow morning, with few people on the street. Evidently everyone was exhausted from Sunday night's fake Wild West show and Brad O'Neal's accidental shooting. In the distance, she saw Lieutenant Fortenbury standing on the street corner talking to Sadie. Lillian frowned.

The pair seemed to see her for the first time and Sadie stuck her nose in the air and hurried off, leaving a trail of smoke from her cigarillo behind her while the officer came toward Lillian, all smiles. "Miss Lillian, so good to see you this morning."

He took her hand and kissed it but Lillian pulled away. "I saw you talking to Sadie."

"I was being polite," he said. "She's only a harlot. I'd never even consider speaking to a lowly woman like that, but she stopped me to ask if I knew how that gambler was. So how is he?"

"Much better. He's pretty tough. I don't think this is the first time he's been shot or stabbed."

"No doubt," said the officer with a cold sniff. "No sign of blood poisoning?"

She shook her head. "I think in a few days, he'll be up and around."

"Oh." He sounded disappointed.

"I had a few things to pick up, and the day was so nice, I thought I'd walk."

"Then it's my lucky day that I happen to be uptown with the Major's buggy, picking up his new pruning shears. I'll give you a ride home."

"I don't want to trouble you."

He took off his hat and bowed low. "Miss Lillian, any time spent with you is no trouble, it's a pleasure."

She blushed in spite of herself. "Oh, Lieutenant, you're so gallant."

"I can't tell you what a pleasure it is to be in the company of a real lady. There are so few of your type in the West, especially Texas." He shuddered. "Probably the only place worse is the desert of Arizona."

"Oh really? I've decided I rather like Texas."

"Dear lady, you must be joking. It's full of horses, cattle, rough cowboys, and scoundrels like that Brad O'Neal. Here, let me open the door for you."

She let him open the door of the general store for her. "Brad must be as he says, tough as a longhorn bull."

"Brad? Now you call him Brad?" His patrician eyebrows went up.

"I meant Mr. O'Neal."

"It's too bad about the accident, but with everyone shooting in the confusion, I suppose it couldn't be helped."

She agreed with a nod. "Someone was either drunk or careless, or a rotten shot."

"Or all three," he joked, but she didn't laugh. She could still see Brad writhing on that bed as Doc probed for the bullet.

"I'm glad you find it funny," she said stiffly.

"I only meant—never mind, you're upset. I'll wait out front with the buggy for you."

She nodded and went on in, waiting for Pug to come from the back. "Oh, good day, Miss Primm. How is the patient?"

"Tell the boys he'll be all right."

"The whole town is ready to lynch whoever shot him."

"I'm sure it was an accident."

"We think the world of him," Pug leaned on the counter. "Him and Miss Lil helped everyone in town at one time or another."

"Oh?"

Pug nodded. "She was good-hearted, Miss Lil was. We didn't look down on her."

She didn't know what to say. Evidently the town and she differed over Lil McGinty's morals.

"You think you can keep the Lily open with Brad hurt?"

"We'll manage." She didn't feel like discussing their shaky finances with an outsider.

Luke stuck his head through the curtains in back. "Afternoon, Miss. How's that lock on your door?"

She scowled at him. "Why is everyone so interested in the lock on my door?"

Luke coughed and disappeared behind the curtain.

"Tell the boys," she raised her voice, "they can come visit him in a day or two."

There was a murmur behind the curtain and Pug looked uneasy. "Don't mind them, Ma'am, they're just Texans."

"Now," she said, "I need some white lacy tablecloths."

"Ma'am?" Pug said.

"I've decided while Mr. O'Neal is ill, I'll fix the place up a little—make it look a little higher class."

"Uh," Pug wiped his hands on his white apron, "Brad know about this?"

She fixed him with a cold stare. "Mr. O'Neal will not be able to conduct business for a few days, so I'm in charge. Are you questioning that?"

"No, ma'am. Brad says anyone tanglin' with a stubborn lady like you has to be loco."

"Indeed. I'm stubborn, all right. Now here's a list of what'll I'll need. We may be having a wedding at the Lily and I want the place to look better than just a saloon."

"Weddin'? Who's walked into the trap?" Pug scratched his face.

She wanted to smack him, but decided it wouldn't be ladylike. "Just wait on me, Mr. Pugsley, I don't need editorial input."

"What?"

From behind the curtain, she heard the laughter of the Town Beautification Committee. "I'll be back for these things. Let me know when they come in."

"You bring your buggy, Miss?"

"No, but Lieutenant Fortenbury has offered me a ride."

Pug scowled.

"What's the matter, Mr. Pugsley?"

"Nothin', Ma'am. But if I was a lady and had a choice between that prissy officer and old Brad, I'd—"

"Please sir, that is my choice to make." She started out, calling back over her shoulder, "Good-bye, boys."

Outside, the Lieutenant tottered to meet her in his high-heeled boots. "Miss Lillian." He had taken off his hat and stood looking earnestly up at her. "It may be too soon, but I know you must have many admirers."

Not a one, she thought, but she smiled at the short man. "You're being too kind, Lieutenant."

He offered his small, sweaty hand and helped her up into the buggy. "What I meant to say was," he paused and fumbled with his hat. "I—I'd like to call on you. Normally, of course, I'd ask your father's permission—"

"I'm an orphan," she said.

"Oh? Brothers and sisters?"

She sighed. "I'm afraid I'm quite alone in the world."

"Oh, I'm so sorry. My heart goes out to you, a defenseless female in a cruel world."

"I'm quite capable of looking after myself, thank you." She hated his presumption that she was helpless. She wasn't sure she wanted Lieutenant Fortenbury to call on her. That was almost the same as saying "yes" to an engagement. Could she see herself married to the man? He did have sterling credentials and was from a fine, aristocratic family, utterly rich and respectable. Those qualities were what she had always wanted in a husband, weren't they?

Yet her mind wandered and she smelled the

shaving lotion and saw the mischievous, crooked grin of the Texas scoundrel. He was so utterly not respectable and very low-class. Her mother had warned her to stay away from men like Brad O'Neal.

"Miss Lillian?" Buford was staring up at her.

"Yes?" She came back to the scene with a start.

"I asked if I could begin to call on you?"

She made her decision then, because this was the kind of man she'd always said she wanted and she wasn't getting any younger. Besides, she didn't like the way that rough Texan kept looking at her like she was a cold mint julep or a juicy steak. If he tried to kiss her, she wasn't sure that she could withstand the temptation of finding out what it was like to be in his arms. "Yes, Lieutenant, I'll think about it."

He broke into a grin and she realized how weak his chin was. "I'm so relieved. I was afraid you might be falling under the spell of that rogue."

"Who? Brad?"

"You again call him Brad?" He looked at her accusingly.

"I meant that rascal of a gambler," she stuttered. "And anyway, I'm on to his tricks. I know a respectable, high-class fellow when I see one, and that's you, Lieutenant."

He smiled. "I wish you would call me Buford."

"All right, Buford." She hated the name. It sounded like a sissy's—and the lieutenant . . . okay, so maybe he wasn't as virile and tall as the gambler, but he had class. Lillian imagined herself in Philadelphia in his fine house, meeting his oh so respectable parents. Yes, this was what she had always dreamed of, what her mother had dreamed of for her. And she owed something to her mother's memory. If she married Buford, she wasn't sure what she would do about the Lily, maybe sell her half to Brad. *If you do, he wins,* she thought. Like the gambler, she was competitive—which was probably frowned on in Philadelphia. Besides, she had begun to like Texas. The people and the land were fiery and independent.

She wanted to change the subject. "I don't know what's getting into Mr. Pugsley. He wasn't very friendly."

The lieutenant shrugged his narrow shoulders. "He's a Texan, and most of these Texans supported the Rebels—like all the cowboys. It makes for friction between the troops and the local peasants."

"I'd hardly call them that," Lillian said.

"Well, they're hardly of our class," Buford sniffed.

That sounded so snooty. "No, I—I suppose not."

"Especially that gambler—what a rascal!"

"He is a rascal," she admitted, "but a charming one. Why, I think half the women in town would simply swoon if he winked at them."

He sniffed. "No accounting for taste. I do worry about your reputation, Miss Lillian, living under the same roof—"

"Would anyone dare impugn my reputation?" She was horrified.

"Not as long as I'm around," he said with a nod, "I'd wipe up the street with them."

She imagined the back-East dandy going up against a Texan and sighed. Fisticuffs probably weren't the officer's strong point.

They drove up the driveway and he reined in, hopped down, and yelled for the Mexican stable boy. "You," he snapped, take these packages for the lady and be quick about it."

"There's no need to be rude, Buford," Lillian said.

"You've got to be firm with these types," he assured her as he helped her down. "Otherwise, they'll just take over."

"I hardly think so." Suddenly, she didn't like him very much. She started up the steps.

He called after her. "Dear Miss Lillian, why don't I pick you up about seven tonight and we'll go for a moonlight drive? Right now, I've got to get back to the fort; the major is planning a practice."

"All right." She waved to him and watched him drive away. Herman paused in his browsing and glared after the departing buggy as if he'd like to butt the uppity officer.

She went inside and called, "Delilah, I'm home."

The cook stuck her head out of the kitchen. "Doc's been here. Mister Brad is askin' for you."

She went into the gambler's room. He sat up in a rocking chair, wearing a fresh shirt and clean shave. "How are you feeling?"

"How how do you think I'm feelin'? My foot hurts, and I've been told not to walk on it, stay in my room and rest."

"You're lucky to be alive," she reminded him primly. "Remember, I told you that plan was dangerous. You could have been shot through the head."

"Don't nag. What kept you so long?"

If it's any of your business, which it isn't, I went uptown to pick up supplies and ran into Lieutenant Fortenbury."

"That pantywaist?" Brad made a face.

"He was kind enough to give me a ride home." She drew herself up proudly.

"We own a buggy," he reminded her.

"It was a nice afternoon. I walked."

"And I'm stuck inside, can't deal cards or drink or do anything fun."

"Are you feeling sorry for yourself?"

"I reckon I am," he admitted. "Help me out on the porch. At least I can sit in the big swing and watch the town."

"Didn't Doc bring you some crutches?"

"Not yet."

She hesitated, not wanting to get physically close to the big man.

"Well?"

She didn't want to explain that being close to him made her as nervous as a cat up a tree. She helped him to his feet and let him put his arm around her shoulders. "Take small steps," she said.

"Honestly, must you give advice about everything?" His face was so close to hers, she could feel the warmth of his breath. She had to slip her arm around his waist to steady him and slowly, they walked out to the porch swing. She deposited him there and backed away.

He patted the seat beside him. "Sit down and visit; I don't bite."

"Mr. O'Neal," she stood stiffly, "being nice to me won't get you my half of the Texas Lily."

"You're a suspicious person, you know that?" He grinned at her. *My, his teeth were white and straight in that dark, rugged face.* "As bad as business is right now, maybe I should sell you my half."

She sat down next to him and carefully scooted as far away as she could get from him. "Even if I had that much money, which I don't, you surely understand that I couldn't step into the shoes of a madam. The thought appalls me."

"Your aunt must have known you'd feel that way, I reckon that's why she suggested to Dewey Cheatum that I offer to buy you out."

Lillian shuddered. "No wonder she was never mentioned at home. I knew that she had disgraced the family, I just didn't know the half of it."

"Don't be so hard on Lil," he said softly as he reached in his shirt for a cigar. "I think she had bad luck and a tough life. Some heel messed up her life when she was quite young and innocent, she said."

She looked at him. "You know very much about my aunt?"

He shook his head. "Under different circumstances, she might have been an elegant lady like yourself. Bad luck."

Lillian shook her head. "I find it hard to excuse sinking this low."

"That's because you've never been in her circumstances. Texans say you should walk a mile in a man's cowboy boots before you judge him."

"I know nothing about her except that she came from a fine family and disgraced them, probably to start with by marrying some low-class Irish brawler."

He grinned at her. "Like me?"

"Probably."

"You are so naïve and innocent, my dear Miss Primm. Why, I'll bet you've never even been kissed."

She felt the hot flush rush to her face at the truth of that. "That's hardly your business, Mr. O'Neal. Respectable young women do not allow men to take liberties until they are engaged."

He threw back his head and laughed, a hearty, male laugh. "My dear Miss Primm, you are a little long in the tooth and way past courtin' age. Perhaps it's time you found out what you are missin'."

She jumped up out of the swing. "I'll have you know I have a suitor, and a very respectable one at that. Of course, that's something you wouldn't know about."

"Lieutenant Fortenbury?" He frowned.

"Yes."

"He's only after your share of the Texas Lily."

"Funny, he says the same about you."

"But at least I'm honest about it."

She felt like slapping him, but of course genteel ladies did not make a habit of slapping even mashers. "Isn't it just possible that he might really be interested in me?"

"Miss Primm, at the risk of being called a liar, I know a great deal more about the cad than you do, and believe me, he is not a suitable beau for—"

"I will not hear another word of this!" she couldn't keep her voice from rising.

"I don't reckon you would believe me anyway."

"Not on a stack of Bibles. When you want to come in, yell for Delilah. I've done enough good deeds for low-class rascals today." She went inside and slammed the door.

Watching her, Brad sighed. She was almost pretty when she was angry, and he had handled this badly. He had no doubt that the prissy officer was after her share of the Texas Lily—which he'd get over Brad's dead body. Of course, if she married the pantywaist, Brad would have to do business with the arrogant Yankee. That would indeed be a problem. The only way to deal with this was to charm Lillian Primm himself. Brad's reputation as a ladies' man was at stake. Lily seemed too smart to fall for a fool like the Lieutenant; she seemed as smart as most men. Naw, no woman was that smart. Of course, that made Lily a real challenge. Brad grinned. He liked challenges.

A few days later, Lillian was at the train station early in the morning. As the train pulled in, she noticed two well-dressed gentlemen step onto the platform.

One of them tipped his hat. "Excuse me, Miss,

we're from New York and in town on business. Can you direct us to the hotel?"

She shook her head. "I'm afraid it burned down this past spring."

They looked crestfallen.

An idea came to her. Now that four girls were gone, there were several empty rooms upstairs at the Lily. Delilah was a great cook, and they needed the money. "Well, I believe you can stay at the new hotel, the Texas Lily. That's my buggy over there at the hitching rail. You get your luggage, and I'll pick up a few things at the store."

They nodded, all smiles.

Lillian went into the general store. "Mr. Pugsley, did my lace tablecloths arrive yet?"

He nodded, got a package from under the counter. "Who are the men standin' by your buggy, Miss?"

"They needed a place to stay and the Lily now has plenty of extra rooms."

Pug frowned. "You turnin' the Lily into a hotel while Brad's down? He ain't agonna like that."

"We need the money," she said, "and it seems like a sensible solution to me."

"But Brad won't like it."

"You leave Mr. O'Neal to me," she said with more assurance than she felt, "I can handle him."

"We'll see," Pug wiped his hands on his white apron and picked up the package. He opened the door for her and the two went outside.

On the sidewalk, Luke stood talking to Dewey Cheatum. Both men tipped their hats.

"Mornin' Miss Primm," Luke grinned, "how's that lock workin' for you? You want I should take it off?"

"Of course not," she snapped. "Does this town

have nothing to preoccupy itself with except the lock on my door?"

Dewey's gray hair stuck up at awkward angles. "Don't pay him no nevermind, Miss Primm, there ain't much in a small town like this to amuse folks."

"I suppose not." She walked to her buggy, followed by Pug with her package.

The two gentlemen from New York stood there. One of them said, "Miss, would you like me to drive?"

"Get in," she snapped. "I am perfectly capable of driving a buggy. Besides, you don't even know where it is."

Sheepishly, the two got in the back seat and Pug helped her up into the front. "Let me know what Brad says."

"I imagine you'll hear him yelling all the way down the hill," she said, snapping her little whip. The buggy took off at a brisk pace.

"This seems to be a very prosperous town," one of the gentlemen in back said. "No wonder there's such a shortage of places to stay."

Should she tell him her place used to be a whorehouse? She decided against it. "We had a second hotel, but it burned down."

When she glanced back, one of the gentlemen was looking around in a nervous manner. "Indians burn it? We heard there was an attack only days ago."

"No, they think somebody dropped a cigar. But of course, with the fort here, you're perfectly safe."

In the distance, the fort's band started up, only slightly off-key. Lillian winced. Major Bottoms should stick to raising roses. "That's the Lily up ahead, gentlemen."

"My, what a beautiful place," said one of the men,

"I suppose for such accommodations, the price will be higher than most?"

She hadn't the least idea what to charge. "Of course, but I can tell you're both gentlemen of quality and five dollars a day, including meals, is not too much."

She heard a sharp intake of breath from the back. Five dollars a day? Was she insane? They probably didn't charge that much in New York City.

"Well, for such a lovely place, that's probably about right," admitted one. "I presume the meals are good?"

"Gentlemen, this is Texas. How much steak can you eat?"

"I don't have any idea," one said.

"Well, we'll find out," Lillian smiled as she drove up the horseshoe drive and Herman raised his head out by the bird bath and shook his horns at them.

"I say, is that goat just wandering free?" One asked.

"Yes, and he's not very even-tempered," Lillian warned. "He pretty well keeps everyone out of that lily bed."

She drove up to the front porch and the stable boy came out to meet them. "José," she said, smiling, "these gentlemen will be boarding with us a few days. Get my packages and their luggage, please." She gathered her skirts and José helped her down.

"*Senorita*, does Mr. Brad know about this?" the boy asked doubtfully.

"He's about to," Lillian said with determination. "Get down, gentlemen. I imagine our piano player, I mean, our check-in clerk, Lem, will be happy to fix you a mint julep."

"What is that?" One asked, as they got out of the buggy and looked around.

"If you like whiskey, you'll love it." She assured him and started up the steps with the men. They both grinned. *Was there ever a man who didn't like whiskey?* She frowned at the thought.

Delilah met them at the door, looking baffled. Before she could say anything, Lillian said, "Here are our new guests. You might get Lem to mix them a drink. And please tell them what time you're serving dinner, will you?"

"What is Mr. Brad gonna say?" Delilah shook her head.

Lillian smiled. "I don't know, but I'm about to find out." She turned to the two New Yorkers, who were looking about and nodding with satisfaction at the piano, the bar, and the red velvet drapes. "Gentlemen, Delilah will show you to your rooms."

"Why," said one of the men, "this looks just like a—"

"But it's not," Lillian corrected him. "The girls on the premises are waitresses."

The men were staring at the poker tables.

"Uh, sometimes in the evenings, the local ladies' clubs host a domino or whist party, complete with tea and sugar cookies."

The mens' faces fell. Delilah was already leading them up the stairs. "Dinner at noon," she said.

Lillian stood in the hall gathering her courage. At the moment, she didn't feel nearly as brave as she had a few minutes ago. Delilah looked down the stairs and shook her head at her. Lillian heard Brad's crutch as he hobbled out of his room. She hurried to intercept him before he saw the new boarders.

They met in his doorway.

"Well," he grinned, "this is a nice surprise." He looked pale and a little thin.

She almost said, 'don't waste your time flirting with me,' but then she remembered she must be charming. She smiled back. "You really shouldn't be up, you know."

He looked surprised. "I'll be damned, you're friendlier than usual."

"You probably will be." She took him by the arm and led him into his room, closed the door, and leaned against it.

He grinned and paused. "Now that really is improper for a Boston lady. Just what did you have in mind?"

"Don't be crude. We need to talk." she motioned toward a chair. She didn't want him to faint with surprise or maybe whack her with his crutch. She helped him to the chair and took the crutch, leaning it against the wall. She leaned over him and smiled again.

"You know, you're really not bad-lookin' for a woman your age."

"Thanks a bunch. You really know how to make a lady's day."

He shook his head in bewilderment. "You're the one who keeps callin' for honesty."

She was, wasn't she?

"Uh, Brad—"

"I'll swan, you are getting familiar." He grinned and winked at her and she stifled the urge to smack him.

"Mr. O'Neal," she said in a voice that would cut ice, "you know that there's no money coming in with you too laid up to deal poker—and the girls—"

"I can't help it about the poker, but you're the one who's keepin' the girls from workin'."

"Well, a couple of them might make pretty good waitresses, and that's respectable."

"What?" He looked bewildered.

She paced up and down. "We've got all these empty rooms, and Delilah is a great cook—"

"Not as good as me," Brad said. "But then, I'm not able to barbecue much, leanin' on a crutch."

"Humility is not your strong point," Lillian said.

"Who, me?"

"Never mind. It occurs to me that with the hotel burned down, the town could prosper more if visiting businessmen had a place to stay and eat besides that greasy cafe over near the Bucket O' Blood Saloon."

He shrugged. "Maybe so."

"You know it's true." She paused and took a deep breath. "Uh, what would you say to five dollars a day?

"For what? Our girls generally get two dollars—"

"Not for that." She hurried to cut him off. "We could rent out rooms and take in boarders for a while." There, she'd said it.

There was a split-second pause before her words sunk in. He blinked. "What?"

"The Lily could be a great hotel and make a ton of money that way and—"

"No!" he roared. "N-O. This is the best whorehouse and gamblin' joint in east Texas and you want to turn it into a hotel?"

"Think about it," she said. "I've already got two customers, businessmen from New York."

"Yankees? Yankees are livin' in my house?" His voice rose.

She would not be intimidated. "You have been doing business with Yankees all this time. It's the perfect answer."

An idea seemed to cross his mind. "Do these, ah, gentlemen play poker?"

"None of that," she said. "I told them the only entertainment was dominoes or whist now and then."

"Lady, you sure know how to take the fun out of life."

"Oh, stop whining. I'm just trying to keep things going."

"Do I need remind you that the Texas Lily was a very profitable business only weeks ago when you arrived and started turnin' everything, includin' my life, upside down?"

"Someday, you'll thank me for taking you out of this disreputable life of sin."

"I don't think so." He tried to get to his feet.

"That just shows what a wastrel you are. Now take a nap or play solitaire. You don't have anything else to do."

"Ain't that the truth?"

She closed his door and left, her mind busy with her project. She already had the girls waxing the wood floors and dusting everything. She'd also hired help with moving things around. She went out into the big room. For the first time, she noted some big, pretty brass vases José had gathered to clean. "José, give those an extra polish and then go pick me some lilies."

"Is Señor Herman in his pen?" The boy looked uncertain.

"I don't know. If not, get Delilah to lock him up."

She called to Fern to help her with the tablecloths.

It was soon dinner time and Delilah's eyes grew round as she came out of the kitchen to ring the bell. "I don't know what Mr. Brad's gonna think about this."

"He'll love it," Lillian assured her, but she wasn't sure. She'd have to be extra charming to the rascal until he got over his surprise. She went down the hall and knocked on his door. "Come in."

He sat in his chair.

"Where's your crutches?"

"I don't do so well with those, why don't you just give me a hand?"

It seemed churlish to refuse. As he hobbled to his feet, she hurried to get his arm over her shoulder. His face was so close, she could see his chin square as he smiled, and smell his soap and shaving lotion. For a moment, they stood there looking into each other's eyes—his were a warm brown with crinkles at the corners. His arm over her shoulder was warm and strong. Something about him made her take a deep breath and pull away. "I—I think you'd better use your crutch." She reached to get it for him.

She took a deep breath and walked out the door ahead of him. "I've made a few changes, I hope you like them."

"Everything was just fine the way it was. Women always want to change things, especially men," he grumbled as he hobbled down the hall behind her. They reached the main room and he paused, wordless in surprise. There were lacy white tablecloths over every poker table, the floor had been waxed, the billiard table was gone, and Lem had his hair neatly combed and wore a jacket. The biggest surprise was the tables. He blinked in shock. A shiny brass spittoon was in the center of each table full of orange day-lilies.

"What do you think?" she asked, "I found the vases and decided to use them. I've really made everything pretty, don't you think?"

"Lily," he shook his head in defeat, "it don't look like a whorehouse no more."

"Good," she said and smiled. "And now, come have dinner with our hotel guests from New York."

Chapter Twelve

As June deepened, Brad graduated from a crutch to a cane and at last, gave that up. He quit complaining about Lillian renting out rooms to travelers. Of course, he often engaged these gentlemen in a game of cards when she wasn't looking and he made a very good profit there. Perhaps Lillian didn't notice, he thought, because she was busy with Fern's wedding. He scowled at the thought.

What was it that was so fascinating about getting hitched that it consumed all the women in town, even an old maid like Lily Primm? Maybe it was because she'd never have one, he thought, but of course he didn't say so. So far, his attempts to charm Miss Primm were getting him nowhere, which was not only unusual, it had all the members of the Town Beautification Committee laughing at him. Worse yet, he knew that snooty lieutenant often took her driving. What did she see in that dandy?

"Now," Lillian said to him as she came into his office with a pencil and papers in hand. "I've told Fern to invite the whole town."

"The whole town?" Brad grumbled, "you know

what that will cost? Why don't they elope and get Reverend Lovejoy to hitch them?"

She scowled at him. He was charming all right, but she wasn't stupid enough to fall for his lies. Why, the man could charm a dog off a meat wagon. "A girl only gets married once so it ought to be nice."

Brad snorted. "This may be the only fancy weddin' in Texas history where half the men in the audience have slept with the bride."

She felt the blood rush to her face. "Don't be crude. The bride deserves a second chance. Anyway, I thought we'd have the wedding out on the front lawn among the lilies—"

"The big bird bath is in the way."

She shrugged. "So the morning of the wedding, we'll move it and lock Herman up."

He sighed. "You invitin' both the ranchers and the soldiers?"

"Yes, and I'll expect them to behave."

"With a little liquor in them, the cowboys'll start yellin' at each other or singin' "Dixie" and then the other side will begin the "Battle Hymn of the Republic," and we'll have a big fight on our hands." He grinned at the thought. "Maybe it will be fun after all—nothing like a good fight to top off the afternoon."

"There will be no fights and no liquor," Lillian declared. "We are serving lemonade and wedding cake."

"That's all?"

"It seems like enough."

"You'll draw a better crowd with beer and barbecue." He suggested.

"This is a wedding, not a brawl."

Brad grinned. "Men would enjoy a brawl better, especially the Texans."

"Cake and lemonade. The rancher's marrying Fern and they'll live happily ever after."

"Doesn't he get to say anything about the arrangements?"

"He gets to say 'I do' when the reverend asks him. The ladies plan the rest of it."

"If he ain't full of beer, he might not say 'I do.'"

"Mr. O'Neal, how many weddings have you attended?"

He thought a minute, leaning on his desk. "So far, I've managed to avoid them all. I was afraid it was contagious."

"I rest my case," Lillian snapped. "It will be lemonade and wedding cake, and all the men will be expected to behave like gentlemen, including the Texans."

It would have been a beautiful wedding, but just before Lillian sent José and Lem out to move the big bird bath, it began to rain.

"Well," she said, "we'll just have to move the whole thing inside. Mr. O'Neal can bring the bride down the stairs and we'll all scoot the poker tables back and have the ceremony in the main room. We can set up the cake and punch in the dining room. Delilah, let's get busy."

Of course Brad managed to open the bar for the gentlemen while they were waiting and Lem struck up a loud rendition of "Buffalo Gals," until Mrs. Bottoms insisted he play something more appropriate. The guests began to arrive and stood or took seats on each side, military to one side, ranchers and cowboys to the other.

Lillian suspected what was going on downstairs, but after all, she couldn't be in two places at once, and right now, she was upstairs with Fern, helping her get dressed. Fern had asked Lillian to be her maid of honor and Lillian had dug into Lil McGinty's closet and found a pale green silk dress that seemed modest enough. Then one of the girls did her hair so that it was pulled back in soft curls with ringlets about her face.

"Gosh, Miss Lillian," Flo said, "you look purty as a speckled pup in a red wagon."

"What?"

"Hit don't make no never mind," the girl shrugged. "It's Texas talk. Is Brad ready?"

"I hope he's not too well oiled," Lillian said. "If he stumbles down the stairs and ruins this wedding, I may beat him to death with the silver cake server. Is Fern ready?"

They went to check on her and she was a vision in white, her dark hair framing her pretty face. "Miss Lily, you think anyone will laugh? I mean, about the white dress?"

"They do, they'll answer to me." Brad stood in the doorway, all dressed up and smiling. He might have been a little bit drunk, too, but he looked so handsome and so charming, Lillian almost forgave him for that.

She felt him staring at her.

"What's the matter, do I look ridiculous in this getup?"

"Miss Lily," he bowed low, "you look like ham and eggs to a hungry cowboy."

"What?"

"You're pretty," he announced soberly. "I never realized just how pretty you are."

She almost smiled at him, then remembered he was so smooth with women, he could talk a cow out of her calf. "Thank you. You look nice yourself—drunk, but nice."

"A Texan is never drunk," he corrected her,

weaving a little. "I've just had a quick snort for courage. Remember the Alamo."

"I don't know what that has to do with anything," she snapped.

"Yankee lady," he leaned against the doorway and grinned at her. "Brave men went to their fate there, too."

"Praise be," said the preacher, coming through the door. "There's a nice crowd downstairs, Miss Primm, and someone has set up a barrel of beer. A lot of the crowd is snockered."

She glared at Brad. "Now, I wonder who did that?"

He shrugged. "You wanted it to be a success, didn't you? You think Texans would settle for lemonade?"

"Well," said the reverend, anxiously glancing toward the stairs, "we'd better get with it before the level reaches the point that the 'Battle Hymn' crowd tries to out sing the 'Dixie' bunch." He started for the stairs, then paused. "Now, Miss Primm, you come down after the music starts, I'll signal you. Once she's almost to the front, Brad, you escort Fern down the stairs."

"I'll do 'er," Brad declared.

He looked like the only way he could make it down the stairs was to fall down, Lillian thought. Outside, the rain pattered gently on the roof and garden.

"Watch out," she warned Brad. "If you fall down the stairs and ruin this wedding, the ladies will kill you."

He grinned a little crookedly at her. "You look beautiful, Lily, as pretty as the bride, you know that?"

"Now I know you're drunk," she admonished.

He sounded so sincere, but she didn't trust him. "Are we all ready?"

"I'm so nervous," Fern twisted her bouquet of white roses, courtesy of the major's garden.

Brad stepped to look over the upstairs banister. "You think you're nervous, you ought to see the groom."

Lillian asked anxiously. "Does he look like he's about to run?"

Brad shook his head, "I don't know. He looks like a cornered calf in a ropin' pen."

Fern got tears in her eyes. "Maybe he's regretting marrying a wh—"

"No, he's not." Brad put his arm around her shoulders and kissed her cheek. "He's just nervous. Gettin' married is a big thing for a man, like maybe goin' into battle. He knows he'll look like a fool if'fen he runs and besides, he's about to do the most important thing he's ever done in his life. He wants to, but he's a mite scared."

Lillian looked at him and their eyes met. "That was sweet. Thank you."

Now he scowled. "I didn't do it for you, Miss Lily."

Downstairs, the music began on the saloon piano.

Lillian took a deep breath, held her bouquet of pink roses and started down the stairs. She looked down into fifty curious faces and for only a moment, when she saw Lieutenant Fortenbury in his best dress uniform in the crowd she imagined it was her wedding. She smiled at him and he smiled back. Down by the bar, she saw the minister, the cowboy groom, and his best friend, all slicked up with their cowboy boots polished. She reached the foot of the stairs and glided over to stand near the preacher. Then she turned and looked up at the balcony. To the strain of the wedding march, Brad, with Fern on his arm, came down the stairs.

If he stumbles and falls and ruins this wedding, I'll kill him, Lillian vowed. As they crossed the saloon, he stared at Lillian and kept on staring as if he'd never seen her before. She felt herself flush and looked down at the floor modestly. Now they all stood before the minister. The ladies in the crowd were wiping their eyes, whether because they were sentimental or because they were getting rid of one more pretty whore who had tempted their men, there was no way to know.

The minister said, "Who giveth this woman?"

Brad had to clear his throat twice to speak. "I do, her former employer."

Some man in the crowd laughed and Brad turned and glared at him. The laughter broke off.

Reverend Lovejoy said, "Now dearly beloved, we are gathered at this place before God and these witnesses—"

Somewhere in the crowd a child whined, "When are we gonna get some cake?" and the mother shushed it.

Brad had taken a front seat now but Lillian was aware that he was staring at her so hard that she almost felt naked. She tried to ignore him and turned her smile toward Buford, but she felt Brad's gaze on her.

Finally the minister said, "I now pronounce you man and wife. You may kiss the bride."

The cowboy grabbed Fern and kissed her soundly while the whole crowd applauded.

Brad stood up and signaled for silence. "I reckon you all are ready for refreshments and we'll also have some dancing, led by the bride and groom."

The crowd applauded even louder and began to move toward the dining room while the piano

struck up a waltz and the cowboy danced his new
bride out into the middle of the saloon. Lillian realized both Brad and Buford were moving toward
her, but Brad elbowed the shorter man out of the
way. "Dear Lily," he said, bowing low, "may I have
this dance?"

"I was going to ask her first," Buford argued.

"Oh, shut up," Brad said and swept her into his
arms, and danced her away.

"My, that was rude." she said, attempting in vain
to put space between them.

"I got there first, remember?" He grinned down
at her and she smelled the scent of bourbon and
shaving lotion. "Did I tell you you look beautiful?"

"Mr. O'Neal, to put it bluntly, you are pickled. I
know how plain I am."

"You make it tough as a longhorn steak to compliment you," he held her even closer.

"Must you hold me so tight?" she complained
and struggled to pull back.

"I must. Now stop tryin' to be so proper, and
enjoy it," he murmured against her hair. His breath
was warm on her ear and his big hands were warm.
She could feel one on her waist and the other en-
trapped hers so she could not get away. Outside, it
had stopped raining and dusk was coming on.

She watched Buford over Brad's shoulder. He
seemed to be summoning up his courage. Finally he
marched over and tapped Brad's broad shoulder.
"May—may I cut in?"

"No, you may not. This is my dance." Brad
snapped.

"Have you no manners?" she scolded as they
danced away.

"None. I'm not gonna to let that Nancy boy take
the woman I'm dancin' with."

She didn't know what to say. She was not used to

having the attention of two men. When she was young, she had always been a wallflower at any dance she was forced to attend, standing on the sidelines, pretending to be laughing with other girls while never being asked to dance. For many years now, she had been the chaperone at Miss Pickett's Academy dances.

It was warm and someone had opened the French doors out onto the big covered porches that surrounded the house. With the coming darkness, a cool breeze blew though. Before Lillian realized what he was up to, Brad whirled her out the French doors and onto the porch.

"What are you doing?" she scolded, "I really need to go see if Delilah needs any help serving cake—"

"Let 'em get their own damned cake." He continued dancing her around the porch.

"What will they think of me as a hostess?"

"Who cares? They all seem to be havin' a good time, let them alone. Did I tell you you looked larrupin' good?"

"Several times," she sighed.

"Purty as an ace high straight," he nodded. His breath stirred the tendril of hair near her cheek.

"Mr. O'Neal, dancing out here in the darkness with you is not good for my reputation."

"Lily, honey, being seen anywhere with me ain't good for your reputation."

"Now that's a fact." she declared. "But I am not yours or anyone else's honey."

"You could be." He paused, looking down at her.

She stared up at him in the moonlight and the burning look in his eyes spoke of hot desire. It was the liquor, she thought. No man had ever looked at her like that before. She was taken aback and it must have shown.

"I wouldn't worry if I were you, Miss Primm. Why

you're so innocent, not even I could smudge your precious reputation. Why, I'll bet you've never even been kissed."

She looked away and flushed. "That—that is hardly any of your business."

"You haven't, have you?" He looked incredulous.

"I—no, but when the right man comes along—"

"Oh hell, lady, you don't know what you're missing."

"Don't laugh at me, please." She looked up at him, into those intense dark eyes and that full sensual mouth. They had stopped dancing but he hadn't let go of her and she didn't try to escape his embrace.

"Lily, does it look like I'm laughin'?" He bent his head and kissed her gently. His lips were warm and soft and tasted faintly of whiskey. His body felt warm and strong against hers as he molded her to him. Her mind told her she ought to pull away, but she simply could not force herself to extract herself from his embrace. The kiss deepened and her heart seemed to pound like the bass drum in the army band. She gasped for breath and now his tongue flicked along her lips. She didn't mean to, but she opened her lips to his tongue and leaned toward him, molding herself against him. The kiss deepened even more until she gasped for air.

He groaned aloud and pulled her closer still. "Lily, oh, Lily," he whispered against her mouth and one of his big hands caressed along her bare shoulders until she was shaking. For a moment, his big hand hesitated on her throat and she willed him to go lower with his caress, into her bodice. His mouth touched her throat and she threw her head back, wanting him to kiss all the way down until his lips would touch the swell of her breast and . . .

Faintly from inside, she heard Buford calling, "Miss Primm, Miss Primm, where are you?"

That slammed her back into reality. What was she doing out here in the darkness with this rogue? She managed to pull away from him. They were both breathing hard and Brad looked as surprised as she felt. *What on earth was she doing?* In confusion, she turned and fled back inside, calling, "Here I am, Buford."

Buford stared at her anxiously as she rushed up to him. "Are you all right, Miss Lillian? You look a bit flushed."

Could he tell by looking that she'd been kissing that low-life Texas scoundrel with wild abandon? Oh Lord, she hoped not. "I—I'm fine."

"Are you sure?"

"I'm sure." Of course, she wasn't sure at all. Her mind returned again and again to that wild kiss on the porch. She shook when she remembered it. "Shall we—shall we have our dance now?"

"Certainly." He bowed low and took her hand in his white gloved one, the other placed carefully on her small waist. He kept a respectful distance between their two bodies as they waltzed. She danced like one hypnotized and when Buford whirled her, she saw Brad come in the door and lean against the wall, watching her. His stare was as intense as his kisses. All she could think of was the hot, virile embrace on the darkened porch where she'd acted like a harlot, letting him devour her mouth, run his hands over her, do everything but take her down in a hot embrace in a porch swing. She had never lost control of her emotions before.

The music was the "Blue Danube" waltz and the young officer kept humming it in her ear as they danced. She hated that. As he whirled her around the floor, she noted the officers' wives nodding with approval. Brad O'Neal stood on the sidelines, watching her. He looked as puzzled and confused as she felt.

As the dance ended, young Fortenbury whispered in her ear, "would you like to go out on the porch?"

"I—I think it's a bit chilly outside."

He frowned. "It's June. All the French doors are open, and it's hot in here."

"All right, let's go out." She took his arm and they headed for the porch. She glanced back over her shoulder and saw Brad O'Neal sipping a mint julep and scowling at her. It made her feel like a slut, that she'd let him paw her and kiss her—but she'd liked it. That surprised her most of all.

She and Buford went out on the porch and stood looking up at the warm Texas sky. It had stopped raining. Under a full moon, the lilies glowed as orange fire.

"Let's walk through the garden," she suggested.

"I'd rather sit in the porch swing," he said, but she ignored him and taking his arm, dragged him off the porch.

"It's a lovely night to walk through the flowers," she said. If she sat in the porch swing with him, would he try to kiss her? She was afraid he might.

"The flowers are nothing but common day-lilies," he snorted as they went down the steps and out along the drive. "I hear Lil McGinty was out here early every morning working in her flowers, but she didn't have much taste. Now, my mother wouldn't have anything so ordinary in her garden. Did I tell you she has a conservatory and raises orchids?"

"How nice," Lillian said as they walked.

He paused and took both her hands in his. "Two aristocratic families uniting as one. What fine quality children we'd produce."

"I beg your pardon?"

"What I'm asking, Miss Lillian, is would you marry me?"

She was stunned speechless. Yet hadn't she already been dreaming of her engagement to this ambitious young officer?

"Miss Lillian?"

Was she an idiot? Of course she should say yes. Oh my, suppose he ever found out about her kissing Brad O'Neal out on the porch?

Her heart yearned for the Texan, but she pushed him from her mind. *Be sensible,* that was what her mother would have said, *Buford's from such a distinguished family, as are you.* "Uh, of course I'll marry you, Lieutenant."

"Buford," he corrected with a smile as he looked up at her. "Now that we're engaged, "may I kiss you?"

She took a deep breath. This should be the happiest moment of her life, so why wasn't it? "Of course, Buford."

He took her in his arms awkwardly and gave her a big, wet smack on the lips.

She resisted the urge to wipe the back of her hand across her mouth. It was so unlike the kiss that Brad had given her. But of course that scoundrel had probably kissed hundreds of women.

Just past his narrow shoulder, she saw a blur of gray. "Look out!"

Her warning came too late. Herman charged the officer, butting him in the rear and tossing him into a lily bed. Then the goat paused, bleating and shaking his curled horns as if proud of himself.

"Oh, Buford, are you hurt?"

He sat up, his white gloves smeared with dirt as he sputtered. "That beast! He ought to be shot and barbecued! He's a dangerous animal!"

She reached out and took Buford's hand,

helping him to his feet. "I'm so sorry. I don't know why Herman has taken such a dislike to you."

Buford was still sputtering as he brushed himself off. "I ought to sneak over some night and kill that goat."

Herman returned to munching flowers and Lillian and Buford started back toward the house. "I wouldn't do that if I were you, Buford, he's really a very nice pet and I'm getting fond of him. Besides, I imagine Brad O'Neal would beat you up if you shot Herman."

Buford snorted. "The owner is as wild and uncivilized as his goat. Honestly, Miss Lillian, you should move out of this place until you can get control of it—before your reputation is ruined."

"I—I can't; at least not now. I've got a big stake in this property."

"My dear mother would not approve."

"Neither would mine," Lillian sighed.

He smiled up at her as they went up the steps and inside. "We're two of a kind, my dear."

There was still a large crowd, but it was mostly cowboys and single soldiers, as the respectable ladies had left. Of course the men would stay until the bar ran dry, Lillian thought. There was a little pushing and minor insults going on between the two sides. Brad O'Neal's expression was black as thunder as she and the Lieutenant returned.

Before she realized what he was going to do, the officer stepped in front of the piano and gestured for silence. Gradually, the room quieted.

"Everyone," he shouted, "I just can't keep this good news to myself anymore. This evening, Miss Lillian Primm, lately of Boston, has consented to marry me!"

Oh, my.

There were cheers from the drunken crowd, but Brad glared a hole in her so that she looked away. Men were gathering around the lieutenant to shake his hand and were offering her good wishes. Brad O'Neal did neither. He gulped his drink, slammed the glass down on the bar, and yelled for another.

She knew she should be happy, but somehow, she wasn't. Buford Fortenbury was everything she had dreamed of in a husband: respectable, upper class, fine ancestors. Yet all she could think of was that wet, sloppy kiss . . . and the smoldering one the Texan had given her.

Chapter Thirteen

Brad was raging as he stood at the bar and watched that pantywaist lieutenant lead Lily back inside the house. She looked flustered and confused, but the short officer looked happy and triumphant.

She wasn't any more confused than Brad was. He'd kissed the prim old maid out there on the porch in his plan to seduce her and get her share of the business. Yet he'd never had a kiss affect him like that. Never.

Brad signaled Lem for another drink. The bartender paused. "You sure, boss? It ain't like you."

"Gimme another drink, damn it!" He ordered as Fortenbury marched proudly across the floor to where the little band played and signaled for silence. "Everyone," he shouted, "I just can't keep this good news to myself anymore. This evening, Miss Lillian Primm, lately of Boston, has consented to marry me!"

There was uncertain applause. The lieutenant was not the most popular officer at the fort.

What the hell? Brad swore under his breath. How could she have been out on the veranda with Brad, kissing him like she was going to surrender her virginity in hot passion one minute, and a few minutes later she was announcing her engagement to that young upstart? Why Fortenbury was so low-down, he'd steal the milk out of a baby calf's bucket. It was all Brad could do not to throw his glass at the man. Of course, he told himself, it was only because young Fortenbury was beating Brad at his own game. Not only was the Yankee upstart going to take her virginity, but it looked like Brad would soon have that pantywaist as a partner. *Not if hell freezes over,* Brad vowed.

Everyone was gathering around the officer now, shaking his hand and offering congratulations. Brad didn't move. Instead, he glared at Lily. She looked at him only once, then glanced away. She didn't look too happy to have just accepted a marriage proposal.

Sadie had sneaked in through a side door and in the crowd, no one had noticed her leaning against the bar and smoking a cigarillo. She signaled Lem for a drink as she smiled at Brad. "Hey, sport, what do you think of that?"

Brad shrugged. "He's after her half of the Lily."

"You don't think he actually loves her, do ya?" She sipped a whiskey, smoke curling around her blond head.

"Of course not." He remembered the surprise of Lily's hot, wild kisses. Now Buford would get those. The thought made Brad grit his teeth.

Sadie winked boldly at him. "You don't look too happy about the engagement."

He shrugged. "Except for the battle over the Lily, why would I care?"

"Why don't you come on over to the Bucket O' Blood, Brad? I got a room there and we could have some fun."

He shook his head. "I'm the host. I can't leave."

"Any excuse is a good one, I reckon."

"What do you mean by that?" he snarled at her.

"Nothing. Nothing at all." She took a big drag on the cigarillo and ashes flew everywhere.

"Be careful with that, Sadie, you'll start a big fire someday."

"Yeah. Well, see ya." She finished her drink and walked slowly out the front door, swinging her hips. She turned and gave him a smile, and nodded in open invitation.

Brad swallowed hard. He needed a woman bad, but he didn't want that slut tonight. Funny, he didn't used to be that choosy, and Sadie really knew how to please a man. He just kept clenching his fists and watching Lieutenant Fortenbury's grinning, triumphant face as he stood now at Lily's side, his arm around her. How dare he? How dare he what? If he was going to marry her, he had a right to put his arm around her waist. He was looking at her like he owned her. That really annoyed Brad.

The Town Beautification Committee drifted over to him.

"Don't say nothin'," Brad warned.

"She took him over you?" Dewey said. "That don't make no sense."

Pug shook his head. "I reckon you ain't the ladies' man we thought you was, Brad."

"I ain't done yet," Brad said, "that lock'll come off her door yet, you'll see."

"Yeah, but for which man?" Lester said, and Brad grabbed him by the shirt collar. "Watch your mouth."

The others grabbed Brad's arms. "Easy, Brad, don't hit him. He didn't mean nothin.'"

"I ain't through yet," Brad said again, "you'll see."

"It don't matter none," Pug soothed.

"It matters to me," Brad snapped. "My pride is at stake. How could she choose him over me?"

Dewey ran his hand through his rumpled gray hair. "You ask her to marry you, too, did you?"

"Are you loco? I may be drunk, but I'm not crazy." Brad leaned on the bar.

"Well," Dewey paused in lighting his pipe. "I think the man that beds her will have to marry her."

The others nodded in agreement.

Brad was tempted to tell them about kissing her on the porch, but he didn't. He'd had a feeling out there that if he'd gathered her up in his arms and carried her out to the barn, he'd have had her clothes off with the two of them putting out enough heat to set the hay on fire. "Just wait," he promised.

The bar ran out of liquor, so the men began to drift away. The bride and groom had left hours ago, but no one seemed to notice. Now as the crowd thinned, Brad marched over to where Buford and Lily still stood accepting congratulations. "Time to go home, soldier boy."

"Are you ordering me out of here?" Fortenbury said.

"I am."

Lily bristled. "You can't do that. I'm half owner."

"Remember, we run a respectable house and it's time for gentlemen callers to leave."

Lily's eyes blazed. Why had he never noticed how long her lashes were and how endearing those freckles?

Lily seethed. "You aren't suggesting we'd do anything improper, are you? Buford, my honor is at stake here."

Brad grinned at her. Surely she didn't expect the

cowardly officer to take a poke at the best saloon brawler in Texas?

"Uh," said the shorter man, wiping sweat from his brow.

Brad said, "I'm merely closin' the Texas Lily for the evening. Good night, Lieutenant."

Fortenbury acted as if he might argue, then seemed to size up just how big the Texan was. "Very well. I'll see you tomorrow, darling."

She held out her hand awkwardly. "Good night, Buford."

He kissed her hand, claimed his hat from the frowning Delilah and left the house.

Lily turned on Brad. "That was rude."

"Yeah, I know, I'm a rude fellow." He couldn't keep from slurring his words.

"Worse yet, you're drunk."

"Also guilty. Good night, Miss Primm." He stumbled toward his room and tripped against a table leg, caught himself, and kept walking.

Behind him, Lillian watched him go. Yes, he was everything that she didn't want in a man: savage, virile, rude, and of no background. The rough Texan was everything the Lieutenant wasn't. She heard Brad stumble into his room and slam the door so hard, the house shook.

Delilah gave her a disapproving frown and began to blow out the lamps. Lillian stood there in the growing darkness, trying to decide what to do. She shouldn't care that the scoundrel was angry with her, but somehow, it mattered. She tiptoed across the room and down the hall, rapped lightly at his door. "Mr. O'Neal? Brad?"

"What the hell do you want?" He sounded annoyed.

"I—I wanted to explain to you—"

"Go away."

She stood there, hesitating. What did she want? This was not at all proper—she knew it and yet here she stood. She should go up to her room and dream about her coming wedding to Buford. Once again she was in the garden, getting that big wet smack of a kiss. She had maybe fifty years of those kisses ahead of her. Without thinking, she wiped her mouth with the back of her hand. "Mr. O'Neal? Brad?"

The door opened suddenly and he stood there, big and virile. "I said, what the hell do you want?"

She was paralyzed with indecision, staring up at this drunken stallion of a man, remembering that wild, passionate kiss. Past his shoulder, she could see his bed and the way he was looking down at her let her know that he was thinking about gathering her up in his arms and carrying her there, making hot, abandoned love to her.

She was completely unnerved at the bold need in his eyes. "I—nothing. I didn't want anything at all." She turned and fled down the hall and up the stairs, closed her door and locked it, stood gasping for air leaning against the door. Why had she done such a foolish thing? Buford was right, she needed to move out of this place as soon as possible.

When Lieutenant Buford Fortenbury left the Texas Lily, he was both angry and humiliated. He figured Lillian had expected him to challenge that rowdy and Buford was not about to do that unless he had an edge. Everyone knew Brad could fight and nobody made any trouble at the Texas Lily.

He mounted his horse and started out, waving his fist at the goat. "Someday, you walking chops and roasts, I'll see you cooked and enjoy every bite of it."

The goat lowered its head and bleated a challenge at him.

What to do now? Kissing Miss Primm that one time had aroused a need in him, but of course he couldn't expect a respectable girl to satisfy his animal instincts. For that, he needed a slut like Sadie. He'd been at the Bucket O' Blood several times since she'd left the Texas Lily.

The place was rough, and he hesitated to go there, but it looked almost empty as he tied his horse out front and went in. He leaned against the bar. "Give me a whiskey."

The swarthy bartender glowered at him, and slid him a drink in a dirty glass. Buford frowned and wiped the lip of the glass with his hand. "Is Sadie around?"

The dirty man nodded toward the back. "You got tokens?"

"Sell me three."

The bartender laughed. "In your dreams, Romeo, but I'll sell them to you anyway. Maybe you can make a watch fob out of them."

Buford looked at the size of the man and decided not to take offense. He laid down six silver dollars and took the tokens. Then he picked up his drink and walked toward the back. "Sadie?"

She opened her door with a smile, a cigarillo in her hand, then the smile faded. "Oh, it's you."

He gulped his drink. "Who were you expecting?"

"Never mind. Anyway, you just got engaged, what are you doin' here?"

"We going to stand out here or can we go in your room?"

She opened the door wider and gestured him in, closed the door. "You got a token?"

"I got three."

Sadie laughed in a way that made him wince. "Well, you're ambitious, I'll say that for you. I only know one man who could go three times and you ain't that man. He's over at the Lily."

He had an urge to hit her across the face and keep hitting her until she was on her knees and begging. "I didn't come here to be insulted."

"I know what you came for, what they all come for." She sounded tired and disappointed. "You want another drink?"

"Sure." He sat down on the edge of her bed while she poured him a drink, pouring herself another. "You don't be nicer to the customer, maybe I won't come back."

She laughed and gulped her drink, then poured herself another. Smoke curled around her blond hair, and she flicked ashes with an unsteady hand.

"Be careful with that smoke," he scolded. "Ain't burnin' down one building enough for you?"

"You know I didn't mean to do that. You was afraid to come to my room at the Lily, so we ended up in the hotel."

He grunted. "You burn down this dump, the locals might run you out of town. They still might if they find out you burned down the hotel."

She shrugged. "There's nothin' in this town for me anyway, just men. And there's always men wantin' to climb me anywhere I go. There's only one man I ever cared about. Now if Brad showed any real interest in me—"

"Brad, Brad." he complained. "I'm damned tired of hearing about that gambler. He ain't so much."

"You kiddin'?" She laughed without mirth. "He's special—a two-fisted Texan that's all man and can make a girl glad to be a woman." She wasn't looking forward to this, but a girl had to make a living. "Your elegant fiancée wouldn't do it for you, huh?"

"She's a lady," he said coldly.

"And I ain't."

He smiled. "We both know what you are, Sadie. Give me another drink."

She poured him another and one for herself. When she'd heard a man's step in the hall, she had jumped up, hoping that Brad O'Neal had changed his mind and come to her. The lieutenant was clumsy and his height wasn't the only thing that was short about him. "Let's get this over with."

He sneered. "You'll treat me with more respect when I own half the Texas Lily. You'll be back working there, too, you and a dozen more whores. I got big plans."

She shrugged and began removing her dress. "Brad O'Neal will let you take half the Lily over his dead body, and I wouldn't go up against him if I was you."

He reached out and grabbed her breast. "He isn't so tough."

"I've never seen him beaten in a fight." She tossed her smoke away and stepped on it.

"Shut up, slut." He slapped her. Then he began to take off his uniform. "Maybe I won't have to fight him, maybe he'll have an accident."

Brad would have killed a man who hit a woman, but he wasn't here. She rubbed her stinging cheek. She cared about Brad, really cared, even though he didn't seem to know she was alive. "What do you mean?"

"Well, he got shot at the Indian raid and almost didn't make it."

"Folks say that was an accident."

Buford jerked her to him. "Was it? Something like that could happen again, and then Lillian and I would own the whole place."

"You really love that prim and proper miss?"

He laughed and sat down on the bed. "Are you

joking? When I marry her, I'll control her and her half."

"Do I fit into this somehow?" She knelt before him and took off his boots.

"Sure, Sadie." He leaned over and grabbed her breast again. "When I own the whole of the Lily, I can do anything I want—like move a mistress in— and she can't do anything about it. Then I'll have two women to sleep with, plus all the whores."

You couldn't satisfy one, she thought, but she only sighed and reached up to kiss him. "Make love to me, tiger."

He was more like a small tom cat, Sadie thought as he struggled to complete the act, and those wet kisses were almost more than she could stomach. Of course, she pretended that it was great and moaned and clawed at him. He finally gave up and then rolled over and snored.

Sadie lay there hot with need and thoughts of Brad O'Neal. She had to warn him about the Lieutenant. Finally, toward morning, she shook the young officer awake and sent him back to the fort.

It was not yet dawn when she sneaked out the back way and walked to the Texas Lily. It was a quiet morning and there was no one about. That was good. She'd just as soon it didn't get back to the lieutenant that she'd come here.

She knew where Brad's room was. She went around back and threw pebbles at his window. No answer. She threw another pebble.

Brad stumbled to the window, raised it, looking bleary-eyed as he looked out. "Sadie? What do you want?"

She looked around. "Let me in. I got important things to tell you."

He nodded and disappeared, then he stood in the

back door, motioning her in. She followed him into his room, but she didn't close the door behind her.

"God, Brad, you look like you been rode hard and put up wet."

"I feel that way, too. How come you're waking me up?"

"It's important." She watched him pour himself a whiskey.

"It better be. I probably would have slept 'til noon."

"You never used to drink like this, Brad."

"That's not any of your business," he snapped. "What is it you want?"

She moved closer. "I got news."

"You said that." He looked at her coldly.

"Boy, you've got the disposition of a mad bull. Livin' with Miss Primm doing that to you?"

"Leave her out of this," he snapped. He slammed the glass down, paced up and down the rug.

"You upset the lieutenant is gonna marry her and end up with half the Lily?"

"Now, what do you think?"

"Listen, he came to me last night after he left here."

"What'd he want?"

She laughed. "Now, what do all men want?"

"And after he's announced his engagement to Lily?"

"Ain't that a joke?" Sadie laughed but Brad didn't.

"Damn," he said. "And she thinks *I'm* a rascal. Tell me what you know, Sadie."

"Okay. The lieutenant hinted that it wasn't no accident about you gettin' shot."

He whirled on her. "That little bastard shot me?"

"Reckon so, from what he said. He may try

again since if he marries her and gets rid of you, he controls it all."

Brad strode up and down, swearing. "I'd tell her what a rat he is, but she wouldn't believe me."

Sadie caught his arm. "What do you care what she thinks? You know I always had a soft spot for you, Brad."

"I know. I'm sorry, Sadie—"

She put her finger to his lips to stop him. "It don't matter if you don't care as much for me as I do for you. If you'd just keep me around and make love to me once in awhile, that would be enough for me."

She looked up at him and saw the need in his eyes. She wished she had been the woman who fired that need, but it would be enough to her to be able to satisfy it. Before he could react, she slipped her arms around his neck and kissed him with all the passion she was capable of. For just a long moment, he let her kiss him and then she felt him pulling away from her, but still she clung to him.

"Well, what's going on here?"

They jumped apart, startled.

Lillian Primm stood in the doorway, arms akimbo, wearing a pale green dressing gown and she looked angry enough to take on a rattlesnake and give it first bite.

Brad jerked out of Sadie's arms. "Lily, I can explain—"

"This is really none of my business," Miss Primm said. "It's just that we're now running a respectable business, that's all. If you must have your harlots, please meet them some place else."

"Why, you—" Sadie began, "I oughta pull your hair out."

Lillian Primm glared at her, her eyes green as

glass. "Don't try my patience. Now please get out of my house."

"*Your* house? This ain't just your house—"

"Mr. O'Neal," Lillian snapped, "Get her out of here." Lillian was shocked to have followed the slight noises to Brad's room and find the pair in a hot embrace. The slut had probably spent the night with the rascal, satisfying that hunger Lillian had seen in his dark eyes last night.

Brad grabbed the indignant whore by the arm and turned her toward the back door. "She's right, Sadie. Clear out and we'll talk later."

"Okay, sport." Sadie cast one defiant glare toward Lillian and marched out the back door.

Lillian watched her go. She was both furious and something else. She wasn't sure what that emotion was she'd felt when she saw the tart in Brad's arms. "If you must bed her, do it at her place." She turned to go.

"Lily, it's not what you think."

"Do you think me a fool?" She raised her voice to an unladylike pitch. "You were pawing each other like you were about to go right down on the rug like two animals."

He reached out and grabbed her arm. "Okay, so we were kissing, but she really came to bring me information."

She yanked out of his grasp. "That's the most ridiculous thing I ever heard."

"Listen, she came to tell me that my shootin' wasn't an accident. Your precious lieutenant deliberately shot me."

"What? Now you've sunk to a new low," Lillian snarled at him. "It isn't enough that you've brought a notorious whore into what I'm trying to turn into a respectable hotel, you try to cover your tracks with a ridiculous story. Well, I don't believe a word of it!" She turned and marched out of the room.

Brad stared after her. There was no use trying to convince her, she'd never believe him. And there was only one way to get even with the dangerous officer. Brad would seduce Miss Primm before she married that rotten bastard and Buford gained control over Lily's half. *Seduce a woman?* Brad grinned. He could do that.

Chapter Fourteen

Dewey Cheatum stared out his office window and watched Lillian Primm driving by in her buggy, headed for the railroad station. Boy, had Lil McGinty made a mess of things by leaving that niece half the Texas Lily. On the other hand, Lillian seemed to be doing a thriving business the last couple of weeks using the big house as a hotel. He wondered idly as he ran his hand through his unkempt gray hair if Brad had ever found that big box in the closet and done what Lil had requested. He must remember to ask him about it sometime. At least Dewey no longer had the responsibility of sending money to that Boston bank like he'd been doing regularly for ten years now.

Somewhere in the distance, he heard the fort band playing, but not too well. Dewey winced as he lit his pipe. The major should stick to growing roses. Then he heard the whistle of the incoming train. He went to the door and looked out, watching Miss Primm alight from her buggy and step up on the platform, no doubt waiting for passengers. He peered down the street at the big white mansion. Yes, the Lily was big enough to make a nice hotel. It would make an even better mansion for a rich family, but of course, no one in town was wealthy enough to use it as a private residence.

The train roared into town, chugging and blowing its whistle. He watched Miss Primm approach three people who got off, a salesman and a young couple. The three nodded, gathered their luggage, and walked toward Lillian's buggy. Dewey grinned. She was a hard-headed little thing, and she might turn the notorious bordello into a respectable hotel yet. That, of course, would be over Brad's dead body.

Later that morning, Dewey saw Brad riding that black stallion into town. He went to the door and signaled him. "Come on in, we'll have a drink and visit some."

The tall man reined in, dismounted and tied his horse to the hitching rail. "You see any of the boys?" Brad asked. "I'd love a little game of poker."

"She's not allowing that, either?" Dewey tried to hide his grin as they entered the disorganized office. He gestured Brad toward a worn but comfortable leather chair. Lillian Primm was the first woman he could remember who had managed to deal with the stubborn gambler.

Brad flopped down in the chair and sighed. "The Texas Lily is now so damned respectable, I can hardly stand it."

"Are you turning a profit?"

Brad nodded grudgingly. "Just barely, but not like before. You know what she's got the gals doin'?"

"Not bouncin' on a mattress, I presume?"

Brad snorted and reached for a cigar. "They're waitin' tables. Waitresses, for God's sake."

Dewey laced his fingers together and grinned. "I thought you was planning on charming her to do anything you wanted?"

"Oh, hell," Brad scowled and lit his cigar, "she ain't—isn't your average woman. I ain't—am not gettin' no place with her."

"That's unusual for you," Dewey leaned back in his chair and put one boot on his untidy desk. "Women just usually fall on their backs for you."

"Well, it may have something to do with what happened with Sadie a couple of days ago." Brad admitted.

"Sadie? I thought she'd moved to the Bucket O' Blood?"

"She has. But the other morning, she slipped into my room about dawn, and the prim old maid caught her."

"Uh-oh. That's kind of hard to explain." *Only Brad*, he thought, *could have women slipping into his room.*

"I tried, but Lily was a mite unreasonable about it."

"Imagine that."

Brad blew smoke in the air. "She caught Sadie in my arms kissin' me."

Dewey threw back his head and laughed. "In some ways, Brad, you don't change."

"It really was innocent," the gambler insisted. "Sadie came to tell me Lieutenant Fortenbury was the one who shot me durin' our fake raid and it wasn't accidental."

"That short, sneaky bastard. He'd steal the butter off a sick beggar's biscuit." Dewey sat upright in his chair. "You tell Miss Primm?"

"Yeah, but she wouldn't believe me." Brad smoked his cigar and thought about that night of the wedding when she'd kissed him out on the porch. She'd raised his desire in a way he'd never thought any woman could, and he'd wanted to sweep her up in his arms and carry her to his bed. Of course he'd never admit that for the world. "I'm beginnin' to think no man can get the drawers off that strait-laced old maid."

"Sounds like the lieutenant is plannin' to."

That thought annoyed Brad no end. He didn't like the idea of losing his image as a lady-killer, and worse yet, he hated the thought of his Lily in bed with that pantywaist. Buford couldn't handle her anyway—he wasn't man enough. "So what should I do about the lieutenant, Dewey?"

"Legally, or as a Texan?" The old lawyer shrugged. "You can't prove anything, and no sheriff or court would take the word of a whore like Sadie—even against a Yankee. I'd just say watch your back and be ready in case he tries again."

"As a Texan, I'm yearnin' to beat the hell out of him."

"You hit him and then Miss Primm will feel sorry for him and think you're a bigger savage than she already does."

"I've got one more idea," Brad smiled and tossed his cigar in the spittoon. "I could seduce Miss Primm and then tell the young bastard so he'd break the engagement. You know he wouldn't take the leavin's of a rascal like me."

Dewey frowned at him. "Kissing and telling ain't something a Texan would do to a lady."

Brad winked. "I'm gonna do more than kiss her. I'll do anything to keep Buford from endin' up ownin' half the Lily."

"Besides," Dewey reminded him, "your charm hasn't worked on her so far."

That really annoyed Brad. "Well, I ain't really put my mind to it yet. I still think I can get her drawers off." He started toward the door and stopped. "You reckon we could get the boys together for poker? I miss the old days."

"Where? At the Lily?" Dewey stood up.

"Are you jokin'? She's even outlawed the bar except for a little wine and maybe some mint juleps. Now what kind of Texans drink wine?" He snorted with disgust and headed out the door. "*Adios.* I'll keep you up on what's happenin'. I just thought someone else ought to know about the Lieutenant in case you find me shot in the back some night."

"Be careful," Dewey warned. "Fortenbury is yellow enough to do that. Maybe you should tell the major."

Brad smiled. "And tell him what? Nope, I think I'll have to deal with him myself. Now I think I'll go to Pug's and see if he's got any doodads that might please a lady."

"Sadie?"

"She ain't no lady. I mean Lily. I got to stop her from marryin' that damned little snot. He's as slick as calf slobber." Brad left and walked down the sidewalk.

It was only after he was gone that Dewey remembered he'd forgotten to ask Brad if he'd found that mysterious box. Oh well, he shrugged. He'd mention it next time. *How important could it be?*

Brad went into Pug's store. "Hey there, *hombre.*"

"Long time, no see." Pug grinned and shook hands. "We ever gonna get together and play poker again?"

"Maybe in Dewey's office. Lily don't like gamblin' at the place no more."

"You lettin' a woman boss you around?" Pug's bushy eyebrows went up.

"She just seems to have the knack of gettin' her

own way," Brad admitted with a shake of his head. "I tell her how it's gonna be and she just smiles and does it her way."

"That ain't like you, Brad." Pug swatted a fly.

"Well, she ain't your average woman," Brad said. "And as a hotel, we're startin' to make some profit. You know, a good hotel will bring lots of new folks into town."

"So does a good whorehouse."

"I meant *respectable* people." Brad said.

"Now you're beginning to sound like her," Pug said.

"I'll go along with it until I change her mind," Brad assured him.

"She don't look like the type to be swayed, that Yankee." Pug swatted another fly.

"Well, I'm workin' on it but she's as stubborn as an army mule," Brad said. "You got any fancy scent?"

"You mean, perfume?" Pug blinked in disbelief.

"Yeah, some fine stuff, not something sluts would wear."

"Here's a dozen bottles in the counter you can sniff."

"You can't tell what it really smells like just sniffin' the bottle." Brad complained.

"You want I should dab some on?"

"Well, there ain't nobody around," Brad nodded. "Put a little behind each ear and then let me sniff it."

Pug shook his head. "I don't know about that."

"You wanta sell some expensive perfume or not?"

"All right, but if I go home smellin' of perfume, what's my old lady gonna say?"

"Tell her you was with Sadie at the Bucket O' Blood."

Pug snorted. "You tryin' to get me kilt?" He dabbed a little from the first bottle behind his ears.

Brad closed his eyes and sniffed. "What's that called?"

"*New York Night.*"

Brad shook his head. "That don't smell like Lily. Gimme another."

Pug splashed some on his bulldogish face. "This here is called *Lady Love.*"

Brad leaned close and sniffed.

About that time, some of the Beautification Committee walked in. "Well, la te da, what you boys doin'?" They were all grinning like polecats. "This place smells better'n a whorehouse."

"Nothin' smells better than a whorehouse," Dimples said.

Brad sighed wistfully. "The Texas Lily used to smell like that. Now it smells like soap, furniture polish, and apple pie. Pug, you got anything else?"

"Well, I got one bottle I let the drummer talk me into buying, but I ain't sold it yet. Costs too damned much for most cowboys and soldiers." He reached into the display case and brought out a fancy bottle. "Here, boys, take a whiff of this. It's called *Passionate Parisian Nights.*"

Brad shook his head. "Even if it smells good, I don't think Miss Primm would be caught dead wearin' a scent with a name like that. It ain't respectable enough for a lady."

Pug scratched his head and then dug into the display case again. "Here's something almost as expensive, called *Spring Blossom.*"

"Now that sounds more like her—and a pretty bottle, too." Brad grabbed it and took a sniff. It was a light floral fragrance. "I think this'll do."

Luke grinned. "You givin' perfume to another man's fiancée? He ain't gonna like that."

"Good!" Brad snapped. "Maybe he'll call me out.

I'd like nothin' better than for Lily to see me whup up on him like a big dog on a mangy pup."

"Lily?" Dimples said, "you call her Lily?"

"Oh, shut up." Brad laid out some money for the perfume and put the bottle in his pocket.

"We still got faith in you, Brad," Luke patted him on the back.

"Nobody can beat a Texan when he really goes after something," Brad nodded. "Wish me luck."

"You're gonna need it with that Yankee lady," Pug said. "She seems as stubborn as any Texas gal."

"Aw, women are all the same," Brad said as he left. But he wasn't sure he believed that any more. Lily was different in a good sort of way, even if she was a Yankee.

He returned to the Lily. Lillian Primm was bustling about, setting tables. "Where have you been?" she asked and she didn't smile. "I've got three new guests besides the two we already have. Delilah is fixing stew but I promised them your barbecue for tomorrow."

"I'll be happy to do that," He gave her his warmest smile. "Reckon you've got a good idea here, Lily, I mean, about the hotel and all."

For once, she smiled back. "And doesn't it feel good to be respectable for a change?"

"I don't know. I've never been respectable."

"Well, now you're about to find out. We're showing a profit already. Soon you won't have to stay up late drinking and gambling, you can go to bed at nine o'clock like respectable people."

Why in the hell would anyone want to go to bed at nine o'clock? He thought as he watched Lily's little bustle on that blue dress waggle as she walked away from him. Well, he could think of one reason.

The last two girls, Rosita and Flo, came downstairs dressed in plain pink dresses with little white aprons. They wore no face paint and they looked as respectable as choir girls. Lily gave them orders and they bustled about, setting tables and putting out white linen napkins.

"Uh, Lily, have you got a minute?" He felt the little bottle in his pocket.

"I told you I was busy." Her voice and expression were cold. It appeared she hadn't forgotten about catching Sadie in his arms.

"All right, it can wait until after dinner then, or maybe this evenin'."

"Good," she smiled. "Now, Brad, you wash up and be charming to our customers. If they like our place, they'll spread the word to other travelers."

Brad? Had she really called him 'Brad'? He liked the way she said his name. "Sure. I'll be charmin'."

And he was charming. He was so charming that two ladies were almost swooning in their soup to catch his every word.

The next morning, he caught Lily walking through the main room. "Was I charmin' enough for you yesterday?"

She frowned at him. "You didn't need to be that charming. Those women were ready to pull off their drawers."

Was she jealous? Lily? Naw.

He tried to look contrite. "I was just doin' what you told me. I reckon you're still angry about Sadie?"

"Now why should I be?" Her voice dripped sarcasm. "I hear a noise downstairs and find a slut in your arms."

"I'm sorry about that, but you know men are just weak, vile creatures whose thoughts seldom get above their belts. That Sadie was there to tempt me."

"If you've got to have her, go down to the Bucket."

"She ain't the one who tempts me, Lily, no matter how much she throws herself at me."

"It didn't look like you were fighting her off."

"She—she caught me by surprise."

"Uh-huh." Her mind seemed busy elsewhere. "You know, perhaps the hotel needs a little gentlemens' lounge where we serve liquor and the men could smoke."

Now it was his turn to blink. "You mean that?"

"Certainly. You could stock some fine brandy, and of course the mint juleps would be nice—and maybe we could serve some sherry."

"Sherry? That's a lady's drink." He laughed.

"I'll have you know, Buford says he prefers sherry."

"I rest my case," he said and then realized he was off on the wrong foot again. "I'm sorry, Lily, I shouldn't have said that." He tried to look contrite. "When I'm around you, I act like a damned fool."

"I won't argue with that." she said.

Touché. A growing suspicion gnawed at his mind like a rat in a corn crib. "Uh, Lily, just where did you intend to set up this gentlemen's lounge?"

She brought her hand to her chin and leaned on it thoughtfully. "Your office."

"My office?"

"You needn't squawk like a turkey gobbler being chased with an axe," she complained. "After dinner, we'll discuss some other changes I have in mind."

Oh, he had to put a stop to this before it got any worse. "Perhaps this afternoon we could take a drive."

"Where?" She looked at him with suspicion.

"Well, I thought we might drive out and see some land I own at the edge of town."

"Hmm, maybe we could sell it and use the money to improve the Texas Lily."

"Sell my land?"

"Oh my, you're squawking again."

"Miss Lily," he said, forcing himself to smile although he wanted to shake her. "The land under discussion does not belong to the partnership. It belongs to me."

"Oh? Well, we'll look at it anyway, now that we're in agreement." She marched into the kitchen.

Agreement? He hadn't agreed to anything . . . or had he? When he was around Lily, she confused him. This headstrong woman thought she could just twist him around her little finger. Hell, she'd find out he was not like Fortenbury.

They had a delicious dinner, complete with a huge beef roast, corn on the cob, apple pie, and homemade ice cream. They had three hotel guests plus five who had come just for dinner. The girls managed to set the table and serve the meal, only spilling soup in a gentleman's lap once.

The guests all leaned back with happy sighs. "Honestly," said one drummer, "that was the best apple pie I ever had and the coffee was hot, just like I like it."

"Gentlemen," Brad pushed back his chair, "would you like to adjourn to the gentlemen's lounge for cigars and brandy?"

All the gentlemens' eyes lit up. "I say, this is a really first-rate hotel."

Lily gave him a nod of triumph that made him want to shake her, but he only said, "Certainly. The Texas Lily is the best hotel in all Texas."

* * *

Later in the afternoon, Brad had the stableboy bring the buggy around front. "Miss Lily," he bowed with a flourish, "I promised you an afternoon drive."

Lillian hesitated, yet yearned to go. "I'm not sure what Buford would think—"

"You don't trust your own partner?" He looked hurt.

Actually, her common sense told her she shouldn't trust him any farther than she could throw Herman the goat, but she didn't want to be rude and say so. "Thank you for allowing your office to be used as a lounge."

He appeared to be gritting his teeth but managed a smile. "My pleasure, dear lady."

She warmed to him. "I'm looking forward to the drive." And she meant it, even while she sensed she was playing with fire.

They went out on the porch and down the steps. Brad put his big hands on her waist and lifted her up into the buggy. For just an instant he hesitated, his hands warm on her narrow waist while he looked deep into her eyes. She remembered the way he had kissed her and took a deep breath, knowing she should never allow herself to be alone with Brad O'Neal. Then he set her gently on the seat.

"I know how to drive a buggy," she said.

"Maybe so, but I'm drivin'." His tone brooked no argument. He was definitely in charge.

"All right. Nice day, isn't it?"

"The weather in Texas is always perfect."

"I don't think so," she disputed. He got up on the seat, snapped his little whip, and the bay horse started off at a brisk trot. "I hear the summers are as hot as hell with the lid off and the winters sometimes have blue northers that freeze people in their tracks."

"For a Texan, that's perfect."

She decided she wouldn't argue with him. The rogue was stubborn and determined. Well, they had that in common. The weather was warm, and the lilies were in the last stages of bloom. "I don't know why my aunt planted only common orange day lilies," she complained. "They're so ordinary."

"Lil was just plain folks, nothing snooty about her," he said as they went down the drive at a brisk trot. Herman glanced up, then returned to eating the flowers around the bird bath. It was almost as if he protected that rusty thing.

"And you think I am pretentious?" She glared at Brad.

He grinned and she was aware of how white his teeth were in his tanned face. "Miss Lily, I don't know that big word. Now, let's not fight like two coyotes over a carcass, let's just enjoy the ride, shall we?"

"You have a way with words, Mr. O'Neal."

He grinned and winked. "Call me Brad."

She was already regretting coming on this drive. She really feared being alone with Brad O'Neal. "Nonsense," she said.

"What?"

"Nothing."

He made pleasant small-talk about the town, but she hardly listened as she grew more and more ill at ease sitting next to him. He took a narrow dirt road and, still within sight of town, reined in. "Here, it is, it's only about five acres, but it's pretty as a Sunday go-to-meetin' hat."

She looked around. "It's more than pretty, with all these big live oak trees trailing Spanish moss. It would make a lovely town park."

"Park? Lady, this is where I plan to build a bigger

and better saloon." He jumped down and came around to lift her down. When he put her on the ground, he didn't remove his hands from her waist. He stood there looking down at her, so close, she could feel the heat from his big body.

Oh my. Now she remembered why she didn't want to be alone with him. She recalled that kiss— that consuming kiss and she was afraid . . . of what? She couldn't decide if she was afraid he would kiss her again or that he wouldn't. *Lillian, are you out of your mind,* she scolded herself. *You are a respectable, engaged woman.*

She managed to pull out of his grasp. "It is a lovely piece of land. Right over in that meadow would be a good place for flowers and some grass."

"It is beautiful, ain't—isn't it?" She felt him step up close behind her. "I bought it last year, when Lil and I was talkin' of expandin'." His arms slipped around her waist. "I brung you a gift," he said.

She hesitated, not wanting to hurt his feelings by correcting his grammar. She stood looking down at those big hands, trying to decide whether to make an issue of him touching her. While she hesitated, he pulled her back against him. "Uh, Mr. O'Neal."

"Call me Brad." His face was so close to the back of her head, his warm breath stirred her hair and raised goose bumps on her neck.

"Remember, I'm an engaged woman."

"How could I forget?" His breath stirred her hair and his big hands seemed to encircle her so possessively. "I got you some perfume."

"You—you shouldn't have done that." Her heart began beating harder.

"I wanted to. When I smelled it, it reminded me of you." He put his face against her hair, sniffing it.

"Uh, Mr. O'Neal, I don't think you should—"

"Call me Brad," he whispered.

She turned in his arms, meaning to protest that this wasn't proper. Then she looked up at him and his mouth seemed so sensual, his brown eyes dark and intense.

"Lily?" He whispered as if asking permission. She must not give it. She must not surrender and lose control of her carefully planned life. "Lily?"

She didn't mean to, but he kept looking down at her, all wide shoulders and virile body. His big hands came up and took her face between them, very gently tilting her face up to his. She must not do this, but she couldn't control her lips opening ever so slightly, her eyes closing as his lips came down to cover hers.

Chapter Fifteen

She gasped and moaned slightly, throwing back her head, surrendering to the tantalizing, paralyzing touch of his tongue across her lips. Without thinking, Lillian not only let him kiss her, she returned the kiss with ardor as it deepened. Her small hands went to the back of his tanned neck as his arms pulled her closer until she could feel the heat and the power of the man all the way down her body. His lips felt soft and full and now the tip of his tongue begged entry to her mouth. She didn't mean to, but she opened her lips as his tongue teased there, then slipped inside.

Lillian trembled, clinging to him, wanting even more. She wasn't sure if it was her heart or his that pounded so hard, but it didn't matter. She felt the cords of his neck under her fingertips and the softness of his black hair that curled in her hands. His manhood was hard and throbbing against the softness of her sheer dress. When she took a deep breath, he smelled of shaving lotion, soap, and tobacco and she tasted the sweetness of his mouth.

Lillian pulled away, gasping. He looked as shocked as she felt.

"Lily, oh, Lily," he whispered and she started to protest that this was not at all proper but his mouth covered hers again and she forgot all that. He scooped her up in his arms and kissed her cheek and trailed kisses down her neck, "Oh, Lily, what are you doing to me?" he whispered as he leaned over and sat her against the trunk of a big tree.

The grass was soft as he sat down beside her, took her hands in his and kissed the backs of them so very gently. The sunlight dappled his face through the shade of the leaves and she was faintly aware that somewhere, a bird sang. She saw her own hands tremble, and she reached out and ran one slender hand through his tousled hair. "I—I think we shouldn't be here." she said. "I am an engaged woman."

He lay his head in her lap and looked up at her earnestly. "If you want to go, we will," he said and waited.

She knew she must say that, but she couldn't seem to do anything but look down into those intense dark eyes.

After a moment he reached up, caught her head in his hands, and kissed her again. She felt her fiery hair come loose and tumble down so that it hung around him like a veil. He tangled his fingers in her locks and pulled her down to him, kissing her, then lay his face against her breast.

Her dress was a sheer green lawn, and through it she could feel the heat of his rugged face against her breast. It seemed to burn like a branding iron. She knew she should scramble to her feet and demand that he drive her back to the Texas Lily, but somehow she couldn't make herself do that. Her pulse seemed to be roaring in her ears and she was intensely warm all over.

He turned his face ever so slightly and kissed her

breast through the fabric. She leaned back against the trunk of the tree and let him nuzzle there. She closed her eyes and felt his mouth, wet hot through the fabric. She gasped, breathing hard, her mouth open as his hand reached up, pulling down the lace neck of the dress so that his mouth was now on her nipple. His tongue teasing there felt like fire and yet she pulled him to her, wanting still more. "Look at me," he commanded, his breath hot against her bare breast. "Lily, look at me."

She opened her eyes slowly and met his smoldering gaze even as he turned his head and deliberately kissed her breast, laving it with his tongue. She knew she should demand that he stop, but all she could do was pull him closer still, until his mouth took her whole breast, sucking hard. His hand pushed up her dress and stroked her thigh through the dainty white lace of her drawers. She had never felt such delicious sensations in her life. If he wanted to slam her down and mount her right here in the open like some common slut, she wasn't sure she could or would stop him.

Instead, she leaned over and kissed his cheek, letting her thighs fall apart as he stroked her thigh.

"I want you, Lily," he whispered huskily. "I want to be one with you in a way you've never done before."

Oh God, she was so weak when it came to this man. Hadn't she fought this feeling since the first time she had seen him? She had to change the subject. "What—what about the gift?"

"Perfume," he smiled. Reaching in his pocket, he brought out a pretty bottle. "Let me put some on you."

As she watched, mesmerized, he took off the lid, put a dab on his finger, and set the bottle on the grass. Then very slowly and deliberately, he ran his finger down between her breasts.

"I—I don't think . . ." she said as his fingers played up and down beneath the lace of her bodice.

"Mmm, smells wonderful," he murmured. He bent his head, sniffing her skin so close, she could feel his warm breath between her breasts.

Oh my! This had been a mistake. "We—we really should go," she began.

"Anytime you say, Lily," he whispered. He kissed her again, and his hand went up her thigh to the opening of her drawers to touch her most private place. She felt suddenly intensely warm and damp there.

She forgot everything but how it felt to be in his arms with his face pressed against her breasts. He came up and took her in an embrace, kissing her deeply, holding her against the tree as his fingers explored the warmth of her very depths. Beneath her, the grass felt soft, and somewhere a bird sang as a slight breeze blew across the wooded landscape. For this moment, there was nothing in the world but the two of them and the slight scent of the perfume he had trailed between her breasts. Nothing mattered but being in his arms.

"You are beautiful," he gasped. "I never realized how lovely you are." He kissed her again with such an intense passion, that it was almost as if he meant it.

No one had every told her she was beautiful before. Her intellect told her it wasn't true, but she couldn't pull away from the heat of this wild embrace. She knew she should stop it, but she couldn't bring herself to do that because she wanted him to touch there—she wanted . . . she was not sure what this emotion was that was raging through her, but she did not reject him or object as the kiss deepened. His hands moved her ever so gently so that

she lay on the grass and as he kissed her, she felt his
fingers fumbling with the buttons of her bodice,
and still she did not object.

Now his fingers felt like gentle flames pulling
aside the lace of her corset cover so that her breasts
were bared to his mouth. She took a deep breath
and trembled as he whispered, "soft as silk—so
lovely."

Her common sense told her she should slap his
face and scramble to her feet in indignation. Yet
with his hand caressing her nipple, she was power-
less to do that. Even as she had that thought, he
kissed along her throat, his breath warm on her
neck. She held her breath, tense with need and ex-
pectation, and then his lips found her breast again.
He kissed and caressed there.

Lillian gasped and arched up to meet his lips,
wanting him to take more of her breast in his
mouth. She put her hands on his neck and pulled
him down, encouraging him to touch and taste and
tease her until she was shaking and gasping for air.
"Oh, Brad, ohh. . . ."

"Tell me you want me." He brought his face back
up to hers and kissed the side of her mouth. "Tell
me!" He kissed her eyelids and her cheeks. He was
breathing harder than she was, his face dark with
desire, his brown eyes intense as he took her face in
his hands and kissed her passionately.

Did she want him? She had never had feelings
like these before. Of course she wanted and
needed him. At this moment, if he could quench
the fire burning within her, she didn't care that
they were out in the woods. She yearned to mesh
like two wild things.

Just as she was about to whisper consent, a sound
drifted suddenly on the breeze—the off-key, discor-

dant sound of the army band practicing, with the tuba going "oompa, oompa, oompa."

Buford. Oh my God. She sat up abruptly, smoothing her rumpled dress. "Are we out of our minds? I'm a respectable, engaged woman. Take me home this instant!"

Brad looked confused and angry. "Lily—"

"Miss Primm to you," she snapped and tried to stand up, but he was sitting on the edge of her skirt. She stumbled and fell back into his arms. "If you don't mind."

"I do mind," he groaned, "but I reckon that's the end of it."

"How dare you!" She grabbed up the perfume bottle and doused him with it. She was still straightening her dress and buttoning her bodice as she marched, nose in the air, toward the buggy.

He stood staring after her, slightly confused and reeking of *Spring Blossom*. He had only meant to seduce the prim old maid, but when he kissed her, passion had taken over. He had forgotten everything but the girl in his arms, the taste of her mouth, milk-white skin, and the most delicate, perfect breasts he'd ever touched. He wanted her as he had never wanted a woman, his pulse pounding in his ears. "Lily?"

Even as he watched, she hiked up her skirts and climbed into the buggy, showing a flash of trim ankle that hinted at long, slim legs. He couldn't seem to move, staring at this vision of unconsummated passion, with her mane of red hair falling about her shoulders, her clothing in disarray. As he stood there dumbstruck, she snapped the little whip and took off at a brisk trot.

"Hey!" he yelled after her. "That's my buggy!"

"It's *our* buggy!" She yelled back over her shoulder and kept driving.

"Well, damn!" He stood there looking after the departing buggy, listening to the discordant sounds of Major Bottoms' band. At this moment, he'd like to stuff young Buford into his tuba. The raucous racket had interrupted the hottest passion Brad had ever experienced. If he'd only had another five minutes to . . . five minutes, hell. He wanted hours of the ecstasy of Lily's arms, hours and hours of it. Not only hadn't he gotten young Buford out of her thoughts, but there was the Town Beatification Committee to consider. They would laugh like a pack of coyotes if Brad didn't manage to seduce the girl.

The buggy was fast disappearing into the distance, and the June afternoon had turned hot and stifling as only east Texas could be. It was some distance back to the house. Brad, like most Texans, wore boots. And as with most Texans, "walk" was a dirty four-letter word that was not in his vocabulary. Well, there was no help for it. He gritted his teeth, ran his hand through his black hair, and started back along the dusty road. He couldn't keep his mind off Lily and how she had surprised him with her hot ardor. In those few moments under the live oak tree, he had wanted her more than he had ever wanted a woman. That scared him because he felt like he was losing control. Brad was always in control when making love to a woman. He was beginning to wonder if he could outwit this headstrong wench. Of course, she was pretty smart . . . for a woman. What was he to do? With a resigned sigh, he set out on the long walk home.

Lillian did not look back at his shout but kept driving. She did not want him in this buggy with her where he might touch her hand or worse yet, slip his arm around her. She took a deep breath. The scent of the perfume came to her, and in her mind, once again his fingers trailed between her breasts. In the distance, the army band played and the tuba went "oompa, oompa."

"Oh Buford, have I been unfaithful to you? How could I, a respectable woman of superior lineage have let myself be pawed and kissed by that low-class Texan? Her mind returned to the taste and heat of his mouth, the soft caress of his lips on her breast. Oh my goodness, how could she ever explain trampy sensations like that to a high-class gentleman like Buford? She couldn't even explain it to herself. One moment they had been looking at the landscape, the next he was kissing her, the next she was on the ground with his hand under her skirts and his tongue between her lips. She must be losing her mind to surrender like Grant took Richmond. She was putty in Brad O'Neal's hands. It wasn't for nothing everyone in town said he could talk a dog off a meat wagon or a cow out of her calf.

Since she couldn't trust herself any more around that randy rascal, she needed to marry Buford as soon as possible to stave off temptation. Surely one man's kisses couldn't be that different from another's. She remembered Buford's wet, smacking kisses and knew she was lying to herself.

She pulled up in front of the Lily and hopped down, calling for José. As he came around the house, did the boy stare at her rumpled appearance, or was it only her imagination? She felt her cheeks flush as she rushed up the steps and into the house. She nearly collided with Delilah, who paused and stared at her. "You all right, Miss?"

She must look a mess. "Of course I am." She marched up the stairs with as much dignity as she could muster, considering her dress had smudges of green from the grass, and there were leaves and dandelions in her hair, which hung in disarray around her shoulders.

That damned scoundrel. He had deliberately tried to seduce her and she had almost fallen for it. Why, he was probably laughing right now. Of course he was having to walk a distance in boots, so he might not be laughing at all. The thought cheered her as she went into her room, closing and locking the door. She must oversee supper for the hotel guests, and Buford was coming to call tonight. Would he be able to look into her eyes and see the guilt there? Even knowing what a rascal Brad was, it was difficult to resist him. Why, judging from his smooth manner, he'd probably made love to a hundred women. The thought annoyed her.

She washed up and changed into one of Lil's dresses, which was pale pink with lots of lace. She put her hair up in a mass of curls. Then she pinched her cheeks and sucked her lips to give them a rosy glow.

Downstairs, she heard the front door slam and the sound of angry boots stomping around in the front hall. She opened her door tentatively and peered over the railing. Brad looked hot, angry, and disheveled. Delilah came out of the kitchen.

"Why, Mister Brad, what—?"

"Don't even ask!"

"Okay, but you sure smell good!"

"Oh, hell!" he snapped, stomping back to his room and slamming the door so hard it echoed through the house.

Lillian smiled. He was tired and out of sorts, which served him right. She floated down the stairs, a serene smile on her lips. Delilah looked at her as she descended. "My, Miss Lillian, you do look like your mother."

"Thank you. When did you meet her?"

The woman paused a moment in confusion, then blurted, "I think one time Miss Lil showed me her picture."

"Oh. Have you supper ready for our guests?"

"Yes ma'am, if'fen I can get the girls to set the table. It would be nice if Mr. Brad would entertain the men with drinks in the gentlemen's lounge. He sure looked mad as a hornet-stung hound dog—wonder what happened to him?"

"I'm sure I wouldn't have any idea," Lillian said airily. "I suppose I can set up cigars and drinks for our guests."

She was still in the lounge when the first of their guests came in. "Hello, gentlemen, there's whiskey in the decanter and fine cigars in the humidor."

The taller man grinned at her. "I do say it's a treat to see such a pretty lady. Are you Mrs. O'Neal?"

Lillian frowned. "Certainly not. We're only business partners."

About that time, Brad came into the room looking freshly scrubbed. He still smelled faintly of perfume. The guests sniffed and looked puzzled, but Lillian only smiled and avoided his gaze.

Brad said, "Good evening, gentlemen, let me pour you a drink before dinner."

The shorter one nodded and laughed. "I do believe this is the best hotel I've stayed in for a long time."

Lillian nodded to him and blushed prettily. "Why, thank you. Do pass the word to other travelers, won't you?" As she started out of the room with Brad glaring at her, she called back over her shoulder, "supper will be on the table in a few minutes. Mr. O'Neal is a master of barbecue. I hope you gentlemen like it."

"Yes," Brad said, glowering at her, "I like to build a fire under everything and let it smolder."

She felt her face flame and she fled the room, leaving the gentlemen to their liquor and cigars. Oh, he was mad, all right. Well, let him grumble. She hoped he had blisters on his feet from the walk home.

Supper passed pleasantly enough and then as they got up, the doorbell rang and Delilah came out of the kitchen to answer it.

"I believe that will be my fiancé coming to call," Lillian said, and she smiled pleasantly at Brad, who glowered at her.

Buford came into the entry hall, twisting his hat with nervous hands. He looked as though he expected Brad to pick him up and throw him back down the steps.

"Buford, dear," Lillian went to meet him with outstretched hands, then linked her arm in his. "Everyone, this is my fiancé. We're to be married soon."

Buford looked around at Brad as if he might break and run like a jackrabbit. "Are you ready, Miss Lillian? I've borrowed the major's buggy."

"Oh, I do love driving with a *gentleman*." She emphasized the word as she got her lace shawl off the coatrack by the stairs. "Don't wait up for us," she announced. "We may be out a long, long time."

"Wow!" Buford's eyes widened. "I mean, anything you say, Miss Lillian. It's a pleasant evening."

"Oh Buford, it's your company that makes it so pleasant." she said and looked pointedly at the scowling Texan. "Well, tootle-loo. We're off."

Behind her as they left, she heard Brad growling under his breath.

"What's eating him?" Buford complained as he

helped her into the buggy. "He looked like he'd tear my head off."

She shrugged as Buford got up on the seat and slapped the horse with the reins. "Who knows? He's just a low-class rascal, and let's not talk about him, shall we not? I want to talk about marrying you, Buford, you're so fascinating."

He perked up. "You really think so?"

"Certainly. I want to hear about all your ambitions and future plans."

That got him started. She hadn't realized how often young Buford used the word 'I'. In fact, he could hardly get through a sentence without it. She kept thinking he might at least mention her and what the future held for the two of them, but he did not. She decided she could let her mind wander if she only nodded and said, "Oh, really?" and, "And then what did you say?" to him while he droned on and on. She tried to listen to him—she really did—but her mind kept wandering back to this afternoon and the wild scene under the big live oak tree with the Spanish moss casting moving shadows as the breeze blew through the limbs. It was a good thing it was dark so that Buford could not see her blush.

Finally, Buford pulled up along the road under some trees. When she looked around, she realized it was the same area where she had been this afternoon.

"Shall we get down?" he said.

"Uh, no, I don't think so." She shook her head. "It—there might be bugs in the grass."

"Bugs? You think so?" He sounded alarmed.

"Definitely."

The grass was probably still matted down where she and Brad had embraced this afternoon.

"Oh." Buford sounded disappointed. "I only thought . . . never mind."

She definitely did not want him to kiss her, she thought, remembering the wet kiss he'd given her the night they became engaged. It was like being licked in the mouth by a friendly hound dog. "Yes, there might be spiders out in that grass, Buford, or even snakes."

"Snakes?" he squeaked. She had his attention now. "I—I never thought of that."

"So we can just sit here in the buggy and enjoy the evening." The seat wasn't designed for hot, close embraces. Unfortunately, the old horse had gas, and sitting behind the steed was fast becoming an ordeal. She coughed and fanned herself with her hand. "Maybe we should go home, Buford."

"Go home? I thought you said we were staying out late?"

"Did I say that?"

"Yes," he nodded, "You looked right at that gambler and said that."

To annoy Brad, she thought. "Let's just drive around the perimeter of the fort," she said.

They drove around the fort and down Main Street. There were cowboys leaning against the hitching rail in front of the Bucket O' Blood Saloon as the buggy passed and they harassed the young lieutenant. "Hey, there, Yankee boy, does your mama know you're out?"

"Hey, there, Lieutenant, how about buyin' some *real* men a drink?"

"Just ignore them, Buford," Lillian ordered. "They're just looking for a fight."

"A fight?" Buford's eyebrows went up and he snapped the reins to make the horse go faster. "I don't stoop to fisticuffs, even though I've had lessons."

She sighed, comparing him to Brad O'Neal. She

imagined the Texas ruffian was good with his fists. "We can sit in the swing out on the lawn at the Lily."

"The goat's usually out there," he said.

"Well, maybe he won't be tonight. Honestly, Buford. You're afraid of a goat?"

"He's a big goat," Buford defended himself.

"I'll chase him off," she soothed. "And it'll be pleasant sitting out under the stars in the dark."

He grinned at her. Why had she never noticed he was slightly buck-toothed? "How romantic. I have a little present for you, my dear."

She was flattered but not too happy. What had she let herself in for? This was getting more and more serious and the thought of sleeping with this man made her shudder.

"Miss Lillian, are you cold?"

"Uh, not at all." She didn't want to give him the excuse to put his scrawny arm around her.

They started up the drive to the Lily and the goat was nowhere in sight. Buford breathed an audible sigh of relief. "I'll just leave the buggy standing in the drive, and we'll sit in that swing out in the lily bed."

"All right." She sighed and wondered how long she would have to stay out here.

He got down and came around to help her out. He tried to put his hands on her waist and lift her, but he couldn't handle her weight and stumbled. She got down quickly to keep him from dropping her. "It is a lovely night," she said. They walked out into the center of the lily garden and sat down on the creaky old swing. She scooted as far as possible to her side.

Buford turned and looked anxiously toward the big house. "You think they can see us out here?"

"I don't know. I don't think so."

Lieutenant Fortenbury stared at the big white

bird bath. "That's an ugly thing. I hope you decide to junk it when you take over here."

"Junk it? I thought it was rather lovely."

"Well, if you think so, keep it then."

"Remember Brad gets some say in this."

"Honestly, Lillian, I wish you'd stop calling him Brad," he said. He turned toward her and took one of her hands. His were small and sweaty, but she managed not to pull away. "I have an engagement gift for you, my dear."

Engagement. Only hours ago, she had been about to surrender her virginity to another man. She had never felt so guilty and unworthy. "Oh really? Buford, you shouldn't have." It was probably a ring and she sighed. How could she marry one man when her lips still longed for the other?

"Well, it's a valuable family heirloom," he explained, digging in his vest. "It's classic and very tasteful, just like you. I know Mama will be delighted for you to have it."

"Oh Buford, I don't know what to say. I'm sure your mother and I will like each other."

He beamed at her. "You are kindred spirits. You'll love Mama, and if we go back East, we can all live together."

"*If* we go back East? I can't imagine why we'd want to stay here." Texas reminded her too much of Brad. She needed to get far, far away from him.

"Here's your gift, my darling." He held out his hand and opened it slowly.

"Oh my! Buford, it's beautiful." It really was so exquisite it took her breath away. The moonlight sparkled on the diamond lily-shaped pin in his hand.

Chapter Sixteen

"Oh, Buford, it's beautiful! I can't tell you how—"

"Here, let me pin it on you," he said with a smile and before she could move, his hands fumbled with her bodice.

"Let me do it," she demanded and took it away from him. She really did not want him pawing her bosom. That made her think of Brad's deft, skillful touch and she gritted her teeth, hating the randy Texan.

Buford rattled on, "Since it's an old family heirloom, I thought you should have it, because you'll be part of the Fortenbury family."

She paused, uncertain about what she had let herself in for. "Buford, perhaps you should wait to give this to me when we're sure—"

"Sure? Of course I'm sure. We'll be uniting two blue-blooded families and produce superior children. Oh, one thing though, my dear Lillian. Perhaps you shouldn't wear it around town."

"Why not?"

He chewed his lip and his wispy mustache wiggled. "Well, you know how villainous these low-class Texans are, someone might rob you."

"I trust all the people at the Lily," she said.

He took her hand in his damp soft one. "My dear, you are so innocent. Why, I think any of them, especially that gambler, would steal it in a heartbeat."

Somehow his sanctimonious tone annoyed her. As much as she disapproved of that Texan, she didn't think he would steal. "All right, whatever you say. It's wonderful just to own it. I've never had anything so fine." She stared at the sparkle of the diamond lily in her hand.

"I think this calls for a kiss." He leaned over and planted a wet, cold smack on her lips before she could move away from him. She pictured fifty years of kisses from this man, and even worse. The thought made her shudder.

"My dear, are you cold? Perhaps I should put my arm around you and—"

"No, in fact, I'm too warm." She scooted to the far side of the seat and fanned herself with her hand.

"You know, now that we're engaged my dear, it's perfectly respectable for us to spoon a little."

"Spoon?" she blinked.

He smiled sheepishly. "You know, a little kissing—"

"Uh, Buford, I'm from a *very* respectable family. Why, my dear mother would roll over in her grave if she thought I would do anything intimate before marriage and our family believes in *long* engagements."

"Oh? Very well." He sounded annoyed.

The swing creaked loudly in the silence. From the stable out back, she heard the faint bleating of Herman the goat.

"I'd like to shoot that filthy beast," Buford muttered.

"If you do, Brad would mop up the floor with you."

"'Brad'? You're still using that familiar name for him?" He drew himself up proudly. "Besides, I'll have you know I've had lessons in fisticuffs at Harvard. I think I can defend myself."

She could envision Brad O'Neal, saloon brawler, turning the prissy officer upside down and slamming him into next week—but she decided it wasn't polite to say so. She turned slightly and looked toward the house. She could see Brad's scowling face as he stood at the window, peering out.

"He's watching us," she said.

"Who?" Buford turned and looked. "I must say he has his nerve, spying on us. What do you suppose he wants?"

"I don't know. He probably wants me to come in."

"What business is it of his? I *am* your fiancé."

Brad came out on the porch and lit a cigar. She could see the tip glowing and his annoyed face in the moonlight.

Lillian stood up. "I think I'd better go in before he comes out here."

The lieutenant stood up. "If he does, I intend to challenge him."

"I don't think I'd do that, Buford. He's a rough saloon brawler and you're a—"

"Gentleman." Buford nodded primly.

"Of course, but ladies hate to see bloodshed." She didn't say whose blood. Brad would kill Buford in a fight. She opened her purse and slipped the diamond lily inside. "Why don't we set a date for maybe next year?"

He caught her hand. "Next year? I was hoping for July or August."

"That's too soon, Buford," she said in a panic.

"A big, society wedding takes at least a year of planning—just ask your mother."

Brad had come down the steps and was now standing on the driveway as if he were about to come out to the swing.

"Uh, we'll talk more later. I'd better go." She turned and fled through the lilies toward the house.

Behind her, she heard Buford sigh and walk across the gravel to his buggy, get in, and drive away.

The Texan stood, feet wide apart, glaring at her as she approached him. "It's about time you came in." he snapped, pulling out his big gold watch and peering at it in the moonlight.

"Are you insane? It can't be later than eight o'clock."

"Right," he nodded, "way past time for a respectable girl to be inside. I saw you out there foolin' around with that pantywaist."

"Fooling around?" She was seething as she leaned closer, speaking between clenched teeth. "You are the low villain who had me in the grass pawing me, only hours ago."

Now he grinned at her. "As I recall, you were enjoyin' every minute of it."

She felt her face flame. "No gentleman would say that."

"Lily, I never claimed to be a gentleman."

"Leave me alone, sir," she commanded. "I am an engaged woman and all you're worried about is Lieutenant Fortenbury getting his patrician hands on some of your filthy lucre."

"Can you speak English, please? Us Texans don't know big words like that."

"Then can you understand these words? I am going to marry the lieutenant. Now stay out of my business!"

She tried to brush past him, but he grabbed her arm, looking down at her. "Lily, I'm sorry, it's just that—"

She felt the magnetism of his gaze again, and it unnerved her. "What?"

Before he could answer, she pulled out of his grasp and marched across the lawn and up the steps. Then she ran up the stairs to her room, closing and locking her door. She leaned against it, breathing hard. Her good sense told her she could not stay in this house with that Texan or he'd have her clothes off. No, that was not acceptable to one of high morals. Brad O'Neal was as dangerous as a mustang stallion. She would marry the dull, reliable officer and lead a safe, respectable life.

She opened her purse and took out the small diamond pin and studied it. It was a beautiful piece of jewelry, and certainly quite valuable. The lily was so appropriate. She went to her bureau and opened the bottom drawer, hiding the pin under a layer of lace petticoats.

Brad had stood looking down at the girl as he grabbed her out on the lawn, loving the way the moonlight danced on her fiery hair and lit her emerald eyes. Why had he ever thought she was plain? Why, when she was angry or aroused, she was just plain beautiful. He had almost kissed her as she looked up at him, defiant and angry. However, then she had pulled from his grasp, and the moment was lost.

He looked down the long driveway at the sight of the prissy lieutenant and his buggy disappearing in the distance. Damn that snooty pup. When Brad had seen Buford sitting close to Lily in that swing and attempting to slip his arm around her, Brad had had to fight the urge to stride out there, grab the young gentleman by the collar, yank him up, and sock him so hard that Buford would knock over the big iron bird bath and end up soaked. He was furious that Buford was being so familiar with Lily.

He turned and walked up on the porch, still angry. Without thinking, he turned and smashed his fist against one of the porch pillars. *God, that hurt.* Now he hopped about, cursing and nursing his bruised hand. "Oh, Miss Primm, my life has been hell ever since you showed up, and it's not gettin' any better."

He held the injured hand in the other and stumbled inside. The house was dark and quiet. Everyone had gone to their rooms. He stood looking up the stairway, rubbing his bruised knuckles. He wanted to go up those stairs, kick her door down and—and what? Kiss her? Make love to her? Turn her over his knee and paddle that little round bottom until she saw the truth about that crooked officer? None of that would work with Lily. She was as independent as a hog on ice.

With a sigh, he strode to his room. He flopped down in his chair and stared at the wall. Just above his head, Lily was getting ready for bed. He imagined her long, red hair falling down her bare, creamy shoulders as she put on a sheer, lacy nightgown and climbed in that big, white bed. "You little vixen," he grumbled. "You've made my life miserable."

He tried not to remember this afternoon on the grass, but he couldn't help himself. No woman had ever roused him like that. No doubt it was Lily's innocence, or maybe the fact that she was so unattainable. Worse yet, he didn't want to admit defeat to his friends.

* * *

Upstairs, Lillian couldn't sleep. She ought to be ecstatic, engaged to marry into an aristocratic family. So why was she so miserable and uneasy? She knew why. When she'd confronted Brad on the driveway a few minutes ago, there was a tension between them that made her nerves taut as a bow string. She'd felt he was about to grab her and kiss her with the same molten passion of this afternoon. In fact, she'd caught herself rising up on her tiptoes to meet him. Oh, he could charm a bird out of a tree, all right, or a woman out of her virtue. One of them was going to have to sell out to the other and move out of this house that was now becoming a respectable hotel. With Buford's family wealth, she wouldn't need the Lily. However, if she sold out to Brad, he'd certainly turn it back into a bordello and gambling den, and Lillian couldn't abide that thought.

Downstairs, she thought she could hear the chair in his room creak. She imagined him sitting there, looking up at the ceiling. She could almost feel his gaze. Was she insane? It was all her imagination. Lillian dropped off into a troubled sleep. In her dreams she got out of bed and ran down the stairs barefooted, wearing only her sheer lace nightgown. She didn't even have to knock. The door opened suddenly and he stood there, looking down at her, his dark eyes burning into hers. "I've been waitin' for you, darlin'," he whispered.

Wordlessly, she went into his arms. He held her so tightly, she could not breathe as he kissed her, really kissed her, and then picked her up, carrying her to his bed. "I've been waitin' for you all my life."

"And I've been waitin' for you," she sighed and reached for him, knowing he was about to make her a woman—his woman.

.She sat up in bed, breathing hard. *Damn him, anyway.* He was dangerous and unpredictable, not safe and reliable like the lieutenant. Staying in this house was like playing with matches in a hay field, but what could she do?

Next morning, Delilah served breakfast to the hotel guests and left the girls, Flo and Rosita, cleaning off the tables as she started up the stairs with a tray. Neither Mr. Brad nor Miss Lillian had come down to breakfast and she was concerned about the conflict between them. *Hm, hm, you two is like fire and kerosene together. Before it's over, there's gonna be a blaze that may burn the Texas Lily down.* She rapped on the door. "Miss Lillian? I got your coffee."

The lady opened the door. She was still in her nightgown, tousled and sleepy. "Why, thank you, Delilah, come on in. I'm attempting to get dressed."

This wasn't like brisk, well-organized Miss Primm at all. Delilah nodded, came into the room and put the tray on a table. "Can I help you, Miss?"

"No, I think I can manage."

But Delilah noted Miss Lillian didn't seem to be managing very well at all as she stood there in her nightgown, looking about. "I can't seem to find my shoes."

Delilah began the search and found them kicked under a chair. "Here they are, Miss." This was strange. Usually Miss Lillian was so precise. Her things, like her life, were very orderly. Now she watched the lady dig in her bottom drawer. "I know I've got a clean petticoat somewhere—"

A sparkly piece of jewelry flipped out on the carpet and Delilah stared in disbelief at the diamond lily as the girl picked it up and put it back in the drawer. Delilah said, "where did you get that?"

Lillian smiled sheepishly. *Oh, she looked like her mother all right.* "Well, it's supposed to be a secret, but a gentleman gave it to me."

So Mr. Brad had taken the pin he had given Miss Lil only the day before her death, and now he had given it to the younger woman. Not that Miss Lil would have minded Lillian having it, in fact, maybe, considering who Lillian was, Miss Lil would have heartily approved. However, the whole thing seemed sneaky somehow, and Mr. Brad had never been that.

"Are you all right, Delilah?" Lillian paused in putting on the lace petticoat.

"Uh, yes, ma'am, I—I'm fine," Delilah lied, and she fled. "I got work to do."

Strange, Lillian thought, staring after her. Maybe Delilah wasn't feeling well, and she was not a young woman. When the Lily could manage it, Lillian wanted to hire more help and retire the old cook.

Lillian shrugged it off, got dressed in a plain dark skirt and white lace shirtwaist, and went downstairs. Brad was seated alone at at the big dining table, drinking coffee and looking disheveled and grumpy. "Well," she said, "as Texans would say, you look like the dogs have had you under the porch."

He glared at her with bloodshot eyes. "I didn't need you to tell me that, Lily."

She sat down at the table. "You need to shave and clean up a little."

"I won't if I don't want to," he snapped.

"My, we are in a bad mood, aren't we?" She rang the little bell on the table and Delilah stuck her head out of the kitchen. "May I have some breakfast, please?"

Delilah nodded, frowned at Brad, and disappeared.

"Well," Lillian said, "what did you do to make her mad?"

"Me?" He blinked his bloodshot eyes. "Delilah and I have always gotten along."

The big grandfather clock in the hall boomed ten times.

"You'd better hurry," Lillian said, "the committee is coming in thirty minutes."

He sipped his coffee and rubbed his forehead with a shaky hand. Perhaps he had a headache. "What committee?"

"The new Fort Floppett Beautification Committee," she reminded him. "They want to plan the Fourth of July celebration."

"What's to plan?" Brad shrugged. "What we always do is put on a parade, then roast a steer and bring out a couple of barrels of beer and some fireworks."

She frowned at him. "That's not at all what Mrs. Bottoms, Reverend Lovejoy, and the ladies have in mind."

He sighed. "You been changin' things ever since you got here, Lily."

"Change is not bad." She nodded her thanks to Delilah as the old woman brought her a plate of ham and eggs and a stack of fresh biscuits. Delilah frowned at Brad again and went back in the kitchen.

Lillian dug in with gusto. There was home-churned butter and homemade blackberry and wild plum jam to go with the light, fluffy biscuits. And to think she used to get by on a cup of weak tea and plain toast. "I told them we could meet in the morning room."

"Morning room? What the hell is a morning room?"

"Don't be profane," she scolded him. "Did I forget to tell you?" She smiled at him over her coffee cup. "We now have a morning room. It's a place where ladies can sit and have tea."

"The Texas Lily now has a morning room?"

"Well, since we're now a respectable hotel, the ladies need a pleasant place to gather and we can charge them for the tea and cookies."

"All the old biddies in Fort Floppett are gonna be gatherin' here for tea?"

"Let's hope so."

He groaned aloud and looked skyward. "Miss Primm, if I could possibly raise twenty-five thousand dollars, would you sell out?"

She considered a moment then shook her head. "I had no idea I had such a talent for the hotel business. We're starting to show a profit."

"Miss Primm," and now his voice had a slight edge. "Need I remind you that the Texas Lily was makin' tons of money before you came along?"

She smiled. "But now you're respectable."

"Respectable?" he grumbled. "There's many a soldier and cowboy who's mighty disappointed to hear how the place has been transformed."

"Now you've only got fifteen minutes," she said looking at the tiny gold watch pinned to her lacy white shirtwaist. "Of course, you don't have to be on the committee. I think we ladies and the reverend can handle it."

"Fine." He snapped and stood up. "Now if you'll excuse me, I think I'll go shoot some billiards."

"Uh, you haven't used the billiard room in a while. I thought you were tired of the game."

He shrugged. "I just haven't had time for a few days. I love my billiard room." He got up and walked toward the back of the house.

Oh my. She sat there sipping her coffee and tensing for the scream. It came about two seconds later.

"Miss Primm, what in the hell has happened to my billiard room? Get in here!"

She took a deep breath, got up, and hurried down

the hall. The big room was on the east side of the house so that the early sun streamed in. She pasted on a smile as she entered. "Isn't it pretty? We finished it up two days ago when you weren't around."

"What in the hell happened here?"

She looked around. The billiard table was gone, replaced by a tea table and dainty chairs upholstered in pink velvet. The room had been wallpapered in tiny pink petunias, and the windows dressed in pale pink chintz. Ribbons were everywhere. There were even little needlepoint pillows on the Victorian chairs.

"Miss Primm?"

"It's a morning room," she explained, taking a nervous breath. "Isn't it pretty?"

"Pretty? Pretty?" he roared like a wounded bull. "This is my hideaway, me and the boys. What did you do with my cigar humidor and my billiard table?"

She cleared her throat. "They're out in the barn."

"My billiard table is out in the barn?"

"Don't you hear well? I said it was."

He marched over and glared down at her.

"Well," she said nervously, "there isn't a need for a billiard table in a morning room, and anyway, there wasn't room when we got the pink settee and the tea table in."

He opened his mouth, but no words came out. He took two deep breaths as if trying to control his temper.

"Are you all right?" She looked up anxiously at him. "Honestly, I think you live with too much stress. That's not good for the body, you know."

"Stress?" he almost whispered. "Miss Primm, I never had any stress until you moved in."

She glanced at her lapel watch. "The committee is due any minute."

"What about my billiard table?"

She put her hands on her hips and considered. "Well, we might get a carpenter to close in the back porch. I think that's big enough."

About that time, they heard the front doorbell ring.

"There's the committee," Lillian said. "Is there anything else, or do you want to stay and help plan the—?"

"No, I do not want to sit with a bunch of old biddies and drink tea and eat sugar cookies. I'm goin' to my room where there's half a bottle of bourbon, to contemplate what I have done to deserve all this." He turned and stalked out.

Lillian hurried to meet her guests. Delilah had already answered the door and ushered the guests into the front hall. "Good morning everyone, so good of you to come."

Mrs. Bottoms looked about. "Goodness, you've done wonders with this place. I'll wager there's not another hotel this fine this side of St. Louis."

Reverend Lovejoy looked about and nodded approvingly. "This is indeed now a respectable hotel. The town will be forever grateful, Miss Primm."

"Some aren't," she said, imagining Brad sulking in his room. "Let's go back to the new morning room," Lillian gestured and led the way while the ladies oohed and aahed over the house.

Mrs. Pugsley said, "it's a real mansion. Too bad it can't be a private residence."

Lillian smiled as she gestured them to chairs. "That would be a dream, wouldn't it? But of course, it would take an enormous amount of money to keep it up, so it'll have to stay a hotel, I'm afraid."

"It's a plus for the community," Mrs. Bottoms

nodded. "We need more women in Fort Floppett like you, Miss Primm."

She felt herself flush modestly. "I'm bringing what little civilization I can to Texas' male rascals."

"Speaking of rascals," Mrs. Bottoms said, looking around, "isn't Mr. O'Neal joining us this morning?"

"I'm afraid not. He's—he's indisposed."

The ladies all looked disappointed. Even the respectable women were charmed by him, Lillian thought.

Delilah came in with a tray of tea and cookies. "What did Mr. Brad say when he saw his billiard room?"

"What?" said the guests.

"Uh, we'll talk about that later," Lillian said.

"Couldn't have been good," Delilah said as she served. "I heard him yellin' clear out in the kitchen."

Lillian gave her a stern look and the cook left.

"Now," Lillian said, "I'll pour. Would you like lemon, or cream and sugar?" She balanced a dainty china cup in her hand and reached for the teapot. Yes, it was lovely to have a morning room. After Brad thought it over, she was sure, he'd see it her way.

The committee talked for almost two hours. When they broke up, it had been decided that there would be a parade and fireworks shot from on the lawn of the Texas Lily. There would also be a parade with little children riding ponies, and of course, the army band would march. A temperance group from Dallas riding in a buggy with white banners protesting demon rum, and a group of very liberal suffrage ladies from clear over at the state capitol had asked to take part.

Mrs. Bottom sipped her tea. "I don't know about that. "You know how those cowboys and soldiers get after a few drinks, they'll be harrassing the ladies."

"Then we'll see they don't get much besides lemonade," Lillian said firmly.

"That'll upset them," Mrs. Darlington said.

"Well," answered Mrs. Pugsley, "it's about time we brought a little order to this town. You know the way the men would celebrate the Fourth is by getting drunk and shooting up the town, riding horses into saloons and shops."

"Not this time," Lillian said firmly.

"Uh, Miss Primm," the Revered said, setting down his tea cup. "Mr. O'Neal was one of those who rode a horse into the railroad depot last year."

"Worse yet," Mrs. Osborn said, "that goat got into a barrel of beer and was so drunk, it crashed through the window at our newspaper."

"Well," Lillian said, "then it's time for the good ladies of Fort Floppett to take control if this is ever going to be a peaceful, law-abiding town. The trouble with these men is that they need strong-minded women to civilize them."

The ladies all said, "Amen!"

The Reverend looked away, wiping his hands on his dainty napkin. "Now if we're finished, ladies, I have a Bible study to prepare for."

"Perhaps," Lillian said, "sometime you could hold your Bible study here. I'm sure our guests would love it."

Delilah had just come into the room with more cookies. "Anybody ask Mr. Brad about that?"

"I'm sure he would approve." Lillian said.

Delilah muttered under her breath as she gathered up the dishes. "When hell freezes over."

Lillian frowned at her, then turned to her guests. "Then it's settled," she said. "Next week this town will have the best Fourth of July ever. We just need to work hard and spread the word that this is a civilized celebration, no shooting up the town or riding horses into saloons."

"Mr. Brad and his friends gonna think that makes for a dull holiday," Delilah muttered.

"Fort Floppett is now respectable," Lillian said firmly and the ladies raised their tea cups.

"Hear! Hear!"

Lillian stood up and escorted her guests out of the new morning room. They were all standing on the front porch making small talk when Caddo the Indian telegrapher galloped up the drive on an old bay horse. He hopped off his mount before it came to a complete stop.

"What on earth—?" Lillian said.

"Just got a telegram," Caddo said, looking unnerved as he waved the paper in the air. "It's for the mayor. He here?"

Lillian shook her head. "Mrs. Pugsley is."

Mrs. Pugsley volunteered, "He's over in Beaumont, ordering supplies."

"Maybe I should give it to Brad, then." Caddo's brown face seemed blanched with shock.

Reverend Lovejoy said, "You can give it to me, Caddo, I'm on the town council and I'll see the message gets around. What's happening?"

"Oh, it's more congressmen." Caddo wiped the sweat from his face. "They want one more look at the town to see if they are gonna close the fort down."

Lillian gasped. "Not again. We all thought that had been settled."

"No, Congressional Budget Committee's still discussin' it," Caddo said. "What we gonna do?"

Everyone turned and looked at each other.

Brad would know what to do, Lillian thought. He was on the town council and a leader among men. "I'll tell Mr. O'Neal about it and the rest of you

spread the word. I imagine Brad will want the
mayor to **call** a meeting. When are the congressmen coming?"

"July Fourth," Caddo gulped.

"That doesn't give us much time," Lillian said,
thinking aloud.

"Oh dear Lord," Reverend Lovejoy rolled his
eyes skyward. "It looks like this time the town of
Fort Floppett is doomed."

"Not if Brad and I have anything to say about it,"
Lillian snapped. Much as she hated to admit it, she
knew Brad would know what to do.

Chapter Seventeen

"Miss Primm," Reverend Lovejoy said, "as an engaged woman, don't you think it would be more proper that you rely on your fiancé?"

"What?" She had completely forgotten Buford. She was ashamed to realize that, and more ashamed to realize she didn't have much confidence in his abilities. "Oh, yes, of course. Reverend, you and Caddo spread the word all over town about what's happened. Obviously we can't have another Indian raid; we've already done that."

"Agreed," said Mrs. Osborn. "Congressmen are pretty stupid, but I don't think even they would fall for that again. No, it will have to be something different."

Mrs. Bottoms said, "What about our July Fourth celebration?"

Lillian shook her head. "I don't know. It doesn't seem very important right now."

Caddo frowned. "Celebrations is always important to Texans, 'specially if there's plenty of beer."

"I don't know," Lillian shook her head. "Maybe Lester can get out a special edition. And in the meantime, the town council has some decisions to make."

"We'll be waitin' to hear," said Caddo. He strode to his horse and mounted up.

The ladies all looked at each other, worry on their faces, then the group got into their buggies and drove away. Herman raised his head from the flower bed and watched the scene, patiently chewing away.

Lillian watched them go. *This is a terrible mess,* she thought, *and just when the Lily was making a profit.* She marched to Brad's room and rapped on the door.

"If it's time for dinner, I think I may drink mine, thank you very much."

"Mr. O'Neal, come out here. This is serious."

"What? Are you ladies stymied on whether to serve sugar cookies or gingersnaps at the July Fourth celebration?"

She opened the door and marched in. "We must talk."

"About my billiard table?" He frowned at her as he leaned against a bedpost.

"Forget the billiard table," she ordered. "We've got a real problem."

"Don't I know it?" He complained. "Pink velvet and little ribbony doo-dads in my billiards room."

From the front of the house, she heard Delilah ringing the bell for dinner and the girls coming downstairs to serve.

"Brad, a wire just came through for the mayor. More congressmen are coming to town."

"What?" His mouth dropped open.

She nodded. "It's true. They'll be here July Fourth. The Congressional Budget Committee still hasn't decided whether to close Fort Floppett."

Brad swore under his breath. "You know how

many jobs are at stake here? The town might as well roll up its sidewalks and close down if the soldiers leave. There'll be nobody for the ranchers to sell their beef to. The Lily won't survive either as a whorehouse or a hotel."

She winced at the word. "And after we've worked so hard. I imagine the mayor will call a meeting. They're all hoping you will have some fresh ideas."

"Me?" he touched his chest. "Lady, you destroy my saloon, redo my billiard room without askin', and now you want me to come up with a bright idea? Why don't you ask your darlin' lieutenant?"

"He hasn't got anything at stake here."

He grinned at her. "Sure, he does, sweet, as soon as he owns your half of the Texas Lily."

She felt like slapping him. "Damn you," she said, "I don't know why I bother." Enraged, she turned and marched out of his room.

Brad watched her go with mixed feelings. He couldn't control her, and he couldn't seduce her. He'd never met a woman like her. She was beginning to occupy every waking thought. That drove him loco. Something had to happen, and soon.

The next night after dinner, the town council and many other townspeople met in the dining room of the Texas Lily. Mayor Pugsley read the telegram aloud and looked around at the circle of anxious faces. "So that's the size of it, folks. The congressmen are comin' in on the train the morning of the Fourth."

Dewey scowled and ran his hand through his gray hair. "Don't them blamed people ever stay in Washington and work?"

"Not if they can find something better to do,"

Brad said, "especially if it involves a free trip and fun."

The major chewed his moustache. "We can't do what we did last time—they might have heard about the Indian attack from those other congressmen."

"I know," Brad frowned and looked toward Lily.

She shrugged. "It's against my principles to be involved in this duplicity."

Everyone looked at each other in puzzlement.

"Say what?" said Pug.

"Miss Primm talks Yankee English." Brad frowned at her. "I'll boil it down to Texan: she won't help stack the deck, even to save the pot if she thinks it's crooked. All she's willing to do is feed and entertain the congressmen all day and see that they get to the parade."

Dewey Cheatum lit his pipe. Lily frowned at him.

Brad said "Smokin' is only allowed in the gentlemens' lounge, gents, unless you want Lily here runnin' around sprayin' you with violet perfume."

Dewey went to the window and knocked the ashes from his pipe while the other ladies nodded approvingly. Brad sighed. Lily was a very bad influence on the other women. If she kept this up, they would all ban smoking and drinking and anything else men did for fun. He frowned, thinking of lace doilies under vases, coasters under every wet glass, and his hallowed billiard room turned into a morning room.

Dewey said, "So what can we do now to show the congressmen how important the fort is to us?"

Dimples scratched his dimpled chin. "Maybe we could tell them the local ranchers depend on the fort as a market for their beef."

Brad snorted. "Now, do you really think some Yankee Republicans is gonna care about the income of a bunch of Southern Democrats?"

"He has a point," Lily seemed loathe to give him credit. "Isn't there any other kind of trouble that we need the army to put down?"

"Well, there's the Saturday night saloon fights," Dewey said with a nostalgic sigh. "Or used to be, before the Lily got so civilized. The Bucket is too small for much ruckus."

Lillian said "Maybe we could try to use intellect and reason with them."

Brad threw back his head and laughed. "Intellect and reason? Please, Lily, we're talkin' about congressmen. They're just takin' an amusin' trip at the taxpayer's expense. They don't give a rat's—" he looked around at the assembled ladies. "They don't care whether our fort closes or not."

Everyone looked at each other, nodding in agreement.

The major said, "Is the town gonna be full of cowboys that day?"

Brad frowned at him. "Ain't it always, Gilbert? You think the cowboys is gonna miss free food and a big dance? There'll be twice as many as there was the last time."

"Oh my," Lily said.

Brad looked at her. "What?"

"The cowboys and the soldiers don't get along too well."

"That ain't news to anyone, is it?" Brad snapped. "That's why we try to keep the soldiers and the cowboys from all gatherin' in town at the same time, much as possible."

Lillian chewed her lip. "Have they ever gotten into a huge brawl?"

The major frowned. "We do our best to avoid that. Why, they'd tear this town down if they ever got started."

Brad smiled at her. "I have a great idea. Suppose we plan a big fight between the two sides?"

"That is not *your* idea," Lily said, "it's mine. But like most men, you always want to take the credit."

He ignored her, warming to his topic. "We could stage a big fight that evenin' just before it's time for the train to leave. The cowboys would get a fake brawl goin' and the soldiers could save the town from burnin' down. Then the congressmen would see how bad we need the fort."

"Maybe the band could play?" Major Bottoms asked.

Someone in the back groaned and Brad hurried on. "Good idea, Major. We could have the congressmen sittin' on The Lily's big front porch with maybe a concert. Everybody would be there."

Dewey snorted. "I ain't sure I'm up for that kind of sacrifice."

"Now Dewey, they wouldn't have to play very long," Brad assured him. "The cowboys would object and start a ruckus."

"I'd object, too." Dewey said.

"Not you, Dewey," Brad said, "you're too old to get into a fight. We could put on a big brawl out on The Lily's front lawn with everybody throwin' punches and shootin'."

"Need I remind you," Lily said primly, "the last time there was shooting, you got shot?"

"I ain't forgot. Ruined a new pair of boots. But we'll be more careful this time."

Dewey nodded. "This plan is full of clever deceit and lots of fistfights. I like it."

"Spoken like a lawyer," Brad said.

Lily protested. "Suppose it gets out of hand and someone gets hurt?"

"Oh, women!" Brad said. "Mayor, we ready for a vote on this?" The mayor called for a show of hands.

The ladies all shook their heads, but of course all the men voted yes.

"Done!" Brad nodded with approval. "We'll talk more later, but now let's get the word out what we're gonna do to save the fort."

Lillian protested "there has to be a better way, an honest way."

"Lily," Brad said as if speaking to a child, "we are talkin' about Yankee congressmen here. 'Honest' is not in their lingo. We aren't about to let Fort Floppett die without a struggle."

"Hear! Hear!" shouted all the men.

"Now that that's decided, we'll all adjourn to the bar for a drink."

"We're all for that!" said the men.

As the men began to leave the room, Lillian smiled at the ladies. "Now ladies, Delilah has some tea and cookies ready, we can adjourn to the morning room."

"What in the hell is a morning room?" Doc muttered.

Brad frowned. "It was the billiard room."

"Where's the billiard table?" Dewey said.

"Don't ask," Brad said.

Lillian ignored him and led her ladies to the back of the house where they sipped tea and complimented Lillian again on her decorating.

Later, the two partners showed their guests out. The crowd stood on the front porch visiting a few minutes in the darkness, then they all left.

Lillian and Brad stood watching them mount their horses or get in their buggies and drive away.

"Yes," Brad nodded, "I can just picture it. We'll stage the fight out here on the front lawn so the congressmen will have a good view."

"This is so crooked," she scolded.

"Well, maybe a bit shady," Brad conceded as they

turned and went back inside. "I had forgotten how honest you are. You make me ashamed of myself."

"Really?"

"Well, okay, maybe not really," he admitted. "But I've got room to change and grow."

"I should have known." She looked around the big empty room. "We got two new guests today— came in from up north with a freight wagon. If we keep growing, we'll soon be one of the best known hotels in Texas."

"Lady, I used to do very well by just dealin' poker. Now you're tryin' to turn me into an upstandin' citizen."

She looked up at him. "You might get some respect."

"Lily, I been buyin' respect with my fists and my poker playin' all my life. It was the best a poor redneck boy could do." He looked around; there was no one else in sight.

Lily said, "Delilah and the girls must have retreated to their rooms—the guests, too."

Brad smiled at her. "Then how about a glass of champagne to celebrate savin' the fort?"

She eyed him suspiciously. "You Texans think you've got to have liquor to celebrate everything. In the first place, I don't drink, as you very well know. In the second place, we haven't saved it yet."

"Oh, but we will." He grinned as he went behind the bar and picked up a bottle, popping the cork. It spewed across the counter and the floor.

"Could you be a little more tidy?" she frowned at him.

"And could you be a little less cross and straitlaced?" He poured two glasses of champagne. *Tonight,* he thought, *he was going to seduce the very proper Miss Primm. And then he would threaten to tell her very proper fiancé if she again refused to sell out.* It was an idea so rotten and underhanded that he felt like a rat. Get over it, Brad, old boy, he told himself. It's a dog-eat-dog world and only the strong survive. "Lily, I told you I was sorry for the way things have gone since you arrived. Don't you think I deserve a second chance?"

"My mother didn't believe in second chances. She believed a person ought to do it right the first time."

"Most of us need a second chance now and then." He smiled at her. "You know, never judge a man 'til you've walked a mile in his boots."

She wavered. He was so handsome and so charming. "I—I suppose I could have just a sip." She looked around. The house was quiet, the lights dim. Everyone, including the guests, was in bed asleep.

He grinned again, picking up the bottle and placing the two glasses on a tray. "Good. Now let's find a comfortable place to sip our drinks and talk."

"What about the swing out on the lawn?"

He shook his head. "Too squeaky."

"What?"

"I meant, Herman would end up with his head in our laps munching on the lace of your dress. What about that lovely morning room you just decorated."

She stared at him. "I thought you were furious about that?" *Did he grit his teeth?*

"Why, no, dear Miss Primm. I'll admit that when I first saw it, I might have been a mite upset."

"A mite?" she snorted. "Why, as you Texans would say, you looked madder than a bee-stung bobcat."

"Oh, but I've decided I was wrong. The room is lovely, and who cares if my fine old billiard table gets rained on out in that leaky old barn? Certainly not me."

"Not I," she corrected without thinking.

He took a deep breath, and she'd have sworn his hand shook. "I'm so pleased you're correctin' my bad grammar. Now, let's go sit back there and have our drinks, shall we?"

He took the bottle and the tray of glasses and started down the hall.

She followed him. "Mr. O'Neal, to my credit, I have spoken to a carpenter about closing in the back porch so you can invite your friends out there to shoot billiards."

"Wonderful," he said. "I can't thank you enough. I see you took down my deer head that hung in the back hall."

"It was too violent."

"Lily, most Texans are violent. Huntin' is part of the Constitution, along with drinkin' and gamblin.'"

"I don't think that's in the Constitution."

"The *Texas* Constitution," he said over his shoulder.

"I doubt that, too." Lillian breathed a sigh of relief as she followed him into the morning room and lit a small lamp. She was so glad he wasn't upset.

She started to light another lamp, and he said, "Don't bother. After all, we won't be here long."

"That's right." She perched on the big pink sofa as he set the tray on the lamp table next to it. Then he sat down next to her.

She started, wishing he had chosen another chair. All she could do was scoot a little to one side, but then she hit the sofa arm. He didn't seem to notice. He handed her a glass and picked up one himself, holding it out. "Here's to the success of the Texas Lily Hotel and our partnership."

She held up her glass and nodded while he made his toast. The glass held a lot more champagne than she'd asked for, but she didn't want to be rude. She sipped it slowly.

"What's the matter? It isn't a good year?"

He was sitting so close to her that it made her very nervous. "Uh, Mr. O'Neal, I wouldn't know a good year from a bad one. I told you I don't drink."

"Well, a high-class hotel generally serves champagne to its guests and they'll expect you to know. Suppose the governor of Texas came to stay and we served him inferior champagne?"

"Be serious. I daresay most Texans, even the governor, wouldn't know champagne from branch water. They don't seem to drink anything but bad whiskey and cheap beer." She tasted the drink. The little bubbles went up her nose and she felt wild and daring. What would her straitlaced mother say about her sitting in an almost darkened room drinking with a gambler who had a reputation with the ladies? Especially one who had almost had her buck naked out under the trees?

He sipped his drink and put his arm across the back of the sofa. *Was it her imagination that he'd moved closer?*

She sipped the drink again. It tasted pretty good to her and she gulped the rest.

Immediately, the gambler reached to take her glass. Their hands touched and she almost felt electricity jump across their fingers. He refilled both their glasses. "You know, this bottle will go flat if we don't finish it tonight. No way to save it, and it's a very fine year."

She didn't know if he was lying or not. She felt very light-hearted. She sipped the champagne. "Well, my mother always said it was a shame and a sin to waste anything."

"Ain't it the truth?" He grinned at her and held his glass up in another toast.

She felt giddy and mellow enough that she didn't correct his grammar. "I've been meaning to speak to you about what happened in the woods the other day—"

"Oh, dear lady." He put his glass down and took her hand, looking earnestly into her eyes. "I owe you a thousand apologies. It was just that you were so beautiful, I was swept away and forgot my manners. Please forgive me."

That was just what a hero in one of the romantic novels she loved would have said. She sipped her drink and felt more kindly toward this rogue. "Mr. O'Neal, you are forgiven. I'm sorry about the perfume."

"I can smell it still." He closed his eyes as if imagining. And in her mind, his face was close to her breasts, breathing in the scent, his breath warm on her skin. "Anyway, thank you for your forgiveness." He kissed the hand he still held. "And please do call me Brad. Would you like some more champagne?"

She giggled, and that shocked her. "Oh my, I—I don't think so. I'm feeling a bit madcap and foolish. I think I've had enough."

He squeezed her hand. "I'll tell you when you've had enough. Do you think I would lie to you?"

Her thinking was a bit fuzzy as he poured them each other drink. He had lied to her plenty . . . hadn't he? Yet he looked so charming as he scooted closer to her.

"I—I think I need to go to bed now." She tried to stand up and nearly fell.

"Careful there." he reached out to catch her hand and somehow when she staggered and sat back down on the sofa, she was almost in his lap. "Now let's toast the success of our mission."

She giggled like a schoolgirl as she held up her

glass and they clinked. "Haven't we already done that?"

"Have we?" He was so close she could smell the scent of his aftershave. "Doesn't matter. Here's to our success. Drink up!"

She did as she was told. "You know, that's tasty. Perhaps I should have just a tad more if I'm going to learn about champagne." She drained her glass and he filled it again. She seemed to be having a difficult time focusing her eyes. She leaned closer to him and looked up at him earnestly. "Mr. O'Neal—"

"Brad," he corrected. Taking her free hand, he kissed it.

"Brad," she said, sipping her drink, "about that day."

"I've said how sorry I was." He looked down into her eyes and she realized how dark his tanned skin was and how a lock of his black hair fell across his forehead, making him look like an innocent schoolboy. Who was she kidding? Brad O'Neal had probably seduced his grade-school teacher.

"I know. I—I just want to make sure you never tell my fiancé about that day. I doubt he would understand."

"My dear lady, you have my promise as a gentleman that my lips are sealed." He made the classic locking motion with his fingers.

She giggled and drained her glass.

He took it from her hand and set it on the lamp table. "What's so funny?'

"I don't think I ever thought of you as a gentleman."

Now he took both her hands in his. His felt big and warm and powerful, almost covering her small ones. He kissed both her hands, leaning closer. "I forgot myself in the woods that day. You were so beautiful and so desirable. Lieutenant Fortenbury is a lucky man."

"Buford," she said without enthusiasm.

"Ah, yes, young Buford. Such a fine young officer," the gambler said with a smile. "But since we're business partners, what goes on between us doesn't count."

She was trying to follow his logic, but her mind was too fuzzy and he was too close. She looked up at him, attempting to focus her eyes. "It doesn't?"

"No, my dear, it doesn't. Just forget that I thought you were so desirable, I couldn't resist kissing you." Before she realized what he was about to do, he took her in his arms and kissed her.

She let him. Not only let him, but put her arms around his neck and kissed him back willingly. His tongue brushed along her lips, begging her to open them, and she did, throwing back her head in surrender as his tongue teased the edges of her mouth and then caressed inside. Lillian took a deep, gulping breath and let his tongue explore her mouth.

"Sweet," he whispered, "so sweet. . . ."

Somewhere in her foggy mind, she wondered if she should be doing this. It wasn't proper. Or was it, since he was her business partner? She couldn't seem to remember any absolutes when she was around this charming rascal. She kept her eyes closed as his warm, soft lips kissed her eyelids and her cheeks. She felt his hot breath on her skin as his mouth moved down her throat. Her pulse pounded like a hammer, but she didn't pull away. He was big and powerful and virile as he held her in a tender embrace. "Lily," he whispered, "my dear, dear Lily. You are so pretty."

No one in her strict, lonely life had ever called her pretty. Her mother had reminded her coldly that beautiful women were apt to fall victim to men's lust and passion. Lily had never even been sure what lust was, but now she knew about passion.

"Brad," she gasped, "I don't think—"

"Don't think, Lily," he whispered against her throat. "Just feel how much I love you."

She didn't open her eyes, but she felt him fumbling with the buttons of her bodice. His breath was warm on her throat as he kissed across her collarbone. She opened her eyes ever so slightly to see his dark, intense face brushing the rise of her creamy white breast above her corset. Then one of his big hands reached to open the lace of her corset cover. In the dim light, she looked from her exposed breasts to his face. He was breathing hard, and his eyes were intense with desire. She took his face between her two small hands and kissed him.

He groaned aloud then and his hot mouth went to the pink rosettes of her breasts. Now it was her turn to moan and arch her back, offering him the feast of her breasts for his ravaging mouth. He couldn't seem to get enough of them, and she wanted him to kiss them and lick them and caress them. Her lower body felt as if it were on fire, a hot burning beginning in her belly and spreading lower. He put one hand on her thigh through the fabric of her dress, and she trembled, wanting him to stroke her bare skin. "Lily?" he gasped.

"Oh, Brad, don't . . . don't stop." She didn't care about right or wrong, or what Buford would think, or anything else but this moment and this man.

She felt his hand going under her skirt, pushing it up even as he pressed her back so that she was lying on the pink sofa. She wore dainty lace drawers with the spilt at the seam as was common. Even as he half lay on her, his fingers stroked up her thigh beneath her undergarment, and then his fingers touched her where he had touched her that day in the park. She trembled hard while he caressed her with his fingers and slipped them inside her heat, even as he reached to kiss her again.

"Oh . . . oh, my." She breathed hard through her mouth as she felt him fumbling with the buttons of his trousers. Was she out of her mind? This was totally unacceptable behavior for a respectable lady, but she must be a tart because she wanted even more. She let her thighs fall apart so that he could stroke the very depths of her. Instead, he moved so that he lay between her thighs and the tumble of her full skirts were pushed up.

"Lily," he whispered, "tonight, I am going to make a woman of you."

She knew she should get up immediately and leave. She should be saving her virginity for her bridegroom, young—, *what was his name, anyway? Oh yes, that prissy officer from Philadelphia, Buford What's-His-Name.* But the man she wanted to give her virginity to was this wild and worthless rogue who was even now creating such havoc with her emotions. "Brad, I—I think I love you."

"Sure," he murmured. "Sure." He came into her slowly.

She tensed.

"No," he whispered. "Relax, it will be easier. You're like wet silk and I never wanted a woman as much as I want you right now."

She desired him as much as he wanted her, and she reached up and pulled him down into her. For a split second, his rigid lance pushed against the silk of her virginity, and she gasped as he broke through, and slipping into her up to the hilt. His mouth covered hers, and he put his tongue deep into her throat. One of his hands stroked her breast until her nipple swelled up turgid, needing the touch of his full lips. "More," she whispered. "More."

His eyes were dark, intense coals as he began to ride her, slowly at first as she pulled at him frantically, wanting more, deeper, faster. He obliged, but it was still not enough as her need grew. The pink sofa seemed to make dull thudding noises as he rode her, driving like a hard, steel rod into her— bare flesh slapping against bare flesh—until she gasped and begged for more, more and more.

Just when she thought she couldn't take further excitement, her emotions rose like a great crashing crescendo of passion. She reached out and clung to him while she bucked under him. Then everything seemed to disappear into an oncoming blackness like a tidal wave crashing over her. "Brad," she gasped. "Oh, Brad!"

At that, she felt him increase his speed and his depth, and then she was swept away with ecstasy, and she no longer knew where she was or what was happening except that she didn't want it to end. Then he stiffened and gulped for air, holding her tightly. For hours, or centuries, or maybe only minutes, they clung to each other, locked in the eternal embrace of desire.

She was drunk and in love, she thought, smiling sleepily. Then she sighed, relaxed, and knew no more.

Brad finally rose up on his elbows. He was hot and felt a sheen of perspiration all over his muscular body. God, he'd never had an experience like this one before. Lily was some woman. "Lily, oh, Lily." No answer. "Lily?"

She was out cold. He looked down into her serene face, soft and pretty in the dim lamplight. He had deliberately gotten an innocent woman drunk and seduced her. That was a new low, even for him. *You rotten, rotten cad!* He cursed himself, but he couldn't have stopped, not even with a gun to his head. He had wanted her too badly.

Chapter Eighteen

Brad stared down into her face. He had accomplished what he'd planned to. So why did he not feel triumphant and pleased with himself?

Lily was out cold and snoring a delicate, ladylike little snore. He smiled. She seemed so human now, and still so innocent. He couldn't leave her here for Delilah or one of the girls to find in the morning. He swung her up in his arms. She hardly weighed more than his Colt pistol. Very quietly, he went down the hall and up the stairs to her room. Laying her on her bed, he rearranged her clothing and pulled the sheet up over her. Then he leaned over and brushed the fiery hair from her forehead and kissed there ever so gently. She smiled in her sleep, and he wondered what she was dreaming.

"Sweet dreams, darlin'," he whispered. "In the morning, this will all be a terrible nightmare."

He blew out her lamp and went down to his own room. Brad went to bed, but could not sleep. In his mind, he made love to her over and over again and remembered that it was the best he'd ever had. But he'd taken her virginity, done something terrible he could not undo, and she would hate him in the morning.

"Since when are you developin' a conscience?" he muttered to himself. "You look out for nobody because nobody ever looked out for you. She shouldn't have been so naïve."

Finally, toward dawn, he drifted into a troubled sleep.

Lily awoke with the first ray of dawn making light-patterns on her bedroom wall. Why did she feel so bad? She sat up and groaned aloud, put her head in her hands. It felt like the local train was rushing through her brain. She blinked as she realized her clothing was in disarray. A dress? Why wasn't she wearing her nightgown?

"Oh my God," she gasped as she searched her memory and found Brad O'Neal, his bottle of champagne and his kisses. Beyond that first kiss, she didn't remember much except that she had wanted more. How had she ended up in her bed? Maybe she had gotten up and walked out of the morning room before things went any further. Looking at her wrinkled and half-buttoned clothing, she didn't think so. When she stood up, her stomach roiled and her head hurt even more. "I've been a terrible fool."

The tears came and she leaned against the bed-post for a long moment, fighting to control her emotions. She, who had always been so frosty and reserved with men, had obviously gotten roaring drunk and acted like a trashy tart with a no-account gambler. *Why hadn't she remembered her mother's warnings?* Because his kisses had tasted so good.

What to do now? She couldn't bear to face him, but she knew she must. Already, downstairs, she heard Delilah and the girls setting tables and preparing breakfast for their hotel guests. As hostess, Lillian had responsibilities. She stumbled to the wash basin and stared into the mirror. Her complexion was ghostly pale and her lips appeared swollen, as if they'd been kissed and kissed.

"Oh my God," she said again, splashing water from the little basin on her face. She felt like going back to bed for the day, but instead she washed up, combed her hair, and put on a fresh green gingham dress. She looked around for her shoes, but couldn't find them. "Now where are they?"

Had she ended up in Brad's room, and they were under his bed? She imagined Delilah or one of the girls finding them while cleaning. "Oh, I can't let that happen."

She went charging down the stairs and looked around to see if he might be at the dining table so she could sneak into his room. No such luck. Still bare-footed, she tiptoed down the hall and opened his door quietly. He lay snoring on his bed, still in his clothes. She tiptoed over to peer down at him. He was sound asleep with a smile on his lips.

You dirty villain, she thought. *I'd like to crack your head open.* She looked around for a vase or something to hit him with but found nothing. Maybe if she'd been in this rascal's bed last night, her shoes would be under his bed. Lily got down on her knees and began to crawl around his bed, looking under it.

"What in the hell are you doin' down there?"

Surprised, Lily glanced up to see him sitting up in bed, staring down at her. "Uh, nothing." She got to her feet and headed toward the door. Maybe he didn't even remember last night.

He blinked and seemed to see her bare feet for the first time. "Mornin' room."

"What?"

"Lily, your shoes are in the mornin' room."

She wanted to cry and scream and throw things at him, but her mother had taught her it was both impolite and unwise to show emotion. Impolite? She was dealing with the biggest rotter in Texas. "How dare you?" she seethed. "How could you have done this?"

"Now, Lily—" He swung his legs over the side of the bed.

"Don't you 'now Lily' me, you rogue. I can't stop thinking about last night."

He grinned. "Me neither."

She must not break down in weak and impotent tears. Instead, she threw one of his boots at him, narrowly missing his head.

"Are you loco? Stop that!" He came up off the bed and before she could move, he was across the room and had grabbed her by the wrists.

"You—you—there's no words low enough for what you did." She fought to get away from him and he held onto her, looking down into her face. She turned her face away so that he would not see her tears.

"Lily, wash your face," he commanded. "We have hotel guests and this is no time for a fight."

"Fight? I want to kill you! Where's your gun?" She broke free of him and ran over to his bureau, pulling a drawer out that hit the floor with a bang.

He leaned against the bedpost and watched her. "Do you know how to shoot a pistol?"

"No, but I'm mad enough that I can learn."

"It's not in the bureau," he said calmly. "Let's go have some coffee, and then we'll talk about this."

"I don't want to talk, I want to kill you!" She pulled out another drawer.

"You've certainly changed from the frosty, distant

person you were when you first arrived in Texas," he said. "Last night—"

"I don't want to talk about last night, you damned scoundrel."

"Tsk Tsk. Ladies don't swear."

She whirled on him. "Have you no shame?"

"None," he shook his head. "You've known that from the first."

Yes, she had been beguiled by the Texas rascal, yet she had known what he was—he'd never made any bones about it. Lily tried to hold back her tears as she glared at him, but they were streaming down her face anyway.

"Lily," he said gently, "you'd better wipe your eyes and go find your shoes before someone else does. We'll talk after breakfast."

The thought of food made her sick. "How can you even think of food at a time like this?"

"Men always think about food," he said. "It's our second most favorite thought. Now go find your shoes and at least come to the table for some coffee."

"You are a cad and a rotter!" She screamed, and then she brushed past him, stopping only a split-second to slap his face as she left.

He rubbed his stinging cheek, wanting to run after her and apologize, but of course he didn't. He had won, but at what cost? "She's right, Brad ol' boy, you are as crooked as a dog's hind leg."

He went over to his dresser, poured water into the basin, and splashed his face. Then he shaved himself, which was difficult because he didn't want to look himself in the eye. Funny, he'd never felt bad about bedding a woman before and this one had been the most enjoyable ever. He'd like some more of that. "Are you loco? That girl wants to kill you now, not sleep with you."

He put on fresh clothes and his boots, then combed his hair and went in to breakfast. Lily sat at the big table nursing a cup of coffee. She didn't appear too well, and she didn't look at him. Two male guests came and sat down at the big table, exchanging greetings. Lily nodded.

Brad pasted on a big smile. "Good morning, all." The men spoke to him. Lily did not. He wondered if she had found her shoes. He was tempted to raise the tablecloth and check her little feet, but decided that was a bad idea.

The girls bustled about, serving breakfast. Lily waved them away with a gasp when Flo tried to put a plate of scrambled eggs before her. Lily looked a little peaked, as if she might get up and run out of sight of the food. Instead, she said nothing. She only sipped her coffee and asked for another cup.

Brad ate with a hearty appetite. After all, he had worked hard last night and used up a lot of energy. He chatted with the two men and the waitresses. Every now and then, Lily raised her eyes and glared at him.

When he pushed back his plate, he said, "I think I'll go out on the porch for a cigar. You gentlemen care to join me?"

Both declined. One had to get ready to catch the morning train, the other had business in town. Brad went out on the porch and sat down in the creaky swing. It was going to be a typical Texas day for the first day of July, hotter than hell with the lid off. He lit a cigar, smoked, and thought. What kind of a mess had he made?

In a minute, Lily came out on the porch and stood there. The tension was as tight as a hangman's noose. He couldn't think what to say. Finally

he blurted, "Well, I see you found your shoes."
Could he have sounded any more stupid and heartless?

"Is that all you have to say to me?"

"It was pretty dumb, wasn't it, considerin'—"

"Are you going to tell everyone in town?"

"Now, Lily," he peered up at her, "do you think I would do that?"

"I think you're an unmitigated bastard who would do anything to get what you want."

He shrugged. "I reckon you know me pretty well. Won't you sit down?" He patted the empty spot on the swing.

"No. I don't ever want to get close to you again." That was a lie, she thought with growing horror. Even now, she wanted to sit down in the swing next to him, throw her arms around his neck, and let him kiss her breathless. "You—you must know I can't let Buford find out about this."

He smiled ever so slightly and smoked his cigar. "And he won't—"

"Oh, thank you," she heaved a sigh of relief. "I was afraid—"

"I'm not finished." Brad blew smoke into the air. "There's a condition."

"What!"

Brad shrugged. "You sell your share of the Lily to me, marry young pip-squeak if your taste is that bad, and go back to Philadelphia with him. He'll never know a thing."

Her face went ashen. "Why, you dirty, rotten—"

"I know what I am, Lily. You don't need to tell me."

She couldn't keep the tears from overflowing her green eyes. She had lowered her guard and let him make love to her, and he was even more rotten than she could have possibly imagined. "You—you planned this to blackmail me."

He paused, smoke drifting from his cigar, and didn't look at her. "Yes."

"You—you no-class Texas scum! I thought there might be something good in you, but you're so low, you could crawl under a snake's belly." She fought to hold back her sobs.

He didn't look at her and when he spoke, his voice was so soft, she had to strain to hear him. "It's a dog eat dog world, Lily. Only the toughest dog survives and he does it any way he can."

"I hate you!" she turned and strode back into the house, blinded by tears. She ran up the stairs and into her room, closing the door. To think she had hesitated to accept marriage and that diamond pin from Buford because she had felt something for this hard-bitten rascal of a gambler.

Outside, Brad smoked his cigar and hated himself. He'd never had any scruples before about how he won. He was one of many children from a poor moonshiner's shack deep in the Lone Star state's toughest area, the Big Thicket. Strangers didn't go there, and if they did, they might not come back. The old man had a bad disposition which only got worse when he lost a leg fighting for the Confederacy, and he beat his children until they were old enough to escape his clutches. No, Brad had never had any qualms before about doing whatever it took to win, but now he felt a new unfamiliar emotion. It might be what he'd heard called 'shame'.

Delilah came out on the porch. "What was wrong with Miss Lillian? She brushed past me and ran up the stairs. Looked like she was cryin'."

He winced at the thought of Lily weeping and all because of him. "Oh hell, who knows what women are thinkin'?" He stood up and tossed his cigar away. "Tell José to saddle my horse. I've got to confab with some of the others about how we're gonna set up this fight for the congressmen."

She nodded and went back inside. After a long moment, Brad went inside, too. He stood at the foot of the stairs, staring up at her door. She was up there crying, and it was all his fault. The prissy Lieutenant Fortenbury didn't seem the forgiving type. Reckon he wouldn't take kindly to the fact that his fiancée had given her innocence to a low-class gambler. So of course, knowing that, Lily would knuckle under and sell Brad her share of the bordello. Brad should feel triumphant, but he didn't. He felt rotten. "Hey, she'll come out all right," he muttered to himself. "You'll give her more than she expects in price."

He still felt rotten. "Remember, you'll have complete ownership of the Texas Lily now." Maybe later he would think it had been worth it. Right now, he wasn't so sure.

Upstairs, Lily washed her face and struggled with her disappointment and the decision she had to make. She had always been a strong person who never let down her guard with anyone. Last night she had, and look what it had gotten her. She had a choice now: back away like a scalded dog and give up her half of the Lily to that scoundrel, or tell Buford before Brad did and hope he loved her enough to be understanding and forgiving. *What to do?*

She decided she didn't have to make her choice right now. Brad wouldn't want to create a ruckus until this trouble with Congress had passed. All that was important right now was saving the fort. She would avoid Brad O'Neal as much as possible for the next several days. Lily squared her shoulders and went downstairs.

Delilah came out of the kitchen, a spot of flour on her dark face. "You lookin' for Mr. Brad? He done gone uptown. I sent José with the buggy to take and pick up hotel guests."

She managed a smile. "Thank you, Delilah. I don't know what I'd do without you."

"Miss Lil used to say the same thing. You all right, Miss Lillian? You don't look so good."

"I—I'm fine."

"Don't look fine," the old woman muttered and returned to her kitchen.

Lillian sighed. She had work to do and couldn't worry over whether her eyes were swollen and red. She'd claim dust or smoke got in them. Over the next hour, she supervised getting fresh linens out and rooms ready for new guests. She made sure there were clean tablecloths on all the former poker tables. Soon José returned with five new guests to check in and make comfortable. Then Lillian took the buggy and went into town to talk with some of the ladies about organizing the Fourth of July festival. Everyone's biggest worry was whether the fight between the soldiers and the cowboys would be authentic enough to fool the congressmen.

"Honey," said Mrs. Bottoms, "you get both sides liquored up, and it'll be authentic enough. There's nothing a Texan likes better than a good fight. Oh, by the way, your lieutenant said he would come calling tonight."

That wasn't something Lillian looked forward to, knowing the gambler intended to tell Buford everything.

* * *

That night at supper, she got through the meal by simply ignoring Brad as if he didn't exist while making charming small-talk with the new guests. Brad seemed to get grumpier and grumpier.

"Well," she said when they had all finished dessert. She wiped her mouth daintily on a white linen napkin and stood up. "I must be going. I have a gentleman caller coming."

The men all scrambled to their feet.

"No, no, keep your seats, gentlemen." She motioned them back down. "You can enjoy coffee and visit, or maybe you'd like to have cigars and brandy in our gentlemen's lounge."

Brad glowered at her. "You're goin' out?"

She simply ignored him. Delilah came into the room to pour more coffee. "Delilah," she said haughtily, "Lieutenant Fortenbury is taking me for a buggy ride. I may not be back until late."

"You better watch out for your reputation," Delilah warned with a frown. "Young ladies shouldn't stay out too late unchaperoned."

She glared at Brad. "Don't worry about my reputation." She sailed out of the room, leaving everyone staring at each other in puzzlement.

Buford had borrowed the major's buggy and now as she went out on the porch in the moonlight, he alighted and came around to help her up. He tried to lift her, but he didn't have the strength. She got herself up onto the seat. As they drove away, she remembered the ease of the big Texan lifting her into a buggy.

She must stop thinking thoughts like that, she scolded herself, and concentrate on Buford's good points—which were . . . well—of course he had some. He was respectable and from a fine family. Then why was it her mind kept returning to the Texan who was not respectable and came from an

Irish white trash family? In her mind, she was in Brad's arms again as he kissed and made love to her. She sighed at the memory.

"My dear, are you all right? You're awfully quiet."

"I—I'm fine," she assured him and struggled to smile and make conversation with him. *When should she tell him about her wild night with Brad?*

How about never? She wasn't sure of Buford or any man's reaction to news like that. Yet she either had to tell him or knuckle under to that Texan. Well, at least she wouldn't tell him tonight. That decision made, she engaged in small-talk, which was difficult because there didn't seem to be much to talk about with the prim young officer unless she wanted to discuss the tuba.

"Why don't we pull off the road somewhere and look at the moon?" Buford said, scooting closer to her on the seat.

That meant more of those wet, smacking kisses. She shuddered in distaste. "You know, Buford, dear, that might put my reputation at risk. Perhaps we shouldn't be alone too much until after the wedding."

In the moonlight, she could see the displeasure on his pasty features. "You don't seem too worried about your reputation while you're living in a bordello and sharing quarters with that slimy scoundrel."

"Why, Buford," she blinked in surprise, "we're only sharing the same building and you know what the situation is. Of course, I could—what is it the Texans say?—'Holler calf rope,' and let him have ownership of the place—"

"No, no, I wouldn't want you to do that. I think you're a brave, liberated woman to take on that rogue and give him tit for tat. It's just that, well," he glanced over at her, "some women find the rascal attractive, and I wouldn't want you—"

"I don't find him the least attractive," she lied, looking upward, hoping God wasn't listening tonight to her bare-faced lie.

"Of course not. You have too much class, Lillian, to even think about him that way."

"What way?"

"Uh, you know."

"Certainly not." For a split second she tensed, waiting for a lightning bolt to come out of the clear sky and burn her to a crisp. In her mind, she was back in Brad's arms, sharing a heated passion that she had never known could happen. She took a deep breath and remembered the taste of his lips and the way his hands had felt under her drawers as they stroked and teased—and the ecstasy of her ultimate surrender.

". . . then maybe I'd better take you home."

"Uh, what did you say, Buford?" She glanced over at him, aware she hadn't heard anything he'd said for the past five minutes.

He frowned. "Honestly, Lillian, are you sure you're all right? You seem so vague and disconnected."

Was it that noticeable? "I—I'm so distracted, being involved in this thing the town is trying to pull off to keep the fort from being closed."

"Oh, that," he snorted. "Frankly, I think I'd be glad if they did close it."

"Why, Buford," she was shocked. "What about all these people who depend on the fort for a living? What about all the soldiers?"

"Who cares about a bunch of rebel Texans?" He shrugged peevishly. "What do I care about the other soldiers? They'd probably all get sent to Arizona to fight spiders, rattlers, and Apaches." He shuddered visibly. "I do care that it would impact the Lily, since we'll own it."

We'll own it. Was Brad right about Buford? Now why would you believe the rascal who seduced you, you idiot?

"Uh, Buford, we'll only own *half* of it. I think I'm getting a headache. Would you please take me home now?"

"All right." He glanced toward her, his voice full of sympathy. "I do hope you're not coming down with something contagious. I have a very delicate constitution and I wouldn't want to catch anything."

"Then you'd better not get close to me—it could be typhoid or black plague or anything."

He scooted farther away from her on the seat.

When they pulled up in front of the Texas Lily, Buford hesitated. "Do you—do you think you can get down by yourself? Just in case you are carrying anything contagious?"

"Certainly." She drew a quick breath of relief, hiked her skirts and clambered down from the buggy. "Good night." She fled up the steps and into the house.

Buford watched her flee. He'd sensed her reluctance to his embraces and kisses. Once he made Lillian legally his, he'd teach her about lust. She'd be his wife and she'd have to submit to anything Buford wanted to do to her, things he couldn't even get the whores at the Bucket O' Blood to do. Of course, to take over, he was going to have to do away with Brad O'Neal. He'd been a poor shot the first time, but he'd do better this time.

He smiled at the thought, slapped the horse with the reins, and drove away. That damned old billy goat was out in the front lily bed next to the big white bird bath, chomping away. As the buggy passed, the goat lifted its head and seemed to glare at Buford. "Just you wait, you hunk of meat. When

I own this place, the first thing I'm going to do is
plow up these common old lilies and have a big
grand opening celebration of the new Texas Lily.
I'll serve you up as some of that slop Texans call
barbecue."

The goat appeared to understand because it lowered its head as if to butt and bleated at him.

Maybe he shouldn't have given Lily that diamond pin, considering how Buford had gotten it,
but maybe no one would recognize it. After all,
Buford didn't remember ever seeing Lil McGinty
wearing it when he'd been in the Texas Lily all
those times, banging first one whore and then another.

"I wonder if the stories are true about money
being hidden in the house?" he muttered as he
drove along. Maybe the gold was hidden in big
trunks in the attic, or even in the walls. Once he
owned the Lily, he could search for it at his leisure.
He winced at the memory of that fateful April
night. "I didn't mean to kill Lil, it was an accident,"
he mumbled to himself by way of excuse as he
drove.

He had sneaked in the back way on the pretext
of lying with one of the whores upstairs. That
damned O'Neal had forbidden Buford to come in
the Texas Lily because he'd caught him cheating at
cards.

It had been an exceptionally busy Saturday night,
Buford remembered, lots of noise and people. The
piano was banging away, the women laughing and
singing, and the poker tables were full. Very quietly,
Buford had sneaked up the back stairs. Lil McGinty
was downstairs. He could see her circulating from
table to table, laughing and joking with the men.
This might give him time to search her room.
Maybe the treasure was in a very ordinary place like

in her bureau or under her bed. He'd paused in the hallway outside Lil's door, looking around. There was no one in the upstairs hall. He'd reached up and turned off the hall lamp, then sneaked into Lil's room. There was only a small lamp lit in there. He would have a look around for the money, and when he came out into the dark hall, no one would notice him with the hall lamp turned off.

His heart pounding hard, Buford had begun rummaging through the drawers of her bureau and the suitcases under her bed. Nothing. Then he had noticed the jewelry box over on the nightstand. He had turned his back to the door and started searching through it. Most of it didn't look that valuable. He had been about to give up when his fingers had found the diamond lily pin. He'd picked it up and held it up to the dim lamplight and watched it sparkle.

"This is exquisite and probably expensive. I can take it, and she'll never know. Sometime when I'm in another town, I'll sell it." He'd slipped it in his pocket.

"What in the hell are you doing in my room?"

Buford had whirled. Lil McGinty, dressed in purple, stood in the doorway. "I—I was just looking, that's all."

"You're a damned thief! That's why Brad told you never to come in the Lily again. I'm gonna call him—"

"No!" Buford had ran at her and grabbed her, putting his hand over her mouth. That big Texan would beat him up for taking Lil's jewelry, so he must not find out. Buford must keep Lil quiet. She was tall, and strong for a woman almost fifty years old. They had meshed and struggled as he'd tried to keep her from calling out. They'd stumbled out into the hall balcony overlooking the big poker room downstairs. The noise and music from downstairs was still loud on that late Saturday night, so no one had seemed to notice their struggle in the dark hall.

At that moment, Lil had bit the hand he had clasped over her mouth and she screamed even as she pulled away from him and lost her balance. She had crashed against the balcony rail and it gave way. She'd screamed once more as she fell.

Oh my God. He hadn't meant this to happen— he was only trying to keep her quiet.

Girls and their half-dressed customers had run out of the adjoining rooms yelling questions.

The noise and music from downstairs had gradually ceased. With a mob of others, Buford had tiptoed to the edge of the landing where the rail had broken away and looked down. Lil had crashed onto a billiard table, breaking it down. She'd lain there staring up, her mouth open in that final shriek.

Then all the women were screaming and men gathered around the table, including Brad O'Neal. With their attention riveted on the dead woman, Buford had run down the back stairs and out into the night.

He smiled now, remembering. Well, he hadn't found the treasure, but he had gotten away with a fine diamond pin. Ironic maybe, but now Lil McGinty's jewelry was going to adorn her naïve old-maid niece. Then all Buford needed was to figure out how to do away with Brad O'Neal.

Grinning to himself at his own cleverness, Buford headed for the Bucket O' Blood. He'd celebrate his bright future by having a few drinks and buying a night in Sadie's bed.

Chapter Nineteen

The Fourth of July dawned hot and bright. Lily awoke, nervous about the congressmen arriving in less than two hours. She dressed in a cute red, white, and blue dress with a saucy bustle and tied up her curls with bright blue ribbons before descending the stairs to breakfast.

The five new guests jumped to their feet. "Do keep your seats, gentlemen, I hope you're enjoying your stay?"

"Very much so," they assured her.

Brad came into the dining room. "My, don't we look patriotic today?"

She ignored his comment as one of the gentlemen rushed to pull her chair out for her. Today was too important, with everything riding on it for the town and the fort. She couldn't risk things going wrong because of petty bickering with this unscrupulous rascal. She nodded to Delilah, who smiled back at her as she poured coffee. "Miss Lil would be mighty proud of you, Miss Lillian. You look pretty as a songbird in a apple tree."

"Thank you, Delilah." She ignored Brad as he sat down and turned her attention to her guests. "Now gentlemen, if you can stay over, you'll enjoy our town festivities. There'll be a parade and a big barbecue—"

"I cook the barbecue," Brad said, "and there's nobody better at it than me."

She frowned at him. "As I was saying before I was so rudely interrupted, after the barbecue, there'll be all sorts of games."

"Poker?" asked one man hopefully.

"I was thinking more on the order of sack races and croquet," she said.

"Oh." The men looked crestfallen.

"Also," Lillian said, "the Fort Floppett band will play patriotic tunes."

Brad groaned aloud and she fixed him with a steely look. "After that, there'll be fireworks."

"There sure will be," Brad said under his breath.

She must not let him badger her. He was probably hoping to bring things to a head and she still wasn't sure what to do about his threatened blackmail. This big calamity could wait until the congressmen left town. She ate a hurried breakfast and stood up. The men all scrambled to their feet.

"No, no, gentlemen, you must stay and enjoy your coffee," she insisted. "I have to drive to the depot to pick up some very important visitors."

Brad hopped up, grinning. "I'll drive you, Miss Lily."

She hesitated, not wanting to share the same buggy with this scoundrel, but she could hardly cause a fuss in front of their hotel guests. "All right, let me get my parasol."

She went up the stairs, silently fuming. What was she going to do about him? He'd been a thorn in her side since the moment she had first seen him, affecting her and stirring her up like no man had ever done before. She would show him. She would

wear the diamond pin today, announcing to the
world that she was engaged to the prominent lieutenant of the Fortenbury family of Philadelphia.
That would annoy Brad no end, flaunting her engagement like that, because he seemed to hate the
young lieutenant so.

Lillian pinned the diamond lily to her bodice,
checked her appearance before the mirror, and
went down the stairs. In the distance, she heard the
whistle of the incoming train.

Brad waited by the buggy. "We'll have to hurry."

He helped her up into the buggy, got up next to
her, and smiled at her. Then his expression turned
into frozen anger.

What had she done to put that frightening look
on his rugged face?

"Where did you get that?" He thundered.

"What?"

"Don't toy with me, Lily, I know that pin."

She glanced down and touched it with her fingertips. "My fiancé gave it to me as an engagement
gift. It's been in his family for generations."

Brad caught her arm and his face was a mask of
fury. "He's a damned liar! That pin belonged to Lil
McGinty. I ought to know, I gave it to her for her
birthday the day before she died."

"What?" She pulled away from him, completely
unnerved. "I don't believe you. Neither will anyone
else. With your reputation, no one would take your
word—"

"Lily, I'm beginnin' to suspect Lil's accident
wasn't no accident, or how the hell did that bastard
get that brooch?"

"How dare you!" she seethed, "I've always known
you have no scruples, but to accuse Buford of being
a thief and maybe a killer? You've gone too far!"
She was so overwhelmed with indignation, she

slapped him hard. In the distance, the train whistled again, coming toward the station.

He looked at her, big and virile and dangerous, as he rubbed his red cheek. "If a man had done that," he snarled at her, "I'd have killed him."

"You don't scare me, you big oaf. Now, I don't have time for this." Her fury matched his. "Get out of my buggy, I've got to pick up the congressmen."

"You don't believe me, do you? I mean about the pin?"

"Of course not!" She was sobbing now, great angry sobs. "You'd do anything to win and get my half of the Lily, you've made that clear. Well, you can forget about blackmail because I intend to tell Buford myself. I'm certain he loves me enough that he'll be understanding. He won't break our engagement because you seduced me."

He shook his head, his dark eyes still angry. "I wouldn't do that, Lily, you'll lose him—him and all his highfalutin' ways and fine family. In the meantime, once today is passed, I intend to corner him and find out about that pin."

"Get out of my buggy, you rascal!" she shrieked again, "I won't ride with you!"

In the distance, she heard the train chugging into the station and the army band started up, playing loudly if not too well.

"Fine. I'll ride my horse into town. This isn't the end of this, Lily."

"You're damned right it isn't." She swung her little whip at him as he stepped down and he caught the end of it, gave it a sudden jerk, pulling her off balance so that she fell forward and into his arms. She could only stare up at him in shock.

He grinned without mirth. "Go ahead and marry your damned lieutenant, but you'll miss this." Before she realized what he was about, he kissed her—kissed her in a savage, wild way that for a moment made her forget everything but the heat and the virile power of the man who held her. The kiss lengthened, and she found herself clinging to him, wanting more and more.

In the distance, the train whistled again and a crowd faintly cheered its arrival.

What was she thinking? She jerked away from him and slapped him as she scrambled to get out of his arms. In answer, he kissed her again even as she struggled. Then he set her back in the buggy. He was breathing as hard as she was and the intense look of his eyes told her he was aroused. Her red finger marks shown on his dark face.

"Damn you," he muttered, "no woman's ever made my blood run hot like you do. Now get the hell out of here!" He whacked the startled horse on the rear with his hand and it took off at a fast trot down the drive. When she looked back, he still stood there, feet wide apart, looking after her with a mixed expression of anger and passion.

The man was positively insane, she thought, straightening her dress and looking toward the station as her horse trotted along. She had no time to think about him now. There was too much at stake for Fort Floppett. The whole town was festooned with red, white, and blue bunting. There were lots of people in town for the July Fourth festivities, including many cowboys from the surrounding ranches. Up ahead, she saw the two congressmen alighting from the train, and the major and the mayor stepping forward to greet them as the band finished its song. She pulled in at a hitching post in front of Dewey Cheatum's law office and stepped down.

The mayor was just beginning his speech. "Congressmen, we can't tell you how proud we are to have you here in Texas enjoying our celebration. You know we are commemorating this date that Texas let the other states join them—"

His wife leaned over and said something to him.

"Oh," he said, "so what we're celebrating is the colonies breaking away from England. Not quite as important to the Texans as the Alamo and our victory against Santa Anna at San Jacinto, but important, nevertheless."

The crowd smiled and nodded approvingly. No true Texan thought anything in American history was as important as those two Lone Star events. Anyone who thought otherwise was either a damned Yankee, a liberal, or both.

The fat congressmen looked about nervously the whole length of Pug's speech. A cowboy finally yelled, "Put a sock in it, Pug, we're ready for the parade."

That line got big applause from the crowd. Now a congressman asked the major loudly enough for everyone to hear "What about these wild Indians my colleagues told me about?"

The major patted him on the shoulder assuringly. "Fort Floppett protects its citizens. Be assured, gentlemen, that there'll be no Indian attack while you're here."

"We're leaving on the evening train," the other said.

"Then you'll be safe enough with all the soldiers in town, who of course won't be here if the fort is closed," the major said.

Lillian stepped forward. "Gentlemen, after the parade and entertainment, José will drive you to the Texas Lily, the best hotel in Texas, to rest. Later in the evening we'll have fireworks. I hope you'll enjoy your brief stay here so much, you'll want to recommend it to your friends."

One of them bowed low and kissed her hand before the congressmen were spirited away by the mayor and the town council to ride in the parade.

As the army band passed her, Buford paused and blinked at her. "Lillian, I thought I told you not to wear that pin yet."

"Well, it was so pretty, I couldn't resist." She wouldn't even dignify that wild accusation of Brad's by mentioning it.

He hesitated. "It's just a bit much for this hick town, don't you think? You wouldn't want the ladies to be jealous." He leaned over and gave her a wet smack of a kiss. It was like being licked in the face by a hound dog. She couldn't help but contrast it with the taste of Brad's hot, full lips. She was puzzled by his attitude about the pin. Most men would be proud to have their fiancée wear their gifts.

"Now Lillian, dear, I've got to go get in formation. We're a big part of the parade, you know."

"I know," she nodded and smiled at him.

From a distance, Brad watched Lily talking to Buford. He wasn't sure what was said, but she nodded and smiled and the officer gave her a kiss. That made Brad want to knock him from here to next week. The pin glittered in the sunlight and Brad was mystified. *How could that young bastard have gotten that pin from Lil?*

About that time, he was joined by Luke and several other members of the old Town Beautification Committee.

Dimples said, "You losin' your touch, Brad? Not a lady-killer anymore?"

Brad took a deep breath. All he had to do was tell them about seducing Lily. They'd believe him, and his reputation would be assured while hers would be smirked and snickered at all over the county.

"Brad?" asked Luke. "Didn't you hear us?"

He realized then that he cared about Lily in a way he had never cared about another woman. And she not only hated him, she was going to marry his enemy. "I'm throwin' in the towel, boys."

"What," they said in unison. "That ain't like you, Brad."

"I know," he said shrugging. "It don't matter. The lady has high morals. She can't be seduced, not even by me."

"What?" Dewey had just joined them. "Brad, you just lost your title."

"I don't even care." He didn't look at them. Instead, he turned and looked at Lily talking to José, who stood with Herman hooked up to a little red cart. The cart had *Texas Lily Hotel* printed in big letters on the side. The goat had been groomed and wore a red leather harness and red, white and blue ribbons tied to his curling horns.

The people were lining up for the parade: the army band, Herman the goat, cowboys on horses, an old man dressed up as Uncle Sam, and some children pushing hoops.

Brad made his way through the crowd and stood next to Lily.

"Go away," she whispered through clenched teeth, "or I'll complain to the sheriff that you're a masher."

"He happens to be a friend of mine." Brad said. "Did you tell your young rotter what I said about the pin?"

"Of course not." She tried to edge away from him. "This is hardly the time and place, and you're making a very serious accusation. As far as the other thing, I'm going to tell him tonight. I won't be blackmailed."

He smiled without mirth. "I have to hand it to you, Lily, you've got more guts and character than I gave you credit for."

"And nobody's got less than you."

He flinched as if she had slapped him. "Reckon I deserved that, but I'm not through with young Buford yet."

Dewey Cheatum pushed through the crowd and joined them. "What are you two in such serious conversation about? Never mind, it might spoil today's fun. Brad, I've got a new bottle of Irish whiskey in my office. What say we celebrate the Lone Star state's birthday?"

"Best offer I've had today," Brad said, and turned away.

"It's not Texas' birthday," Lillian said patiently. "It's the birthday of our country."

"Texans can celebrate our birthday any time we want," Dewey said. "We don't have to wait for a particular day."

"Hear! Hear!" Brad grinned.

There was no reasoning with a Texan, she thought with disgust as she watched the two head for Dewey's office. She strode over to join Mrs. Bottoms and the other ladies setting up tables with all sorts of food. The booths were a riot of red, white and blue crepe paper streamers.

"We're hoping to raise enough money to buy the town a park," the major's wife said. "We've been working on this for a couple of years now."

"The town doesn't even have a park?" Why had she never noticed that before? Under a tree, she saw a cold barrel of beer with a line of thirsty cowboys and soldiers waiting. "Don't Texans ever get enough to drink?"

Mrs. Bottoms shook her head and laughed. "Maybe it's the miles and miles of hot, dry plains, but they're always thirsty. My, what a lovely pin."

All the ladies gathered around to inspect and admire it.

"Thank you," said Lily modestly, "Lieutenant Fortenbury gave it to me."

They were visibly impressed. Mrs. Darlington said, "He's from a fine old family and, I hear, quite wealthy."

"Must be," put in another plump matron, "or he wouldn't be able to give a gift like that."

"Now that charming rascal, Brad O'Neal, is the one that takes my eye," said another with a nod.

"He's an absolute rascal," Lillian informed her.

The other woman sighed. "Isn't that what makes him so attractive to women?"

"I'm sure I wouldn't know," Lillian snapped.

The major's wife asked, "You ready for tonight, my dear?"

"All I'm providing is the location for the evening's party," Lillian reminded the lady. "The rest of it is against my principles."

"I saw you in intense conversation with Brad. I thought you were engaged to young Fortenbury?"

"I am," Lillian assured her. "You know that gambler and I are just like fire and kerosene. We don't mix well."

The older lady smiled. "Makes a hot fire, though."

"Or an explosion." Lillian tried not to think about that night in the morning room. Hot fire indeed. As far as she could remember, it was a wonder they hadn't set that pink sofa ablaze. She tried not to think about the passion she'd found in his arms. None of that was important. What was important was respectability and a fine family. Her mother would have been horrified about her fall from re-

spectability, and Lillian could only be relieved her
stern, cold parent hadn't lived to see this happen.
On the other hand, her mother would have been so
proud of her engagement to Buford Fortenbury.

About the time the parade began, Brad and
Dewey stumbled out of the lawyer's office. He was
probably drunk, she thought with disgust. She
frowned, wishing she could push him in the horse
trough out front. As the parade assembled, José got
in line behind the army band, leading Herman and
the red wagon.

Oh no. Brad stumbled out and took the lead
rope from the Mexican boy. He fully intended, it
seemed, to walk in the parade. All the men were
laughing good naturedly. She could just kill him.
She wished she had a cannon so she could blow
him clear out of Texas.

The gambler bowed to the crowd and tipped his
hat to the ladies. Many of the women were shouting
his name and waving their hankies. She'd had
enough. She marched out to him and tried to whisper, "You're making a fool of yourself and the Texas
Lily."

He looked at her a little cross-eyed. "I seem to
have a habit of makin' a fool of myself, especially
with you."

"If that's an apology, it's not acceptable. You
need to apologize to the Lieutenant for smearing
his name."

"Not if hell freezes over," he vowed.

"You're impossible."

The parade started off and she hurried to get out
of the way. The band was ahead of the goat cart and
she was thankful for that. At least Buford wouldn't
have seen this encounter. The band struck up
"Marching Through Georgia," which set off a
chorus of boos from the mostly Southern-sympa-

thizing Texans. The major immediately stopped, switched over to "The Yellow Rose of Texas," and got cheers as the band began to march.

In truth, it wasn't much of a parade. Besides the band, the congressmen and the town officials and the sheriff rode in buggies bedecked with red, white, and blue streamers. A children's Sunday School class, a handful of elderly Confederate veterans, a riding club, and two ladies' groups from Dallas completed the lineup. Of course the two ladies' groups represented women's suffrage and temperance, but by now most of the men in the crowd were liquored up enough to be genial—even toward liberals from Dallas—so they refrained from pelting the ladies with road apples. The parade marched the three-block length of Main Street and then broke up.

She hurried to meet the congressmen as they alighted from their buggy over by the train station. "Gentlemen, let me escort you to our food and some lemonade and cookies."

Brad stumbled over. Oh God, she hoped he wasn't going to embarrass her again. "Gentlemen, what about some cold beer?"

The congressmen's eyes lit up. "Sounds good."

"Also," Brad said, "when we get back to the Lily this afternoon, I have a bottle of twenty-year-old Scotch and a box of fine imported cigars."

The fat one grinned. "I'm beginning to like this town."

So she stood glaring after him as Brad O'Neal hijacked her guests.

Buford strode up, his pale face red with the heat and the big tuba wrapped around his thin shoulders. "So what did you think?"

"About what?" She was still staring after Brad.

"About my tuba playing, of course."

"Wonderful," she said. Frankly, she couldn't remember how the band had played.

"I thought you were going to take off that pin?"

"Of yes, of course." She took it off and put it in her reticule. "Although I think everyone knows by now we're engaged."

"Let's get some food," he took off his tuba. "I'll put this in the wagon with the other band instruments, and we'll eat."

She smiled at him. "Buford, you do look handsome in your uniform."

He smiled and his wispy mustache wiggled. "My mother always said that, too."

There was a big crowd under the shade of the trees in the livery stable lot. People were lining up to get a plate full of fried chicken and all the fixings or walking over to where Brad served barbecue. Lillian fumed, watching him smile and nod to the ladies as he served them. Some of the women lingered near his booth, flirting with him.

She decided she would skip the barbecue and eat fried chicken so she wouldn't have to confront Brad again. There was a heaping platter of chicken, along with homemade hot rolls, corn on the cob, deviled eggs, potato salad, baked beans, cole slaw, and every type of cake and pie one could imagine. Most of the men seemed to be drinking beer, but the ladies all had huge tumblers of iced tea or lemonade.

Buford joined her and began filling his plate. "You know, I'd like some of that barbecue, but I don't think I want to have any contact with that drunken gambler."

Was he afraid of Brad? She took a deep breath. "I—I'll get you some, dear." She marched over to Brad with a clean plate and held it out.

"Ah," he said with a wink, "do you like it rare, medium, or well done, my dear Lily?"

"I am not your dear Lily," she whispered hoarsely. "And I'd like it well cooked, like most civilized people do."

"I like mine rare enough that it almost moos when I stick a fork in it."

"Of course you would." She turned to walk away.

"Hey," he called after her, "after dinner, there'll be games with prizes."

"I'm sure Buford and I will compete." She kept her voice cold.

Sadie sidled up just then, trailing smoke from her cigarillo. "Hey, Brad, honey, why don't you and me compete?"

Lillian glared at her. "I think Mr. O'Neal is too drunk to compete at anything."

Sadie looked up at Brad with longing. "I don't know about that, he used to be pretty good when he was drunk. Of course you wouldn't know about that." She glared at Lillian.

Lillian held her breath, but Brad didn't say anything. She turned and walked back to the table where Buford waited. "Here's your barbecue, dear."

"What was that tavern wench saying to you?" Buford asked. "I couldn't hear what she said."

Why was he so nervous?

Lillian shrugged as she sat down and began to eat. "Nothing much. She's flirting with him."

"Humph," Buford sniffed. "He always did attract women like bees around a honey pot."

Wasn't that the truth, and she had fallen victim to his charm. She knew she had to tell Buford about her lapse from grace, but she didn't think now was the time. Maybe this evening, although she dreaded it.

* * *

After everyone had had all the cake, pie, cookies, and watermelon anyone could hold, the mayor called for games out in the middle of Main Street, since there was no town park. Lillian checked on the congressmen. They seemed as happy as pigs in a mud puddle, with plenty of food and beer, and some of the whores from the Bucket O' Blood were flirting with them.

Pug stood up and held up his hand for quiet. "First is the three-legged race, so you gents get your ladies and line up."

There was much giggling and blushes from the ladies as someone began tying the couples' legs together. She watched Brad and Sadie being tied together. They had their arms around each other and were evidently enjoying it.

Lillian fumed. "Disgraceful."

"Isn't it, though?" Buford stared at the couple with disapproval. Never mind, Lillian, we'll beat them."

Along came Dimples, who tied their ankles together. "Now put your arms around each other's waists," he instructed, "and get on the starting line."

She hadn't realized that Buford, besides being short, was thin and flabby. She remembered Brad's hard, muscular body with a sigh.

"All right," Pug yelled, waving a pistol. "Ya'll get ready and I'll fire my pistol to start this race."

She and Buford had their arms around each other's waists. Lillian looked up and down the line. There were five couples racing. Brad looked strong enough to pick Sadie up and carry her if she fell.

"Ready, set . . ." The pistol fired and the couples started. At least the rest of them did. Buford and Lillian got their feet tangled and went down on the first step. She lay there in the street, watching Brad and Sadie win the race.

It took some help to get the two back on their feet and untied.

Buford said, "I think that gambler cheated."

"No, he didn't," she snapped and then realized she was defending him. "It—it's just that there's no way to cheat on something like that."

Finally late in the afternoon, the games broke up. Sadie and Brad had won almost everything. Lillian watched and fumed as Brad gallantly handed the prizes to his partner. Lillian managed to get away from Buford, who had to report to the major, and gathered up the congressmen, who by now were feeling no pain.

"Remember the Alamo!" One shouted as she steered them toward her buggy.

The other raised a mug. "I'll drink to that."

They probably thought the Alamo was a saloon, thanks to Brad O'Neal. Lillian took a deep breath. "You gentlemen can rest awhile and this evening, the crowd will gather on our hotel's front lawn and we'll have music and fireworks."

If everything worked out as planned, that's when the soldiers and cowboys would turn the party into a brawl then the army would have to dash in and restore order. The congressmen would realize how badly the fort was needed in east Texas.

"Mr. O'Neal promised us cigars and good scotch," the fat one reminded her.

"Would you settle for iced tea or lemonade?"

They both glared at her.

Damn Brad O'Neal. "Of course there will be scotch and cigars at the hotel."

Now they grinned and climbed in. The fat one said, "That gambler sure is a devil with the ladies, ain't he?"

"I'm sure I wouldn't know." But of course she

did. She was only one in a long line of conquests for the Texan. *How could she have been so stupid?*

She drove away from the depot, heading for the Lily. So far, so good. It was only a few hours before the planned brawl and then putting the congressmen back on the train. She wouldn't draw an easy breath until this was over.

She pulled up before the big Victorian house and the congressmen mumbled approval. José came around the porch. "José, take these gentlemen to their rooms so they can freshen up. Mr. O'Neal will be along shortly to entertain them."

She stopped by the kitchen to make sure Delilah would have a good supper ready. The old woman said, "How was the parade?"

"Well, Brad made a fool of himself."

The old woman paused, spoon in hand. "That ain't like Mr. Brad. He's acted like a stallion who's been eating loco weed ever since you came here, Miss Lillian." Abruptly her gaze fasten on the diamond pin. "You wearin' that?"

"I told you, a gentleman gave it to me."

"Damned cheap of him," Delilah muttered, "I'd have thought better of him than that, givin' you Miss Lil's pin."

"What?" The words soaked in and Lillian shook her head. "No, you're mistaken, Lieutenant Fortenbury gave me this—it's been in his family for generations."

The old woman paused, staring at her. "Reckon there could be two pins alike," she admitted.

Lillian started to say something, then shrugged. Obviously the old woman was getting senile. Or maybe Brad had made her part of his lying plot. Yes, of course that was it. "You don't like him, do you?"

Delilah didn't look at her as she stirred her pot. "Who?"

"You know who, Lieutenant Fortenbury."

The old woman hesitated. "I don't think your mother would like him, ma'am."

"Now how would you know what my mother would like? I'm sure she'd approve of Buford."

Delilah just kept stirring her pot. "That Mr. Brad, now there's a real man."

For a split-second, Lillian was back in Brad's arms as he kissed her and conquered her. She shook off the memory with a sigh. "He's an absolute rascal." She turned to go.

"That's why the ladies love him." The old lady smiled and busied herself slicing tomatos.

"Not this lady." Lillian started to leave the kitchen, turned. "Say, there's a box I noticed up in my closet. You know anything about it? I thought I might take a look."

"Hmm," Delilah was stirring and singing to herself, obviously only half listening.

Well, it was in her Aunt Lil's closet, so it now belonged to her. Lillian left the kitchen and went up to her room. She splashed cold water on her face, took off her dress, and sponged herself. She'd lie down for a few minutes and then put on a fresh dress. Maybe her Aunt Lil had something she could wear that was modest enough. She began digging in the closet and found a pale blue dress. She wondered if there were shoes to go with this outfit. Lillian could see that intriguing big box on the top shelf of the closet. She dragged a stool over to the closet and stood up on it. The stool was rickety and she swayed for balance, but it might make her tall enough to reach the big box with her fingertips. Shoes, maybe, she thought, or maybe hats. The box was covered with dust as if it hadn't been touched for a long time. Lillian hesitated as the rickety stool creaked under her, wondering what she was about to find.

* * *

Down on the porch, Brad had arrived, seating the congressmen in comfortable wicker rockers and passing out cigars. Dewey rode up just then and mounted the steps. "Good afternoon, gentlemen, I hope I'm in time for a mint julep?"

Brad grinned. "I'll see to the drinks." He went inside and made up the juleps. When he passed the kitchen, he yelled at Delilah, "Hey, Delilah, you seen anything of Miss Lily?"

"She's up in her room." The old woman stuck her head out of the kitchen. "She's awful mad at you."

"So what else is new?"

"You see she's wearin' Miss Lil's pin?"

Brad scowled. "Yeah. I'm not sure how the Lieutenant got it, but I'm gonna find out."

"I had thought you give it to her."

He shook his head. "And I thought you took it."

"Me?" Delilah touched her chest in surprise. "No, sir." She shook her gray head. "Miss Lillian said something about a box up in the closet. I didn't pay much attention."

"Hmm." Brad yawned and got a tray full of refreshments and went outside and passed the drinks around. The congressmen looked as happy as dead hogs in the sunshine.

"Ah," Dewey said, "no one makes a julep like you do. Where's Miss Lillian?"

"In her room," Brad sipped his drink.

"Did you ever get into that box of Lil's?"

"Box? What box?" Brad leaned back in his rocker.

Dewey frowned at him. "You know, the box I told you to have Delilah take care of."

Brad blinked. "Honestly, Dewey, I forgot about it until you just mentioned it."

Dewey frowned. "Seems like it was important to Lil or she wouldn't have mentioned it in her will."

"Uh-oh." Abruptly Brad remembered the conversation he'd just had with Delilah. He stood up and set his drink on the nearby table, feeling a premonition of impending disaster.

"What's the matter?" Dewey asked.

"Never mind." He hurried inside the house, looked up the stairs. "Lily? Lily, you up there?"

Delilah came out of the kitchen. "Trouble, Mr. Brad?"

"I don't know yet." Without another word, he headed up the stairs, taking them two at a time.

Chapter Twenty

Balancing on the rickety stool, Lillian peered up into the closet at the big box pushed way to the back of a top shelf. Now what was in that? Suppose it was the fabled treasure? A box like that could hold a lot of money. Her excitement began to build. The fragile stool groaned under her as she stood on tip-toe and tried to reach the box with her fingertips.

Behind her, she heard someone pounding up the stairs, but she didn't look back. She was intent only on reaching that box.

Brad ran up the stairs and burst into Lily's bedroom. She stood poised on her tiptoes, wearing only pretty lace underwear, and she was reaching upward. "Lily, don't!"

She shrieked in surprise and lost her balance as the stool tipped. Brad took two steps and caught her as she fell. The big box tumbled down at the same time, strewing dusty papers and faded photographs everywhere.

She struggled in his arms, surprised and indignant.

"What are you doing? Unhand me, you villain!" She fought to get out of his arms, looking around for something to cover herself with, and she finally found her robe at the foot of her bed.

"I don't think this was meant for you." Brad began to gather up old letters and photos and return them to the box.

"Well, it's in my aunt's closet, so I guess it's mine." She sighed in disappointment as she knelt to help pick up the strewn pages. "I thought I had found the missing treasure. It's just old papers and photos."

"I don't know what this is, I just know Delilah was supposed to get rid of it." He looked as mystified as she felt. He went down on one knee, gathering up all the dusty papers that were now scattered across the Persian rug.

"Get out of my room," she demanded. "I'll pick this stuff up."

He shook his head and kept gathering the dusty photos and returning them to the box. "I caused you to drop it, the least I can do is help pick it up. Nothin' looks important."

"Let me decide that." She tried to brush him aside so she could see all the scattered items. "I thought it might be the gold everyone says Aunt Lil hid."

"Oh, I never believed that old tale." He wondered privately why Lil had left instructions for Delilah to deal with this box. Nothing looked important, but he owed it to Lil to follow her instructions. There was evidently something here she didn't want the whole world to see. "You get dressed and I'll clean this trash up and get rid of it."

"I don't trust you, you rogue." She paused, looking through the documents, old letters, and photos.

"For all I know, there may be some valuable bonds or a map to the gold."

"I doubt that." Brad kept gathering the dusty papers. Frankly, he was mystified.

Lillian didn't speak. She reached to pick up an old, dim photograph. It was of two young women and a baby girl. She peered at it. She recognized the older woman as her mother. The other woman looked like mother, so that must be Aunt Lil. Lillian had only seen her aunt once when she came to visit all those years ago. Aunt Lil was holding the baby. Puzzled, she turned the photo over. Across the back was scrawled: *'My baby with sister Mollie.'*

"Mollie," she mused aloud. "My mother's name was Mary. Mollie is an Irish name. Did my aunt ever mention having a child?"

She heard a gasp, looked up. Delilah stood in the doorway. "Miss Lillian, what you got there?"

"A picture of my mother, my aunt, and a baby. It kinda looks like me."

Brad shook his head and tried to take the photo from her, but she resisted. "Lil with a child? No, but then, I didn't know everything about her."

Delilah said "Oh Lord, Miss Lillian, put that stuff back in that Pandora's box afore you regrets it."

Lillian was even more puzzled. "Why would I? It's just a box of letters. Why, here's an old one from my mother to Aunt Lil. And here's some more photos of Aunt Lil with a baby."

"Miss Lillian, you give me that." Delilah rushed to them, looking alarmed. "You got no call to be digging through Miss Lil's personal stuff."

Lillian resisted. "Here's a letter to my mother

from Lil that was returned unopened." She began to open the envelope.

Delilah looked toward Brad. "Please, Mr. Brad, don't let her look at this stuff. There's some things best left secret."

Brad said, "She's right, Lily, we've got no right to be digging into the ghosts of Lil's past."

Lillian began to get horrible, uncertain suspicions. "Does it—does it concern me?" She looked at Delilah and the old cook hesitated.

"Put it all back in the box, Miss Lillian and let me destroy it."

"No," Lillian shook her head. "I think I have a right to know." She sat down on the floor and began to dig through the things. Some of them were letters to Lil McGinty from Lillian's mother, and some of them were letters Lil had sent that had been returned, unopened. "You two know something I don't?"

Delilah had tears in her eyes now. "I warned you, Miss Lillian, and now you gonna find out something you don't want to know."

Lillian turned a questioning look at the gambler. Brad shook his head. "Lily, I don't know anything, I really never knew that much about Lil's past. I was supposed to deal with this, and I forgot." He cursed under his breath.

Lillian looked up at the old woman. "What is it you know, Delilah? What is everyone trying to hide? Did my aunt have a little girl? Do I have a cousin somewhere?"

Tears ran from Delilah's eyes and down her wrinkled black face as she shook her head. "No, that ain't it. Miss Lil never wanted you to know, and she couldn't do much for you. So she gave you to her respectable sister to raise and sent money, as much as she could."

Lillian felt herself go ashen with shock and horror. "I—I don't believe you. Are you telling me I'm Lil McGinty's daughter?"

Brad looked blank, but Delilah nodded.

"No, that's crazy." Lillian shook her head. Mother's maiden name was Winters. My aunt married an Irishman."

"Miss Lillian," the cook sighed, "Miss Lil was never married."

"Oh God," Brad whispered, "it's worse than I thought." He began to curse under his breath. "I'm so damned sorry I forgot to destroy the box."

Lillian clutched the photo and wept. "It can't be true," she shook her head. "I'm not a low-class bastard. I'm from a fine, high-class family with a noble background. My father died at sea going over to check on his inheritance."

No one said anything.

"I—I'll prove it," Lillian gasped and began to dig through the pile of letters. "It can't be true, my own mother wouldn't lie to me."

"She did it to protect you, Miss," Delilah said softly, "Miss Lil told me her sister had changed her last name, made up a fake background, gotten rid of her Irish accent, and pretended to be a high-class widow, all to protect you."

"So I'm not only the daughter of a whore, I've been supported all these years and educated, not with a scholarship and money from my father's estate, but from the earnings of this—this bordello? Oh, God, it can't be true!" She buried her face in her hands.

Brad reached out and put his hand on her shoulder. "No, Lily, you're the same person you've always been, not the one you thought you were. And what difference does it make?"

"I don't even know who my real father was. No wonder I'm having trouble finding the papers to join the Sisters Noble of British Society." She began to dig through the letters, reading snatches here and there, then looked up at Delilah. "You know, don't you?"

The old woman nodded, sat down on the bed with a sigh. "The McGintys were a poor immigrant family, having a hard time finding work because of the prejudice against the Irish, so your Aunt Lil took a job cleaning the home of a rich saloon owner. She was just a young girl."

"And he took advantage of her?"

Delilah nodded. "Her family threw her out. The only one willing to help was her sister Mollie. They made a deal to protect you in the only way they knew how. Mollie was too sickly to work, and Lil was pretty, so she earned money the only way she could."

Brad sighed. "Don't judge a person 'til you walk a mile in his boots. Rather than be angry and ashamed, Lily, you should be proud of them. They both sacrificed, thinkin' only of you."

She took a deep breath, unsure what she felt about anything. "Buford. Oh, Lord, Buford must not know." She looked over at Brad beseechingly. "You scoundrel, you'll enjoy telling him, won't you?"

He shook his head. "No, Lily, I won't tell him."

"I don't believe you!" she wept. "You'll use this against me, and he won't want to marry me if he knows."

Delilah sighed. "Miss Lillian, you know Mr. Brad wouldn't do that. Only the three of us knows and it can just be our little secret. Let me burn this box of stuff now and you can forget it ever happened. Miss Lil didn't want you to know anyway."

"No," she shook her head, "I—I want to read it all, know everything about them both."

Delilah gave her a sad nod and left the room.

Brad watched Lily and he had never felt so sorry for anyone in his whole life. "Delilah's right, this can be kept secret. Lily, I have been a rascal and I know it, but I swear I'll make it up to you."

"I don't trust you."

She sat on the floor, her face tear-stained, her red tousled curls falling around her white shoulders. At this moment, in all her grief and vulnerability, he thought he had never seen such a beautiful woman. More than that, he loved her. He loved her for her spunkiness and her hard-headed stubborn personality, and her weaknesses, and her pride. Pride goeth before a fall, and she had fallen so far.

"Lily," he whispered, "we will burn all this stuff and no one need ever know—certainly not that knuckle-headed Buford."

She shook her head and sobbed some more. "I don't believe you. Buford won't want to marry me."

"Then Buford is a stupid rascal," Brad snapped, "because I'd marry you in a minute." He paused, shocked himself at what he'd just said.

"You're a liar and a scoundrel. You're after my half of the Lily."

"Yep. I'm so low, I could crawl under a snake's belly, but I love you, Lily. You hear me? I love you and I don't give a damn anymore about the business." He tried to take her in his arms and she resisted.

"I don't even know who I am—my whole world has been turned upside-down—and I don't know what to believe anymore."

"Well, believe this—I love you, Lily, and I don't blame you for doubtin' me. I don't give a damn where you're from or who your folks are. All that counts in this world is who you are. And I love that about you, your pig-headed stubbornness, your silly pride. *You,* Lily, *you.*" He stood up and pulled her to her feet, looking down at her. Their faces were so close as she looked up at him, green eyes blazing, that he wondered, how in the hell could he ever have thought her plain?

She said, "You want the pleasure of telling him about me, don't you, Brad? Oh, what a sweet revenge that will be for you for all the trouble I've caused you."

"Oh hell, Lily, you are so stubborn!" he muttered. He jerked her to him and kissed her with all the heat and passion he had never realized he was capable of. For a long moment she clung to him, returning that kiss. He wanted to hold her in his arms forever, protect and comfort her, and kiss the tears from her cheeks.

But now she pulled away from him and slapped him. "All you wanted was a plaything."

He rubbed his cheek, his anger at her disbelief growing. "No, Lily, I think I'd like to have you forever." And he was stunned to know it was true. "After I've behaved like such a heel, I know I'll never have that chance—but I want you to know I'm sorry about everything, and you have my word that I'll never tell anyone about us or about your past."

She was sobbing now, tears streaming down her anguished face as she looked up at him. "Get out of my sight! I'll tell Buford myself and hope he won't care. That way, I don't have to worry about your blackmail."

"I said I wouldn't tell." He turned and went out

of the room, leaving her sobbing and crumpled into a ball. There was nothing he could do to comfort her, and she didn't trust or believe him. That was his own damned fault. Well, there was one last thing he could do for her. He went out onto the porch where Dewey Cheatum sat drinking his mint julep.

Dewey looked at him curiously. "What's goin' on in there?"

"Nothin'," he lied. "Dewey, I need you to do something for me."

"Now?" Dewey looked surprised.

"Yes, now—legal stuff."

Dewey frowned. "Look, the fireworks and the festivities will be starting in about an hour. It'll soon be sundown."

"I don't care, this is important. I'll have José bring around the buggy." He left the surprised lawyer and went to find the stable boy.

Soon, José brought the buggy around and Brad helped the older man up onto the seat. As he got in the buggy, Brad told Dewey what he wanted.

Dewey's eyes widened. "Are you drunk or just loco?"

Brad sighed and snapped the whip at the bay horse and it started down the drive. "Well, I'm not drunk, and maybe I'm loco—but I love her, Dewey."

Dewey laughed without mirth. "Unbelievable. The great ladies' man finally brought down by a plain little Yankee schoolteacher—"

"She's not plain," he defended her hotly. "She's got beautiful eyes, and hair like a prairie fire, and the palest skin. And she's smart, smarter than most men."

Dewey lit his pipe as they drove toward town. "Yes, you got it bad. You tell her?"

She doesn't believe me. This is what I got to do to prove it to her."

"That's a big sacrifice to make, Brad. I'd think twice about it."

He shook his head. "I've got to do it, Dewey. I've helped mess up things for her, and now I got to try to make things right."

Dewey smoked his pipe as they drove down Main Street. "All right, but what about the lieutenant?"

"I can't do anything about him—she thinks she loves him."

"Ha! Women are such fools!" Dewey snorted.

"Don't I know it? But she's like a spirited filly. I just got to give her her head and not rein her in. Maybe she'll realize what a rascal he is before she goes down the aisle with him."

"You're a good shot, Brad. I'm surprised you don't challenge him to a duel."

"Don't think I ain't thought of that. I can't, because she loves him, and I've caused her enough heartbreak."

"He doesn't know what a lucky Yankee bastard he is then," Dewey muttered.

Back at the house, Lily dug through the box, reading the letters between the two sisters, and looking at the photos and documents. Now she knew it all. She was Lil McGinty's bastard child, sired by Joe Murphy, the rich owner of Murphy's Saloon. Lil had been a young innocent girl working as a maid in Murphy's house when he had seduced her and gotten her with child. He had fired her and refused to help her in any way. A few months later, Joe Murphy had been shot and killed by a jealous husband of another woman he was seeing. Lil had given her baby to her sister and had been sending money to support them all these years, including the private school education that Mother had said was funded by a scholarship.

By now, the evening shadows slanted into the room and she had read everything. At first she had been horrified and furious at the duplicity. Now she was saddened for the two sisters who had both sacrificed so much—and all for her. Tears came to her eyes as she studied the dim photo of the two women and the baby. Yes, Lillian looked like her mother all right, just as Delilah had said weeks ago. Lil McGinty looked sad, so sad as she held her baby. Lillian's heart went out to her. "I've been a judgmental snob and a fool," she whispered. "I'm not nobility, I'm a bastard, and I'm as Irish as Brad O'Neal. Well, so what? People who judge others on their bloodlines ought to be breeding livestock, because it's who you are inside that counts."

She sighed, unsure what to do now. After the way she'd behaved, Brad would surely tell Buford about sleeping with her and about her scandalous background, and she wasn't sure she blamed him. It would be a fitting revenge after the way she'd been so high and mighty. Lillian made a decision then that she'd better tell Buford herself tonight after the Fourth of July festivities were over.

The Fourth of July festivities. That thought jolted her back to reality. The fading light slanting through the window let her know it was dusk. No matter how she felt, she had duties to take care of. She boxed the letters and documents, putting them back in the closet to save them. Then she took the dim photo and lay it carefully on her bureau. She intended to frame it and display it proudly. Two women had loved her enough to make great sacrifices, and from this moment forward, Lillian must show herself worthy of that sacrifice. Tomorrow, she would go out to the cemetery and put flowers on her mother's grave and ask her forgiveness.

Lillian went to the basin and washed her swollen eyes and combed her hair. Then she put on her mother's pale blue dress and made ready to go down for the evening celebration. She went into the kitchen and Delilah looked up and nodded sympathetically.

"I'm sorry you had to find out that way, Miss."

"You knew all along, didn't you?"

The old woman nodded. "Not everything, but enough. I never would have told you because she tried so hard to protect you. Lil was a wonderful, generous woman and I'd have given my life for her."

"But you didn't know about the box?"

"No, ma'am, or I would have burned everything to keep you from findin' it. I thought you maybe was up in that closet lookin' for the gold folks think she hid."

"Guess there isn't any."

"Reckon not, except for the diamond lily pin."

"The diamond pin?" Lillian asked.

Delilah nodded. "The diamond pin Mr. Brad give her for her birthday the day before she fell off that balcony."

So Brad had been telling the truth about the pin. There had to be a reasonable explanation. She didn't know what to think. Lillian grabbed the edge of the table to keep from collapsing.

The old woman came to her side. "You all right, Miss Lillian? You look like you seen a spook."

She took a deep breath. Of course, Brad had told Delilah to say this so that Lillian would think Buford a rotter. And to think, she had been about to change her mind about Brad. Oh, he was an oily one, but she would not be fooled now. "I—I'm fine," she lied. "We'll talk more later. Right now, we've got guests to entertain." She looked out the kitchen window to the porch. "You seen Mr. O'Neal?"

"Saw him leavin' in the buggy with Dewey Cheatum."

Lillian frowned. Crafty fox that he was, Brad was probably not losing a moment of time having Dewey draw up the papers she'd need to sign to keep him from telling her secret to Buford. Of course he'd demand she give up her half of the Lily. Well, he could forget blackmailing her because she intended to tell Buford herself tonight. She was certain Buford loved her enough that he wouldn't care and his family must be wealthy.

She stood looking out the window. In the dusk of the hot July evening, people were already gathering out on the front lawn. "Oh, we're running late, Delilah. Call the girls and let's start decorating those tables we've got set up on the lawn."

Lillian pasted a smile on her face and went out on the porch. The two congressmen sat there in the porch swing. "Are you gentlemen having a good time?"

"We certainly are," said the fat one from Ohio. "Why, that Brad O'Neal mixed us up something called mint juleps that were real tasty."

"In a few minutes, the whole town will be here and we'll have even more food and a band concert and fireworks."

They leaned back in the comfortable swing and sighed. One said "You know, this seems like the perfect sleepy little town. Why, I'll bet a dog could sleep in the road for a week without being disturbed. I think maybe our colleagues were wrong about the town needing a fort for protection."

Oh dear, this wasn't good.

"I realize it may look that way," Lillian said, "but there's all sorts of violence just seething under the surface in this town. We really need to keep the fort open."

Both congressmen looked out across the lawn. Herman the goat stood placidly chewing grass out by the big iron bird bath. In the distance, the town seemed quiet as a graveyard. This called for drastic measures. "Here, let me get you both another julep."

She took their glasses and went inside to get the two men more drinks. She didn't know much about how Brad made these, but she poured in extra whiskey just in case. Then she took them out to the porch and handed them to the beaming congressmen. After that she went down the steps to direct the women setting up punch bowls and big platters of cake. Some of the women had brought freezers of homemade ice cream.

She told herself that if she kept busy, she wouldn't have to think about anything that had happened today. Nor did she want to think about the diamond lily pin. There must be a reasonable explanation. She would straighten this all out with Buford later.

As darkness fell, the crowd got bigger and more boisterous. There was so much to do, Lillian had no time to think, which was good. The giant front lawn of the Texas Lily was now covered with people bustling about. She looked up to see the band

Epilogue

Headline in the January 12, 1901 *Fort Floppett Daily Bugle*

IT'S OIL!!

Texas' first big oil gusher blew in this week at a place called Spindletop near the town of Beaumont. One local well-respected family, the O'Neals, own much land in that area and are now instant millionaires. Mr. Brad O'Neal has announced that the family will close their nationally renowned hotel, the Texas Lily, and turn it into the finest home in the Lone Star state. While the mansion is being renovated, Mr. and Mrs. O'Neal and their large family expect to tour Europe.

Mrs. Lily O'Neal, the leader of local society, has pledged donations for countless public projects, including special funds for unwed mothers and immigrant families. "After all," Lily O'Neal said, "I am the child of immigrants myself, and these people are the backbone and the future of America. While some may raise an eyebrow over my other charity,

I have particular compassion for unwed mothers who have no place to turn."

Readers will remember that several years ago, Brad O'Neal generously donated a valuable piece of land on the edge of town for a city park christened *Lil McGinty Park*. The O'Neals intend to improve that park immediately. Major Gilbert Bottoms, now retired, has just been hired as head gardener. At Mrs. O'Neal's request, the land will be planted with thousands of common orange day-lilies, so beloved by her mother.

The town, especially the military, has fond memories of Lil McGinty, remembered now as a town benefactor and a paragon of local society.

We here at the *Fort Floppett Daily Bugle* join the whole town in wishing the O'Neals a happy trip and a safe return. *Bon Voyage!*

coming down the driveway in smart formation. As they approached the house, they played "The Eyes of Texas," to the delight and applause of the crowd. As they passed her table, Buford nodded to her, his cheeks all puffed out with the effort of his tuba. She smiled and waved. He wasn't as tall as Brad or nearly as handsome as the Texan, but she was sure that he would make her a good husband.

He nodded to her again and kept playing as the band marched up the driveway. People gathered on the porch around the congressmen, who were grinning like polecats. Evidently someone had given them some more mint juleps.

People lined up at the ice cream booth, and Lillian kept busy serving up the homemade ice cream. She managed a quick spoonful and it was delicious, cold, and creamy. When she got a moment, she put a big slice of chocolate and Lady Baltimore cake in a dish and spooned some ice cream over it. Mmm, it tasted so good that for a moment, she forgot all her troubles. A warm darkness fell across the crowd and the band finished its concert. In the torches set up around the lawn, she saw Buford working his way toward her. Now she would have to tell him, and she dreaded it.

Out of the corner of her eye, she spotted Brad O'Neal and he frowned as he looked at her and then at the approaching Buford. "Everyone!" he shouted, "it's time for the fireworks!"

The crowd cheered. Lillian cheered, too, but she was as tense as a barbed wire fence. After the fireworks was when the fight between the soldiers and the cowboys was supposed to begin and it had to look convincing for the congressmen. The town's future was riding on it. Out in the crowd, she spotted Sadie. The girl seemed to be having a good time flirting with all the men. Lillian abruptly saw Sadie as a girl who had had rotten breaks and had been treated badly by life. Perhaps Sadie was a lot like Lil McGinty, just struggling to make it in a tough world. Tears came to Lillian's eyes.

Buford joined her in the booth as everyone turned and looked expectantly toward where Brad and some of the others were setting up the fireworks. "Hello, my dear Lillian. Did you like the concert?"

The army band hadn't played any worse than usual, so she smiled and nodded. "Just as always."

He grabbed her hand and kissed it, and she managed not to wipe the wet kiss off against her dress. "Dear Lillian, after this evening is over and the fort is saved, we'll sneak off and spoon a little."

Wet kisses. She needed to tell him her secret, but she hesitated. Did he really love her enough to accept her for what she was instead of what he *thought* she was? And did she really want to marry him? She was more and more unsure. "Buford, we need to talk."

"Later. They're going to set off the fireworks."

He was right, she thought. This was no time to tell him all this grave and important information.

The fireworks display began—Roman candles shooting into the black sky as small children squealed and the crowd applauded. Firecrackers and rockets blasted into the warm Texas night while cowboy and soldier alike shouted with approval. She loved Texas, Lillian realized suddenly, really loved it. It might be more savage and different than what she was used to, but there was something special, and ornery, and independent about Texans—from the virile strong men, to the thousands of acres of rolling prairie and pale blue sky. She wouldn't be happy living back East again where the skies were often cold and gray, and the cities were crowded. She had changed over the past few weeks. Texas had changed her—or was it a Texan?

Buford shouted to her during a lull in the fireworks. "What did you want to talk to me about?"

How to begin? "Maybe we should go where we can have some privacy."

"And miss the rest of the fireworks?" He shook his head.

"I—I wanted to tell you I found a box up in my Aunt's closet."

Immediately, she had his attention. He grabbed her hand. "You found the gold everyone knows is in the house somewhere, right?"

She shook her head. "No, just papers and photos. Buford, I really doubt that treasure story."

He looked crestfallen. "Oh well, we'll have half the Lily. If managed right, it could make plenty of profit."

She shook her head. "Buford, I've got lots of things to tell you, but one of them is that I'm going to let Brad have my half of the Lily. You and I can go back East and—"

"Give up our half of the Lily? Hell no! Have you lost your senses?" He roared at her as he grabbed her shoulders and shook her. If it hadn't been for the noise of the fireworks, someone might have overheard him.

"You don't understand, Buford, I just found out—"

He shook her again. "I don't care what you found out, we aren't gonna give up the Lily. Why, it's a gold mine, and we can be rich if we turn it back into what it was before."

She tried to pull away from him but he hung on.

"No, Buford, don't you understand? I can't be part of running a bordello."

He put his face close to hers and there was no tenderness in his eyes as he hissed at her. "As my wife, you'll do what I say. You hear me?"

She was too astounded to do anything but stare back at him in the sudden silence as the sound of the fireworks died away. The air was full of acrid smoke from the burned gunpowder as people milled and talked. It was time for the big fight, Lillian thought. Even as she thought that, a fuss broke out between a bunch of soldiers and cowboys over near the porch. Instantly, insults and fists were flying.

"Fight! Fight!" Yelled the crowd, and they pushed forward to get a better look.

"Ain't nothing a Texan likes better than a good fight!" Brad yelled as he struggled to get through the crowd. Instantly, a soldier grabbed him by the shoulder, whirled him around, and hit him.

Women screamed, and horses reared and neighed.

Brad strode toward Lillian and Buford, his dark eyes bright with anger. "I've been waiting for this a long time!" He snarled and then he hit Buford in the mouth.

Lillian could only gasp as Buford went down— then he stumbled to his feet swinging his fists.

Brad sidestepped easily. "Lily, get up on the porch," he ordered, "I don't want you to get hurt!"

"I beg your pardon!"

"You heard me!"

She started to argue with him, then decided he meant it. She ran for the porch, sidestepping the fighting men to get there. All the women and children had scooted to the sides of the lawn to watch.

Lillian ran up on the porch. The two congressmen were watching the fighting, big-eyed with shock.

"My God," yelled one, "I never seen anything like this before!"

The fat one nodded. "Just like our colleagues said, Texas is a wild and uncivilized place! They need all the soldiers and law enforcement they can get."

"Ain't it the truth!" Lillian declared. "Oh, gentlemen, you have no idea what it's like to live in Texas."

The three of them watched a hundred cowboys and soldiers fighting on the front lawn. In the midst of it all, Herman walked through the battling males, calmly munching lilies.

"You know," one of the congressmen said to Lillian, "I think maybe we ought to get an even bigger appropriation for the fort here, more money and more soldiers."

The major stepped on the porch just then. "Gentlemen, that's a wise decision."

The fighting was still going on but in the distance, the incoming train whistle echoed and reechoed.

One of the congressmen frowned. "That's our train, but we want to see the rest of the fight."

"I think the fight's about over," the major said, firing his pistol in the air. The brawlers all paused and looked toward the porch. "All right, that's enough! You cowboys get out of town—and my men, get yourselves back in formation or I'll throw someone in the guard house."

The men stopped, rubbing bruised jaws and wiping bloody lips. Only Brad and Buford were still fighting out in the middle of the lily bed near the big bird bath. It looked to Lillian like they intended to kill each other.

"Stop it!" yelled the major, but the two kept slugging it out.

Lillian took a deep breath. "Someone stop them!" she pleaded. But the two men seemed intent on killing each other, and no one else interfered. She lifted her skirts and started down the steps and across the yard.

As she passed Sadie, the saloon girl grabbed her arm. "You're makin' a bad mistake," Sadie muttered, "Buford ain't no good. Let Brad whip him."

Lillian paused. "You're wrong."

"Am I?" Sadie grinned. "Brad's a right guy. I loved him, but he ain't interested in me, it's you he wants. That Buford, he's been comin' to the Bucket to sleep with me."

"I—I don't believe you," Lillian pulled away from her. "Why, we're engaged."

Sadie laughed. "I'm leavin' on the evenin' train, so I got no reason to lie. That diamond pin he give you? He stole it outa Lil's jewelry box. He was up in her room snoopin' to find that treasure. When she caught him, there was a struggle, and she went over the balcony."

Lillian stood blinking at her. *No, she would not, could not believe this.* In the meantime, the two men still fought, and the other men gathered in a circle to watch. "Brad, stop that!" She ran across the grass and the crowd parted to let her through.

Brad appeared to be giving Buford a terrible beating. Buford pulled a knife, and Brad grabbed the officer's arm, twisting it until Buford howled and dropped it. Then he hit Buford one last time and stepped away as Lillian ran up. "You love him, Lillian, so I won't kill him."

"You uncivilized rogue!"

Brad grabbed her arm. "Lily, I need to tell you something."

"Whatever he's got to say," Buford wheezed as he struggled to get to his feet, "don't listen to him. I do love you, and we'll get married."

She whirled on Brad. "You see? He does love me."

Brad merely looked down at her, and she had never seen such sadness in a man's eyes. "I love you, too, Lily, and I hope this proves it. Here." He reached into his coat, thrust a piece of paper in her hands. "I've got my bag packed. I'm leavin' on the evenin' train."

"What?" She blinked and tried to see the print on the paper by moonlight and the lit torches.

"What is it?" Buford stumbled toward her.

She ignored him, trying to make out the writing in the dim light. Then she was almost speechless with disbelief. "Why—why you're giving me your half of the Texas Lily!"

He nodded. "It's legal. Dewey drew it up for me late this afternoon."

Buford put his arm around her. "It's probably a trick, Lillian, don't trust him."

Brad's face furrowed with anger. "It's no trick. And you take good care of her, Buford, or I'll come back and beat you like cornbread batter. I love her, and I want her to be happy." He turned and started walking away. In the distance, the train whistled again as it approached the outskirts of town.

Lillian stared after him, still holding the paper in her limp fingers.

Next to her, Buford laughed. "Hey, this is great. What a fool! You know how much money we can make running the Lily?"

Lillian's eyes burred with tears as she stared after

the tall, broad-shouldered Texan striding away from her and out of her life. He was walking toward the buggy where Sadie and the two congressmen already waited. In a few minutes, he would be on that train and gone forever. She had what she wanted— the Texas Lily and she had Buford. *Mrs. Buford Arthur Reginal Fortenbury.* And Buford need never know about her past now.

At her side, Buford said, "Well, say something. Aren't you happy? The idiot is giving us the whole thing."

Yes, she could have it all and be a part of Philadelphia society as she had always wanted. Money and social position. She could close the door on her past forever—and the two women who had sacrificed so much for her. And yet. . . .

Brad was almost to the waiting buggy now. He was a rough, uncivilized Texan, but she loved him. "Wait, Brad! Wait for me!"

Brad paused and whirled, surprised.

As she hiked up her skirts and began to run, behind her Buford shouted, "Are you crazy? He's just a low-class Irish Texan."

"Low-class shanty Irish, just like me!" she yelled back over her shoulder. And then she was across the grass where Brad held out his arms to her. She ran into his arms, and he kissed her like he would never let her go, while the crowd cheered and applauded.

"Marry me," he whispered, "and we'll turn the Lily into the best damned hotel in all east Texas!"

"Done!" She said and kissed him again. "Now take your bag out of that buggy."

"Yes, ma'am." He grinned and winked as he strode over to do so, and she turned back toward Buford.

To My Readers

The town of Fort Floppett as well as all my characters are fictitious. So where did I get the idea for this story? During the last round of America's military base closings in 1995, I read a newspaper article about a fort in the Western desert that had been built in 1860 to protect Pony Express riders from marauding Indians. This fort was still open and operating and a small town had grown up around it. The government was attempting to close this fort because the Pony Express ceased operating in 1861. The local townspeople were protesting that the fort was still badly needed—if nothing else, to provide jobs and income for the local townspeople. I have no idea whether the committee closed it or not.

The first big oilfield in Texas was Spindletop, drilled near Beaumont in 1901. That gusher began a rush of oil drilling throughout Texas, and many fortunes were made and lost during the next hundred years.

Some of you know my hobby is gardening, and I love the antique "cabbage" roses. You might be interested to know rose oil is more expensive, ounce for ounce, than gold. The majority of this oil, used for perfume, comes from Bulgaria.

If you've been reading my books, you know they all connect. You've met Brad O'Neal's younger brother Blackie, and the Reverend Lovejoy, in my earlier book: *To Tempt a Texan*. You've met Major Bottoms' sister-in-law, the widow of his lawman brother, Sam, in my last book, *To Tease a Texan*.

So what story will I tell next? You've now met two of the O'Neal brothers, Blackie and Brad. In my next story, you'll meet their younger sister, Bluebonnet.

The year is 1895, the middle of the so-called Gay Nineties. Back East, the famed John L. Sullivan has lost his boxing championship title to "Gentleman Jim" Corbett.

Enter our hero, handsome Jack "Cash" McCalley, a former cowboy and now a fast-living Dallas promoter/gambler. Charming Jack decides he can make a lot of money if he sets up a fight in Dallas between the new champ, Corbett, and rising star, "Fighting Bob" Fitzsimmons. Boxing is illegal in many states, including Texas, but Jack sees no problem. He's always been on the shady side of the law.

Meet his problem. Young, but already twice-widowed librarian, Bluebonnet O'Neal Schwartz Purdy, is in Dallas for the annual meeting of The Lone Star Ladies for Decency and Decorum. Strait-laced Bonnie is president of this group and is horrified to learn that a bloody, uncivilized prize fight is in the works. Of course she and her ladies will stop at nothing to prevent this, and Jack will do whatever it takes to win—even seducing the staid president of the protestors.

Expect another humorous battle of the sexes with the two characters more attracted to each other than either cares to admit in my new 2008 romance that may be called *To Wed a Texan*. Remember, title and release dates are always subject to change.

Based on an actual event in Texas history that involved a lion, the boxers, four governors, Bat Masterson, the infamous Judge Roy Bean, the Texas Rangers, and the Mexican Rurales, the contested prize fight became a legal circus as folks in Texas chose sides.

Some of my earlier books are still available by order at your local bookstore or check my publisher's website: www.kensingtonbooks.com.

I also have a website with up-to-date news: www.nettrends.com/georgina gentry. Or you may write me c/o Box 162, Edmond, OK 73083-0162. Please include a stamped envelope for a reply.

Remember, don't judge someone 'til you've walked a mile in his boots.

Georgina Gentry

From the Queen of Romance
Cassie Edwards

__Enchanted Enemy
  0-8217-7216-4 $5.99US/$7.99CAN

__Elusive Ecstacy
  0-8217-6597-3 $5.99US/$7.99CAN

__Portrait of Desire
  0-8217-5862-4 $5.99US/$7.50CAN

__Rapture's Rendezvous
  0-8217-6115-3 $5.99US/$7.50CAN

Available Wherever Books Are Sold!

Visit our website at **www.kensingtonbooks.com.**

More Historical Romance From
Jo Ann Ferguson

Say Yes! To Sizzling Romance by
Lori Foster

__Too Much Temptation
0-7582-0431-0 $6.99US/$9.99CAN

Grace Jenkins feels too awkward and insecure to free the passionate woman inside her. But that hasn't stopped her from dreaming about Noah Harper. Gorgeous, strong and sexy, his rough edge beneath the polish promises no mercy in the bedroom. When Grace learns Noah's engagement has ended in scandal, she shyly offers him her support and her friendship. But Noah's looking for something extra . . .

__Never Too Much
0-7582-0087-0 $6.99US/$9.99CAN

A confirmed bachelor, Ben Badwin has had his share of women, and he likes them as wild and uninhibited as his desires. Nothing at all like the brash, wholesomely cute woman who just strutted into his diner. But something about Sierra Murphy's independent attitude makes Ben's fantasies run wild. He'd love to dazzle her with his sensual skills . . . to make her want him as badly as he suddenly wants her . . .

__Say No to Joe?
0-8217-7512-X $6.99US/$9.99CAN

Joe Winston can have any woman—except the one he really wants. Secretly, Luna Clark may lust after Joe, but she's made it clear that she's too smart to fall for him. He can just keep holding his breath, thank you very much. But now, Luna's inherited two kids who need more than she alone can give in a small town that seems hell-bent on driving them away. She needs someone to help out . . . someone who can't be intimidated . . . someone just like Joe.

__When Bruce Met Cyn
0-8217-7513-8 $6.99US/$9.99CAN

Compassionate and kind, Bruce Kelly understands that everyone makes mistakes, even if he's never actually done anything but color inside the lines. Nobody's perfect, but Bruce is about to meet a woman who's perfect for him. He's determined to show her that he can be trusted. And if that means proving it by being the absolute gentleman at all times, then so be it. No matter how many cold showers it takes . . .

Available Wherever Books Are Sold!

Visit our website at www.kensingtonbooks.com.

"Buford," she said, "I know about everything."

"I didn't mean to kill Lil," Buford sobbed. "I was looking for the treasure, and she caught me taking the diamond pin—"

The major walked up with two soldiers. "I've heard enough. I think you're headed for a court martial, Lieutenant, or maybe a transfer to Arizona. Come along."

Buford groaned aloud and kicked at Herman, who was munching lilies. Then he leaned over to pick up his hat. The sight of his rear must have been too tempting to Herman because the goat suddenly lowered its head and charged at Buford.

"Look out!" Someone yelled, but it was too late. Herman's horns caught Buford in the pants and threw him hard into the big bird bath. With a resounding clang, the man slammed against it and it toppled over.

Almost in disbelief, Lillian stared and the crowd gasped audibly.

"Brad," Lillian called, "Come look, quick!"

She was barely aware that Brad had walked from the buggy and put his arm around her. "So there was a treasure after all!"

They both stood blinking at the base of the toppled bird bath. Gold coins poured out of the bottom of it, thousands of dollars worth of gold coins. They ran over to it, knelt, and ran their fingers though the shiny cartwheels and silver dollars.

Brad said, "So this is what Lil was doin' early in the mornings when no one was up. She was hidin' money in the base of the birdbath. Why, there must be thousands of dollars."

Lillian smiled at him. "You're rich, Brad."

He put his arm around her and kissed her cheek. "No, *we're* rich," he corrected her. "There's plenty to hire employees, do some improvements, and turn the Lily into a first-class hotel. I thought Lil didn't care about me, but I reckon the old girl did after all."

Lillian felt the tears come to her eyes. "She must have been a wonderful, generous woman. When we have time, I want you to tell me all about her."

He kissed her again. "She'd be so proud of you. She took care of you in the only way she knew."

"I've been such a snob, such a heartless fool."

In the distance, the train whistled as it chugged toward the station.

One of the congressmen said, "Hey, we might miss our train. Let's get this buggy moving."

José nodded, climbed up on the seat, and snapped the little whip. The crowd stood staring after the buggy as it pulled away with Sadie and the congressmen.

Sadie turned once and looked back at Brad with tears in her eyes. "Take care of him, honey," she shouted. "He's a good one."

"I will," Lillian promised and smiled, looking after the girl who had loved and lost. *There but for the grace of God. . . .*

She turned toward Brad. "Can you ever forgive me?"

"Nothin' to forgive." He swung her up in his arms and kissed her again, then yelled at his lawyer. "Hey, Dewey, gather up all that money, will you?"

Dewey stepped tentatively from the crowd. "Will Herman butt me?"

Herman shook his beard, bleated, and returned to munching grass.

"No. It seems he had a particular dislike for the lieutenant. Old Herman gets the run of the place from now on," Brad said with a grin. He started toward the big house, carrying Lillian. "Do you mind if I call you Lily?" he whispered.

"Not at all," she snuggled up against him and waved to the grinning crowd that was now dispersing. "I love you, Brad, only I didn't know it until I saw you walking toward that buggy."

He held her very close as he strode toward the house. "Honey, when I get you inside, I'm gonna make you glad you didn't let me leave."

"In the morning room?"

"Nope, in a big old comfortable bed. Tomorrow you can help Mrs. Bottoms and the ladies plan the biggest weddin' east Texas ever saw."

Delilah stood grinning on the porch as they approached. "Miss Lillian, everything all right now?"

"It sure is, and please call me Lily," she said as Brad carried her up the steps. "Yes, everything's all right—better than all right now."

Delilah grinned. "Miss Lil would like this. She'd be so proud."

"I hope so," Lily said, "and I hope that she'd love those Texas grandchildren I plan to give her."

"Amen to that," Brad said. Then he kissed her again.

The Town Beautification Committee stood on the porch, blinking in disbelief. "Hey, Brad," Luke said, "you ain't givin' up your title as Champion Ladies' Man, are you?"

He grinned at them. "I sure am. I'm gettin' married, and you're all invited to the weddin'." He carried Lily through the door, up the stairs to her room, and kicked the door shut. "Darlin', you want me?"

"I want you," she answered and held out her arms. He laid her on the bed, went to lock the door, and came to her. "Come here, little gal, I'm going to love you like you've never been loved."

"I can't wait," she sighed. She closed her eyes for the kiss she knew was coming. His mouth covered hers in the sweetest, deepest kiss she could imagine as his hands went to unbutton her dress.

"I love you," he whispered. "Oh, Lily, I love you!" And he kissed her deeper still, even as he reached to open the lace of her bodice.

Lily sighed with pleasure at his touch. It was going to be a long, long night of love, and many more thereafter. She could hardly wait.